COPYCAT

Jennie and Martha became friends when Martha moved in next door to Jennie. At least, Jennie thought they were friends. Jennie admired everything about Martha—her house, her gorgeous husband, her bohemian clothes and exotic children's names. And Martha seemed to take to motherhood so effortlessly and confidently, while for Jennie it was all such an effort. Martha tolerated Jennie, took her on holiday, helped her with the children—but all the time she was wondering how much longer she could stand living next to her. As time went on, the roles seemed to reverse. As Jennie became more independent, more successful, Martha's life was falling apart. At times they seemed less like friends, more like sworn enemies. Their relationship became bitter, twisted—a relationship that only one of them could survive . . .

COPYCAT

Gillian White

CHIVERS PRESS
BATH

First published 2003
by
Transworld Publishers
This Large Print edition published 2003
by
BBC Audiobooks Ltd
by arrangement with
Transworld Publishers Ltd

ISBN 0 7540 1944 6

British Library Cataloguing in Publication Data available

Printed and bound in Great Britain by
Antony Rowe Ltd., Chippenham, Wiltshire

For Elias and Megan Newton-White and Jemima Bamforth: three incredible, brand new people, precious and mega-special

PROLOGUE

It's funny how certain labels take precedence over all others. Murderess will be the one society pins on me when I'm gone, and so all those little strived-for succeses, from 'good girl' to 'wife and mother', are obliterated as if they'd never been. Oh and I wanted so hard to be good. Murderess (perceived as so much more evil than murderer) would probably replace far more noble states than I ever achieved; at a push 'prime minister' might still stick, but underneath the greater truths of 'wicked, deranged, ruthless'.

Here lies the murderess. Name, age, state, what about them? Doesn't matter.

If by some miracle I could win a Nobel Peace Prize, that would come second on my grave. It might not even get a mention.

I ought to be grateful, I tell myself when I'm searching for something positive to think about my life. Thoughts of my children I push away—they are far too painful to dwell on. But I ought to be grateful when I think of Ruth Ellis and I remember that so few years lie between my crime and hers, both crimes of passion. And when she said goodbye to her child she knew it would be for ever. I still have the small hope that one day my children and I may be reunited.

Other women in this open prison talk of nothing else but their kids and their men. They keep photos of them in their rooms (yes, rooms, not cells, although of course we are locked in at night. The missing bars are just an illusion in the same way

1

that the flowers we plant are illusions, pointing to life as it was and can never be any more.) I have a photo above my bed but so far I can't look at it.

It is their choice of men that makes it impossible for me to relate to them. All but the rarest inmate has opted for destruction by proxy . . . but their obsessions with these monsters are real and I am an expert on dangerous obsessions. I don't give advice, and nor do I take it. But I am sorry for being a murderess; oh yes, please believe me, I repent every second of every single day.

It's hard being cleverer than the screws; they know that I am and they resent it, so half my time I spend attempting to be crude and silly. You have to adjust to the norm in here, and that norm is becoming younger, more violent and increasingly aggressive. Drugs flow. Knives flash. I turn away from trouble, still trying, in my way, to be good without being seen as sissy.

People say life is a dream and it would be so good if it was. It would mean I hadn't killed anyone, I hadn't destroyed my children's future by depriving them of their mother and tagging them with my own dreadful label. Suppose the whole of my life has been just a kind of troubled sleep, sluggish mostly, but feverish at times with periods of real nightmare? Certainly, the things I have done I seem to have done in a dream, and the person I killed is like a dream person.

The obsession that overtook her and me is a curious phenomenon, a chemical process. 'Love' sprang from somewhere like a witch on her broomstick, a separate and menacing power, distorted. This kind of attraction makes billions of atoms rush together, lights conflagrations in the blood that reach nerves, heart and brain, chest and stomach. Any sensations of exquisite delight come with acute distress.

After years of anguish caused by obsession came a frenzied craving, a physical need for relief from the tension so acute it could not be ignored. She seemed almost invisible when I approached her that last fatal time in the garden. She was myself, but shapeless and without substance. The buzzing of the insects was loud, and in that blazing heat the whole world hung as if enchanted.

The pain of it drove me, soft-footed, towards her. She saw me coming, she saw the rug, she opened her eyes and frowned, then stared in a disgusted way, then burst out laughing. She laughs when she's hurt instead of crying, I know that so well. She sat and watched me as I came nearer, her face rigid, her eyes enormous. She watched me with indulgent confidence. The proximity of her was too hard to bear.

It was then that she turned away and I was able to make the cut.

It was then that her eyes turned frightened and, in the ladder of light that slanted over her shoulder, a million tiny things danced in scarlet.

'For the love of God,' she begged.

She was bleeding. But nothing she said could have stopped me.

Now she is gone there is little of me left, nothing but scraps that take time to find.

Nothing more can happen to me now, and I am glad.

CHAPTER ONE

Jennie

Can you hear them?

As I walked down my garden a moment ago I thought I heard—no, I did hear, I'm not deaf—I heard laughter. Collective hatred. Ill wishes. Thistles and weeds choking my roses under such a clear blue basin of sky.

As the DJ insists on telling me, it is six o'clock precisely, and at six o'clock on a Monday and Thursday it was my habit to leave the house by the stable door, go along the path to my back fence and reverse the whole procedure to let myself into Martha's kitchen. This ritual was so deeply ingrained it was more on the lines of sleepwalking, me blundering along like a blindfolded child with a tail to stick on the donkey, arms outstretched, a junkie groping my way towards the shameful fulfilment of my need.

What a sad and pitiful fool.

*   *   *

But Martha's kitchen was warm and crumbly like home-made biscuits on blue and white plates and it beckoned me like the ghost of something— childhood stories and fairy tales. She had so many knacks that I lacked. Martha picked flowers in handfuls and rammed them into muddy brown jugs while I took time with mine and missed that spontaneous effect. Snipped and brittle in

Worcester china, my arrangements ended up formal as flowers made out of blown glass.

And now I can't go there any more it feels like a desolation.

I am reduced to standing motionless, peeping out between my curtains till my eyes ache and *it hurts it hurts, dammit, it hurts.*

Something like this happened at school. They have counsellors to prevent it these days, but looking back on those faraway times it was no more than a painful game. God help me, this is real.

*   *   *

How I would look forward to Mondays and Thursdays at six o'clock. You couldn't compare it to Graham's homecoming; it was balmy, better than Graham's returns. It wasn't the signal for manic activity—making sure the kids were changed and pushing a shepherd's pie in the oven, scraping toys off the living-room floor so that Graham could walk safely across without stamping on a Fisher-Price game or breaking a careless ankle.

No, when Martha came home from work the sherry bottle would be brought in slatternly triumph from dresser to table, her shoes would be kicked off and the day's events chewed over, along with any old Twiglets she might find in her rusty cracker tin, while she rubbed her poor blistered heels.

I have never seen Scholls so distressed as hers and the soles of her feet were bleached and splintered, rough as those chewed-up blocks of wood.

'It's my time now, damn you, you little buggers,'

Martha would shriek at her children—wiry, olive-skinned creatures with peepy eyes like infant orang-utans—who were unfazed by their mother's excesses, not nearly so ultra-sensitive as my little Poppy and Josh. 'Old Mother Frazer's been working all day chopping kindling for the stove and now she needs some quality time for herself.'

Mondays and Thursdays. And with Martha at work on those two days a week, I used to depend on these evening half-hours and know they would make me happy because in those early years I was closer to Martha than to anyone else in my life.

She'd always threatened to get back to work as soon as she possibly could, but for some defensive reason I never really believed her. I suppose I imagined that I was so happy with our slow and often hilarious days that she would be as reluctant as me to change the status quo.

How stupidly mistaken.

'I am a woman of no substance,' she moaned. 'Kids, cats, carrots, cold custard, curtains, curses. This is my life I'm talking about. As soon as these brats go to nursery school I'm off like that bat out of hell.'

It was like a threat of bereavement. I used to say, 'Yes, it would be nice, for the money mostly,' but I never meant it. And anyway we were lucky, Graham earned enough without me working.

Martha and Sam named their house Beavers after Sam's grandfather, some bigwig in the navy, and nobody laughed at them for that. Graham and I, we would never have got away with it.

Mondays and Thursdays.

Martha's words spun round her like cat's cradles, she strung them about her with gestures while I sat

7

across the table waiting. I listened to Martha slack-jawed, like a kid eating popcorn at the cinema, chewing up every nuance as in her husky, smoky voice she set out her colourful, tempting stall and went through the bric-a-brac of her day.

She knew what I had been doing, of course; there was no mystery surrounding my life. What continued to surprise me was the fact that Martha could like me. Once I asked her why she did. At first she said she didn't know and then she admitted it could well be that she had felt sorry for me, I looked so vulnerable and pathetic crabbing down the ward after stitches. So shy and frightened. Trying to stand up for myself against those pushy nurses. All I remember about that time is laughing so much that the stitches pulled, and being shocked at the lengths she went to in order to have a smoke.

If you smoke, they say, you'll have a small baby.

'Who wants a large baby anyway, for Christ's sake?' was Martha's answer to that. 'Big, fat, sluggy wartime things. That can't be healthy.'

The boot-faced midwife said to Martha, 'You are a very crude and selfish young woman.' And the whole ward screamed with laughter, for we were a charmed circle.

*   *   *

When she went to work I was her backstop. If Scarlett or Lawrence was too ill for school she would pop them over the fence still warm in their night clothes, like a new recipe to be tasted, and I would automatically take over.

God, how I loved those kids.

Beautiful but oblivious to it, just like their mother.

I despised myself for the disloyal way I wished mine were more like hers. Easy, laid back. They didn't whine for hours on end after a fall or a fight. They didn't nag for attention from her—they knew that was a waste of time—but all the same they had no doubt that they were the apples of Martha's eye.

Did I resent my role at that time? Since she accused me of this I have asked myself the question, but the only answer I can come up with is, if I did resent it I wasn't aware.

I must be honest, I suppose: I did resent Martha going back to work even though she gave me fair warning. So I wasn't enough for Martha? Why not? We had good times, didn't we? Why did she need more in her life? I understood that staying at home was threatening her sanity, especially given the highhanded way she allowed herself to be treated by Sam. She needed more independence and I could sympathize with that. I babysat for her during interviews although most of the jobs were inappropriate—agony aunt for *Marie* magazine— and I meanly rejoiced when she got turned down.

'But, Martha, you haven't got time for a job,' I used to say to make her feel better after another rejection.

'I need other people to reflect who I am. Without their approval I feel that I'm drowning. You're lucky, Jennie, you're far more self-sufficient than me. You don't need anyone.'

But she knew how much I needed her and that was part of the trouble.

We used to be honest together. There was no rivalry between us.

But Martha was right in that I was contented with just a few close relationships. Awkward with strangers, hopeless at parties; those meaningless, superficial friendships you pick up and put down at whim leave me cold. It takes me years to make a friend, and then Graham calls me loyal to a fault.

This remark annoys me, and the grudging way he says it. 'How can anyone be loyal to a fault? You're either loyal or disloyal, surely?' I'd ask.

'But you don't have to make such a song and dance about it.' And I'd be hurt, shocked by that, because when did I make a song and dance? And I wasn't used to Graham being critical. We were united in our disapproval of the way Sam used scorn and criticism in his treatment of Martha. In my eyes she was a martyr the way she put up with Sam, but then she adored him, worshipped him and their relationship was seriously physical.

Sometimes I looked at Sam's hands—active, roving hands, all muscle and bone—and compared them to Graham's . . .

And now I am betrayed.

Undone. That formal classical stuff should never have gone out of fashion. Woe is me for I am undone. Cursed be the day I was born. Undone, unravelled, ravished, cut into pieces to make little labels, like Christmas cards turned into gift tags.

There are some things so precious they shouldn't be shared, secrets which should never be written down. To betray the confidence of a friend in exchange for fleeting popularity—that heart-squeezing sense of self-disgust the moment you close your mouth. You instantly know what you've done. But when you betray yourself, you don't realize it until later.

I used to think the ultimate betrayal must be that of a man who has left his wife for another woman. A bodily betrayal, those bedroom/bathroom secrets, secretions, tingles and squirms.

Sex.

But I was wrong.

Martha and I had a meeting of minds and that was exciting and sweet, not so much striking a chord as composing a whole concerto, and the only person who can know the pain I'm feeling now is Martha. Martha with the flashing laughter.

Who won't speak to me.

Who puts the phone down when I call.

Who refuses to answer my notes.

And who is breaking my heart.

*   *   *

There's a drifting of spirit from our house since Martha stopped whisking in carrying hysteria like a cloak about her shoulders, melodramatic, full of ideas, life swishing in velvet around her.

But it is worse than that.

The way it began was worse than that, watching Poppy and Josh being hurt, really, truly, deep down hurt for the first time in their lives. Ten and seven is too young to feel those pangs of anguish and I thought Martha was bigger than that. We might not be friends any more but we should have tried to prevent the feud from touching our vulnerable children.

'You're splendid at catastrophes, Jennie, so go away quietly and indulge.'

Those were the last unkind words she said. A crumbling Ayesha . . . that was me. I felt that I had

11

suddenly aged and was quite unable to cope.

I tried to explain exactly what happened but Martha refused to listen.

I was awed by her fearful anger, blinded, groping towards the truth.

*   *   *

I would have preferred an older house and Martha said, nastily, that was so I could empathize with its pain. But the Mulberry Estate wasn't bad as they go. The architect had made an effort; every house was that little bit different and the gardens were a decent size. They were called executive lodges and Graham and I, being the first ones in, were presented with a bouquet and a beribboned bottle of bubbly. The first three lodges were only just finished when we moved into ours through the muddy wastelands of Mulberry Close, and we lived with strips of thick brown paper over a mustard wall-to-wall carpet provided by the company.

Inducements indeed—built-in Scandinavian hob, fridge freezer, Bosch dishwasher and washing machine. We had put our name down for the first house on the day Graham and I got engaged, but because it wasn't ready in time we had to move in with Graham's mum.

*   *   *

A lawn brittle from over-mowing. A bungalow neat and gloomily solid. A pirate head from Majorca, glass-fronted cabinets, G-plan Sixties furniture, and pot plants, a timid green in the passionless air, sitting sadly in spindly wicker stands.

'What do you two get up to all evening, hiding away in your bedroom like this? You can't possibly be comfortable. For goodness sake, come in and join Howard and me in the lounge. We won't eat you,' said Graham's mum, Ruth, aggrieved.

But Graham and I, cuddled up on the bed watching telly, were just happy to be together, at one, married, a front to the world.

Graham said, 'Leave us alone, Mum. We'll come through if we want to. We're fine.'

'Well, excuse me for interfering.'

Because I worked I didn't have time to help with stuff like laundry, shopping or housework but I knew Ruth expected more of me, and sitting with her and Howard in the evening seemed to be part of the deal. We ate with Graham's parents even though we had made it clear we would rather eat alone. Gravy with everything. Stewed fruit in various guises in shell-shaped dishes of watery green. On the day after we moved in I came home to find the table set for four.

'Ruth, you should have left that,' I said. 'I'd have done it.' But my voice trailed away as I undid the buttons on my mac while she tied on her apron.

'You can do the potatoes, dear, if you really want to help. Let Graham and his dad watch the news in peace.'

Oddly, as if she resented me, Ruth seemed deliberately to do her chores in an order which made it impossible for me to help. I simply was not there to do my duty, so her irritation was self-induced.

The dishes could never be left to drain. 'We don't want smeary china,' she told me. She eyed me through a stiffening distaste. 'In this household,

13

Jennie, we have always dried up.' And then she watched me carefully. 'One plate at a time, dear, please. I've kept these plates for twenty-five years and I don't want chips in them now.'

Clean sheets would be folded and pointedly left on the end of the bed every week, as if she guessed ours would be stained. Every Friday, top sheet to bottom and a fresh one on top. I said, 'Please don't bother to iron our sheets, Ruth. They really don't need ironing.'

And Ruth smiled staunchly.

I don't think Ruth disliked me, but maybe she was trying to tell me something I had failed to grasp about marriage. Graham and I were married now and so the romance was over. As a wife, self-sacrifice came next on the list and this was a mild initiation.

I would look at Graham reproachfully but all he could do was shrug his shoulders.

When we drank wine it was secretly and in the morning Graham smuggled the bottles out of the house in his briefcase, rolled up in serious newspapers.

Another couple would have made a fuss but not me and Graham, oh no. We hated to argue, we dreaded scenes and we felt so grateful to have found each other. Neither of us had imagined we were special enough to be chosen, neither of us had had a best friend; we were so similar in that kind of way. Middle of the road, fifteenth in a class of thirty, sixth in a team of twelve, friends with everyone but special to no-one.

Fair to middling. Could do better.

One of the best things about being married was sharing somebody else's name. There was strength to be had in this pooling together; a name was a stout wooden fence and meant we could peer at the world through the knots. And Gordon, a good strong name, was near the front of the alphabet whereas my maiden name, Young, had kept me last in life, near the back.

Every day during that first summer we went to look at our sprouting house, pacing round it and imagining what our new furniture would look like inside. I would walk up and down the stairs, running my hand along the smooth wooden banister. Graham planned out the garden. Unsure of the house to begin with, I came to start loving it then. It signified such a great escape and I whispered to it, 'Oh hurry, house, hurry up, please hurry.'

*   *   *

Heaven. We could breathe again. Truly together for the first time ever and he carried me over the threshold. We were proprietorial, understandably I suppose, and kept an eye on the couples who came to see over the show lodge, the last house to be sold in the frying-pan-shaped close.

We weren't in longer than a month before the red SOLD sign went up on numbers two, three and four, even though the men were still working inside. We saw this as a good sign: we'd be able to sell quite quickly when we came to move on, we believed. I was already pregnant. Poppy was due the following spring and I had already resigned from the bank, having no real interest in the job.

'I know him,' said Graham, shamelessly spying on the couple coming up next door's path with the

15

keys to number two in their hands.

'Oh?' I stared as rudely as he, fascinated by the blowzy woman with the wild mane of hair, more pregnant than anyone I'd ever seen and wrapped in an emerald curtain. She was big. No shame. She flapped along penguin style in large ethnic sandals, her hands kneading her back as if she was about to give birth. Her coarse guffaws of laughter were unreasonably disturbing; after all, she was the stranger, I already lived here—me, Graham and a few sick saplings.

'Sam Frazer, he runs his own advertising company and goes to the Painted Lady for lunch. I've seen him in there with his mates.'

'What's he like?' I felt uneasy but didn't know why.

'Seems like a decent kind of guy.'

'Perhaps we should make them a cup of tea . . . and go round . . . be friendly, you know.'

Sensing my tension, Graham held my hand. We stood together warily in our house of brand-new wood, breathing sawdust and turpentine, paint and putty. 'Jennie, no more "shoulds" for us, this is our house, we don't do anything we don't want to and we can be as unsociable here as we damn well like.'

Martha would have been the first to echo this sentiment. She might even have raised a smeary glass in a toast, had she heard it.

*   *   *

Dear God, how I wish that I'd never met her.

CHAPTER TWO

Martha

Dear God, how I wish that I'd never met her.

*   *   *

So there we were, in our superior executive lodge. I must say I never expected to end up on a half-finished estate in bloody Essex.

But then I had never expected to get married or have my own baby. Nor did I think I would ever reach twenty, or grow breasts, menstruate, throw away my black leather skirt, die, or stop watching *Neighbours.*

Unlike the co-ordinated house next door ours was a jumbled mixture: tumbledown sofa strewn with throws, assorted chairs with various cushions, lamps and pieces of twisted oak, because we'd been meaning to buy an old cottage over the border in Hertfordshire.

Piglets Patch was my dream house. Honeysuckle, thatch and roses.

It fell through when I was eight months pregnant. We had sold our flats and we needed a home, we had buggered about long enough. So we bought the house and its dandelion lawn in a state of panic. We hadn't intended to stay for long, but life is full of little surprises.

I didn't expect to settle down here round a fading mulberry bush but, dear God Almighty, far more extraordinary than that was being knifed in the back by the woman I came to call my friend.

*   *   *

It was a wet and blustery March when Jennie and I entered the dark world of breeding.

All night long the women in our ward were kept awake by pitiful cries from the adjoining delivery suite.

Sam rushed me to St Margaret's when the pains came every five minutes and within an hour Scarlett was born.

Nature's disgusting.

Nature hurts.

That animal smell, blood and Johnson's and the visitors' freesias.

Sam stayed and watched and afterwards we stuffed down chicken sandwiches, holding Scarlett in our arms and getting used to the words 'our daughter'. Oh, the glory! Kissing her black, bloody hair. I had to use half a box of tissues to wipe Sam's proud tears away.

Perversely I had the natural birth while Jennie endured the forceps.

I recognized her in the morning when they wheeled her into the ward with the teas, drooping like a dunked digestive. I had caught sight of her only once, yesterday, when we moved in. I had made the sandwiches to tide us over until the cooker could be wired up. We never imagined we'd have no time to eat them.

'I know you, don't I? You live next door to me.'

Jennie's matching slippers sat waiting on the floor by her bed. White with rosebuds, signifying innocence, same as the nightdress she changed into. All that whiteness made her waif-like. She lifted her head from the pillow and eyed me, unaware of where she was or what she was supposed to be doing.

Nosing into the pink blanket in the perspex cot beside her I said, 'Great, a girl. They'll be neighbours, they'll be best mates.'

Jennie's moan of distress was tragic.

'Leave Mrs Gordon alone,' said the nurse. 'She's had an exhausting time.'

Well, naturally I was indignant. I'd been spoken to like a child, but I managed to rise above it because my main concern was getting to the loo for that first morning cigarette.

As I passed Jennie's bed, fags deep in Sam's dressing-gown pocket, she whispered to me with her eyes tightly closed, 'That's it. Never again.'

*   *   *

One of the first subjects Jennie brought up was the way she was bullied at school. I think she had a thing about this and it influenced all her behaviour.

We were in her house at the time, in her bedroom. I sat on Graham's side of the bed while she, with her wet hair wrapped in a towel, sat beside me bottle-feeding Poppy after a careful sterilization routine. With her hairline reduced by the towel Jennie looked almost childlike, quite impish. And with her small bones and snub nose she put me in mind of a freckled pixie. 'Why did they pick on me?' she asked, still bewildered all these years later. 'I didn't stand out in any way. I wasn't fat or spotty or smelly, I didn't have a squint or a harelip. They were girls I'd had to my party, and they made fun of my mother.'

'What was wrong with your mother?' I teased, my sticky nipple in greedy Scarlett's mouth. I was always finished way before Jennie because it was essential that Poppy drained the lot, was winded at least six times during her feed and by the time the torment ended Jennie's lips were as sore as my tits; she bit them continuously. She kept Lipsalve in the pocket of her special feeding apron. She changed the brand of milk weekly, even venturing into goat's when Poppy went through a long phase of colic.

'Nothing was wrong with my mother,' she snapped. 'That was what made it hurt more. My mother was really trying, she'd made such an effort to get everything right. My God, how I hated kids' birthday parties, but you had to have them and you had to go to other people's if you were invited. Does any kid honestly like them?'

'I did.'

'Honestly?'

'I was a pig. I went for the food and the presents.'

Jennie propped Poppy against her hand and the baby burped and puked. Jennie looked worried. 'Damn damn damn.' Her agitation was catching. 'I'm going to get no sleep again tonight.'

'Leave her downstairs where you can't hear her. It won't hurt her—not as much as you being so tired.'

Of course she didn't listen to me, why would she? Letter by letter, word by word, Jennie was following the latest book. Following rules, like believing in God, like measuring recipes, like testing her hair before colouring, was an essential part of her nature.

'My mother had veins on the back of her legs.'

I looked at my own. 'Join the club.'

'No, Martha, not veins like that. Horrible wormy veins. She was always in having them done. She had to wear special stockings. It was the veins they started whispering about—Barbara Middleton and Judith Mort.'

She even remembered their names. 'Kids are so foul.'

'They scrawled on the blackboard, thin wispy scrawls with red and blue chalk. Nobody knew what they were but me. And they wrote underneath in mauve, "legs eleven". But they didn't stop there, they went on and on.'

'Only because you let them.'

'What do you mean?'

'You should have fought back. Thrown their books down the loo.'

'And then some other kids joined them. People I thought were my friends.'

'Picking on somebody else is a way to make sure they don't pick on you.'

'I know, I know.' At last Poppy drained that dratted bottle. Jennie tried to smile, a tired one, purified by pain. She started to tidy her layette, a basket in pink waterproof gingham in which she kept her oils and creams, half-opened packs of this and that, sacred ceremonial ointments. 'It sounds obvious now, but it wasn't then. I used to break my heart at night thinking how hurt Mum would be if she knew. She kept asking me what was the matter. She asked so gently, so tenderly, how could I explain?'

21

That first spring at Mulberry Close was so wet the earth gave out seaside smells and the rain went on interminably. To venture out meant getting covered in mud. The heart-shaped leaves of the mulberry tree which stood on the green in the centre were splashed with tar and cement. Sam could do nothing with the new garden. The clay was too heavy to move, so the patio slabs, the sand and cement stayed stacked at the back of the garage, and when the roses arrived in their little brown sacks we dumped them in the shed and forgot them.

I grew fatter and slacker and more depressed, while next door Jennie smiled radiantly and oozed with an eerie confidence, her whole house organized to create an aura of peace and goodwill.

On the few dry days her washing was out on the line by eight thirty. Although it never properly dried outside, she disapproved of stringing it, dripping, round the kitchen as I did.

I was the only one allowed to peep behind this maternal serenity and this was because, with my Safeway bag full of Pampers nappies, my dribbled-on bibs and sticky dummies, I was no competition.

For Jennie everything had to be right.

When Poppy caught chickenpox, every individual spot was dabbed at with the calamine while I watched in mad exasperation.

The towels in her bathroom matched her flannels.

Her kitchen sink stayed clear of dishes and her windows sparkled.

She needed to be reassured that she was a

marvellous mother and she was, at some cost to herself as, like a superhuman, she liquidized all Poppy's food, had her weighed weekly, boiled her snow-white terry nappies, disinfected rattles and crept round the house while her baby slept, with her voice in mellow mode. But she was draining her own vitality.

Everything was done to rote, nothing was ever spontaneous.

'Isn't this lovely?' she seemed to be asking. 'Look—I am a safe and natural mother.'

But she wasn't safe. Not safe at all.

*   *   *

I thought of her mother's terrible veins and wondered how she got them because Jennie, programmed like this, was following some destructive pattern.

If I encouraged her to try to relax she would twist and protest with all the strain showing. 'Let Graham help more,' I suggested. 'He's a genuine new man. You should make more of him. Now if you had Sam as a partner, I could understand the state of your nerves.'

'What state of nerves?' she'd ask sharply, biting a trembling lip.

In the end, seeing she was close to collapse, I ordered her to sit down.

'I'd better not drink,' she sniffed when I offered her wine, head down like a sulking bird.

'Nonsense,' I said. 'Get this down you and stick your feet up on this chair.'

'You don't know what it's like,' she groaned. 'Mothering comes so naturally to you. It ought to be such a simple thing. But Scarlett's such an easy baby, she's never woken more than twice a night.'

'I find her almost impossible to cope with,' I told Jennie truthfully.

With a voice contorted with fresh distress she confided her terrible secret. 'What would you say if I told you I sometimes hate Poppy so much, I'm frightened I'm going to kill her?'

'I'd say you were normal,' I answered, amazed that she thought otherwise.

'If I said that to Graham he'd never understand. He would think I was a freak.'

'If only you'd stop pretending,' I said.

And I wondered in how many other ways Jennie and Graham pretended. And why.

I made her go out, to fetch stamps from the post office. She hadn't left her house since coming home from the hospital after the birth. 'Walk, take your time, don't use the car.' Such a little step. I made her leave Poppy with me.

She came back happier but fearing corruption.

And the next step after that was enrolling for aerobics.

*　　　*　　　*

Sam said, 'Why is that damn woman always here when I come home? And she looks so sheepish, as if she's doing something wrong. I don't know how to react to her, she seems shy and uncomfortable with me.'

'That's because you're so gruff,' I said. 'Not everyone appreciates your sick sense of humour. Be gentler with her. And perhaps we should have them over for supper.'

24

'Oh no . . .'

'Don't start. We could ask the Fords, too. I think Jennie is lonely, out of her depth. I mean, she cries if her cakes don't rise and she has no-one but me to talk to.'

'We don't want to live in the neighbours' pockets,' Sam said predictably, 'nor do we want to get involved.'

'It would be the first time that poor woman has left her house at night since Poppy arrived,' I informed him. 'I'm going to suggest a babysitter.'

'Martha, I just can't face it. She'd bring the wretched child with her.'

*   *   *

So that was how it first started, ten years ago.

Life with Jennie was never easy, but the fatal cracks appeared much later.

When Mrs Forest rang me up I couldn't believe what I was hearing.

I was stunned. 'But Jennie Gordon's a friend of mine, she only lives next door. If this bullying has been going on for so long, why the hell didn't she tell me?'

'She says she did bring the subject up, but that you took it very lightly,' said the teacher. 'All I can say is, apparently Poppy has been frightened to come to school from the beginning of this term. Yesterday afternoon she went missing.'

'Because of Scarlett?' Ridiculous!

The telephone hummed with tension. There must be some misunderstanding. Scarlett and Poppy, inseparable since infancy, had their desks moved last term to stop their endless gossiping.

25

They chose to open their Christmas presents in each other's bedrooms. They insisted on the same hairstyles. Snow White and Rose Red they might be, but somehow they managed to look alike.

'I think you and I need to talk this over,' said Mrs Forest sympathetically. 'Come into school and collect Scarlett early.'

Stranger and stranger. As I backed out my car I thought I saw a movement of curtains at number one. Jennie was nervous. More persecution, more victimization, and I began to wonder if victims were made by a parent's genes or some unidentified chemical.

*   *   *

And I think she never learned how to love.

CHAPTER THREE

Jennie

And I think she never learned how to love.

*   *   *

By some kind of mystic osmosis the Frazers drew their neighbours around them like the Lord drew his disciples, like bony prophets drew frenzied crowds to their deserts of biblical brown.

Come unto me and I will refresh you.

Not a bad thing if you've got the knack, but me, I grew irrationally jealous, gleaning my pleasures from pain as Martha would later put it.

At least the Frazers' popularity and slatternly nature meant that the Close the compulsion to compete with the pr... Joneses. The Frazers drove an expensive Cherokee jeep which they never cleaned, inside or out; it was filthy and pranged in several places. Instead of buying a second car Martha ran Sam to work every morning—no more than a ten-minute drive—while back at home there'd be some calamity: her washing machine would be flooding the floor, she'd have let a stew boil over. Rather than a costly playhouse with a gate and pretend garden flowers, their kids used a ramshackle den built by Sam, with corrugated iron as a roof and walls made of rough bits of four-by-two nailed together. Martha refused a cleaner. The poor woman wouldn't have known where to start. They owned a ride-on mower but it leaked petrol and rarely worked.

Their magnetism was a mystery to me. Although they weren't a glamorous couple, they had this charismatic, enchanted quality which I so envied but couldn't define and which I remembered meeting before at the miniature desks of childhood. To be around these special people gave you an air of exultation. Excluded, you could feel neutralized.

The green-door factor.

The door was built with clever whispers.

The door was chained by knowing eyes.

You had to know the password.

Ostentatious they were not, but the Frazers certainly went short of nothing. Sam was in fashionable advertising and the name of his company sometimes rolled by in the credits on ITV, but in spite of this Martha dressed like a psy, choosing outlandish material and running up her own flowing clothes—vivid, sloppy and tasty like burnt home-made sweets—and her kids lived in patched dungarees, baggy jumpers and multi-coloured boots.

Natural taste, I thought to myself, knowing that I had none.

She went to the hairdresser only once a year to have her curly black locks cut short.

She was quickly bored.

She blossomed in company.

She collected cats and her homely house had a feral smell about it.

I felt a pleasant kick of satisfaction each time I was included in Martha's disorganized plans, but I couldn't escape the slump of misery when the Frazers were asked to supper by my neighbouring rivals.

Yes, it's true and I have to admit it, I saw them as rivals right at the start of my friendship with Martha.

I was haunted by the most ludicrous trivia.

Unable to keep my distress to myself, I would moan to Graham with my voice mean and sharp. 'Why the hell would they want to go round to the Wainwrights' again when Martha swears she can't stand him? She calls him the flasher because of his mac.'

And:

'Fancy Christine inviting Scarlett to Jody's sixth birthday party. Scarlett's a baby . . .'

Or:

'Martha says she feels sorry for Tina, that's why she keeps going round for coffee. That's the trouble with Martha, everyone wants her. She

28

makes them laugh.'

Graham protested between the silvery bones of his morning kipper. 'Does it matter? Do you care? Why are you so bothered about what Martha Frazer is up to? You spend most of your time round there gossiping, anyway. I should think you'd be glad of a chance to catch up.'

'What do you mean, catch up?' This, as always, hit a raw nerve. I was always well ahead of myself. Like his mother, Ruth, and my own mother, Stella, I kept a neat and tidy house.

'By the way you keep tabs on Martha anyone would think you were jealous.'

This accusation came as a shock. 'That's absurd. Of course I'm not jealous.'

'Well then, leave it alone. What does it matter to you if Martha's garden is littered with kids? You wouldn't want them round here. If she doesn't mind the mess and the mud, good luck to her. She's crazy.'

Graham would have had a heart attack if our garden was abused the way hers was. Scarlett's little sandpit had been spread, partly by kids and partly by cats, so it overflowed onto the patio. Pastry cutters and plastic watering cans, mostly broken, and punctured beach balls lay around rotting with little pats of mud inside them. Sam had laid turf which had not properly taken, so the surface of the Frazers' lawn was uneven, not billiard-table smooth like ours, for which Graham had sensibly sown grass seed and used the roller on it for weeks.

'You might as well do things properly if you're going to bother to do them at all,' he used to say, fairly often.

On the few days it was warm enough for Poppy to toddle outdoors I struggled to keep her on the patio, for Graham's hard-working sake.

We made an earnest pair, Graham and I, so proud of our house; but Martha's attitude was undermining, she was so unconcerned about hers. It made us look so uptight and conventional, so materially obsessed, forever fiddling with curtains and mats, and I suspected that Martha found my loo-seat cover amusing. We weren't like that—not really.

But we were certainly going wrong somewhere because the atmosphere in her house was so much easier, while ours still smelled of new paint no matter how often I opened the windows.

In the evenings, later, when the kids were safely in bed and we went round for a slapdash supper at Martha's warped and crayoned table, her hysterical kitchen of half-burned candles and battered pine— with its baggy cushions, chipped china, bright yellow walls and cats on the Aga—managed to give out an ambience of sophisticated French café life which we could never achieve with our matching candles in our beige dining room.

*   *   *

My little triumph.

Against all the odds my children were bigger and heavier than hers. Probably because they were used to regular meals and not fed scrapings out of the fridge at whatever time was convenient for Martha. And in my opinion, the bottle gave them a better start.

'I thought mine would be giants like me,' said

Martha rather ruefully. 'Not scruffy street urchins with lanky loins, like a Dickens illustration.'

'Martha can be far too casual,' I gloated to Graham self-righteously that day. 'It's all very well her telling me to relax, saying I do too much or I worry too much, but you can see how it pays off in the end.'

'Martha's a slut,' said Graham.

'But nice with it,' I had to say.

'Yes, a very nice slut,' he agreed.

'Do you sometimes wish I was more like Martha?'

'Christ, no, why would I? She is melodramatic, loud and lazy. She would drive me demented. I couldn't live with her for a second, and you couldn't live with Sam.'

Would he like to screw Martha? I wondered.

Men looked at Martha, men were enamoured in spite of the hair under her arms.

I was too stiff. It was hard to bend. Compared to the voluptuous Martha who admitted she preferred sex in the kitchen I felt like a frump, although I was not yet thirty. People have called me aloof, mistaking my shyness for haughty disdain, and the way that my nose turns up doesn't help.

'But as we're going on holiday together,' said Graham with a sigh of gloom, 'we'd better just hope that we all get on.'

As the months sped by, we proud mothers watched as our little girls smiled their first smiles, grew their first teeth, gurgled their first words and crawled their first few yards. Those were the days. The best of times.

*   *   *

31

But eight years on and the tables were turning.

The bullying had been going on for weeks before I found out about it.

Thinking back, yes, Poppy had been quieter, but then she'd had more homework to do as she came to the end of her last year at junior school and I knew she was dreading the move to the comp.

I was frantic and frightened when I discovered her skiving off school. Thank God I did find her and managed to stop it happening again before it became a dangerous habit. I came across her in the mall, sitting among a gaggle of wrinklies on a bench outside Marks & Spencer.

At first I couldn't believe it. I assumed she was on some project. I even smiled to see her there. 'Poppy! What's going on? I didn't know you did this on a Wednesday.'

But where were all the others? Why did she look so pale?

She hung her head, empty of answers, and then her blue eyes filled up and she began to cry.

'Whatever's the matter?' I fished for a tissue. 'Poppy, look at me now! What's going on? *What are you doing?*'

She stared at me in utter misery, sucking the end of her hair.

'Are you on your own? Where's Scarlett?'

The horror of this, of her vulnerability, of what could have happened to a child her age, made me suddenly furious.

I raised my voice. *'And nobody knows? No-one at school knows you're here?'*

Poppy shook her head forlornly. She twisted one thin, scabby leg round the other.

'You're coming straight home with me right now and we'll talk about this until I know what's going on. The thought of it, Poppy, *Jesus Christ*, the thought of you being here on your own . . .'

'I'm quite safe here, Mum.'

I went cold in the pit of my stomach. 'What? What are you telling me? That you've done this before, this isn't the first time?' I was staggered. We were close. I truly believed that we had no secrets and now this—my God.

'This is the first time. I couldn't help it. I just couldn't stay there any longer. I'm sorry.'

'I daresay you are. And so am I. Daddy will be sorry. Mrs Forest will be sorry . . .'

'Please don't tell them,' she pleaded with me. *'Don't tell Mrs Forest.'* And she broke into floods of tears again.

This was impossible. I bent down to her level and held both her arms. 'Listen, Poppy,' I began, determined to be gentle and soothing. 'Nobody's going to shout or be cross. All we need to do is talk this through till we understand what is happening here.'

'But I can't tell you!' she stormed.

I looked at her hard. She was as stubborn as Graham.

'But what can't you tell me, darling?'

'I can't tell you what's been happening, I can't tell you what you want.'

I made my voice extra cajoling. 'Why not, Poppy? Nothing's so dreadful that you can't tell me, or Daddy if you'd rather. Or Martha? D'you think you could talk to Martha?'

'It would only make things worse,' she hiccuped.

I looked across the busy arcade with panic-stricken eyes, at all the ugly, misshapen people, and brought both hands to my head. '*Worse*? Worse than you hanging around, seeking refuge in this God-awful place? Surely not worse than this, Poppy? When I think of what could have happened to you. And what about the work you're missing? I can't imagine how they didn't miss you.'

'I'm never going back there, Mum,' she said, rubbing her eyes which were swollen and red. My heart broke to see my child so unbearably unhappy, drooping, head down and swaying slightly like a small corpse on a gibbet. 'Whatever you do and whoever you speak to, I refuse to go back to school.'

*   *   *

The first thing I did was go round to Martha's, although she denies this now.

'It's Scarlett,' I said desperately, 'Scarlett and that Harriet Birch.'

Heavy with complaint, I had to make her know how she'd wronged me.

She moved the Brie and the plasticine. She pushed me a cup of coffee. She lit up one of her foul cigarettes: Samson Shag. She used to roll up with an angry urgency, believing these were better for her health, but her cough was worse if anything.

She turned irritated eyes on to me and said, 'I haven't liked to say anything but it seems that Poppy resents Scarlett's friendship with Harriet and it's been quite difficult for all three of them.'

Oh no, this wouldn't do. This was denial. A twisted truth. 'They have been deliberately unkind to Poppy,' I said, 'and it's been going on for a long

34

time. She says they watch every move she makes and my God, Martha, she's been suffering in silence . . .'

'Jennie, I don't want to sound unreasonable, but that's not the way I heard it.'

'I can't believe this. You knew? *You're saying you knew and you didn't tell me?*'

'Jennie . . .' She sighed, sitting back and allowing her ash to fall sloppily off the end of her bent-up rollie. 'I don't want to sound as if I think that Poppy has a problem.'

'Sorry?' I put down my cup, gaping at this unfairness. 'A problem? *Poppy?*'

'And I don't want to suggest you are over-protective.'

Then she had the nerve to smile.

What a gross simplification! 'Even if I am over-protective, you have to admit this is hard for Poppy. She and Scarlett have been best friends ever since they could walk. And now here comes Harriet Birch and all of a sudden Poppy is treated with less sensitivity than you'd use on an old handbag.'

Martha leaned forward and said gently, 'Hang on, Jennie, you mustn't evade the real issue here.'

'If you know what the real issue is, maybe you could enlighten me.'

'The real issue is that Scarlett has been carrying Poppy for years and she's just got tired of it.'

Jesus! I couldn't believe it. Martha, renowned for her bluntness, had cracked my heart so hard it took all I had to draw breath. I lowered my face as if I'd been slapped. I was pink with indignation because deep inside I knew what she meant, but couldn't bear the way she had said it. This was my child we were discussing, my vulnerable, frightened, unhappy daughter, and I expected more from Martha than this. I thought guiltily back to the times we had said:

'Go with Scarlett, Poppy, she'll take you . . .'

'Keep your eye on Poppy, she's frightened of dogs . . .'

'Tell Scarlett if those kids start on you. She'll sort them out, she'll see them off . . .'

Both of us had understood that Scarlett, as Martha's child, was more confident than mine and might enjoy the role of keeper.

But Scarlett had never complained.

Not until now.

In fact she seemed to enjoy the part of defender of the weak. She took it upon herself naturally. Nobody forced her, or put her under pressure.

Then Martha said, 'I think we have been expecting too much from Scarlett lately. There's exams coming up and a change of school. She's only ten after all.'

This was outrageous. I blinked hard and fast. 'So is Poppy. And I notice you don't seem interested to hear the details of what's been happening. They have been very cruel, you know.'

My best friend sighed again. 'Children are, I'm afraid. Shit, you of all people know that, Jennie.' This was disloyalty in the extreme.

I was going to tell her anyway, whether she wanted to hear or not. 'They've been ganging up on her, picking on her. Hiding her books and throwing apples, making sure she's chosen last when teams are being selected, whispering in the playground, and I heard there was some money missing . . .'

'Yes,' said Martha. 'I know about that. Poppy accused Scarlett of stealing. She sneaked off and told Mrs Forest that she'd seen Scarlett and Harriet take the money from a gym bag in the cloakroom. It turned out to be lies—just a pack of lies.'

By now I was shaking with rage and shock. I had never liked Harriet Birch, a sly and cunning child. I felt so hurt. So betrayed. 'Poppy did see them take that money.' What I hated most was that Martha seemed pleased that all this had come out in the open.

Martha said briskly, 'And you are so unconditionally uncritical that you honestly believe her?'

It struck me then that Poppy, holed up like an animal in her room, had no circle of friends, unlike Scarlett. Friends who might back her story. Friends to walk round with during break. Take Scarlett away and Poppy was all on her own. Is this why I felt so protective towards her, is this why I had to fight so hard? Remembering how it was with me when I was Poppy's age?

And frightened.

And alone.

And then Martha said, 'Look, calm down, Jennie. You've come here to talk, so let's do that. We can't get anywhere while you're behaving as though Scarlett has committed mass murder.'

Huh. The flippancy I so admired before disgusted me then. I didn't need Martha. I didn't need anyone. I got up and stiffly left her house, drained and exhausted.

*   *   *

Oh yes, ours was an uneasy friendship.

37

CHAPTER FOUR

Martha

Oh yes, ours was an uneasy friendship.

*   *   *

Our babies had started to walk and talk. Sam and I had argued for weeks over whether to ask the Gordons to come on holiday with us that year. Sam liked them well enough, although he and Graham had little in common. 'He'll never rise above middle management,' said Sam at his most pompous. 'He hasn't got the thrust to succeed.'

'You mean,' I told him, 'that he's just too decent.'

Today was not a good time to broach it. The TV was on and Scarlett was crying.

'One more worry we don't need,' Sam complained. I had made him peel the apples and he was being deliberately clumsy, cutting most of the apple away along with the core. 'It'll spoil everything,' he went on. 'They won't get on with Emma and Mark, and you're up the duff again. Poppy is such a whinger they won't make the dining room in the evenings, and we won't feel free to leave the hotel no matter how good the babysitting is.'

'But Jennie needs a break and a laugh. Look at the shadows under her eyes and that old twitch is coming back. If it wasn't for that I wouldn't suggest it, but she'd be so lonely left here for two weeks . . .'

38

'Jesus, Martha,' and another mutilated apple was flung into the pan. 'That woman's got a drag behind her like she's held down by an anchor. Damn damn damn. So who else are you inviting? Anyone in the Close with a problem? Why don't you put up a sign? You are not responsible for Jennie so why do you allow yourself to be so put upon by your neighbour?'

'She's not just a neighbour, she's a friend,' I told him wearily. But Sam, like most men, doesn't understand about friendships. 'Don't be so petty. She is bowed down by routine and a warped sense of duty.'

Incoherent dark mumblings and then Sam said, 'One holiday won't change that. She'll drag all her chains along with her. She needs them, Martha, can't you see that? She uses pathos as a weapon and wins hands down every time. She needs those shackles for safety.'

'And whose fault is that?' I enquired coldly. He was such a selfish, uncaring bastard. 'Men. Men who undermine a woman's self-confidence so she builds these pitiful walls . . .'

'Balls balls balls. You're talking about Graham Gordon, remember? He's more of a bloody woman than she is.'

'You don't know the half of it. Jennie hasn't had much of a life.' I tried to explain matter-of-factly; Sam despised sentiment. I pushed him away from the sink. He always managed to look wrong there— just one of his more irritating knacks. I might as well do the apples myself. 'She hasn't had much fun or freedom. She grew up with a neurotic mother who carried a hideous grudge against a father who sodded off and left them. Try to imagine it.' But I

39

knew Sam couldn't. Men with narrow vision, like him, don't have vivid imaginations. 'Jennie was the only child and had to grow up quickly and that's why she's so serious and that's why you don't like her. Isn't it?'

*   *   *

Oh, how Jennie suffered during those toddler years.

And sometimes when she confided in me, I had the urge to shout *'Shut up, stop, don't tell me that, it's too private.'* Instead I squirmed and my toes curled up. She trusted me implicitly, far more than I trusted myself.

Did she think of me as a healer, able to make her whole again?

'I've never told anyone this before . . .' Starting another confession, she would look trustingly up at me with those large pale eyes. I think she thought I ought to feel flattered, but I wasn't and it was hard to respond. I now know that a shrink would have helped her, a long and profound course of therapy. There were personal issues that needed sorting, present problems and past ones.

And why had she shacked up with Graham?

Their sex life verged on the non-existent.

They made love once a week, on a Friday, to pacify him, I suppose. So on a Friday I'd think about them plodding upstairs in that awful cold way, knowing they had to do it whether they wanted to or not, and I imagined him in blue-striped pyjamas and Jennie in rosebud winceyette. I knew they didn't dress that way, of course: he wore an M&S nightshirt and she white broderie anglaise nighties; rather charming as nighties go. I had sat on their bed often enough in that apathetic bedroom of theirs. I had seen the neatly folded garments on the individual pillows, not a crease in either of them, while I bottle-fed Scarlett to keep Jennie company.

Sex and flesh.

Bodies disgusted Jennie.

I wished I'd not pushed that third sherry on the day she chose to unburden herself of her sexual problems. She didn't drink much, ever, nor did she trawl the dark side of her nature. With her face set and her shoulders tensed, she picked at the wooden swirls on my table as she described her mother's reaction when she found poor Jennie touching herself. And this was followed by the bowel movement saga. How important it was, in her mother's house, to perform at a regular time every day and how she was smacked if she failed the inspection. So much was disgusting, so much was called rude. I listened to Jennie's halting account with mounting disbelief and pity. Her embarrassment and shame were awful to see, so why was she telling me?

I laughed it all off. Was this the wisest reaction?

But she carried on as if in confession; such sad little sins had been eating her up. And I thought that I was helping her by absolving her of all blame. I know now that she didn't want that—she liked to endure, she enjoyed her guilt. A whip to scourge her back would have given her more relief than forgiveness.

'So what would you do, Martha, if you found Scarlett with a vibrator?'

'Well, if she wasn't just two years old, then I

hope I'd respect her privacy and be happy that she could enjoy such pleasure. Your mother was obviously a woman with problems.' I got up to turn down my boiling beetroot.

'She did have problems. A hard life. She worked herself to the bone.'

To the bone? What an odd thing to say in the late twentieth century. That mother/daughter relationship sounded vaguely abnormal to me.

'I don't feel a thing with Graham,' she said in a small stiff voice. 'It could be a finger up my nose.'

'So perhaps it's time you had a fling, a bonk with somebody else.' I was joking.

'Oh Martha,' she said coyly. 'Trust you.'

'Did you never feel anything?' I asked out of interest. 'Not even at the beginning? Not even with anyone else?'

Then she blushed virtuously and I thought she was like a nun, spiritual, she hardly existed in the flesh. 'There was nobody else before him, and I could never cheat on him. I love him. I might not like him in bed with me, but I really do love him a lot.'

*   *   *

Graham was a white-meat eater, he was suspicious of red and that's probably why he fell for Jennie. The largest part of him was his face, round and ponderous; below that he was thin, almost gaunt. Despite that, I felt he'd be heavy in bed. He had old-RAF-film dusty red hair, decent and boyish in the mess alongside David Niven. Graham was quiet with a quick, dry wit, coming out with the odd one-liner that made even the cynical Sam weak with laughter. I suspected he was afraid of me and considered me far too vulgar.

So could it be this serious, considerate man who put the squeeze on Jennie, so she felt she should clean, bake and scrub, remove her shoes at the door, wash her baby's hair every day and vacuum the inside of the car on a Saturday? And regularly vote Conservative—the natural response to inferiority?

Or was it the dire magazines she used to digest so avidly?

Whatever it was, I suspected that Graham disapproved of my friendship with his wife. You could see how disconcerted he felt when she and I shared some secret joke. But although I was a bad influence, he must have recognized that his duty-bound wife had to be able to let go sometimes, had to escape that antiseptic house, or go stark staring mad.

*   *   *

That holiday was a solemn affair.

Lists lists lists. Trips to Mothercare, the surgery, the chemist, the bookshop for advice about travelling with baby because the world across the Channel was a dangerous place where the heathen hordes lay waiting.

What I considered went quite well, Sam called an unmitigated disaster. OK, the flight was a nightmare due to Jennie's concerns over Poppy. With a mother so tense and tortured, of course her baby screamed.

She complained to the stewardess about a loose screw, pointing it out, on the wing.

Southern Italy was far too hot, dirty and cruel to animals.

Nothing but veal and more veal, and she wasn't about to feed veal to her toddler. Poppy was allergic to sunshine, so out came the calamine bottle again. The pushchair fringe wouldn't fix properly. Sam, me, Emma and Mark went off for days in the hills leaving Graham and Jennie imprisoned in the hotel. 'At least the room is cool,' she said, 'and we can boil the water.'

Emma and Mark, old friends of ours, had shared our holidays before. 'You must have known it was going to be hot,' Emma told Jennie quite fairly. 'So what made you come in the first place?'

'There's heat and heat,' said Jennie, flapping an overlarge sunhat. She'd resented Emma immediately in spite of the fact that, as mothers, she and I had more in common than my old soulmate and college buddy. 'This is a nasty dry heat which sticks in your throat, it can't be healthy.'

We ate out, drank wine, enjoyed most of our meals under vines.

But the bugs, dark and purple as the local plonk, bit the babies and Poppy cried.

The Germolene came out of the bag.

The rash spread.

The sea stank of sewage. 'That's not shit, that's seaweed,' said Sam, floating belly up on the water with a giggling Scarlett, brown as a berry in spite of the warnings, balanced precariously on his chest. But Graham knew best; after all, he did work for Essex Water.

Vegetables were plentiful but even so Graham, nearly a veggie but not quite decisive enough, found it hard to choose from the menu. There were times when we waited twenty minutes while he made his impossible choice. Sam knew exactly how long because he secretly timed it.

'Never no more,' he said, eyes rolling, in the privacy of our bedroom. 'And I blame you.'

I threw him a towel. 'Don't be so negative.' Tanned all over except for his bum, he knew he looked good and was showing off. 'It's not affecting your holiday,' I said, 'only theirs, which is a shame. I'm feeling guilty now. Maybe I shouldn't have asked them?'

'You, my sweetheart, are a manipulative, interfering old tart.' He put his hand over my mouth to stop me being boring, covered me with sand from his hairy chest, and we made love. *Again*.

*　　　*　　　*

So bearing in mind my tolerance and goodwill, eight years later when the bullying story came out, you can understand why I couldn't believe it when Mrs Forest rang to talk to me about Scarlett.

The situation was getting out of hand.

Why had Jennie complained to the school with me just across the fence? What the hell had got into her?

I'd been gobsmacked by the confrontation after she'd found Poppy alone in the mall and by her crude interpretation of that troubled little threesome, especially when I'd gone to such lengths to make damn sure they included Poppy the time Harriet Birch came to stay.

I could hardly stop Scarlett from having friends, and threesomes rarely work; even with adults they can be tricky. Little girls can be bitchy, but I'm not always first to spot the clues, unlike gloomy Jennie, forever on the lookout for Satan's cowpats to splat down on her innocent head. Sam calls it invoking the devil. I'd rather wait till the worst happens before I start clearing up the mess.

But there had been clues. I should have noticed the surface friction. I remember Scarlett called Poppy mean, and there were other pointers, but nothing firm or consistent enough for me to take too seriously. She'd said, 'Poppy's mean but you won't see it. She sneaks behind our backs. And she told me that Graham called you a slut.'

This is the kind of kids' conversation I switch off when it starts. I think I just said, 'He calls me a slut because Jennie's so neat, she works so hard. And the same applies to you, young ladies. Look at you, Scarlett, look at Harriet! When's the last time your hair saw a brush? Your hands are encrusted with grime. You're revolting.'

I was busy and life was hectic.

Sam delighted in telling me that he thought I was overdoing it, working on the *Express* full time, starting again when I got home, and later on having to deal with Lawrence's croup.

And then, was it the following week or the one before?

'Poppy's always hanging around. She won't leave us alone, will she, Harry? She won't take the hint. Why does she always mope around here?'

'Scarlett, you sound so horrid,' I said. 'Poppy is still your friend and just because you've found somebody new, that doesn't mean you can dump the old one. No. It won't do. You and Harry must try to make sure you don't exclude poor little Poppy. Be kind, please. Show her you care.'

46

'But why doesn't Poppy have other friends?'

My first glass of wine, downed too quickly, must have dimmed my brain; there was no sharpness left. I liked to be well into my second before I started cooking the meal. 'Poppy is shy and you know that.'

I scarcely noticed how Harriet kept her hands clasped in front and her small eyes fastened on Scarlett, but the half-smile on her face announced her enjoyment of this little scene. I wasn't sure I approved of Harriet. 'Poppy's not shy, she's sly, like Princess Diana.'

I had a thousand things to do and the kids were pestering, in the way. And where was Lawrence? I'd called him in ages ago. My eight-year-old son was turning native. I hardly ever saw him until he started coughing his lungs up at night. We lived our lives in the kitchen, not in specially designated areas like they did next door, and at times like this when I needed to cook I regretted our slovenly lifestyle.

'Don't speak ill of the dead. You've been listening to your father.'

'Poppy told Mrs Forest she saw me and Harry take some money from Kirsty Sullivan's gym bag.'

Hey. What was this?

'Poppy told Mrs Forest. And when Mrs Forest looked in my gym bag Kirsty's fifty pence was in there, exactly where Poppy said.'

This was more serious. 'When did this happen?'

'On Monday, but it's OK because Mrs Forest believed me and Harry.'

'But why the hell would Poppy say that?'

'And,' said Scarlett, a knowing sparkle in her eye, 'Poppy said that Jennie had it off with Daddy at a

47

party.'

'Oh?' I said, and Harriet Birch gave an unpleasant snigger. 'This is ridiculous. Poppy's imagination running riot. Go somewhere else with your scurrilous gossip and for God's sake wash your hands.'

*   *   *

Sometimes I wished that she was dead.

CHAPTER FIVE

Jennie

Sometimes I wished that she was dead.

*   *   *

When we went to Italy Martha was pregnant; by the time we got home so was I. A triumph when you think of the sweaty sheets, the failing fan and the weak sexual charge that Martha said existed between me and Graham. Italy was the first time Graham and I went away together, apart from those months with his mum and the odd weekend with my mum, Stella, below ground in her Walthamstow basement.

Hardly holidays.

We managed to rescue a broken-down donkey from a scar-faced peasant with teeth like dominoes. In tears I turned from the plight of the dogs, the dying hens . . .

*　　　*　　　*

Everybody accepts the fact that the sort of stress you have with your baby, especially your first, is bound to affect you as they grow. I had stress all the time when poor little Poppy was born. Martha did not. Martha and Sam did not have to suffer the tensions of wearying visitors. Their families' homes, being bigger and grander, offered nothing but happy respite, and when Martha went to her mother in Dorset, she came home refreshed and rested.

Stella, my mother—in her late forties, so a long way from elderly—was turning the colour of bone and her hair was mouse brown and tightly permed. She moved in for a fortnight after Poppy was born and, quite apart from the traumas she caused, she interrupted my new friendship with Martha. I hate to admit this, but for the first time in my life I felt desperately ashamed of her and the values she represented, of her hostile attitudes and her mean-sounding voice, of her cleanliness fetish and her love of hard work.

'I come all the way here,' she said, 'and all you want to do is gad off next door to gossip with that dreadful woman.'

'She's good fun.'

Stella's blancmanges with skin on top lay heavily on my still-swollen tummy.

Poor Mum. Born to be useful and neutered by life, she would rather I was tucked up in bed, an invalid dependent on her, clinical and kept sterile. And I loathed the way she fawned and simpered when the midwife called, still deferential towards anyone medical.

And the fuss she made before the midwife's visits.

Shipshape and sweet-smelling—not just me but the whole house—me sitting in a chair, daisy-fresh, not a suggestion of torn flesh about me and Poppy already up and bathed, a frilly doll in her lacy cradle. The washing got dried out on the line, free of all by-products of the body, the sink was clear, my home clean and hoovered.

Sluggish and mournful in the middle of this, like a sloth in a roomful of monkeys, I did my best to enlighten her. 'She's only a midwife, Mum. We don't need to do all this. She's not going to whisk Poppy away if the house doesn't come up to scratch.'

But she fought me every inch of the way. 'That's no attitude to take. You're a mother now and you need a routine. We certainly don't want people thinking . . .'

I turned off. I refused to listen. This phrase, the scourge of my childhood—*we don't want people thinking*—meant milk bottles sparkled on our step, I never left home without my bran flakes, I wrote thank-you letters by return, my hair was cut in a basin-shaped fringe and we never ate chips in the street.

What was Stella so afraid of?

But I had been indoctrinated at too early an age to recover, Martha told me.

After a submissive farewell to the midwife, Stella would keep the door open to watch the nurse's arrival at Martha's. Knowing how much I admired her, Stella viewed Martha with derision and pity. She gloried in the fact that my neighbour's door was frequently opened by 'a slattern in a dirty nightie', with Scarlett screaming in her arms. 'What does she look like? How the heck did she find a husband? And that poor child, what a start in life . . .'

But I noticed the midwife stayed longer at Martha's. That was where she stopped for her morning coffee, although Stella had laid out a tray with a doily and three neat biscuits.

Did Martha not notice, or did she not care about Stella's blatant disapproval? Either way I was so relieved. I didn't want to lose her as a friend.

'Interesting,' Stella observed, 'Martha's mother hasn't taken the trouble.'

'She did offer, actually, but Martha would rather not have her around.'

'Huh, and I can imagine why.'

'Mum, *you don't even know her.*'

'And you do, Jennie, do you? You met her at the hospital. And you don't need to be on intimate terms to know what sort of person she is.'

As far back as I could remember, Stella was judgemental, rather cruel, putting down other people who didn't conform to her petty standards. I knew this was a kind of defence, a way of being superior, and God knows she had little enough to be superior about.

Martha laughed at the way Stella tried to potty-train Poppy at one week old.

'It's the cold plastic feel on their bottoms that does it,' Stella said, looking pained, stung by Martha's criticism. She used a special apron whenever she handled Poppy; it matched her hands, so white, so starched. 'It triggers them off. Mark my words, Poppy will be dry in no time.'

'But the poor little mite can't sit up yet.' Martha laughed, unaware of the tensing effect on Stella. 'It's just a waste of time. She'll be dry in the end whatever you do.'

Stella sniffed and made her point with a flaring of eyes and nostril.

Martha and I would try to relax while Stella slopped around, moving a bucket of nappies to the washing machine, dragging the next load forward, puffing and damp with urgency and her tight brown hair frizzy from the effort.

'You just sit there,' she told me and Martha, and the thing is she honestly meant it. 'Leave this to me, you need your rest.' And then, over-politely, 'Mrs Frazer, another cup?' How many times must Stella be told to call her Martha? And one cup of coffee took so long; it meant rattling sounds from the kitchen and sighs, as if a full-blown meal was being cooked. The suffering that went into the process! Presentation was all-important. If the saucer was wet, it had to be wiped. But Stella's kindness was double-edged; no gift could be freely given.

'Goodness knows how you'd cope if I wasn't here.'

Of course I preferred Martha's house.

Watching Martha with Scarlett was like taking off a tight pair of shoes after a long and painful walk.

Yet when Poppy was asleep, we were made to creep round the house. It felt like a morgue, a place for the dead rather than a home for one newly born baby, and the smell of disinfectant could well have been formaldehyde.

But Martha mostly flopped like a whale on her

52

shabby kitchen sofa, reading or watching some junk daytime programme, smoking and slurping coffee. Scarlett was never far from her side, at her feet in that lumpy carrycot, or propped up dangerously on a nearby cushion, while Poppy, at Stella's insistence, always slept in her crib in her bedroom. No noises, sudden or otherwise, appeared to disturb the slumbering Scarlett and nor did Martha seem even slightly concerned about the skulking cats.

She always seemed pleased to see me and disappointed when I left Poppy behind. But I would rather leave Poppy at home; I was frightened by her fragility and I dreaded her waking up, that mewling wail and the way it began with a series of warning snuffles.

Martha's house was full of people who came and went without fuss. Martha would call, 'Wine in the fridge if you want it, coffee on the side.' And she could throw a lunch together, just tuna and cold potato, in five minutes flat at her breakfast bar. To her, numbers never mattered.

At our house sudden visits were frowned on. 'How thoughtless to call like that, unannounced,' Stella would say after the visitor left. 'How rude. What's the price of a telephone call?' Not that unexpected visitors were a common event when I was small.

And my own early experiences must have made me the mother I was.

My own mother didn't bother with friends.

When I told her how it was next door, she tutted and mentioned railway stations.

Next door was a brand-new world to me, where the word mending was unknown and babies were

53

hardly mentioned. *But could I ever step across?*

I used to watch Martha, bright-eyed and beautiful even in Sam's overlarge torn sweater, and marvel.

I mostly left when Sam came in from work. I would sit at home remembering how hard it had been to fit in when I was still in my mother's house. 'There must be more suitable people round here who you could make friends with, Jennie,' Stella would say to me, her listless daughter.

'Well, there aren't.' I was being defiant.

'What about the girls at the bank?'

How Stella annoyed me when she went on like this. Didn't she understand? Until I was twenty-three years old I lived with her in Walthamstow, and after we married Graham and I spent those difficult months with Ruth and Howard. I never had much opportunity to bring friends home. As a child I would play round at my friends' because Stella was so unwelcoming when I tried to bring them home, except on special occasions such as birthdays, when she went over the top. Other people had parties with hot dogs and beans, chips and mayonnaise. I had hundreds and thousands, balloons and games, and Stella worked very hard, of course, what with all the extra mess and expense to cope with.

The bullying went on for around two years but I hadn't dared to bunk off like Poppy. It was partly for my mother's sake that I set my face and went on going to school, half blind with misery, sitting alone in the playground or at the front of the class, pretending to be happy to read and have lunch on my own in the noisy canteen.

Those varicose veins. What else was wrong?

Packed lunches instead of school dinners. White socks instead of black tights. Oily hair in a childish style. Bad at catching. Bad at batting. Hairy legs. Unable to swim. Nylon shirts instead of cotton, and I had been seen in church on a Sunday.

It was the worst phase of my life until now.

I yearned to make things right for my mum and for me.

I wept distraughtly every night.

I learned to make myself small, to live on the outskirts of life, observing. To walk close to walls with my head down but still able to see around me, alert for the next crisis. I hated myself more than they hated me and oh how I longed to gain favour. I used to dream I would do something brave, rescue someone, go blind or be chosen as Child of the Year. Or my father would suddenly turn up and turn out to be Richard Branson.

But best of all—Stella would die. I saw it all so clearly. The secretary would call me out and take me off to her office where the lilac-scented headmistress, waiting with a box of tissues, would gently break the sombre news.

I would be escorted home while the class was informed. Some of the girls would sob for my sadness and when I returned three weeks or so later they'd be falling over themselves to get near me, to comfort me, to be my best friend.

But Stella refused to die for me, and I, broken-hearted with sorrow for her and for my wicked fantasies, knew how much she would suffer if she knew how badly I was being treated. And all this in spite of her hard work, her efforts, her daily trials and tribulations. I had failed her by not making friends. If I caught sight of her anxious face while walking home from school, I would edge towards the nearest group and pretend to be one of them for her sake. And when Judith Mort stole my purse and removed my scratchy photo of Stella, when she ripped it in half and trod on it, it was as if she had torn out my heart.

*   *   *

So I could relate to my bullied daughter and was so relieved that Poppy, now her suffering was out in the open, felt she could talk to me about her unhappiness. To me this meant she did not feel responsible, not in the way I had felt about Stella. At least we'd got that the right way round; she hadn't failed me and she didn't need to protect me. And I went to see Mrs Forest because my daughter's torment did not stop. Poppy protested that taking it further would make things worse, so I went to the school during lesson time when I knew she would not see me. This bullying had to be stopped at all costs. I had to have words with her teacher.

My chat with Martha proved fruitless. And it was hard to catch her these days, insistent as she was on working full time, even though the Frazers were not short of money.

'Poppy's looking ill,' I told Mrs Forest, who looked too young to be a sixth-former, let alone a class teacher. I wasn't there to have a discussion: I was there to tell her just how it was. 'And she eats like a bird. There must be something you can do to turn this situation round. Scarlett lives next door to us and that makes the whole matter much worse.'

We sat in an empty classroom decorated with

fern and leaf and behind us two fat hamsters chomped through their paper shavings. I sat on a miniature chair while Mrs Forest perched, bird-like, on the edge of the nature table. It felt like this should be a happy place and I was angry to think of my daughter's pain. Childhood doesn't last long.

'This awful bullying.' The situation was unforgivable and I could not accept excuses. The school was responsible, they ought to have known; this was not my fault. *I was not a carrier, Poppy could not be infected by me.* 'You must have seen something was wrong before it got this bad. Poppy tells me this trouble started right at the beginning of term.'

I noticed how clever the plaiting was of Mrs Forest's braided hair. She looked Swiss, like Heidi, with a fresh and rosy alpine complexion. She smiled faintly before her defence began and I smiled back from politeness. 'This is difficult . . . I don't know how . . . if anything, I would have said Poppy was fine. I would have said Scarlett was more upset by the rift, and the animosity, subtle though it is, seems to have come mostly from Poppy.' She paused to check my reactions before she went on in the same vein. 'I did notice the turn of events and, in many ways, poor Harriet is merely the catalyst for something that was bound to happen. The truth is, Mrs Gordon, that for some time now Scarlett and Poppy have been growing apart. They have different interests. They are both growing up, individuals with varying needs . . .'

Suddenly I felt nauseous, with pinpricks of alarm that tickled my back and underarms. I had not bargained for this. 'So you are trying to tell me that Poppy will not accept this? You are saying that

Harriet Birch has nothing to do with this behaviour, that it's all Poppy's fault?'

'Mrs Gordon,' she went on gently. 'As you must know, Scarlett is a lively and popular little girl. A happy-go-lucky child. Poppy finds making friends harder and until now she has tended to shelter under Scarlett's wing. This worked fine through infants' school and in the first years here, but at ten years old socializing takes on a more complex form . . .'

'*Yes?*' Why the pause?

'We ought to have acted earlier, that's true. We should have split the two girls up to allow this transition to happen more naturally. Poppy has been under too much pressure trying to keep up in Scarlett's group.'

'Oh?' I continued to listen, dismayed and distracted as Mrs Forest droned on. So between the two of them, Harriet and Scarlett had concocted a believable tale. It's always the prettiest, most popular children who get the teachers' approval and I'd even heard that attractive names could influence attitudes. But her name, Poppy, was attractive. I could have understood matters more if we had called her Janice or Sue.

*   *   *

I don't know how I got home that day.

Graham was insufferable, no support at all, told me I was paranoid and why would Scarlett suddenly turn nasty? I should get the two girls together in a non-threatening atmosphere and talk to them both about finding a way out.

But to me, this was the day when Poppy would

58

be left behind in the race. No longer one of the chosen, but the one left behind to pick up the chaff.

It was so unbearably sad.

I saw this as the day when she would be sent to a slower, less challenging class. She would mix with less able pupils. She would lower her own expectations. One day soon she would wake up feeling cheated; she would suffer that raw awakening that comes when you face mediocrity and watch the privileged ones move ahead—not because of superior abilities but because of their natural appeal, and their cunning.

The day when your dreams are betrayed.

It was all so unfair, UNFAIR, UNFAIR.

I was ashamed of the strength of my feelings.

Like my daughter, Poppy, like my mother before me, my unhappiness was making me vicious.

*   *   *

And this after everything else that she and I had been through.

CHAPTER SIX

Martha

And this after everything else that she and I had been through.

*   *   *

Jennie got pregnant with Josh because I was

pregnant with Lawrence. When I first said this Sam called me paranoid, but there were other clues that I failed to mention—and not just buying strappy sandals or getting a furious urge for Pot Noodles. It was illnesses, unbelievably—not just ours but our children's.

This wasn't like Munchausen's Syndrome; it was no straightforward cry for expert attention using Poppy as bait. And I haven't yet seen a label put on these particular symptoms, but after the initial shock there was no doubt left in my mind—she was *copying*.

*   *   *

It beats me how Jennie conceived in all the dire misery of that Italian holiday. I can only presume that their Friday night date was too much of a habit to break.

Of course, she had known that I was 'carrying', 'with child', 'up the spout'. When I first suspected, panicked, cursed Sam's loins and his creeping hands, she hurried straight round to the nearest chemist to pick up a pregnancy testing kit.

Positive. But please, *please, could it be wrong?* We hadn't planned this. This was too soon.

Every morning, expectantly, she would enquire into my condition, and then take my dramatic reaction at face value (it was more the response of a shocked prima donna). She was at her most priggish when I said I'd get rid of it.

'But you can't. *You can't possibly.*'

My arguments were with myself. 'Why not? There are too many kids in the world already.'

'It's murder,' she said, 'taking a life.'

'Bollocks. Don't come round here spouting that mumbo-jumbo. I'm not a pro-lifer and nor are you.'

'You don't have to be a fanatic to know what's right and wrong.' And that little self-righteous nose tilted at the sharp end. 'You have no reason to have an abortion. You should have behaved more responsibly.'

'Oh yes? Like you and Graham?'

OK, that was unkind, and Jennie was taken aback. 'What d'you mean by that?'

I got up to rescue Fishcake the cat from Poppy's inexperienced maulings. She treated my cats as if they were toys; I was glad I didn't own a pet Rotty.

'Jennie, I know you're on the pill and that's very commendable, but I am too fat to do that and that's why we use a more hazardous method.'

'Yeah, your repulsive old cap. No wonder it failed, it must be rotten. And you never keep your appointments, so that must mean you subconsciously wanted this baby.'

Jennie was right; my cap was disgusting and I felt uncomfortable wearing it. And I do mistreat the stuff I dislike. My jug kettle in hearing-aid beige, a wedding present from an old aunt, is stained and unpleasant and handled roughly because I want one I can use on the Aga. Same with my torn, brown ironing board. Same with my shoes: I prefer my old Scholls or I would rather go barefooted. Oh yes, my cap was a nasty sight and I shouldn't have left it out in the upstairs bathroom, but then I didn't expect my friends and neighbours to be up there rooting about.

Once Jennie asked, 'Have you got piles?'

Surprised, I said, 'No, but Sam has. Why?'

'I just wondered.'

61

Now that was a lie, I knew. She had been in my bathroom cabinet. 'But he'd hate anyone to know—his health image. His vanity.'

And another time she gave herself away. 'Why does Sam use an old-fashioned razor?'

'Because he's like Esau, an hairy man, and nothing else will do the job properly. Why?'

Jennie shrugged.

'For the record, I use his old razor blades.'

At that time her questions weren't too out of line, as we frequently discussed more personal matters than those. What really baffled me was why she was interested. I rarely bit back whatever she did. Already, a level of consciousness warned me that I must be careful with this sensitive friend, who was flattened by crudely gesturing drivers, floored by brusque checkout girls, felled by rude ticket collectors and fatally wounded by frosty doctors. She rolled all these tiny insults up and threw them into the air and they fell back around her in clusters and stuck like she was a figure, trapped, in a glass-ball snowstorm.

I understood how reliant on me she was growing. She didn't attempt to disguise this need and I did feel the first stabs of unease. Sometimes she made small attempts to explain, but I hated to hear her demeaning herself and I worried because she sounded so vulnerable. 'I wish I was more like you, Martha.'

How little she really knew me.

'I feel so alive when I'm with you.' And her voice was tremulous, almost religious. Perturbed by this as I watched her finger moving over my table squiggles, I busied myself looking for a missing sock which Sam had raged about that morning. I

62

delved around in the empty washing machine. I sorted through the ironing pile. I had promised to go to Marks and buy him a new triple pack. 'I miss you so much when you're not around.'

Tears threatened behind her voice.

'What would I do without you?'

*   *   *

It was after this curious episode that she started being offhand with my friends. Again, it was hard to nail this down. It wasn't outright rudeness, but she was cold, she was abrupt, in a way I hadn't noticed before.

I wished I could talk all this over with Sam, but he was the type to misconstrue it. 'Dyke' would be his gleeful reaction. Sam was hysterically heterosexual; he had no time for gays and he made a point of staying up late to watch any film with an adult warning in the corner. Mostly, they sent him to sleep.

Sexual preferences should be kept private, Sam maintained, while happy to broadcast his own smutty wit with the lads, given the chance.

And anyway, this wasn't a problem with Jennie. There were no sexual undertones here—it might have been simpler if there had been. I could have just told her that wasn't on.

*   *   *

For the second time Jennie was pregnant and I was pregnant, so once again we were thrown closer together. We passed going to and from the clinic. I started the iron pills, she finished hers, I was over

63

the morning sickness while she still spent hours with her head down the loo.

We bought our daughters baby dolls in an effort to lessen the sibling blow and encourage that helpful, motherly instinct that I was certain I had missed out on. Poppy poked the eyes out of hers and Scarlett buried Rosebud in the sandpit.

I got up one morning and, sick with horror, discovered bloodstains on my sheets. *How? Why?* I was never ill. My body was a perfectly functioning machine despite the smoke that was dragged down its throat.

Sam scooped Scarlett from her cot and whisked us to St Margaret's where they tilted me up on an iron-hard bed and kept me in for a week under observation.

When I got home, Jennie moved in.

'You're a fool. You must rest,' she ordercd, 'and come to terms with the fact that you are as vulnerable as everyone else. You can't carry on with your terrible habits. You have to stop going riding with Emma. You can't meet Jayne for those raucous reunions. You've got to cut down on the booze and the fags.'

'Oh piss off, Jennie.'

'You must think of the baby now, not yourself.'

'Bollocks. And, I suppose, if it was a question of saving mother or baby, you would happily give up your life?'

'Yes, actually. Yes, I would.'

She never failed to amaze me.

*   *   *

Next, dear God, I caught her telling my old friend

Stevie that I was too ill for visitors.

'Who was that on the phone?' I asked her. I was pretty annoyed that she'd answered it. It was my house, dammit, I could still walk and talk.

'No-one important.'

Christ! 'Jennie, tell me who it was!'

'It was Stevie.' She gave me a sideways glance.

I'd have liked a chat. 'What did she want?'

'She wanted to come over for lunch.'

'Oh?' I was pleased. I was bored. 'What time?' The question hung in the air.

'I told her she couldn't.'

'*You what?*' I turned savage. Being stuck indoors, resting, was driving me nuts. 'You had no bloody right, you've got a goddamn nerve . . .' I went to the phone and dialled Stevie's number.

'You don't understand.' Jennie crumpled, wringing the dishcloth between her hands. 'I can't bear it! *Why* do you want to be with these people? I'm never enough. You pretend to be friends, but you just feel sorry . . .'

'*Stop it, Jennie! Now!*' I was livid. 'Why can't you think of me for a change?'

'I just can't stand it,' she cried. 'Not one more minute. It goes on and on and it just won't stop and I just dunno what to do . . .'

I put the phone down quietly. 'Look, Jennie, I do try to understand how unhappy you are, but I can't change my life to suit you. You make me feel guilty, responsible for you, and that's not fair, that's too much. You talk about friendship but this isn't . . .'

She wasn't listening. She was irrational. 'You twist every single thing I say, when I only want what's best for you.' She backed away. 'Go on, call

Stevie. *Call her!* And no doubt you can have a laugh about that dumb woman at number one . . . Here . . . here's a bottle of wine, crack it open with your precious Stevie and fall about the room together.' Like a mad woman, she ransacked the kitchen drawer for the corkscrew. She thrust the wine into my face, then picked up Poppy and rushed from the house, leaving the door wide open behind her and that damn jug kettle boiling furiously.

'I can't solve all your problems for you,' I called out after her, but she didn't hear.

I smoked two fags in a row. I wondered if I should follow her over.

The next thing I heard was Graham's car pulling into next door's drive.

I was worried. 'Everything OK?' I called. Feeling like a louse, a nosy neighbour.

'No!' he shouted dementedly, dashing towards his door with his keys in his hand. 'Jennie's just been on the phone. My God, she's started bleeding.'

*   *   *

There was Jennie, washed out and subdued, rocking like a knitting granny but clutching her stomach with anguished hands.

The washing machine beside her was whirring, its soapy window frothing pink.

Bloody hell, had I brought this on with my temper? I couldn't do enough to help. 'Hang on, sweetheart, hang on, we'll soon have you in hospital. Don't give a thought to anything here. I'll take Poppy, I'll look after Graham . . .'

'Let's just get her out to the car.' And then Graham asked, as if suddenly struck by it, 'Why didn't she call you first?'

I knew very well why she hadn't called me. 'What about an ambulance?'

'No, the car will be faster.' He handled Jennie so gently, with so much love. He supported her completely and she leaned on him as together they swayed down the drive and he lifted her into the car. I was struck by how tiny Jennie looked, all bone and sinew with such narrow, childlike shoulders, and wondered how much of this was my fault.

After the car drove off I took Poppy home, called Tina—my neighbour on the other side—to come and watch the babies while I headed straight back to number one to clear up the mess. Blood spreads in such a sinister way, like oil burning in Kuwait, black and red—both such dangerous colours.

Their bed was in total disarray. I'd never seen it so messy before, as if someone had had nightmares in it. The duvet was pulled back to reveal a rumpled underblanket, but of the sheet and of Jennie's clothing there was no sign.

Jesus Christ. She couldn't possibly have stopped in the middle of all that mayhem to clear up after herself, like a bitch when it's given birth?

And then I remembered the washing machine.

I made coffee and sat at Jennie's table, smoking and mindlessly watching the machine going through its cycle, the water getting pinker and pinker. How the bloody hell had she managed, in the face of all this, to clean up after herself *and turn on the washing machine*?

Everything in Jennie's kitchen was carefully in its place, save for one drawer which was slightly open. I went to the drawer beside the cooker where Jennie kept her herbs and spices, neatly arranged in their pots of course, unlike mine in screwed-up paper bags. It was Jennie's habit to empty everything into her matching containers: even her cornflakes and her spaghetti; even her milk went into plastic bottles with cows and daisies chasing round the sides.

Only the flavourings and colourings were allowed to stay in their little glass bottles.

I took out the cochineal and lifted it to the window.

I ran my finger round the lid.

Nothing.

But I should have known.

It was also a habit of Jennie's to wipe round rims before screwing on lids.

I paused at the sink to inspect her cloth but it hung hygienically, whiter than white, over her gleaming taps, and beneath it her blue washing-up bowl, not congealed with old fat and gravy, sat upside down, clean as a dinner plate.

What the hell was the matter with me? Why was I so suspicious? Good God, if this was revenge, what did that turn Jennie into? What I was thinking could not be true and I felt ashamed of myself. Here I was, prying and poking through my friend's kitchen when I ought to feel flooded with sympathy over the fear she might lose her child.

Smiling at the sight of her airing cupboard, I remade Jennie's bed in a way that I never made mine. If these responses portrayed psychological states, then I was the mad one, not her. I concentrated on hospital corners and stayed to fiddle with the end result until not a crease, not a dent in the pillow, remained. A photo of Jennie and Graham on their wedding day sat in a silver frame beside the lamp on Jennie's bedside table and I pondered on the wisdom of that, to come to bed and be reminded of that stark, unnatural day full of tight, unnatural smiles; the promises made, as old as the ark.

It was Graham I felt sorry for now.

They might not suit each other in bed but Graham and Jennie were friends. He must have been on the receiving end of Jennie's recent emotional turmoil.

Dear God, what had I done? And was this my fault as well?

*   *   *

If only we could have stopped it there.

CHAPTER SEVEN

Jennie

If only we could have stopped it there.

*   *   *

To appreciate how desperate we feel living here at the moment, it's important to have a rough idea of the layout of Mulberry Close. Most people say it's a frying-pan shape but I see it as a mirror with a handle, like the one the wicked queen used to consult in *Snow White*.

> *Mirror, mirror on the wall*
> *Who is the fairest of us all?*

And in the Close, Martha would win. Sadly, for me, there would be no contest.

The handle of the mirror is a box-hedged road, and when this road meets the green with the mulberry tree in the middle it swings round in an oval. Around this oval sit our six lodges, ranch style, the most prestigious on the estate, most of the others being semi-detached and completely cut off from us higher mortals.

Yes, ours was an exclusive zone.

A ten-minute walk down the road there's a small shopping centre, horribly utilitarian—a Mace, a laundrette, a post office-cum-deli. The fish and chip shop at the end of the block means the place is always strewn with paper and thick with flies.

At night this is a no-go area. The predatory young congregate here and it's sad to see their lethargy, their low expectations when, after leaving the swirly-carpeted pub with its revolving stools, its chips with everything and its squirty plastic sauces, they are reduced to sitting on benches, bedecked with noserings and tattoos, shouting and making trouble, with nothing to energize them but extra-strong cans of lager.

The girls sit cross and solemn beside them, tough little arms dangling out of tight T-shirts.

People have warned us that investing money in a house attached to such an estate shows a serious lack of judgement. But as Graham insists, wherever you live you're fifteen minutes from trouble these days; even far-flung country villages attract teams of thieves from the cities.

Our lodges were built fully fitted with alarms and safety windows.

But even though the location is dodgy, most people admire the houses themselves. Their wood fronts shine, as if polished, under two triangular roofs, one rising above the other for a splendid 3-D effect. The small gardens in front are open plan— which does attract passing dogs—but the backs are fenced and large enough for a reasonable game of badminton.

So when Martha described Piglets Patch, the cottage she first had her eye on, I understood immediately why the Close and her didn't quite fit.

'But the children will thank you one day,' I said. 'They'd hate to be dumped in the middle of nowhere; streams and puppies and picnics. *Adventures.* Fiction. A fantasy. Mulberry Close is more realistic.'

And I wondered what Martha would say if she saw the place where I was brought up: Stella's Walthamstow basement, dug out between advertisement hoardings. I had told her some of my past, but not all.

But Sam was the snob, not Martha, and he, so happy to broadcast the fact, forced me to defend 'the underclass'. He turned me into a loony lefty.

He was postage-stamp close to Hitler. 'Castrate the buggers', 'string 'em up', 'deport them'.

Martha smiled but did not argue and her lazy attitude drove me wild.

She said, 'He says these outrageous things to annoy you. You're not going to change him, so why

71

bother to argue?'

I bothered because he made me feel stupid and I knew how he'd sneer if he guessed at my background.

Martha used that same sad smile when Stella ranted on at her most vindictive. 'Hang, draw and quarter . . . send them back where they came from . . .' Her remarks made me wince, I was so ashamed.

'*Shut up, Mum,*' I would groan in despair, making sure Martha knew that these views weren't mine. In her bovine complacency she said nothing.

And when, at her worst, Stella's face contorted, when she said that her neighbours came straight from the jungle, when she said hooray for the National Front, Martha would merely change the subject.

I saw this attitude as a weakness. 'You would do anything to avoid a scene,' I said accusingly.

'But there's just no point, Jennie, why can't you see that? It's a generation thing, you can't change her. And fat people are known to be easy-going.'

She was just the same with Sam. It incensed me to see how she rushed around him while he treated her with such casual arrogance. If Martha had planned to go out for the evening and the precious Sam had made other plans, she wouldn't ask him to babysit. No. Scarlett would be dumped at our house where me and Graham would be happy to have her. And when Martha was trying for that first part-time job, Sam was disparaging, no help whatsoever.

'It seems like he doesn't want you to work.'

'He doesn't care either way,' said Martha. 'Just as long as he's not affected.'

'He's so selfish,' I told her warily.

'Yes, he's a bastard,' was all she replied, absent-mindedly stroking Scarlett. But I saw how unhappy Sam made her and I knew that he had a wandering eye.

Although Sam could have helped with the feeding, he never got up in the night for the babies. And if one night was particularly fraught, he would move to the spare room for peace and quiet.

When we enrolled for water aerobics, Martha's main reason for going was Sam. She wanted to get her shape back for him. And when we went to Italy, it was Martha who put down her knife and fork after the babysitter's intercom call, it was she who went upstairs every time to get Scarlett back to sleep.

And yet she had such strength and confidence. She so easily coped with two squalling babies, saucepans overflowing and telephones ringing, while Sam, the slob, sat around eating toast and reading the *Independent*'s sports pages.

'It's not fair,' I said. 'Sam should help more.'

'It's just not worth the hassle,' she answered. 'He is clumsy, inadequate,' and then she laughed, 'but not in all departments.' And I cringed. How I loathed it when she talked like that. She could be unpleasantly coarse at times.

*　　　*　　　*

Scarlett was not even a year old when Martha started scanning the local papers.

It was a dismal time for me.

'Why don't you look for a part-time job, Jennie?' she asked with a pencil between her teeth and rigid

73

with concentration as she sat up at her breakfast bar. 'Get out and about a bit.'

'I never want to go back to work. It was more boring there than it is at home.'

'You meet more people, get a better perspective. You don't want your brain to disintegrate and end up riddled with gaping holes.' She was swamped by her latest fashion creation and her scraped-up knot of hair wobbled wildly. 'Taxi drivers' brains are larger because of the information they store.'

'Well, I use my brain more at home than at work.'

'Go back to school, then. Take up a challenge.'

And I wished that I was a doctor, a surgeon, a lawyer or even a teacher, to shine more brightly in Martha's eyes.

*   *   *

The last time we went to Safeway's together—long ago now but I still remember—we stopped for a coffee and a bun, and Martha laughed so much she choked and spouted a mouthful over the table, her greedy fingers gleaming with butter.

*   *   *

At the park I didn't tell her that her skirt was hitched up in her knickers and a passer-by tapped her on the shoulder.

*   *   *

She struggled from the changing room in Gap, hopelessly overweight as ever, to show how the

74

press-studs refused to meet and her bulges dangled over her skirt. 'These mean little people that take size ten,' she said in a voice brimming with malice. I thought I would wet myself in the shop. I left at once with my legs tightly crossed.

* * *

Whatever we did and wherever we went was a fun event with Martha. Even a torpid day in the garden watching the sprinkler's liquid branches was a joy. So was a winter afternoon watching old films with the kids asleep and a bottle of Safeway's Bulgarian wine and the room fugged up with Martha's smoke.

My mother would have had a stroke.

But Scarlett was a year old and Martha wanted her life extended; tea and fruit buns weren't enough.

She was after something spicier.

* * *

I shouldn't have hinted at how needy I was. *Was she uneasy in my company now?* I had made myself pitiful and unequal.

But I had such confidence in her wisdom: if she had some idea of what I was suffering, maybe she could sort me out. All she did was to suggest a hobby. 'Perhaps it would help if you took up painting.'

Was there a name for my addiction? Was it so uncommon? Maybe I was not alone. There might even be a cure.

If only someone could make it right.

Was it possible that I'd told Martha the truth

about my embarrassing feelings for manipulative reasons? If she knew how I felt, might it strengthen the bond? Why did I desperately want her attention? Round and round in my head it all went till the feelings themselves seemed to fill my eyes.

It had started off with jealousy, and I hadn't even recognized that until Graham casually pointed it out. And that was soon after we met.

Then came that empty feeling; I was half a person without her.

After this came the longing to be her, to emulate not just her style, but to actually turn into Martha, to be the person I so admired.

Don't think these were just passing niggles which nagged at me every now and again while piercing the tomato purée tube, scattering the daffodil bulbs or trying to prise out a new toothbrush. I woke up with this obsession first thing every morning and it kept me awake, tossing and turning, each night. I imagined crazy scenarios: me and Martha forever together, her need for me turning stronger than mine, or me suddenly possessing some marvellous talent that Martha would have to admire.

God knows what this must sound like to people who haven't been through it—this moving away from grace towards a serious corruption.

It had no name. *Was I queer?* All the time this worried me. Did I want to take Martha to bed? See her without her clothes? Touch her? Stroke her or, in some way, like a man, possess her?

I imagined her body brought to me on a trolley, docile flesh decently covered. Would I uncover it if I could?

And if not, what were these ecstatic emotions? Surely something as fierce as this must have sex at its core?

Even now I can't answer these questions, but I can swear on my children's lives that I never consciously felt any of these physical manifestations.

The little I had confessed to Martha—my growing dependence, my jealousy—only made her more anxious about me. She agreed that this state was unnatural and became as keen as I was to sort something out. Laughingly, she once called it a crush and when I wailingly disagreed, 'It's far more powerful than that,' she told me she thought there was nothing more powerful than that adolescent first passion. 'There was this boy called David Fuller. Jesus, I used to give him money. Horrid, spotty little bugger.'

'I just hope it doesn't last,' I said, still hoping for an answer, as if this was thrush or cystitis to be looked up in the *Well Woman's Guide.*

'These things mostly burn themselves out,' she decided, rattling ice cubes with nonchalance.

But that was nine years ago, so obviously she was wrong.

Sometimes, horrified that I'd told her too much, I wondered if Martha had spoken to Sam. *And what if this got back to Graham?* He wouldn't begin to understand. But no, Martha wouldn't tell Sam. They didn't swap news like we did and she'd know that Sam would snigger, and he was indiscreet in his cups. No, I felt fairly safe that Martha would keep my sickness to herself.

*   *   *

We should never have discussed it, because after

I'd let those first feelings out my behaviour began to deteriorate. I had thought she might make concessions.

Her friendships were increasingly hard to bear.

I begrudged any interests that excluded me.

And my excuse for my moody behaviour was that tired and meaningless phrase, *'But, Martha, you don't understand.'*

It's a wonder it took her so long to hate me. I was walking on dangerous ground.

Once again, as in childhood, I grasped at weird straws, wishing that something dramatic would happen so that Martha, a fat woman with holes in her tights, would make a fuss, would notice me. If our house burned down, if Poppy was ill, if Graham crashed his car . . . Nothing fatal, of course, just enough to get Martha's undivided attention, so she would spend more time round at my house—or, better still, me at hers.

So that in the end I began to will it, and if Graham was late home from work I would look at my watch and start hoping . . .

And if Poppy had a temperature, I would dip the thermometer in warm water to send it up a degree or two before I rushed over to show it to Martha.

Oh yes, yes, *I did these things.*

And this was ME, such a dull and middling, straightforward person. ME. A frump. The mother of such an adorable child. Reduced to this. If anyone had told me this would happen, I would have laughed in their faces. You flick through stuff like this in the hairdresser's: I MARRIED A ONE-LEGGED MONSTER; MY BABY WAS NOT MY BABY; I WATCHED MY MOTHER KILL MY FATHER; I FELL IN LOVE WITH MY NEXT-DOOR NEIGHBOUR.

I hid my face in my hands and wept.

*   *   *

And I couldn't begin to know, at this stage, how bad this was going to get.

CHAPTER EIGHT

Martha

And I couldn't begin to know, at this stage, how bad this was going to get.

*   *   *

There was something fishy behind the idea: why would Jennie, of all people, want a pool in her garden when she could barely swim? On our Italian holiday her crab-like breaststroke only just kept her buoyant. If waves lapped at her chin she panicked.

She was disturbed. I suspected her motives and went round feeling guilty for being so damned uncharitable.

She hugged her knees gleefully. 'Just think about it,' she enthused. 'Just imagine. The kids can turn into water babies while we spend the summer getting tanned, and think how good you'll feel with some exercise.'

Oh yes, I could well imagine, and saw myself stranded beside Jennie's pool, having to use it to prevent confrontations which were gradually turning more bitter. It seemed that she would do anything to tempt me from going back to work.

And now this.

I prayed that Graham would see sense. The kids were too young, the weather in this country doesn't merit that kind of expense and, above all, no matter what you do, a pool in the garden attracts hectic swimmers. Kids. New 'friends'. Pushy neighbours. *And the mess.*

My prayers, as usual, went unanswered. I think God had sussed me out by then—I was not a dependable fan. Graham thought a pool might cheer Jennie up. She was expert at getting round him and I wished I could learn that knack for myself.

'Everyone will be able to help,' Jennie went on, eager-faced, quite pretty, and all smiles for a change. 'We'll start after Christmas. A joint project!'

Even in those days I had to tread carefully. 'You can say goodbye to your precious privacy. Think of the swarms of people in your garden. Wet towels, wet floors, litter. Everyone using your lav. And the racket. My mum's got one. They're hard work.'

Out of everyone I had ever known, out of everyone I'd ever heard of, the thought of Jennie playing hostess to a mass of wet fleshy bodies dripping their way hither and thither across her carpets was the most unlikely. The most ludicrous. She would not survive the ordeal.

The casual way our own house was used as playground, free pub and women's collective set Jennie's teeth on edge. So for her to turn the tables in such a perverse way was a worrying signal of how far she was prepared to go.

So, damn the consequences, I faced her head on.

'I'm not going to play your mind games, Jennie. We both know what's behind this idea and you're crazy if you honestly think that a pool would make the slightest difference to me wanting to work. If I wanted a pool, I'd build one myself.'

She flashed me the falsest of bright smiles. 'Martha! You're so self-obsessed, it's incredible.'

OK, OK. Perhaps I was neurotic. After all, a pool was an excessive move in the small game Jennie was playing. Maybe the idea would die a death after Christmas. Jennie would surely be cured by then and we could all get back to normal.

*   *   *

'Love thy neighbour.'

That Christmas was a blighted occasion. It should have been one of the best, with Poppy and Scarlett at two and a bit, perfect for tinsel and Father Christmas and sacks and reindeers and babies in mangers.

Poor Jennie suffered miserably with Graham's parents, Ruth and Howard, and her own purse-lipped mother, Stella, for a week.

When she told me they'd invited themselves, I said, 'No way! Tell them you just can't cope, what with Poppy and a baby on the way—dammit, a baby you nearly lost.'

She'd been kept in hospital overnight and then sent home, ordered to take things easy. She never said much about it. Thank God it was just a false alarm.

I was eight months pregnant and huge. Jennie was only four months gone but still being sick, cramming herself with vitamins and pills for her swollen ankles. 'This baby's not right,' she kept saying, 'I just know it.'

I hated to hear this mother's curse. 'Don't say that, Jennie. The scan was fine.'

'Scans don't pick up everything.'

As if she was willing it. More of that sadness pheromone.

And if she was genuinely worried, why the hell had she agreed to put up that dismal crowd for Christmas? And if she lacked the confidence to say no, then Graham should have said it for her.

I raised the subject with him, but his answer was predictably feeble. 'If they don't come here we'd have to go there, to the bungalow. And Jennie hates it.' It seemed too revolutionary to point out that they didn't have to spend Christmas with anyone.

*   *   *

Of course, I invited them all to our party and for drinks on Christmas morning. Although we'd moved in only two years back, the tradition was already established.

'I can't bring them,' groaned Jennie. 'I can't. They'd ruin everything.'

'Well, leave them at home with the Bristol Cream and you and Graham come anyway.'

This, however, was out of the question. 'The height of rudeness,' Stella would call it, 'going off out and dumping us here as if you were ashamed.'

'But,' Jennie moaned, 'it'll tear me apart hearing the music and all that laughing and me stuck inside playing Scrabble with that lot.'

Someone had to make up her mind. 'You're

82

bringing them over here. Sod it, there'll be enough people to blot them out.'

'They'll go on about it afterwards—in a spiteful, mean way. They do when they see people having fun.'

'Fucking hell, Jennie, that's their problem. Don't let them get to you like this.'

But Jennie was fighting a split personality; her family knew her by her skirts and blouses, by her neatness, competence and earnest demeanour. There had been times when she'd worn her jazzy waistcoat, but even that had been known to raise eyebrows. In the last few months, however, in spite of being pregnant, she'd gone into jeans and skimpy tight skirts above the knee. She looked good. She looked like a gentler person. And once I saw a small hole in the heel of her black stockings! Around the house, too, she was less dutiful. Apart from this destructive obsession with me, she had begun to ease off and let go. Graham had acclimatized gradually, but her visitors would find the change shocking.

'A week,' she fretted. 'All those puddings. And how can we fill seven whole days and pretend to enjoy ourselves? Help me, Martha, *help me.*'

Any woman would sympathize. Somebody must do something soon to reduce Christmas back to two days and cut the rising suicide rate. There must be a ban on 'Hark the herald' until one week before, and no Teletubby adverts allowed.

*   *   *

Christmas Eve.

Jennie, Graham, Howard, Ruth and Stella were

the first guests to arrive and although I shouted at them from upstairs to help themselves, I knew damn well they wouldn't. They'd be wandering round, or sitting expectantly, minding their manners, waiting to be served.

'I couldn't hold them back,' hissed Jennie frantically. 'It was fatal to tell them eight o'clock.' Jennie suspected that this year Stella had surpassed herself and bought her daughter a new steam iron. Hints had been dropped. Ruth and Howard had pinned envelopes to the Gordons' tree, book tokens for Jennie and Graham, a savings bond for Poppy.

Damn. So I was forced to abandon my shower, and when I went down in my red kaftan—the outfit Sam borrows to play Father Christmas at the cricket club party—Jennie's relations were sitting round the room in funeral-parlour mode. Paper plates were handed out, and food trays meant for picking at later, never designed to be lifted, were politely offered and accepted gravely.

'Nice tree,' commented Stella, casting an eye on our decorations, so straight away they looked degenerate, their brightness faintly savage.

The atmosphere was catching. No matter how effervescent, guests met by this Stonehenge effect, boulders on chairs and refusing to mingle, were instantly subdued. Formal chatter began to predominate. Hell. I looked at Sam and shrugged my shoulders; booze should put a stop to all this.

Jennie was knocking it back alarmingly and gin was known to go straight to her head. I understood her anxiety, but she had no need to blame herself. It was our party, we'd deal with it.

In the end, Sam was forced to ask Jennie's group

84

to move. Their presence killed any spark of fun. 'You might find it quieter and more comfortable to sit in the conservatory,' he said, with what I considered admirable charm, and as their long faces moved away the tinsel and flashing bow ties went on.

Poor Jennie—it was 'Lady In Red', combined with the magic-grotto effect in the playroom, that was her downfall. Earlier, in the afternoon, when Sam was stringing the fairy lights I'd warned him about the possibility of epileptic convulsions.

Flitting around in my favourite role, it took me a while to twig that the same song was playing over and over, so off I went to investigate. There, in the playroom, swayed the drunken Jennie, tears rolling down her face, strap of her dress hanging immodestly and half of one tiny boob exposed. Lost in the mob of happy dancers, she floated, the dying fish in the tank.

' "Lady In Red" should be your song,' said an old boyfriend of mine here with his large-buttocked second wife, while admiring my scarlet dress. My *'Oh God, no'* must have surprised him. Could this be some meaningful message for me, or was it merely coincidence that Jennie kept playing this sloppy old song? Never before had anyone declared their love for me so romantically . . . The thought that Jennie might be doing just that was an excruciatingly toe-curling thought. I pointed a serious finger at Graham. 'She's had too much. She needs rescuing, *right now.*'

But Graham was letting his hair down for once, and as the music his wife kept playing became increasingly inappropriate, to my relief Sam said, 'It's OK, I'll go.'

That terrible family were still plonked there in the conservatory, putting a damper on the proceedings with their strained and courteous faces. While they stayed, the conservatory—a good room for resting—remained a no-go area. They were even demanding cups of tea. They refused to get off their arses. Bloody hell, *why didn't they go*? Don't tell me they believed that manners required they stuck it out till the end?

Upstairs, Poppy and Scarlett slept through the racket like lambs.

As it was Christmas Eve no-one stayed late, nobody wanted to spend the next day being sad and hugging the loo. Taxis arrived and the crisp air outside was snappy with calls and shouts.

For the last hour Sam and Jennie had been smooching round the playroom, Sam innocently acting as hitching post for our helpless, drunken neighbour. That damn family were still sitting there and I wanted my bed, so I decided it was time I went to Sam's rescue.

Two couples shuffled round the now darkened room, oblivious to anyone but each other. But where the hell was Jennie, I worried. Had Sam abandoned her?

He hadn't. I found them upstairs together.

'I put her to bed,' he said quickly, standing, his hands clasped behind him. 'She's in no state to go anywhere. We can't let that po-faced mob see her like this.'

'I see.' I felt vaguely unsteady. She looked like a crumpled doll spread on the bed like that, a well-loved tree fairy, dragged out every year for sentimental reasons. My heart knocked wildly when I asked Sam, 'Wouldn't it have been better—

safer—if you'd called Graham or me?'

'Safer? I did look for you. I couldn't find you,' Sam said. 'And anyway, she's heavy.' My anxiety was misdirected. Sam had saved the day, this was no 'other woman'. *This was Jennie.*

So I sighed and let it go, replacing it with a yearning for hot scrambled eggs. 'I'll go and tell them she's ill,' I said, 'but they're bound to know she's just pissed.'

'God help her tomorrow,' said Sam. 'I wouldn't like to be in her shoes.'

'I wouldn't like to be either,' I agreed wholeheartedly.

Of course, I know now that nothing went on, in spite of her later lies.

*   *   *

Why did I ever trust her?

CHAPTER NINE

Jennie

Why did I ever trust her?

*   *   *

On and on, on and on. It was exasperating and wearying, not just for me but for Martha too. '*What do you want from me, Jennie? If only I understood what you wanted,*' she'd say. All too often.

I wished I could give her a straightforward

answer. The closest I got was to mumble feebly, 'I think I want to belong to you and be special like Scarlett.'

'So what if I go along with this and tell you that you are special?' said Martha with a sigh. 'Would that make you feel any happier?'

What a stupid question; unworthy of her. I shook my head. 'You'd be playing games just to make me feel better.'

'So I'm in a no-win situation,' Martha said. 'You're allowed to play bloody games but I'm not.'

*   *   *

Lawrence was born in January. A curly-haired monkey, and his baby-blue eyes soon turned a haunting black, like Martha's and Scarlett's. His body was wiry, like Sam's. Having a son was important to Sam—fishing and football and all that stuff—and I wondered how he would have reacted if Martha had had another girl. Graham would be happy with either.

Martha still smoked and drank, of course, and moaned about getting back to work, although how she could think about that with so much on her plate was beyond me.

'It's more important now, not less,' she said from the depths of her squalid kitchen, trying on a purple home-made hat (she thought she might take her hats to the market and sell them) while she sipped gin and bitter lemon. 'Alas, I could be dead, the world wouldn't miss me. Sam says I've started to smell like a baby, all milk and turds. I am swamped.'

I wished the birth was over for me, too. I thought

I'd never forget my first ordeal, when I swore I would never go through this again. And yet, over time that memory had faded. But now it was back, vivid with pain.

'You must have an epidural, Jennie. Forget about natural childbirth, it's simply inhumane. You're not a beast of the field, however else you despise yourself.'

I had to agree.

'And maybe,' she said casually, 'while you're at it, you could ask the doctor about your depression—and everything else.'

We didn't know how to refer to it. 'Everything else' meant my obsession, but how could they put a stop to 'love', because that was the nearest comparison I could make. 'If they could stop me, they'd be swamped by a horde of broken-hearted, would-be suicides clamouring for the same cure.'

Martha disagreed. 'This isn't love,' she said sternly. 'I thought we'd been through this and decided. This is some kind of transference caused by a childhood trauma and, who knows, psychotherapy might bring it to the surface. For God's sake, Jennie, it's worth a try.'

Martha had started making a rug 'to stop my hands tearing at myself', but it was more to do with giving up smoking. 'For God's sake, look at me,' she went on, her rug-making tool behind her ear. 'You're not the only nutter round here and it's all caused by being stuck at home.' She was silent for a moment and still, before she suddenly exploded, ripped off her purple hat and said, *'And I think Sam is seeing someone else.'*

I turned pink, gobsmacked. 'Oh Martha, no! What makes you think that?'

'He's done it before, the wanker.'

'You told me. But nothing serious. And not for years. He's that sort of man—you accepted that.' And I'd always considered her laid-back attitude towards his lechery crazy.

'But I've never felt so vulnerable as I feel now,' Martha said quietly, rubbing her cheek with soft purple felt. 'Shit. Never so needy or so dependent, and he's stopped reading the morning papers.'

She could be blaming this on my phone calls— calls I felt impelled to make, no matter how foolish I felt, just to hear her voice and know she was there. When the phone was answered, I put the handset down quickly. No good her trying 1471, our number was withheld.

'You're up every night with Lawrence,' I said. 'You're tired and you've got post-natal depression. You've no cause to think Sam's cheating again. It's all going on in your head. You're a prat.'

'I've got my reasons. Which one d'you want first?' Martha answered, to my surprise. 'He's gone off sex—my fault I suppose. I don't fancy bonking in the few spare minutes I've got. Lawrence is a pain in the arse, I'm shagged out all the time.'

What a selfish, thoughtless husband Sam was. 'What else?' Did I want to know?

'He comes home late.'

'He's got that new contract . . .'

'I know that,' she snapped, 'but then there's the phone calls.'

'What?' My heart sank. The phone calls were mine. I could feel the blood draining . . .

'At first I took no notice. I don't go round looking for trouble, unlike you. But now it's almost every evening, sometimes three or four times, and

90

when I answer I'm cut off.'

'If Sam was playing around, why would he risk her behaving like that?'

'Dunno.' She shrugged. 'Unless he's dumped her.'

I shook my head, avoiding her eyes. 'It doesn't make much sense to me. You're jumping to the worst conclusions.'

'Maybe I could get the calls traced in case it's some nutter. I said that to Sam and he agreed.'

'Well then, you've got your answer.' I got up quickly to make some coffee.

'Tina says I should tell Telecom.'

I whirled round. *'You've told Tina?'*

'Yes. Carl did this to her. Once.'

'Since when were you that close to Tina?'

'Oh Jennie, not now, please don't start . . .'

I knew how aggravating I was in spite of my craven desire to please. I felt my eyes narrow into slits. But Tina at number three, with the snap-shut handbag, silver shell suit, smutty novels, lacquered hair and Beanie Baby collection? Surely not. I couldn't find the words. I just couldn't bear it. *'But why didn't you tell me first?'*

'Because you've got enough problems.'

I wished I could stop my own voice from speaking. I knew how much I was going to annoy her. *'But I'm your best friend.'*

'Yes, you are.' She was cautious. 'But I'm not like you, I need other people.'

'Why?' God, I was pathetic.

'You know damn well why. Different experiences, different approaches. You can't get it all from one person . . .'

'I can.'

'And well I know it. So you're lucky then, sod you, Jennie . . .'

'I'm sorry I'm sorry I'm sorry.'

I'd have to tell Martha about the phone calls; one more reason for her to despise me. I had such a horror of exposing myself and yet in this situation I had no pride. I was shameless, without inhibitions for the first time in my life.

I closed my eyes. 'It was me. The phone calls.'

She'd forgotten what we'd been talking about. She'd picked up her old guitar and was strumming it sadly, some slow blues number. At the end of the chord she looked up, frowning in disbelief.

I said again, *'It was me.'*

'You are joking, I hope.' And her laugh was cold.

'Please don't look at me like that.'

'Bloody hell. But you should have spoken. If you'd asked, you could have come over . . .'

The wretched words were hard to find. 'I can't come every night after Sam gets home. What would he think? He'd soon get annoyed . . .'

How Martha loathed the necessity of tackling this subject again. As soon as one symptom was dealt with, another would rear its lamentable head.

I was desperate for her constant attention. She had to focus on me all the time.

I was taken aback by the frostiness in her voice. 'I'm losing patience, Jennie, I warn you. You've got to ask someone for help. This is getting right out of hand. What if I'd accused Sam to his face? I honestly thought the wanker was up to his old mucky tricks again. Who knows what the outcome might have been if I'd had it out with him like I planned? You know damn well that I'm not feeling strong, what with Lawrence so small and my job

92

applications getting me nowhere.' Martha's eyes began to fill with water. 'I'm sodding well pissed off with it all. I've had enough, Jennie. This is it.'

'It's not much fun for me either,' I cried, overwhelmed with misery. 'Believe me, if I could stop this I would.'

'I do believe you, Jennie,' she said, still grappling with that wretched hat, afraid I would lose control and cause a scene if she spoke to me too harshly. She knew my moods so well by then, she was forever watchful. 'And whatever you think, I do care about you and that's why I'm saying you must find help, because what's going to happen next? I mean, *this thing is a bloody medieval possession . . .*'

Martha was right, it was a possession. But how would my doctor see it when I described my unnatural complaint? Madness was another word for it. I'd be sent straight to a shrink.

Graham might find out.

And in an inexplicable way this germ of madness growing inside me did not want to be cured. It fed off misery, it heightened emotion: the agony and ecstasy were addictive. Weird as it was, the focus of my life was now so enormous that the pressure was off everything else.

Like a greedy louse I sucked and gorged; my brain spun with plots and plans, with my fantasies, with my heightened awareness of music and my yearnings for the 'Cloths of Heaven'. The sadness and wistfulness of being with Martha sent me dancing on their clouds.

She was my inspiration, my reason for being alive.

So what else could it be but love?

Martha gave me a frown of concern before she

dropped the bombshell. 'If you don't do something about this, Jennie, I'm not going to see you at all.'

I went cold. I was begging. *'No no no . . .'*

'For your own sake, not mine. I've handled this badly as it is and maybe . . .'

I collapsed. 'I will get help, *I swear.* The next time I go, I'll talk to the doctor. *Only don't ever think of doing that, Martha,* I really couldn't stand that . . .'

'OK, OK. Now help me finish off this old pasta.' Heavily, distrustfully, Martha left the subject alone, and rummaged in the depths of her fridge. The door knocked off her purple hat.

*   *   *

Ten minutes later, back at my house: 'Help me, it's Poppy! She banged her head. *Now she keeps going to sleep.'*

As I knew she would, Martha dropped her defences and drove the jeep at breakneck speed to the casualty department at St Margaret's. I leapt out with the listless Poppy, holding her out to the nurse like a sacrifice. 'I must stay with her, she'll be terrified without me . . .'

'Don't worry, I'll wait,' shouted Martha, dishevelled, full of concern. 'Everything's going to be OK and I'll let Graham know where we are.'

'Graham? Oh yes, you tell Graham.'

The acned young doctor stared deeply into Poppy's eyes. 'Please tell me what happened, Mrs Gordon, as clearly as you can.'

'She fell out of her highchair,' I cried. 'She's learned to rock it and before I could stop her I saw it going over in awful slow motion. I tried to reach

94

her in time, *I tried . . .*'

'Yes?' Meanwhile, a nurse was taking her pulse.

'I always kept my eye on her. I was afraid this might happen one day. And the next thing was she went all woozy and I couldn't get her attention . . .'

'You did the right thing, bringing her in. The actual wound doesn't look too bad, but I am concerned by this apathetic response.'

'What d'you mean?' And my voice was barely audible.

'She's not responding as she should and her pupils are dilated,' said the doctor, turning to face me. 'She can't have got hold of anything, can she?'

'Like what?'

He shook his head. 'Pills, medicines, some cough mixture that an adult could take but that might have a bad effect on a small child?'

Dear God, dear God, how had he . . .

I wrung my hands as I hovered over my child, a bad angel.

'Please don't worry,' he went on calmly. 'You can stay with your daughter, but I think we will keep her in overnight for observation.'

What was the doctor doing now? The studious young man was examining the fresh red mark on Poppy's forehead. It had been easy and quite painless: it only meant rubbing gently with a sheet of sandpaper, backwards and forwards, and the tender baby skin roughened and tiny blood spots appeared. She didn't cry—if she'd cried, dear God, I would have stopped. It looked as if she'd had a knock and she was sleepy anyway after three teaspoons of Benylin.

I closed my eyes against the stark lights, feeling sick.

My teeth, I couldn't stop them from chattering.

To see my baby lying there so sweet and defenceless broke my heart. Poppy whimpered in her sleep and I couldn't hold back the tears. I sobbed with relief that no real damage was done, but more than that, I wept at the evil act prompted by my obsession. Martha's threats of total withdrawal had thrown me into a panic. There was no forward planning. The idea had taken hold of me suddenly and before I came to my senses I'd done it.

In just the same impulsive way, I had staged that threatened miscarriage months ago.

Before I knew it, that mark was there on Poppy's head and the medicine had been given.

The frenzied regret came seconds later. I screamed for Martha, more stricken with horror than I would have been if the highchair story was true.

I had turned into a monster.

God help me. For my child's sake I should seek help and confess. NOW NOW NOW. Tell them, my conscience screamed at me. Martha was right—what next? If I could do this hellish thing to Poppy, the one I cared about most in the world—except Martha—then I was capable of anything.

And all this—for what?

Martha's attention?

The certainty that she would forgive me?

A small measure of her pity?

What was this demon that possessed me? What in God's name was living inside me?

And this in the name of love.

*　　　*　　　*

If only we had been able to talk to somebody wise.

CHAPTER TEN

Martha

If only we had been able to talk to somebody wise.

* * *

Tina Gallagher might not be wise but she was a damn sight wiser than Sam, who wouldn't have known what I was talking about if I'd turned to him for advice. I confided in Tina Gallagher, the brassy popsie who lived next door, on the day she found me hunched and demoralized, quite overcome in my kitchen. I had confided in Tina before—she was nice—about the times I was suspicious of Sam and the despair I felt at being trapped at home. I'd even told her about small irritations, like when Sam was being deliberately unhelpful and refusing to call at the nearest Spar on his way home.

Feeling particularly ugly and bloated on that fatal day (Lawrence's birth had played havoc with my weight), I played straight into Jennie's hands. And the self-contempt caused by my feeble reaction has bugged me ever since. Not so much because of what happened, but because I *allowed* it to happen, knowing how fragile her warped state of mind was.

I let Jennie down. I should have been stronger.

Somebody wrote that to experience the whole

spectrum of life's emotions you must spy on your country, commit murder and make love to someone of your own sex.

Oh yes? A pretty rounded sort of person is what I thought myself to be at the time.

And up until that fateful day, I had missed out on all three of those highly charged activities.

*   *   *

Jennie despised Tina and Carl, the Gallaghers—my neighbours. In the morally superior manner of her mother, she considered them the wrong friends for me. And now, when I think back to the way I allowed her intrusion into my life, I have to wonder at my own sanity. But when you're marooned at home all day, surrounded either by blubbering kids or women trying to find themselves, deprived of outside diversions, you can lose or confuse your identity.

*   *   *

Jennie's son, Josh, had arrived in April, and thanks to the epidural his birth was a piece of cake. Mother and baby came home the next day, and we celebrated the day after, raising our glasses to the fact that this time she'd managed to avoid having her bossy mother to stay.

This old swimming-pool thing. She refused to drop it. It was now time, Jennie decided, to press on with the project. A community effort sprang to my mind: if Jennie could be persuaded to make this a shared activity, maybe, just maybe, she would open up, make friends, and this infatuation might die a death in the process. What about time and labour in exchange for reasonable use? I'd read about something similar in a magazine—some village in Essex had tried it and it was working well. In the faint hope that she might agree, I dropped a couple of hints and couldn't have been more astonished when she agreed without a mega-trauma.

I see now that her reasons were devious. First, she was after approval from me. And secondly— and this seems incredible—she actually believed that worming her way into our neighbours' affections would make me jealous.

If it wasn't for me, there'd have been no project. Jennie was not the most popular resident in the Close. On top of her shyness there were these mood swings and nobody wanted to share a pool in the snooty Gordons' garden. I curse myself now for my misguided decision to influence the opposition—I certainly didn't want it and Sam didn't care. Wishful thinking underlay my response; I so hoped this major diversion might cool her ardour.

'Your garden would be better,' said the neighbours with one voice.

I explained to the small meeting, on a day I knew Jennie was out, that because these were her plans and her original idea I honestly thought it would work.

'I don't see why,' said Hilary Wainwright from number four. 'I haven't spoken a word to the woman since we first moved here. Lord knows why, but she seems to resent us. I'm lucky to get a terse nod. Otherwise, I'm ignored. With the best will in the world, why would she expect anyone to join in a scheme like this? It's so vague—"reasonable use"—knowing her, we'd never get in.' A silky, sensible woman who more often than not wore beige, Hilary had an enviable job in teaching.

'What does Sam think about it?' asked Angie, the builder's wife from lodge number five, dressed from top to toe in pink denim. Presumably she believed that her Alex, being a builder, would do a better job.

I had to be honest. 'Sam doesn't care one way or another. To start with he never believed the project would get off the ground, but that's Sam, profoundly negative. But as Graham is the expert on water round here, and as this is his plan and he thinks it's good, we ought to at least think about it.' I pointed out the man-hours that Graham had calculated would need to be put in in exchange for free swimming. 'You can see it's all been well thought out. Graham must have worked very hard.' Yes, driven by Jennie, I thought.

After a struggle which lasted an hour, they all agreed to think it over and meet at the Gordons' house to view the site on the following Saturday.

'But Jennie's so unstable,' said Tina, to my surprise, after the rest had gone. Tina was easy to talk to; she was understanding and discreet.

I had to admit, 'She can be odd.'

'She behaves very strangely round you.'

So people had noticed? 'What d'you mean?'

'She's so peculiar, you can't have missed it,' Tina said. 'She craves your attention, she stares at you with doggie devotion, she can't do enough to please you.'

Hell. This was all I needed. I'd have to warn Jennie. This nonsense must stop. 'Jennie has problems,' I said defensively, 'same as we all do

100

round here.'

*   *   *

I wasn't half so guarded the next time Tina called.

'Martha, Martha, *what's happened to you?*'

'Don't ask me,' I sobbed, half undressed and flat on the floor in an effort to pull myself together. *'Just don't ask, OK?'*

'You're ill.' And yes, I must have looked close to death, with my face so blotched, my hair wild and witchy, while Tina stood there with not a strand out of place, slim and together in her silver shell suit. 'You're either ill or you've been doing battle.' Tina stood back and stared down at me, her eyebrows raised like distant seagulls.

'Battle,' I muttered, 'and I lost.'

'Come on, Martha, have a soak in the bath and come over to my place for a brandy. Where are your kids? Or is that it? You've dismembered them and hidden their bodies?'

It was then that I broke down completely, great fat sobs and bubbles streaming from my nose and mouth. I cried out dementedly, 'Don't mention the kids to me. I'm no mother.'

'It can't be that bad.' Tina stooped to gather me in her capable arms. Her deck shoes were in a matching silver and so was the sporty band in her hair.

'Don't touch me, don't touch me . . .'

She recoiled in shock. 'But, Martha, what on earth . . . ?'

I lost control of my face completely. It collapsed in miserable folds like a bloodhound on the scent. 'There's no-one to blame but me,' I sobbed, 'and

101

that's the worst thing about it.'

I needed to talk but what words could I use and what about the malicious rumours that might circle round the Close?

I supposed I could try, 'I've just been to bed with another woman . . .' Or, 'My neighbour has just made love to me—she's devoted to me, by the way . . .'

And who would believe my pitiful excuse? 'I never dreamed it would go that far. She got into bed for a cuddle.' Yes, a cuddle that quickly got out of hand.

I loathed myself for my weakness. I was withered up like a dead leaf.

I started in the simplest way. 'You're not going to believe this, Tina.'

'You've got me wrong, sweetheart,' she said. 'I believe anything.'

'Can I ask you a personal question?'

'Go on,' she said, but she looked jittery.

'Have you ever been to bed with a woman?'

She began to crow with relieved laughter. 'My God, Martha, is that all? What d'you want me to say—*how could you?*'

'It's not funny. It's a long way from funny . . .' And I picked myself up with some semblance of dignity. I pulled up my socks for a start.

'Don't tell me,' said Tina, 'let me guess. Jennie. I knew it. I suspected she had lesbian tendencies.'

My eyes might have turned in Tina's direction, but I concentrated firmly on the wall behind her. This was such personal stuff. 'Jesus, I'm shaking. I'm still in shock. And Jennie, God knows what she's thinking now.'

'But what were you doing down there on the

102

floor?'

'I reached this far, but my legs gave way.'

'So what was it like?' Tina reached for the bottle, the half-empty bottle of wine on the bar.

I refused the glass she offered. 'No more, never, I'm now teetotal.'

'Was she good with her hands?'

This wasn't a joke. 'This is serious, Tina, if only you knew . . .'

'But I don't, so why don't you tell me?'

'Jennie's at home now, hugging herself, thinking her love is reciprocated. She's probably convinced herself she's a dyke, but this is something far deeper than that . . .'

'If Jennie thinks you enjoyed yourself, you must have given her that impression.'

I perched on a stool at the breakfast bar, running my hands through my crazy hair and wishing like hell I could take back time. In one way I was grateful for Tina's light-hearted reaction, but she'd got it so wrong it worried me sick. It wasn't simply the fact of what had happened, it was the future implications.

Christ, this was hard to talk about. I moved across to the sink and splashed cold water on my face. That was better. Tina sat waiting at the bar, her chin propped up on the wine bottle.

'We were fed up. We turned on the music, downed a few drinks, made the most of our freedom—you know what it's like when the kids aren't around?' But Tina was childless, so she couldn't imagine. 'We were being silly—dancing, shouting, flinging ourselves around the room . . .'

'God, I can't see Jennie Gordon . . .'

'You don't know Jennie Gordon,' I reminded her

tartly. 'And suddenly I felt exhausted, what with Lawrence's teeth and his rash. I was desperate to go and lie down. So I left Jennie down here, went upstairs, tore off my clothes and got under the sheets just as I was. It was gorgeous, just giving in, bed in the afternoon. How degenerate . . .' At this point my voice trailed away, as I remembered with shame what happened next.

Could I trust Tina?

Could I trust anyone?

Why worry about that now? But this was a serious humiliation. When Tina yawned her skin didn't crack and her make-up, I noticed, was perfect. But she showed no shock, so I carried on regardless.

'Well, she didn't go any further than touching, but I did nothing to stop her, did I? Shit, shit.'

'Martha, you enjoyed it. *Admit it.*'

'Did I? Really?' I tried to think back. Salty bodies and damp hair, weird in an afternoon. The curtains had thrown sunny shadows and made all movement seem dreamlike, and yet when the ashtray fell off the bed and Jennie said she'd fetch a dustpan, I giggled; I couldn't stop laughing, even when I was naked against her. I told Tina, 'You've seen the video, well now I've got the T-shirt.'

Tina whistled. 'How fascinating. How very grown up. But it sounds to me like you can't blame Jennie.'

'When did I say I blamed her?' I snapped. 'Haven't you heard a thing I've been saying? It was my fault for not stopping her and that's the whole trouble, that's where it gets dangerous.' That white world of sheets against Jennie's green eyes. I had itched to thump her away, but I hadn't. All I had really craved for was sleep.

'Well.' Tina considered my dilemma, staring at me through her wine glass. 'You've broken the rules, but nobody's hurt. So apart from it being unexpected and unlikely to be repeated, I don't really see your problem.'

So then I had to say more about Jennie and her manic possession.

Tina said she wasn't surprised. 'Quiet types, they're always the worst.'

'You're missing the point. Jennie's at home thinking all sorts of unlikely thoughts . . .'

'You're going to have to put her right. You're going to have to explain and be honest.'

'If you only knew how sick of all this I am. The responsibility for her mental condition. The way this obsession is crushing my life. It's Jennie, Jennie, always Jennie—trying to avoid saying the wrong thing and causing more scenes, more dramas and more of her sodding suicide threats. I've suggested giving our friendship a rest, but no, she won't have that. And now, dammit, this happens.'

'It certainly takes the biscuit,' said Tina.

'A more enlightened response would be helpful,' I told her. 'And if Sam should hear about any of this, there is no doubt he'd divorce me,' I warned her.

'What a powerful position I'm in.' And she gave her languid, most feline smile.

'He would most probably never believe you.'

'Don't worry. Trust me, sweetie, I am as discreet as that proverbial clam.' And that was true: Tina might jest but I knew I could trust her.

*   *   *

How had it ended?

I must have slipped into a drunken stupor because when I woke up Jennie was gone.

I dragged myself downstairs, trying to remember precisely what had happened and what part I had played in the action.

With that thoughtless and primitive response of mine, I had failed myself and Jennie.

It was time we had a serious talk.

*   *   *

If I could take time back and start all over again, I would.

CHAPTER ELEVEN

Jennie

If I could take time back and start all over again, I would.

*   *   *

That cunning Gallagher woman stuck to Martha like a mussel to a rock. *Easy.* She and Carl had no children, she was a materialistic go-getter, and because she worked from home on her state-of-the-art computer, updating holiday brochures for the English Tourist Board, her time was her own.

At first, flying high on the thought that she loved me back, this didn't worry me too much. She loved me—*she loved me.* OK, her response hadn't been passionate, but she hadn't kicked me out in disgust. Mine was a total, ecstatic joy. I made frantic plans in my head: one day we would sail away together and live on some sun-soaked Greek island, run a beach bar, teach English to students, or even get work as couriers if all else failed.

Martha had let me touch her in a way you only allow those you love best.

Her lack of response meant little. *It was what lay behind it that counted.*

This was a pure and perfect love, not some freaky manifestation.

I was strong with a boundless energy, like some arthritic on steroids, but no longer would I waste my efforts on scrubbing my house, my kids, my body. There were no bears beneath pavement cracks, nothing was going to leap out and devour me if there was fluff on my carpet, egg on my teaspoons, or butter in the marmalade. My powerful obsession crushed all these others.

Even my urge to see her diminished because of her reciprocal love. I went through the hours in a dream world, sucking up strands of spaghetti with my eyes tightly closed, fantasizing through my Arctic Roll; Martha and I shared this special secret which bound her to me the way nothing else could.

*   *   *

So when she said, 'Jennie, we've got to talk,' it flayed me to hear her say that the closeness we had shared must not be repeated, that she was appalled by what we had done and if I'd thought it meant something, well, I was wrong, the messages were not intended. She was too confused to analyse her motives, but if I wanted to keep her friendship, she didn't want that afternoon referred to ever again.

Calamity. I said, 'Is it Sam?'

She fixed a firm frown to her face. 'It's nothing to do with him. This is between you and me. I was tipsy, tired, depressed. Maybe I wanted comfort . . .'

Hardly able to cope with the nausea, and trembling from head to toe, I started, 'I suppose you are saying I took advantage . . .'

Her interruption was brisk, sharp. 'Don't you dare start on that self-pitying crap. I'm not blaming you. I could have stopped you but I didn't. Now it's over, finished with, and if I misled you I'm sorry. If you use this against me, I will never forgive you.'

I sat at her table, a dejected heap. 'It sounds like I'm your enemy.'

'You're dead right, you are. You're a threat.'

I winced. 'I never wanted to be.'

'I daresay not,' Martha said, with a hostility that frightened me. 'But that's how it is. I never know when you're going to blow. I'm sick of drama, hysterics and tears between declarations of undying devotion. Of making excuses for your rudeness. I don't want these things in my life any more. I want it to stop—*right now*!'

'But how can I stop?' I wailed, despairing.

'Jennie, you can, *you must.* For God's sake, don't you think it's time that somebody round here started behaving bloody normally?'

*   *   *

How could I eat? How could I sleep?

I couldn't confide in Graham, but my world was crashing around me.

'I've fallen out with Martha,' I told him. I had to give some reason for my swollen eyes, my lack of appetite.

'What's new?' And he turned over to *Newsnight*.

I pretended to read as I sat beside him, but my head was spinning in turmoil. The printed words were like soldier ants devouring the page before my eyes—and they came through to my brain with no meaning. I stared at him over the top of the book and, in spite of my own pain, my heart melted. How could I hurt him? Graham, so steadfast, such a sensible man and so contented, wouldn't have the vaguest understanding of my relationship with Martha. It dismayed me to think about his lot, one relentlessly boring routine as the web of responsibility held him: up early for work, midday sandwich, home at six thirty, sex on a Friday, squash on Saturday, golf on Sunday. Life's loathsome confining walls. But, for an agonizing while, my passion had carried me over on wings . . .

It was anguish to sit there quietly all evening, pretending all was well, fighting the urge to rage, pace the floor, ring Martha, dash over and plead for forgiveness.

I hadn't meant to go so far when I got into Martha's bed. If I was queer, I was not a freak. If I enjoyed what I did, I was natural. Maybe not quite as natural as a heterosexual, but acceptable all the same. I pushed away the destructive thoughts that told me it hadn't felt right and I reassured myself that although I had needed to do what I'd done, just like Martha, I felt no desire to repeat it.

All it suggested was that Martha loved me in

109

some kind of sexual way.

A mistake.

I lay next to Graham, wide awake, listening to his contented snores while I curled and uncurled in my misery, in that hot, lumpy bed. I wrote letter after begging letter in my head—it's so much simpler to say it in writing, and in the night when defences are low. It was useless to stay there and hope for sleep, so I crept downstairs to the kitchen and sat there with a mug of tea, warming my now frozen hands, as I composed my hundredth letter.

I spread my photographs over the table: Martha stuffing her face at a barbecue but still looking amazing as the camera caught her laughing eyes; Martha and me on our last London trip when we lost the pushchair in the Natural History Museum; Martha struggling in the snow with her bald old Christmas tree, two fingers in the air and her red scarf blowing.

I traced her profile with my finger.

She couldn't have made her feelings clearer, but still the idea that my burning emotions were only a bore and a cause of distress refused to take hold in my head.

I transferred my intense thoughts onto paper.

I wanted her to read this NOW, or, at the very latest, first thing in the morning.

I knew her routine as well as my own. Tomorrow she was going to the dentist. She would take Scarlett and Lawrence to the minder's, drive Sam to work and then bring the jeep home.

I could stick my note onto the jeep.

The need for instant relief made me reckless; passion drove me to act. I gave no thought to the risks involved: what if somebody saw me creeping across my garden into next door's drive; what if the wind got up in the night and blew my letter away; what if Martha, furious, tore it up without reading it?

Why did it never occur to me that Sam might find it first?

*   *   *

The begging letter. A sympathy bid.

I was making myself ridiculous again.

I had used this same device at school in an effort to make myself popular when everything turned so black and it felt as if the world was against me.

I took it to Barbara Middleton, the worst of my tormentors, when I caught her alone in the loos drying her hands.

She gave me a questioning glance. 'What's this?' She put my letter in her satchel.

'Don't show it to anyone else,' I stammered, before rushing off.

I arranged my books with elaborate care, passing time. I sat in that muggy classroom all that endless afternoon, listening to the classroom clock and the window blinds as they clacked in the heat. I screwed and unscrewed the top of my pen with wet hands. I shut my eyes and prayed for a miracle. But what had I done—trusting someone as spiteful as her, giving her the ammunition she needed to destroy me? I remembered the words of that letter by heart; it had taken me more than a week to compose.

Dear Barbara
I want to say how unhappy I am and to ask you

to help me. My mother has a boyfriend and he has begun to abuse me and I don't know anyone who can help. He said he would kill me if I told on him and I think that if she had to choose, my mother would choose him, not me. I hope you will understand. I need someone to talk to about it.
Love
Jennifer Young

While Miss Ridley had her back to the class pinning up a map of Africa, I saw Barbara's hand move down towards her satchel which was on the floor beside her.

It was like waiting for death.

Shaking with anticipation, I watched her remove the envelope and stealthily pull it open. Judith Mort, in the desk beside her, stretchcd across to see what it was, but Barbara jabbed her with her elbow.

I must have bitten my lip in half. By now I knew my face would be scarlet.

She read the note quickly, glanced round and turned to the front again.

The next words cut my senses like knives. 'Bring that paper to me, please, Barbara.'

'Oh, miss . . .'

'Don't argue. Bring that paper to me now and put it on my desk.'

Huffing and puffing and with a brief glance towards me, Barbara handed in my note and the lesson went on without further interruption. But all my concentration was focused on the centre of misery—which spread through my whole body, burning it up. The shame. The humiliation.

What had I done?
Would my mother find out?

The rest is sadly predictable. Barbara Middleton spent the next break whispering behind her hand to her friends. Eyes were turned in my direction. I saw no sympathy in them but a kind of malevolent glee.

'Jennifer Young,' said Miss Ridley, as she went on her way round the class, 'I'd like you to stay behind for a minute after four o'clock.'

My knees went weak. Half paralysed with shame, I could hardly walk. I stood beside the teacher's desk while she flattened that damn piece of paper and looked at me for an explanation.

When I stayed silent, she asked, 'Is this true?'

Too embarrassed to admit the lie, I nodded and whispered, 'Yes.'

'Would you like to talk to someone about it?'

'No,' I said quickly, 'no, not really.'

'Well, Jennifer, we can't leave it here, dear. Come with me now and we'll find Mrs Valentine.' And she smiled in an understanding way, revealing oddly pink plastic gums.

It was better to play along with this than admit the pitiful truth.

That walk—I will never forget it. That walk along the corridors side by side with Miss Ridley was endless. *Squeak squeak* we went on the polished lino, as it pulled at the soles of her open-toed sandals. Through the windows I saw a group of girls. The one doing the talking was vicious Barbara Middleton.

I waited outside the headmistress's office for what felt like a lifetime. Being such a desperately middling child I had never had the summons before.

Mrs Valentine opened the door. She was a sweet woman with a bun of white hair, an icon like a crucifix who we turned towards in prayers every morning.

'Sit down, dear.'

I obeyed like a robot. Her lips gave out a lilac aroma.

'Miss Ridley has shown me this note which one of her girls was reading during geography this afternoon.' She paused to take a look at me over the top of her half-glasses. 'I presume it's yours, you wrote it?'

'Yes, Mrs Valentine.'

'And your mother knows nothing of this?'

I hung my head. No answer.

'Tell me, Jennifer, how long has this been going on?'

I ran my foot in a tight little circle round the pattern on the carpet.

'Don't you think, dear, that it might be better if your mother was told?'

I managed a squeaky 'No, Mrs Valentine.'

'And why do you say that, I wonder?' I heard her sit back and smelt her body as it shifted in the still air of the room. Her voice was as sweet as the inside of soft orange chocolate. When I stayed silent she asked, 'Are you frightened that if she knew, your mother might go off and leave you?'

'She wouldn't believe me,' I ventured.

'And he might hurt you,' she continued, following the line of the shameful letter, 'as he has already threatened to do? What is this man's name, Jennifer?'

My lips were sealed; I had no idea.

'You do realize, I hope, that this cohabitee of

your mother's is no more than a common criminal?'

'I know,' I said in a muffled whisper. I looked at the teacher's cushiony chest and wished I could disappear in its folds.

'And therefore the police will have to be told.'

I wanted to die. If my mother ever heard about this, she would freak out. She would collapse. In my eyes she was sexless. She would no more dream of living with a man than put unwashed milk bottles out on the step or leave her support stockings off on a sunny day.

'Talk to me about this, Jennifer,' said Mrs Valentine kindly, moving to sit beside me, taking one of my sticky hands in her cool one. 'All I am trying to do is help. You know that, dear, don't you?'

'But . . .'

'But what?'

'But I don't want anyone's help.'

'That's not what it says in your note.'

How could I answer? The room was stifling. I craved a glass of water because my throat was so parched I could hardly swallow.

'*You've made all this up, haven't you, Jennifer?*'

This jerked me awake. The shock stopped my heart. 'What d'you mean?' I whispered.

'This letter of yours,' and she held it out between finger and thumb as if disposing of a used condom, 'is nothing but a crude device to attract attention.'

'No . . . no . . .' I was crying now.

'Jennifer, I don't want to bully you, but it really is time you told me the truth. Making accusations like this is a very serious matter. I don't know whether your mother has a male friend living at home, but if

115

she—'

'She hasn't, *she hasn't* . . .' I blurted out, searching for a tissue. Mrs Valentine handed me one. There was a pile on the edge of her desk and I wondered how frequently she had to replace it.

'Your mother does not live with a man. Is that what you are telling me now?'

I shook my head. 'She's not. She can't. She wouldn't—because of her legs.'

'So nobody's done anything to you?'

'No. No.' I wished to God they had. How I wished that everything I had written in that wicked note was true. How I hated my mother for being unsupportive.

'Well then, Jennifer; in that case you may as well get on home.'

'But you won't tell her, will you?' I pleaded.

'My dear child.' The headmistress fixed her eyes on my face. 'Of course your mother will have to know.'

I hated the teacher and I wanted her dead. I had put so much into this attempt and what had it gained me? Nothing. Nothing but the increased spite of the girls who made me so frightened. I knew they would discover the truth. Somehow they would find out. And my mother would be hurt and disappointed that I could think up such sick accusations.

I should have learned then that letters, like stomach acid, have a habit of coming back and are therefore never the answer.

*   *   *

It would seem that I had learned nothing as I

stepped out into that dewy night with a coat over my shoulders, as I tiptoed across the misty grass which was striped by shafts of moonlight, and stuck my precious letter to the handle of the dirty jeep.

At once I felt easier. My heart lightened as I crept back up the stairs and slid into bed beside Graham.

Martha would understand. Martha would forgive me. We could renew our close friendship, with this stain wiped out—forgotten. I would always love her, of course. I couldn't lie and pretend that had changed, but I knew now my feelings were not about lust and nor was I gay. My love for Martha was purer than that, because although I had enjoyed the closeness of our bedroom encounter, the thought that it would not happen again didn't worry me unduly. Although I loved and worshipped Martha, I didn't need her as a lover.

*   *   *

If only forgetting had been so simple.

CHAPTER TWELVE

Martha

If only forgetting had been so simple.

*   *   *

The phone woke us up at seven in a panic. The news left me bereft. Our wonderful, kindly, trustworthy, beloved babyminder, Hilda, was dead.

Just like that.

Our kids adored her. No-one else would do. She was like the Lord, she suffered little children.

'I can't tell you how sorry I am. Please let us know if we can help,' I weakly told her daughter.

'Damn,' said Sam, when I put down the phone and wiped away the stinging tears. 'That puts the cat among the pigeons.'

'*You really are a selfish bastard,*' I turned on him in fury. 'And if I didn't know your nasty ways were a cover-up for inadequacy, I'd have sodded off out of here before now. Scarlett and Poppy—how can we tell them? Where can we say Hilda's gone? They love that woman more than us. My God. *My God, how terrible.*'

'Tell them she's playing pit-a-pat in the sky. Tell them she's sprouted the same tinfoil wings she made for them last Christmas. But that settles it— you'll just have to cancel the dentist, or get a bus. I'll take the jeep this morning.'

My whole schedule was turned upside down. 'Oh yes, sure, *with both kids*?'

'Dump them on Jennie.'

I searched for a plausible excuse. 'She's very low at the moment . . .'

'So when is she anything else?'

'The dentist will think I'm chickening out the same as I did last time. He'll charge me the full rate, of course.'

'Sod the dentist. You don't have toothache. It won't hurt to leave it a week or two.'

Total despair set in. 'How the hell are we going to cope without Hilda?'

'Now who's the selfish bastard? It's me me me

with you, isn't it?' he joked, picking up his portfolio. 'The funeral should be a jazzy affair, well worth keeping a window open.'

'Just go. Get out. *She's irreplaceable.* We're going to miss her so much. A really sweet, decent woman. How could I leave them with anyone else?'

'Last night you were talking about adoption.'

'Oh piss off, you arsehole, just shut up and go.'

*   *   *

I was quick to the phone. 'Hello?'

'It's Jennie.'

I stiffened and my fingers flew to my hair when I attempted a casual 'Hi, Jennie.'

'I saw Sam take the jeep this morning.' That tense tone of voice alerted me. *So she still watched our every move.* What new mischief was this?

Before she could start, I said, 'Yes, he took it. Hilda's dead.'

I didn't expect the phone to go down with quite such a crash. OK, Jennie was fond of Hilda—we all were. But how typical of Jennie to take this tragedy and make it her own. How self-absorbed that woman was, even suffering gave her a buzz. Well, I wasn't prepared to go over and comfort her, or to share her grief. She could play the bleeding Madonna as much as she liked, it no longer cut any ice with me.

I sat and debated what to do, then I fed Lawrence, dressed Scarlett and read the paper, expecting Jennie to come over here. I was surprised when she didn't arrive and I hoped that my strict talk with her had hit home at last.

What an absurd situation. If it wasn't so crazy it

might be funny, and if I'd been working I could have laughed and put the whole incident down to one of those cringing blunders of life that are never easy to rise above. Tina's worldly attitude had been refreshing, although she missed the point entirely. No-one could really know the ferocity of Jennie's twisted passion. The swimming-pool project was about to start and I prayed this would distract her.

There was nothing more I could do to help her.

*   *   *

Sod's Law.

In the post that same morning came my first invitation for an interview, after months of faithful form-filling, CVs and crawling letters. I'd just about given up, but not quite . . .

Shit, *not much time,* they expected me to be there the next day. I panicked—the kids! The first thing they'd want was a reassurance that my child-care arrangements were foolproof. Now there was no Hilda, *where else could I turn?* After what had just happened, to involve Jennie would be playing into her hands again. It would give out the wrong signals. I needed to distance myself from her: to ask her help would be to draw closer. She'd fall over herself to help me, I knew. There was nobody else in the Close I could use, no-one *that* desperate for funds. One's own kids were daunting enough, let alone somebody else's.

My passport to sanity beckoned.

But now, what the hell should I do?

I paced up and down, planning what to wear, what to say, figuring out what sort of person they'd want me to be.

120

I ought to forget it, Sam would say. To him, this would be no more important than cancelling the blasted dentist.

The thought of turning down this chance I so longed for—to be part of the real world again, to leave behind these breeding years, to mix with sane people, to have conversations that didn't include shit and bile—the thought of turning my back on all this was enough to make me feel suicidal.

How long had I waited for this very moment?

My brain was so addled I couldn't remember.

The walls of my house closed in on me and the children's cries were steel bands round my head.

But faced with dependency on Jennie after the awkwardness between us, I knew very well what I ought to do—I should turn down this job. Right now.

And apart from that, was I seriously considering leaving my darlings with a nutter?

*   *   *

At last Lawrence went for his morning sleep.

To try and soften my crashing dreams I got out my oils and a canvas—it was the only therapy that might lift me out of this well of depression. I covered every inch of the kitchen with old newspapers so that Scarlett could join me in my madness. Once, before I got hitched, I had been considered quite an artist and most of our walls were splodged with what Sam called my primitive efforts. But deep emotions are hard to express with a three-year-old at your elbow, let alone that inane, encouraging chatter.

'Who's that, Scarlett? Oooh yes, a house, a dog

and a pear tree . . .' My daughter was brilliant and I beamed at her proudly; she was advanced for her age, a likely genius. *Noddy* was on the telly and we sang the well-known songs together, shivering at the spooky goblins, eating biscuits and drinking milk, and making the sort of unholy mess Jennie would weep at if she saw.

I decided to ring the *Express* and cancel my interview.

I punched in the number and covered one ear to block out the sound of Noddy's damn bell.

'Hold on, I'll just put you through.'

I waited. The tears didn't show, they were deep inside me.

'Look, Mummy . . .'

'That's excellent, Scarlett. Do some more while Mummy—'

But Scarlett needed the potty, so I left the phone and scuttled to fetch it. I undid her dungarees and picked up the phone again. 'Hello,' I cried desperately, in case someone important was there. I positioned Scarlett on the pot, handed her her lop-eared teddy and glanced at the mirror over the phone, and gawped to see the state of me: saggy-eyed, dishevelled and vacant, with green smears of war paint over my nose and dried milk streaked round my lips.

'Mrs Frazer?' came a calm voice from some distant planet.

'Oh yes, hello, is that Peter Taylor?'

'So good of you to apply. We've whittled down the applications. Hundreds applied. They think they're qualified to do this job with just a Bic and a spiral pad. I'm looking forward to meeting you. Sally Ince says she worked with you once . . .'

'Oh, how is Sally?' I'd forgotten my buck-toothed old mate existed.

For a quarter of an hour we chatted like this and finally the editor said, 'How would it be if we ducked the interview and met for lunch at a pub instead?'

I'd got the job! I knew it! *I knew it!*

I heard myself saying a casual 'Fine.' If I caught the twelve o'clock bus, I might just make it.

I put down the phone in a euphoric trance.

Someone out there was truthfully looking forward to meeting me in person!

Someone had said I was good at the job!

Somebody wanted to pay me!

And just two days a week—it was perfect!

Lawrence woke up and wanted his bottle. Scarlett was painting the floor with her pee. Big Ears was saying something banal, and I had to ring the plumber because the loo was blocked.

Half an hour later, in a moment of calm, when I'd satisfied every demand on me, I got on the phone to Jennie.

*   *   *

'I'll come over,' she said with alacrity. She seemed to be coping with poor Hilda's death.

'Of course I'll do it,' she said, 'if you really are determined to go.'

'I'll pay you, of course.'

She adopted her most wounded expression. 'You know there's no need for that. Please don't drive me any further away.' She was more muted than usual and I noticed she watched me expectantly as I charged round the house searching for clothes,

123

ironing, washing my hair, cursing the muddied state of my only decent pair of shoes. Jennie was at her most downcast, but I was so thrilled and excited that I put her depression down to the fact I had found a job at last.

The door of the doll's-house prison was opening. I could see light. *Just one extra shove . . .*

Scarlett, Poppy and I experimented with the scrappy contents of my make-up bag. It had hardly been used since I'd become a mother—no free ten minutes by the mirror each morning—and, as I wasn't going anywhere anyway, why take the trouble? Jennie watched us tensely.

'What d'you think?' I turned to face her, smacking my lips over pale pink gloss.

'That's nice,' she said, uninterested.

'Hair up—or down?'

'Whatever.'

I refused to take this boring bait. She was upset by my rejection and the thought of another intense discussion wallowing in her murky mire was more than I could endure. I tried to humour her out of the sulks. 'Two days a week, for God's sake. It's hardly emigrating to Australia.'

No doubt she wanted to discuss our improbable sexual encounter. She carried the weight of the world on her shoulders and this morning there was a veil, a kind of thin blue sickness, over her duller than usual eyes. Was she ill? Was she in mourning? Whatever—I did not want to know.

*   *   *

The lunch went well. I knew I had landed the job. I was elated when I got home and spent the

124

afternoon making plans, tearing round the house looking for suitable clothes, and compiling lists. All being well, I could start work in two weeks' time. I'd convince Sam somehow that this was something I had to do.

I heard the jeep. Sam was home early. But why was he striding towards next door? Graham wouldn't be home yet and Graham was the only reason why Sam would go next door—to discuss the wretched swimming-pool plans.

I was quite unprepared for what happened next. My hackles rose when I heard the screaming. I flew to the door, cold with fear when I saw Sam striding down Jennie's path pursued by a screaming, weeping woman trying to clutch at his feet.

'*Sam?*' I tore out to meet him. *'My God, what's happened, what have you done?'*

Jennie kept after him, panting and sobbing, until she reached our front door. 'But you must let me see her, you must.' She flung herself down on the mat, buried her head in her hands and gave way to a torrent of tears, a penitent in terrible remorse. 'I love Martha, I love her so much.' And when she looked up, she was crying so hard it looked as if she had no eyes left.

Oh. Dear. God. So Sam had found out about us. Somehow.

*　　　*　　　*

God, how I hated her then.

CHAPTER THIRTEEN

Jennie

God, how I hated her then.

*   *   *

Shame slammed at me in tidal waves. 'Jennie,' said Martha with frost in her voice. 'Stop these dramatics and get back to your house. You silly bitch—*are you satisfied now*? Go on, go on, destroy me completely. Happy now, are you, damn you?'

Sam stood beside her in stony silence, and oh the guilt and the racking anguish over something impulsively done that could not be undone.

Inside me day turned to night . . . all over . . . nothing left but a shell. And deep, deep within, I was screaming; I writhed in agony.

Neither one put out a hand to help me.

He'd appeared on my doorstep quite out of the blue, standing there, tyrannical, as if he had rights. 'You're going to tell me, 'cos I know Martha won't.' He thrust the note under my nose. 'This letter'—he shook it, his disdain pouring out—'it's absolutely pathetic. What are you, for God's sake, some closet dyke?'

His sneering sarcasm burned me, but over all that was the awful knowledge that Martha's friendship with me was over. Sam's intolerance of minority groups, particularly of the sexual kind, was the one which he harped on most often. All day I had been waiting for something, from that first dreadful moment when I saw him drive off to work in the jeep. I'd expected him to attack Martha; I hadn't reckoned I'd be the first victim.

His face was a grimace, his arms were crossed tight, and dislike filled his half-closed eyes. Thank God he spoke quietly because of the neighbours, but I wished he would come inside. The terrified Poppy was trying to push past me and I didn't want her to hear his tone. But he said, 'What the fuck have you been doing to my wife?'

'*I didn't mean . . .*'

But he didn't wait for any excuses. 'Come on, what happened? Something did.'

I longed to reach up and shut his mouth. If only I could wipe that half-smile from his face.

'It happened—once—it was my fault. Martha . . .'

'Oh? And what did Martha do while you were busy satisfying your perverted desire? Scream for help? Fight you off? Tell you to stop being so fucking obscene? What did Martha do then, Jennie?' His eyes stared intently. Sharp as pins, they missed nothing.

I stayed silent. At a loss. He gave another of his ice-cold smiles.

'And do you make a habit of sneaking to the nearest house and having it off with whoever's around? Aren't you getting enough from Graham, is that it? You can only stand him one night a week.'

I stiffened with pain and cried, 'Did she tell you that?'

I forgot how to stop crying. A proper smile broke out on his face. His next few words came with amusement. 'Oh yes, Martha told me everything. She is my wife, in case you'd forgotten.

127

Husbands and wives do tend to share secrets, although you probably wouldn't know about that.'

I needed to cling to him, to convince him, but his brain was closed to reason. 'It happened once and Martha's been sick ever since. It never would have happened again—she didn't want to, I didn't want to . . .'

'*Oh, I see, I see.* So my wife's charms didn't impress you. She failed to live up to your expectations. Tits too big, I suppose?'

Poppy was whining behind the door and I was afraid to move.

'You know what you've done, Jennie, don't you?'

'No!' I cried out through my tears.

'You've really messed up with your sly perversions . . .'

'*But I love her!*' Was that my voice, so strong, so clear, that shriek from out of nowhere?

'I am so sorry for you. I really, honestly am. So you love her, well, do you really. Let's see how Martha feels about that.'

And with that he walked away down the path with my letter in his hand like a flag, and me behind him, crying and begging. A child again and powerless.

*   *   *

Those words were meant for Martha's eyes only. But now they were cheap and crass. I cringed when I remembered them. A flood of outgoing love when I wrote them, they were now no more than self-abuse.

Dearest Martha

To write to you is such a relief.

Please don't let what happened between us make you give up on the rest of it. I know what I did was out of line and although I know that it was wrong, I can't forget how happy and natural I felt with you in my arms. Strong and good. I think about you all through my days and my nights are full of fantasy. Even writing to you, like I am now, gives me such a rush of elation, knowing you're going to read what I'm saying. If I thought that, after what happened yesterday, you would want to end our friendship, I don't think I could stand the pain of it. I will do anything, go anywhere, be anyone you want me to be, just as long as you stay near me and care.

All my love

Jennie

I spoiled it all. Ruined everything.

Everything whirled in a scarlet blur, so I couldn't know who else in the Close had observed the confrontation, or who kept watching as I crawled back to the hole which was my house. I wouldn't have noticed a multi-car pile-up inches from my nose.

'It's OK, Poppy, it's OK.' My eyes gazed at my daughter, unseeing. 'Sam and Mummy are only playing a silly game. Daddy will be home at five, so let's see if we can finish our soldiers.'

Yes, Daddy was coming home.

I had the rest of the afternoon to teach my grief-stricken face how to smile. To somehow swap this unbearable misery for the trivia of everyday life. I could say I had a headache and head for a darkened room; I could pack a bag and run away, a quiet walk to the station . . . going back to Mother, they call it. But thousands of women go missing each year and are never heard of again. They drift into rivers, they fall off bridges, they disappear down cold country roads. Or I could adopt a disguise and spend the rest of my life stalking Martha and making silent phone calls.

But did I want to exist like this, drained of energy and purpose, my head split as if cleaved by an axe? Day after day, despair and inertia until slowly my brain gave way?

I could end it all, of course, and lift this exquisite pain. How lovely that white emptiness seemed when my future was surrounded by darkness. There was no point in living without Martha's friendship, and I fantasized that they found me hanging by a rope in the garage. Or perhaps I would take a more gentle route and use the car exhaust fumes.

Sam would feel the most guilty.

That monster who treated Martha like the dust that flew daily out of her old vacuum cleaner, how he would regret his cruel words; how he'd stand, shamefaced, by my coffin as they trickled the earth onto the lid, cursing himself for his insensitivity, his ego, his flippancy and his deranged aggression.

*   *   *

That same day, praise be, my mother, Stella, dropped dead and all I could think of was that at last, apart from the animal act of birth, she had done something positive to help me.

My salvation was as miraculous as Christ

130

appearing after death. The phone rang while Graham was bathing the children and I sprang to get it . . . *it might be Martha.*

It was Mrs Miles, my mother's neighbour.

'Is that you, Jennie?'

Not Martha. My heart dropped as I said yes. I had no other interest in life except my cocoon of agony and I wanted to slam down the phone.

'Jennie Young that was?'

As I heard the background of Walthamstow traffic, heavy at that time of evening, my mind slipped into gear. 'Yes.'

'I have some terrible news, I'm afraid, my dear.'

I knew at once that Stella was dead because this was part of such an old fantasy . . . all those occasions when I'd prayed to hear those words at school, elevating me instantly to the heights of noble martyr while the flames of tragedy licked my feet. And I used to imagine my poor mother winging her way to heaven and passing my vile thoughts, like belching chimney smoke, on the way up.

And would my betrayal be such a surprise? *Had she honestly never known?*

But if Stella had done as I wished and died while I was at school, it would have been a wasted gesture. This was a far, far better thing she did now, but I squashed the rising flash of excitement.

Having acted out this part so many times, it was hard to guess at the proper reaction because nothing came to me naturally—no deep sense of grief, no shock, only a calm acceptance and woodenness of emotion.

Had I ever loved her?

Had I ever loved anyone?

131

If no to both these questions—did that make me a psychopath?

Mrs Miles was saying, 'And, of course, they're waiting at the hospital until they know what to do with her. All that side still needs to be arranged, and then there'll be the flat to clear. I presume she left a will, but as far as I know you were her only kin.'

Kin? Kith, and dear ones. The departed and the dearly beloved. Words like white lilies, saved for death.

I assured Mrs Miles that I would take care of everything. Graham would know exactly how to deal with this melancholy business, and of course Martha would have to be told.

'Who was that?' Graham asked, coming downstairs with little Josh wrapped in a towel, and Poppy trailing naked behind them.

'Stella's dead.'

'*Oh, Jennie, no . . .*'

'She died in hospital this afternoon. She was admitted this morning with a brain haemorrhage and they've been trying to trace me ever since.'

'Oh, Jennie, how awful, oh no . . . no. Poppy, come here. Mummy doesn't want you crawling all over her just now. Mummy's upset. Where are those Fuzzy Felt pieces you were playing with before? Go and see if you can find them.'

'I'll have to go and sort it all out.'

'I can make most of the arrangements from this end.' Graham was so reliable, so practical, so sweet and considerate to me. 'All you'll have to do is clear out the flat at some point.'

'She didn't have anything we would want.'

'No,' said Graham, aware that everything in that

132

dreary basement would end up in the council tip. 'But you better go and make sure. There have to be personal bits like photos, books and papers. When you've done that I'll get hold of a clearance firm.'

'She was only young. She was fifty-one.'

'I know,' said Graham. 'It's awful.'

'She was always so unhappy.'

'But that wasn't your fault, Jennie.' He tied Poppy's dressing-gown cord in a special butterfly bow. He started to dress the baby, while I sat motionless by the phone trying to make sense of the mess. 'Why was she so unhappy?'

'Because her life was so unfulfilled, I suppose, and she was lonely. She never recovered from being abandoned all those years ago, and she never forgave my father.'

Graham said, 'Her life was a struggle. She was short of money. She had to work hard.'

But that was no excuse for being so bitter and twisted. 'Lots of people are short of money, but they don't go through life bearing the cross she lugged round on her shoulders. Think of her face— so closed and ungiving.'

If these were ordinary circumstances Graham knew that I would need Martha. He knew his compassion wasn't enough and he said, with so much concern in his voice, 'Why don't you slip over to Martha's while I put these two little devils to bed?'

My chest was bursting with new-found hope. 'Would you mind?'

'Don't be silly,' said Graham. 'Martha would want to know, anyway. First Hilda, now poor Stella. Two deaths in forty-eight hours. Who will be next, I wonder?'

133

*   *   *

I crept up my neighbour's drive with an indescribable dread.

'*Jennie!*' Sam's eyes narrowed, confusion spread. '*What the hell . . . ?*'

'I know, Sam. I'm sorry.' And I burst into tears. 'Mum's dead.'

He took one wary step backwards as if he suspected a lie. 'What? When?'

'This afternoon,' I told him with my head down, unchallenging. 'And I just wondered if you would mind if I had a quick word with Martha.'

He could hardly throw me out of the house—not now. *Bless you, Mother.*

'But . . . I didn't know Stella was ill.'

'Nobody knew. It was sudden.' I remained on the porch. I wouldn't go in unless invited.

Sam said, 'Well, you better come through.'

'Thank you, Sam. I hope I'm not disturbing . . .'

'No, no, it's OK.'

'Listen,' I told him, a red-eyed penitent, 'I want you to know that I'm so very sorry and if I could take time back I would . . .'

Sam sighed and softened. He looked weary. 'Jennie, don't let's go into that now. Come and find Martha and have a good cry . . .'

When death strikes people hold their breath, and Sam and Martha adored their own mothers.

I stepped inside to the same general disorder. Martha had been crying. They must have been in the middle of an almighty row when I so brazenly interrupted. She looked up at Sam, then at me, and she hesitated before stepping forward. Sam said solemnly, 'Stella's dead.'

'Oh Jennie, no!'

Martha drew me towards her and we sat down on the battered old sofa, my vile indecencies quite forgotten in the gravity of the moment. How simply it had turned out after all. Who would have thought that such a short time ago I was thinking of topping myself?

'I just feel so sad for her,' I whimpered to Martha. *'Nothing good ever happened . . .'*

'Shush, shush, don't think like that,' said Martha at her sweetest, and I knew I was halfway to forgiveness. 'Good things did happen to Stella. She had you, she had Graham and two wonderful grandchildren.'

'Drink?' asked Sam, giving me a chance to smile and share some new understanding.

'I never loved her, perhaps she knew that,' I sniffed in my distress.

'But you did love her, Jennie,' Martha argued, soothing the newly bereft, stroking my hand. 'Look how much you cared when those girls at school were so cruel. It was your mother they were attacking and you felt so hurt for her, not for yourself. You tried to protect her, you went through hell so she wouldn't be distressed. And you did this when you were only a child. You did love her. I'm sure you did.'

'You're going through the kind of guilt everyone feels when someone dies,' said Sam, rallying to my pitiful cause. 'And let's face it, Jennie, Stella didn't make it that easy for anyone to love her.'

'And I worry that I'm too like her,' I went on, dabbing my eyes. Both Sam and Martha protested at this. I looked up to show them how much I appreciated their comfort. Everyone likes to feel needed and here we were in a marvellous vortex, gurgling down a comforting hole, and all was going to be well again.

If I'd never loved my mother before, then I certainly loved her now.

When I left their house later that evening it was as a special guest, wrapped in their concern, strengthened by their love and in the certain knowledge that we could start afresh.

*   *   *

What a blessing that it's not possible to see into the future.

CHAPTER FOURTEEN

Martha

What a blessing that it's not possible to see into the future.

*   *   *

I, too, blessed Stella's timing, but these coincidental dramas whenever there'd been an 'incident' between me and Jennie were becoming uncanny. If I hadn't known for certain that Jennie was next door all day, and that Stella had died under the eagle eye of professionals, I would have suspected murder.

A murder of convenience.

136

I have never seen Sam so driven as on the day he arrived home with that note, pursued by a hysterical Jennie. It was scary. I had no defence. I had 'been to bed with that woman', and it was, as Sam told me quietly, 'more gross than any normal bloody infidelity'. And how the hell would I have felt if he'd been caught in some public bog with his prick up another man's arse, or coming out of our bedroom wearing my bra and knickers?

And what the fuck was he supposed to do now?

It was a waste of time telling him it was a 'one-off', never to be repeated, one dreadful mistake. He refused to listen. 'What's done is done,' he said with meaning. And how could we possibly return to any semblance of married life—'Especially with that nympho next door. Nothing but a farce,' he sneered.

Now was not a good time to mention the hypocrisy of his self-righteous rage, the unimportant fling he had with the daughter of his sales manager; Fiona, with the lifeless eyes, the dead hair, but the alarmingly lithe and firm body. Or his weekend with the lovely Sarah, one of the designers at work; Sarah who flashed her thong at the world every time she bent down. He would have preferred not to work quite so closely with Sarah, he said. But funnily enough—although he disliked her and called her a tramp—he ended up shafting her, then calling her 'nothing much'.

And then there were the nearly times when he flirted shamelessly with my friends, fawned over women at parties, made passes at other men's wives, and when I saw how easily they fell under his spell I wanted to shout a warning, 'Beware, this man is debauched, don't touch him, he'll hurt.'

137

And how many times had I warned him that I wouldn't have him back again?

If I had screwed another man I had no doubt that would end our marriage, and until Jennie came to the door with her devastating news, I almost believed that Sam would pack his bags and go.

But death is hard to deal with, especially the death of a mother. If mine had died I couldn't have borne it and Sam felt the same about Caroline. And under that hard-boiled exterior, Sam is a soft-hearted fool. He caved in at the sight of poor Jennie in mourning, and only I detected that gleam of triumph in her eye. By the end of the evening I couldn't believe it when I heard Sam say of our 'warped liaison', 'It's the age we live in, these things happen.' Although by then he was on his fourth brandy.

*　　　*　　　*

I went to the funeral with Jennie.

'But surely Graham should be the one . . .'

'Please, Martha. I need to feel strong, and with you alongside me I will.' And Graham seemed only too happy to stay at home and mind the kids.

As we drove through the dull grey streets, past terraces, towering blocks of flats and broken houses, we marvelled at the way some small, proud gardens basked in green and white spring daisies before the dust of London withered their freshness away. The privets along the railings were gold, the uniform trees were spread with the pink and white of may, or draped with the mauve of lilac. It was odd to smell the sweet fragrance resting on the air,

138

mixed with fumes and garbage.

Jennie said, 'I could have gone to visit her in the chapel of rest, but I didn't think that was a good idea.'

'Very wise,' I told her, 'what would be the point?' But I couldn't use the old platitude, 'Remember her how she was when she was alive,' because in Stella's case she would probably look happier and more relaxed in death.

The dead. And their poetry.

'*It hath pleased God Almighty to take unto Himself . . .*'

'*He cometh up and is cut down like a flower . . .*'

'*In the midst of life we are in death.*' Well, Jennie's mother was certainly so.

It was all the essence of courtesy. Sympathy flowed, from the men who carried the coffin down the aisle to the priest on his soft feet, but no amount of kindness could obscure the fact that the crematorium chapel was empty and that nobody— not even her daughter—mourned the fact that Stella's body lay under the purple drapes.

When the soft machinery started to hum and the coffin moved towards the furnace, I wondered how many times she had left her house with no-one to wave her goodbye. *And was this a measure of success*—how many people wept at your funeral?

*   *   *

Afterwards, at the basement flat, someone had puked on the steps outside. Mrs Miles, the neighbour who gave us the key, said greedily, 'Let me come and see what's left before you finally lock up, dear.' And when Jennie looked at her stonily, the woman said with total conviction, 'Stella would have wanted that.'

We drank two strong cups of tea before we felt able to sort through the remnants of somebody else's life. Everything had a doleful look, once special and new, now soiled and unwanted. It was quite an eye-opener for me. So this was where Jennie grew up; her dreams had been formed in this dismal basement, her view from the window obstructed by chimneys, tenements and a railway line. Limited horizons.

'That was my school.' Jennie pointed to a red-brick factory, its walls tangled with barbed wire. This wasn't the dark, mysterious poverty that moved poets and writers—booze, babies, batterings and Bridewells—this was quiet and respectable, with dingy net curtains and no vibrancy. Immediately beyond the factory was a playground. The clues were the climbing frame and tyres; otherwise it was more like a disused bomb site, a prowling ground for thin brown dogs with tails that curled up over their backs.

'What do I want out of here?' Jennie cried, holding out a pink candlewick bedspread, a deadly thing, as if she felt she ought to claim it and not abandon it to its fate.

'You really don't want that,' I said, 'and put that lampshade back where you found it. You've got to be selective. Stella's dead. Turning down her bits and pieces isn't going to hurt her now.'

But Jennie put the button box, an oriental lacquered tea caddy, into one of the boxes we'd brought. 'The awful thing is,' she said, looking round hopelessly, 'Mum worked so hard for all this crap and look at it! *Just look at it!* All that scrimping and scraping—for what? It would have been better if she'd given up and gone on the dole.'

I pressed her hand. 'Pride,' I said, but knowing sod all about the stamina required of women like Stella. If I was ever in need, I would damn well make sure I claimed the last penny. And if things were that bad, I might well turn to crime. But Stella's pride had not been passed on to her daughter, except in the superficial concerns that kept Jennie scrubbing and cleaning.

No, unlike the miserable Stella, Jennie had no pride at all.

*   *   *

'Look at this! What is it? It looks like a letter from your father!'

I'd been delving in a musty box that reeked of damp. I had found it under Stella's bed.

'Let's have a look . . . oh . . . there's a photo . . .'

I was astonished when I realized. *'Haven't you ever seen this before?'*

'No.' Jennie sounded shy. I watched her face as she picked up the picture, taken by one of those Instamatics and sticky with fingerprints. 'That's not him,' she said firmly.

I took it from her and stared. 'How do you know? It's with all the letters, and here's a wedding photo, my God!'

Jennie snatched it off me. She said nothing. Her father was a funny little man, shiny like a salesman, wearing a crumpled suit, and the picture was taken between cars, on the pavement outside some register office. Stella wore white. A white linen suit with shades of Oxfam, and white high heels that

141

made her feet look overlarge and her legs peculiarly skinny. But the very obvious surprise was that she bulged like a balloon at the front. There was no doubt about it. Stella was pregnant.

'So much for all that moral high ground.'

But Jennie ignored me. In the same low voice, she said, 'I never dreamed he would look like that.'

'I know. You hoped he'd be Richard Branson. Well, now you know.' I was suddenly struck by a wonderful idea. 'Jennie, *why don't you trace him?*'

'I don't want to trace him,' she said quickly, and she folded down the top of the box and put it on the take-home pile.

'But he's probably alive. Stella was only fifty-one. You could search for your roots. It'd be such fun.'

'I don't want to find my roots. *Leave it alone, please, Martha.*'

I was taken aback by her vehemence, but I did what I was told.

*   *   *

It was astonishing how deviously Jennie, at her most submissive and artful, penetrated Sam's macho abhorrence and turned him into a kind of protector. She was a weak and feeble woman, and that appealed to a dominant male who would secretly have preferred me to be more needy. I talked him through our awkward relationship: how Jennie's infatuation had spiralled, without encouragement, into this manic obsession from which we could see no way out. He, at his most benevolent and surprisingly grown up, finally accepted that sex was not at the core, that neither of us was the dyke he suspected and our squeamish

142

reactions proved that.

I had to admire the way Jennie spun her web around him, using every wile she had to get herself forgiven and accepted. All I wanted was peace to reign and if this was the best way to achieve it, then that was OK by me.

Sam and I both reluctantly agreed that the only real way to help Jennie out of her emotional turmoil was to include her in our activities and to try to treat her as normal. So when Betws-y-Coed came up, Sam said, 'OK, let the Gordons come, but Emma and Mark won't be too chuffed and it is their cottage.'

'It would mean such a lot to Jennie,' I said, not mentioning how many chances my neighbour had already been given, and blown. 'It would signal your absolution and you know how she cares about stuff like that.'

'She's mad, not bad,' Sam said, full of his own self-importance again, expert as he now was on obsessions. 'But let's hope that's water under the bridge.'

And I dared to remark, 'We've all done things we're not proud of.'

And Sam said, 'Jennie hasn't got a clue how sodding lucky she is, and there's old Graham going round in the dark, thinking he's got the perfect wife.'

'She must be hell to live with—all those moods, and the kids so mollycoddled, waited on hand and foot.'

'Well, just as long as they don't expect us to pander to that when it's pissing with rain in Betws-y-Coed for a whole sodding fortnight,' said Sam.

On a Monday and a Thursday, as soon as I got home from work, Jennie would come over to return Scarlett and Lawrence. It became a routine which was never broken and it meant that I could never stay late for a drink with my office friends after the paper was put to bed. She waited for this precious time, watching the road through her curtains for the moment when my second-hand Mini shook rustily onto my drive.

And because she stubbornly refused payment, I felt obliged to entertain her with talk of my day in exchange for services rendered. It became an unspoken pact. We'd get out the wine and I'd kick off my shoes, and Jennie would sit at the table and wait, like an overstuffed seagull chick waits on roofs, behind chimneys, for its scrawny, worn-out parents to provide grubs. And I felt more guilt at abandoning Jennie for those special two days a week than I felt for my own children.

She handicapped me. If circumstances had been normal, I would have found a new childminder to replace Hilda and paid her so that I could do the hours I wanted—maybe cover the magistrates' court or do some council meetings. I daren't even bring up the subject with Jennie; she might regress into lengthy despair and I couldn't tolerate more of that crap. We were going well. I mustn't rock the boat.

She was trying her hardest.

She deserved encouragement.

She must have known how close she had come to ruining our marriage, and maybe hers as well. If it wasn't for the kids and the fact that we were next-

144

door neighbours, I doubt that Sam would have been so forgiving. Mercifully, nobody else appeared to have seen or heard that frightful drama played out on our doorsteps. If they did, they never mentioned it.

So I was surprised when Tina Gallagher confronted me over coffee at her house. 'I hear you're taking the Gordons on holiday with you again.'

'To a cottage in Wales, which some friends have just bought.'

Tina looked at me hard. *'And you think that's wise?'*

I was taken aback. 'What d'you mean?'

'Well,' said Tina, avoiding my eyes, 'after that dreadful business.'

I dipped a finger in sugar and sucked it, attempting a casual response. I wished I hadn't confided in Tina, but at the time I was so desperate that it felt like the only thing to do. 'Oh, that's over now.'

'That's not what I heard,' she said.

I wanted to leave, but how could I? I needed to know what she meant.

'Well, Jennie's grown chummy with Angie Ford,' said Tina, 'and she told me that after that bloody great row, Jennie came crying to her, saying Sam had no right to treat her like that after what he'd done at your last Christmas party.'

'What?'

'Apparently, Jennie was rat-arsed and Sam had to take her upstairs . . .'

'Yes, I know. He put her to bed, mainly to hide her from that wretched family . . .'

'Well,' said Tina, eyeing me over the rim of her

145

mug, 'apparently that's not all he did.'

'*Balls*,' I said. 'Bollocks, Sam would have said. He tells me about his women—afterwards. That's all part of the thrill.'

Tina raised her eyebrows before going on. 'Don't get me wrong, Martha sweetie, I am merely repeating what I've been told, what the whole Close has been told, for your own sake. *Sam took advantage of Jennie, and you have a serious problem with booze.* Those are the rumours spread by you know who. Nobody believes a word, of course, we all know Jennie Gordon by now. But when I heard about this holiday, I thought you two must be off your chumps. Why you don't just cut yourselves off from that blessed family, I can't imagine. That woman's trouble, red hot, believe me.'

*   *   *

When was this whole mess going to end?

CHAPTER FIFTEEN

Jennie

When was this whole mess going to end?

*   *   *

The cottage was nothing like I'd imagined. They all decided we should meet in the garden rather than travel in convoy, as I had suggested; they also turned down my idea of getting together at a café in town with toilets and water for the children.

We assumed we would find the place without any trouble. We had it circled on our Ordnance Survey and Graham, a scout for so long, was an expert at reading maps.

I was sick of chanting, 'Just another few minutes, we're nearly there. Poppy, darling, be patient . . .'

I couldn't believe it when we drew up. 'No!' I peered out frantically, because Poppy was retching every few minutes and Josh was screaming so hard in his seat that I thought he must have developed a temperature. 'No, Graham, this can't be it. It's derelict, nobody lives here, and how would anyone get in?'

'Up the path, of course.' Graham, at the end of his tether, slammed his sunglasses down on the dashboard in temper. He got out and wandered along the lane that ran alongside the high stone wall. I watched him straining to see over. He stuck up his thumb, slid back in the car and drove bumpily off the road and onto an uneven, grassy slope that bordered the ramshackle building.

Sheep pooh. God. *Disgusting.*

I had to admit I was wrong when he pointed out the name, Last Resort, which was so silly and typical of Mark and Emma; although—to be fair—it was named that when they bought it. It could have been called that for hundreds of years, going by the state of the crooked sign. You'd never have spotted it from the lane.

'Oh look, Poppy,' exclaimed Graham at his most encouraging. 'I think a wicked witch lives here . . .' And I could have shaken him. He knew very well how sensitive Poppy was to suggestion.

How could we possibly wait in this garden?

Masses of tall weeds and brambles with wasps, bees, dragonflies and beetles, at their most industrious, hovered and bothered round hairy stems. Thank goodness I'd had the foresight to bring the wet wipes and the Wasp-Eze, the bug spray and an assortment of blankets.

Graham nearly demolished the gate in order to get through. He trampled down a space on the so-called grass, so we could spread out a rug and have somewhere to sit. Of course, Mark and Emma, being childless and showing no signs of wanting a family, wouldn't consider this hazardous. They had assured us the place was perfect.

'But you must admit,' Graham said, happier now that he was out of the car and draining the last drop of tepid tea, 'the place is idyllic.' For Heidi maybe, yes. We were surrounded by steep green hillsides, almost mountainous in places, while below us a forest meandered down to the distant slither of river.

The sounds were of buzzing insects, bleats of hidden sheep and the faraway splashing of the river, while the smells were of hot vegetation and pine.

'Oh yes, charming if you're in the SAS doing a course in orienteering, or a hermit in training for total seclusion. But how far away are the shops? Don't forget, we've got two babies, and I'm more concerned about basic survival.'

'For once, why don't we try and relax?' said Graham, who was crossing his legs and letting his head fall back. His sandy hair tickled his neck. He leaned forward and took off his shirt.

'You'll get bitten,' I warned him. 'You're asking for trouble.' I sorted out Poppy's sun hat, even

148

though she would tug it off when I wasn't looking. Luckily I had remembered the sunshade for the carrycot because, my God, it was hot.

*   *   *

'You clever things, you've arrived already, super.' Emma leapt lithely over the side of the Morgan and hauled out a gigantic hamper. 'We hoped we'd be first. We wanted to have the grub all unpacked and ready.'

Graham shook hands with Mark and relieved him of the raffia umbrella. 'Bang it in the ground somewhere, while I fight my way in and find us some chairs.'

We'd been on holiday with them before, but not in such close proximity. In Italy we'd all stayed in a hotel, where we did our own thing and had our own rooms. In many respects, Mark and Emma were like strangers: because of their laid-back lifestyle, their endless money and their freedom, they seemed like kids, much younger than us. I felt drab and boring alongside Emma. Were they happy to have us here for a fortnight at their cottage, or had they needed persuading? When Emma and Mark were around, even the steady, sensible Graham talked faster and louder and tried to be wittier.

But in my case, feeling inferior, my awkwardness made me clumsy and dull.

The cottage door was open now and Emma had disappeared into the kitchen. I felt I ought to be helping, although I had enough on my plate with the children tired, hungry and hot. I followed her into the rustic hovel.

She expected me to know what to do with the

149

strange bits and pieces she brought from the hamper. Most of it was probably cordon bleu and therefore unsuitable for the children. But I couldn't cope, *I just couldn't cope.*

'Don't worry, I'll do it,' she said. 'You just take the stuff outside. The table ought to be up by now, and Mark will sort the wine.' She turned to Poppy and gave a huge smile, but Poppy just sucked her finger and clung tightly to my skirt.

'She's shy,' I explained, made inadequate again, and unfairly annoyed with Poppy who could be bright and fun if she tried.

'It's a long journey for them, isn't it?' Emma attempted to draw Poppy out. 'You're hungry, aren't you?' she said, ruffling Poppy's hair, so that my daughter frowned and straightened it again.

'I wish I had hair like that,' said Emma.

But she had. Poppy's hair—straight and honey-blonde—was as fair as Scarlett's was dark. It was just possible that Emma's hair was dyed blonde, but I guessed that it was natural. Its glossy texture seemed effortless too. She and Mark were 'natural' people, mostly in shorts or swimwear, and they sported glowing, advertisement skin.

They probably ran along the sand hand in hand, or rode across it bareback.

But no matter what I spent on clothes, I couldn't achieve that born-into-them look, and I was too thin to swing when I walked, like Emma did.

I whispered to Graham nastily, 'Trust the Frazers to be late. The worst'll be done by the time they arrive.'

'Knowing Martha, she planned it that way.' But Graham's remark was jokey, whereas mine had been meant spitefully. I felt slighted; I was out of my depth but I was determined to make it seem as if I was having a wonderful time.

'While we're waiting for the others, could we take some of our stuff upstairs and see where we are all sleeping?' I thought it impolite that Emma hadn't already shown us round—after all, we were her guests.

She was too busy fiddling in the kitchen for manners. 'Top of the stairs,' she said. 'Duck your heads, turn left and you're at the end of the little landing.'

I prised Graham away from Mark—if men can do nothing, they will—and reminded him that our car was still loaded. 'You want me to do it right now?' he asked with an unnecessary sigh.

'Whatever you like, Graham. Up to you,' I said coldly. But he knew how angry I was. At this point, I knew that the fortnight was doomed.

*   *   *

I was left to unpack on my own while Graham minded the children. An outsider already, I kept watch through the latticed window that overlooked the garden. The bedroom floor creaked and slanted like the deck of the *Mary Rose*. The beams were placed precisely to be a hazard for the unwary. The furniture was antique, black with age, but the fabrics Emma had chosen were gorgeous— patchworks, ginghams, and crisp fresh cottons, which reminded me of a Wendy house I had once played in, in a rich friend's garden. Ours was a comfy double bed, while the kids had bunks in their little room, and Josh, in his carrycot, could sleep at the bottom. As the sun streamed in through the

151

window, it brought with it the scent of red roses. Briefly, foolishly, I felt cheered.

'Hey, you all, they're here.'

I wouldn't go down to meet the Frazers. I would stay up here and see how long it took for Martha to come and find me.

I stood back and watched.

She looked as amazing as ever: her hair, scraped up in a band to the top of her head, fell down round her face in untidy spirals. She might be large, but because of her style she was glorious. Her skimpy sundress was a feminine pink.

Mark swung Scarlett round in the air while Emma cuddled the gurgling Lawrence. Their kids responded. *Why couldn't mine?* 'Take him away before I get broody,' Emma called, laughing, to Martha. She would never have said that about little Josh, who was going through a sickly patch.

Corks popped as the wine was opened, as it had not been for us.

Compelled to make these pathetic comparisons, naturally I was hurt.

'Truly delightful,' Martha cried, as she stood back to admire the cottage. So far, it seemed that she hadn't missed me.

'It's idyllic,' said Sam, 'you clever things.'

Martha gasped at the sight of the table, now laden and looking delicious. 'When did you do all this, Emma?'

'I cheated,' said Emma. 'I brought it all with me. Jennie and Poppy helped. Are you hungry?'

I waited, but still Martha did not ask where I was. I needed Emma and Mark to know how important I was to my friend. Something must be wrong. But what?

'Bloody starving,' said Martha. And, 'Bloody starving,' Scarlett repeated, and everyone laughed and began to tuck in and talk about the cottage and all its idiosyncrasies—how the previous occupant had died in Emma and Mark's very bed, how the locals had nosed in to meet them.

'Where's Mummy?' whispered Poppy. I saw her tugging at Graham's sleeve. I saw her lips move when she asked again.

But everyone was talking so loudly that nobody could hear her.

*   *   *

Were we here because they pitied us?

I tried to slip into the group unseen, cross with myself for being the cause of my own ordeal.

They all made out they were pleased to see me.

The revelling mixed with more mundane activities, as Mark cut the grass with a museum-piece mower aided by Graham and Sam. Between them they stripped and repaired every part of that blasted machine.

Was this their idea of holiday fun?

Eventually a stream was revealed, a stream that sploshed its way through the natural rocks and reeds of the garden. Poppy and Scarlett were in seventh heaven, splashing and paddling in the altogether, and harvesting jars of God knows what.

Martha was watching me. There was a new wariness in her attitude towards me. And strangely, when I went to feed Josh she didn't pick up Lawrence and come with me. I watched from my window and a little while later Emma came out and gave Martha Lawrence's bottle. Was she

153

deliberately ignoring me? Why? Why? What had I done? She sat beside Emma to feed him; they sat in those hard director-style chairs, the ones with the loose striped covers.

They were perfectly happy without me.

They dug out an old gramophone and some scratchy records which Mark had discovered in an outbuilding. 'Lazy River', 'What A Wonderful World', and then a deep singing voice, 'What Is Life To Me Without Thee?' The others laughed. But it made Emma cry.

At six o'clock I decided to try to put Josh to bed. Predictably, the water in the bathroom was stone-cold, so like a killjoy I invaded the party and asked about hot water.

'It's a cunning device,' said Emma lightly. 'Push the switch on that ugly boiler and the water comes out instantly hot. I can't think why we don't get one in London. Here, Jennie,' she said thoughtfully, 'take a drink up with you.'

Graham didn't ask if I needed help, or if he could bath Josh for me. If I asked him I knew what he'd say: 'Let's give it a miss tonight.' At least *he* was having a marvellous time, drinking too much, talking too much and making quite a fool of himself.

I was in the kitchen heating up a jar of vegetable broth—there was nothing suitable to liquidize and no sign of a liquidizer—when Martha came in.

'Is everything OK?' I asked timidly.

'Why wouldn't it be?' she replied.

'Oh, I just thought . . .'

'*Well, don't think, Jennie.* Why don't we make this fortnight a trial period when you make an effort not to think at all? And perhaps we could live

154

without hurtful rumours about Christmases spent in bed with other people's husbands. D'you know what Sam said when I told him? He laughed. He said, "Give me some credibility, sweetheart, I'm not that desperate." But I still can't believe you said it. My God, Jennie, what are you?'

I winced with pain. *'What have I done?'*

'It's what you've said, as you know very well,' she answered coldly. 'Rumours. Lies. They always get back in the end, Jennie. I've come here to relax and enjoy myself and that is what I intend to do. And I'll drink as much as I damn well like without you turning me into a pisshead. Now you can do what you must, so long as it doesn't involve me in any more of your nasty messes.'

'I can't bear this. I'm going home.'

'You do just what you like, it's no concern of mine, as long as you leave me out of it. If you want to go home—go! Just don't make a drama out of it.'

And then she left me alone in the kitchen.

*   *   *

I felt sick. Stunned.

My life was plunged into chaos again, but this time nobody would die and save me.

I couldn't go home. I couldn't leave Martha hostile like this and then spend fourteen days in agony, unable to make things right. I knew what she was talking about. I never dreamed she'd find out what I'd said; the only reason I'd lied about Sam and me at the Christmas party was to make myself more interesting. I needed friends . . . I had to tell lies. And Martha did drink too much, everyone knew that. So what harm had I done?

They lit a bonfire and sat round it, Mark playing his guitar and the crickets chirping merrily. Poppy and Scarlett, up way past their bedtimes, sucked their thumbs and tried to join in with sleepy little voices. If I insisted on leaving, I would be depriving my daughter of a longed-for holiday with her best friend.

Graham was having a good time, too, and since he worked so desperately hard all year, how could I, for my weird, selfish reasons, drag him back to the Close again?

Gripping the edge of the bedroom window I watched with white knuckles, listening to Josh's deep breathing behind me. How thoughtless they were. When everyone came up to bed they would disturb him—especially Poppy, by the time she was settled in the bunk directly above him. And then she'd not sleep for fear of Graham's witches.

We were stuck here for two endless weeks. The only option I had was to try to act as normal as possible, pretend to be enjoying myself, and make more of an effort to get on with Emma and demonstrate to Martha that I could survive without her approval.

So far, she had failed to respond to my new friendship with Angie Ford. She had shown no signs of the jealousy I'd hoped for; I doubt that she'd even noticed. She was very involved in her work these days and the goings-on in the Close played a minor role in her life.

I had wanted to see how Martha would react if she discovered that boring, dowdy old Jennie became more popular than her. I took advantage of her two days a week absence to try and draw

156

closer to some of our neighbours. Angie Ford was the easiest: a buzzing little lady with freckles, short curls and denim outfits. What the hell was I trying to prove? Did I hope that Martha might be hurt? Might consider me disloyal? That she might value our special friendship more?

When Angie asked me about the affray outside Martha's house on that awful day when he'd found the note, I lied about me and Sam at the party. It made me more worldly, more glamorous. 'It's just one of those things that happen,' I told Angie glibly. 'Of course, it's all over now.' Well, I could hardly tell her the truth and expect her to speak to me ever again.

Pretty harmless stuff. It would never get out, I'd thought at the time; just me trying to find a way in, and there were more opportunities now the pool project was under way. It brought our neighbours to my house—where I could befriend and influence.

*　　　*　　　*

Bravely we stayed on at Last Resort.

Apart from that one kitchen confrontation and occasional peculiar glances, Martha was superficially friendly. The worst part of that holiday was seeing how Poppy and Josh were left out of the fun so much of the time. I knew why, but the fact still hurt me. Scarlett was such an outgoing child, happy to be thrown in the air or dunked in the water, to ride a donkey or travel in the back of Mark's breezy Morgan, while Poppy tended to cry and whine and hide behind my back.

Poppy had a horror of being dirty.

And, of course, the carefree Martha never worried if Lawrence was plucked from his cot to be played with or tickled, to be gurgled at, to be poked; whereas once he was resting, it was essential that Josh be left undisturbed because it took him so long to settle.

*   *   *

Everything to do with that woman seemed to be filled with so much pain.

CHAPTER SIXTEEN

Martha

Everything to do with that woman seemed to be filled with so much pain.

*   *   *

She was so transparent it was pitiful; and I was so angry to hear what she'd done, it was hard to stay civil. Surely she knew that malicious gossip had a habit of boomeranging back. And what a vicious lie to tell. As if Sam would look in Jennie's direction—she was hardly his type. But if the Close decided to believe that I was a drunken lush, so be it. I could live with that one, but not the other.

That appalling holiday.

It was such a mistake to invite them.

Instead of sticking to me like glue, Jennie went breezily off every morning with Sam or Emma or

Mark, whoever volunteered for the supermarket run. And if there was no table for six at a restaurant, guess who chose to sit apart . . . If anyone left the beach to buy ice creams, it was the new, independent Jennie. Incredibly, this odd behaviour was designed to make me feel jealous. *She really could not get into her head the fact that I'd had enough,* and I understood that she'd spread these tales about herself and Sam in order to join what she called the 'in crowd'.

The *in crowd*. My God! What a laugh. If Jennie's idea of an in crowd was the mismatch of neighbours in our Close, she needed a shrink to sort her out. If I hadn't been tied to the house with kids, I wouldn't have got involved with them at all. Oh, they were OK, *they were fine,* but not the kind of friends I would choose, and anyway it's a grave mistake to get too chummy with the neighbours.

Dammit. *What made me feel so responsible for Jennie's wretched kids?*

Probably the same reasons that struck me when I first saw her struggles to survive in that damn maternity ward. Yes, I was worried about Jennie's kids. Hell, I loved them almost as much as my own.

Poppy whined, 'Scarlett's Barbie is nicer than mine.'

Jennie said, 'Well, you could have picked the same one.'

'No, I couldn't.' And Poppy, frustrated, battered her new doll's head on the floor. 'Emma chose them for us.'

Emma laughed. 'Poppy, that's not true. I said you could choose the doll you wanted. Scarlett chose that one, and you spent the next half-hour fiddling with every one in the shop.'

Scarlett, watching, seeing Poppy's crumbling face and the way she was stripping the clothes off the doll, handed hers over. 'You have this one, Poppy, we'll swap.'

'Oh, no . . .' Jennie started to say, but then went on, 'well, if you really don't mind, Scarlett, that's very very kind.'

Scarlett adored Poppy and Jennie.

And later in the beach café: 'I don't want chicken nuggets, I want what Scarlett's got.'

'But you don't like spaghetti bolognaise, Poppy. You said you wanted nuggets. Come on, darling, eat up.'

'Let's share.' These little scenes made Scarlett uneasy. They dragged on and tainted the atmosphere. 'You put some of yours on my plate and you can have some of mine.'

And if—on those warm Welsh evenings dogged by midges—Scarlett was settled on Mark's knee, Poppy would fidget and whine until Mark was forced to scoop her up, too. Then Scarlett would climb down to find somewhere more comfortable. But Poppy wouldn't stop at that. She would follow, whatever Jennie said.

This behaviour, though irritating, was no big deal, but it made me sad when Poppy asked Jennie pathetically, 'Why does everyone like Scarlett better than me?'

Cut to the quick, Jennie replied, 'Darling, whatever makes you think that?'

But if other kids with their buckets and spades came to play in the same rock pool as ours, if any little naked strangers arrived to watch, as toddlers do, Poppy immediately stalked away and sulked on Jennie's knee. Instead of sending her daughter packing, Jennie would say consolingly, 'Don't worry, darling, they'll be gone in a minute.' And then she'd wonder why Poppy was finding it hard to make friends.

*   *   *

Back in the Close, there was that time when I'd found learning-to-read flash cards stuck to every piece of furniture in Jennie's house and I'd asked, 'Aren't you taking all this too seriously?'

'Poppy's terribly bright, Martha,' said Jennie, 'so she needs the stimulation. And it's so much better if they get a good grounding before they go to nursery school.'

*   *   *

So naturally I was concerned about Jennie's children. And to an extent I blamed myself, wondering guiltily if Jennie's over-compensatory mothering might be a symptom of her relationship with me.

*   *   *

Home again. One more crisis over and I screwed my courage to the sticking post and told Jennie matter-of-factly that Scarlett was going to nursery school for two mornings a week in September. This would give me extra time to do more hours at work.

'How could you? She's far too young,' Jennie said disapprovingly. 'I'll have her, if you really feel you have to do this.'

161

'I don't have to do it, Jennie, it's what I want to do. And I'd rather she went to nursery than stayed at home with you—for the social experience.'

I'd known Jennie would offer to have her, but Scarlett needed diversity. A show-off like her would love a nursery; she would be in her element.

'But that means Poppy will have to go.'

'Rubbish,' I said. 'Of course she doesn't have to. But it wouldn't hurt her to do a few hours, maybe on the days Scarlett wasn't there?'

Jennie looked shocked. 'Why would I send her on those days? She'd want to be with Scarlett. How can we split them when they're so close?'

'I know, I know.' I proceeded with caution. I'd seen the look on Jennie's face. 'But wouldn't it be more fun for them to have a change now and then?'

Jennie said, 'I don't see why. Unless you don't like Poppy's influence!'

'Oh come on, Jennie, that's absurd. Of course, if you really feel they would be happier together, send Poppy along as well. I only thought . . .'

'What are you trying to do to me, Martha, *alienate me altogether*?'

The anguished look on her face made me say, 'That's not true. You know I'm very fond of you, Jennie.'

'But how can I know that when you're so cold? You're so offhand with me sometimes. And in Wales . . .'

'In Wales I was livid with you. *What reaction did you expect?* You'd gone around slandering my bloody husband, not to mention saying that I'm a lush . . . OK, you say you've put it right now, but there's no smoke without fire.'

162

'But I need you, Martha.'

'I know, I know . . .'

'And I get so hurt . . .'

'Yes, I know that, too, but I don't go around being deliberately unkind.'

'If only you needed me, too.'

'I do need you, Jennie. What would I do on Mondays and Thursdays?'

'I don't mean like that.'

'Then how?' God, how I loathed this soul-searching. If I didn't sidestep most of it, I'd be wallowing around in Jennie's trough most of the time we spent together. This was the type of discussion she enjoyed best of all and she could often get her way no matter how hard I resisted.

Jennie mused as I waited. 'I suppose . . . I suppose what I really honestly want is for you to feel the same way as me.'

I tried to joke. 'My God, what sort of state would we both be in then? Both of us wandering around lovelorn and lost.'

'I'm so unhappy,' moaned Jennie. 'How I wish this obsession would stop. I am so sick and tired of it all, of the stuff it makes me do.'

'So am I, Jennie,' I said. *'Believe me, so am I.'*

*   *   *

She liked to harp on about how lucky she was to have met Graham. 'When you think about his parents and my mother, and I was his first girlfriend and he was my first boyfriend, too.'

They met at the bank where she worked. Graham went in for some travellers' cheques and that's how it started. So I was vaguely surprised when she told Angie Ford that they had met at a party.

But I let it go.

It was unimportant.

Maybe it made Jennie feel more exciting.

It was the following summer. We were a small and lazy group, sitting in Jennie's garden one hot weekend, drinking home-made lemonade and being sexist, watching the men do their time on the swimming-pool project. The hole had been dug. The pipes were going in. The mess had mostly been cleared away now, to Jennie's great relief. We were almost at the exciting stage of attempting to fit the liner.

All the materials for the venture were paid for by the Gordons, but the work had been done by the rest of us. As soon as the liner was fitted, we would fill it and pray for an Indian summer.

'Ruth and Howard resented me on sight,' said Jennie. 'They told their son he could do much better, and Stella was downright rude when she realized Graham and I were an item. She called him "nothing much" to his face, but, of course, Stella never did like men.'

When I raised an eyebrow she added, 'Because my dad left her when I was two.'

'The little I saw of Stella certainly didn't make me warm towards her.'

'My childhood was very unhappy,' said Jennie, going off at a tangent she thoroughly enjoyed. 'That's partly why I'm so determined to make it better for Poppy and Josh. That's why I refuse to go to work. I was a latchkey kid. The children suffer, there's no doubt about that. What's more, the statistics prove it.'

164

'So Martha's a bad mother for a start,' Angie pointed out wryly.

'I wasn't referring to her,' said Jennie too defensively.

I smiled. I knew she was. 'I'd be worse if I stayed trapped at home,' I said, refusing to rise to her bait.

And then out of the blue she said, 'Scarlett has had to harden up very quickly.'

'*Sorry?*' I couldn't have heard right.

Jennie repeated her quiet statement. And then she added, 'I've watched it happen. I notice it more than you, Martha, being the one who looks after her . . .'

'You've never mentioned this before, and anyway, what d'you mean—*harden up*?'

'I have seen that child being hurt and you taking no notice,' accused Jennie.

'She'll be phoning the social services next,' said Angie, trying to lighten the tension.

I just couldn't help retaliating. I'd had enough. 'Well, perhaps I don't notice every time, but mine could be a more natural response than taking on your child's every slight and making it your own.'

'*You really hate me, don't you?*' screamed Jennie, so loudly and so startlingly that everything stopped and everyone turned incredulously in our direction.

'OK, come on, let's leave it alone.' Angie tried to intervene, but she sat up so quickly her sunglasses flopped back foolishly onto the end of her nose. 'It's too sodding hot for this . . .'

'*Shut up, Angie,*' screamed Jennie, in that same harsh, lunatic voice. '*What d'you know about anything? She's always trying to put me down and make me feel stupid, just because I'm a mother and I happen to care about—*'

165

I said, 'Stop it, Jennie, you know that's untrue.'

'*You can't get at me,*' she roared, '*so you try and attack me through the children.*'

Shocked and embarrassed, I rose to leave.

'*That's right, that's right, just turn your back on me, pretend the problem doesn't exist.*'

There was no point in reasoning. It was too late to be rational. In a minute she'd let out her shameful secret and she would regret that far more than me.

Graham came hurrying out through the French windows. 'Jennie? What's this? What the hell's happening?'

Sam pocketed his spanner and muttered, 'Let's go.'

Everyone else trailed out of the garden, toes curled to be witnessing such a bizarre scene. I wondered how many of them already regretted their involvement in the swimming-pool project. And, no doubt, were blaming me for promoting it.

'Martha, can I come with you?' Poppy pleaded, all twisted and frightened and backing away from Jennie.

'*Oh no you don't,*' shrieked Jennie, more hysterical than ever. '*Oh no, you damn well don't take my kids away from me!*'

'Be a good girl and stay here, Poppy.' I bent down to comfort the sobbing child. 'Mummy will be OK in a minute.'

Graham quickly picked her up. 'I'm so sorry, Martha,' he began, shock and bewilderment creasing his face.

'It's OK, Graham, it's quite OK.' I hurried to reassure him.

'*I really don't know . . .*'

But we were gone like everyone else, over the grass and through the door to the safe harbour of our cosy kitchen.

*   *   *

'Shit,' said Sam.

'What's the matter with Jennie, Mummy?'

Every nerve in my body was jumping, so I plunged into the old washing-up. 'Jennie's not very well just now.'

'But you have to go and get Poppy,' Scarlett demanded nervously.

'Don't worry, Poppy will be perfectly OK.' I crashed around with a burnt pan and a scrap of filthy scourer.

Scarlett refused to leave it alone. She started on Sam, tugging at his trousers. 'Go now, Daddy, and bring Poppy here.'

'I can't, sweetheart, she's in her own house.'

'But it's so horrible there.'

I turned. I knelt down. I felt like that ghastly freak in the Fairy Liquid ad, but I wasn't bothered by bubbles or hands. 'But you like going to Jennie's while I'm at work. You're happy there, aren't you, Scarlett?'

'Not when Jennie gets like this.'

I tried not to show too much concern. 'And does she often get like this?'

'Sometimes,' Scarlett sobbed.

I had to ask. 'Does she shout at you?'

'Not at me—at the telly and the cooker and the washing machine. And sometimes she breaks plates . . .'

I looked up at Sam over the top of our

daughter's head. He raised his eyebrows. Careful to be casual, he asked her, 'So what do you do when Jennie shouts?'

She was getting bored with the subject; we'd been dwelling on it too long. She was trying to climb onto the chair to reach the soaking dishes. 'We pretend it's all right and go on playing, but sometimes we hide under the stairs.'

Sam paused for thought. And then he turned to ask gently, 'Would you rather not go there any more when Mummy goes to work, Scarlett?'

She sniffed and rubbed her nose. 'I have to go. To be with Poppy.'

'So where the hell does this leave us?' Sam demanded, hands on hips.

'Dear God, I just don't know.' I passed Scarlett a plate to wipe. 'And I'm too messed up to discuss it right now. We'll talk tonight when her ladyship's in bed.'

'She's as mad as a fucking hatter,' said Sam.

'Please don't use that word when Scarlett's around,' I reminded him angrily. 'Or "mad", for that matter. It really doesn't help.'

*   *   *

But was it true? Was she insane?

CHAPTER SEVENTEEN

Jennie

Was it true? Was I insane?

*   *   *

I know that I ought to have been on my knees. Martha had been more patient with me than I had any right to expect. If the children weren't involved, she'd doubtless have cut me off months ago, and this last fiasco—my moment of spontaneous combustion—could well mark the point of no return.

I'd finally flipped. Such raw, grotesque and naked emotions in full public view. My mask had split and left me exposed, and all my neighbours had seen and heard my preposterous outburst. They'd be whispering behind closed doors. How was I going to face them? *We would have to move.*

'Don't be silly, Jennie.' Graham pointed out that by the time the house was sold and we'd gone, the worst of my purgatory would be over. 'Everyone has their breaking point,' he said kindly, attempting to pull a blind over the wretchedness of my situation. 'You just cracked, that's all, and no wonder—your mother's death could have triggered it off, and on top of that you've only recently had a baby . . .'

'Last year,' I bleated weakly.

'These things take time.'

This conviction of his could well be more for his

169

own protection than mine. But his blind devotion shamed me. When would he learn how unworthy I was? What if he knew the truth?

And I worried about what alternative plans Martha would make for Mondays and Thursdays. Could I approach her even now? Was there anything that might make things right?

No, not this time. *How could there be?*

I wallowed in self-pity yet I knew I'd brought this on myself; or rather, it was the creature that raged inside me, the alien being that stoked my obsession.

Was I schizophrenic? Would I hear voices next?

*   *   *

With a broken heart, leaving Graham in charge, I hobblcd bleakly to my bedroom, unable to face anyone, not even my caring husband. This was the end of any scheme to start a swimming club in my garden next month, because none of my neighbours would risk involvement with a neurotic hell-hag like me. And anyway, it wouldn't work. I hated having people round. I'd spend my whole life hiding—waiting for them to dry off and go. Oh God . . .

I dragged the boxful of Stella's things from the bottom of the wardrobe.

I reread her pitiful letter, the one begging Stan to come back.

I wished my father's name wasn't Stan.

I read his reply—just three lines on cheap notepaper—dated six months later, with no forwarding address.

I tried to imagine her frantic wait, all alone with

a baby. And it was even worse than I'd originally thought—he hadn't hung around for two years, he had taken off the week I was born. And she, stuck in that basement flat surrounded by strangers, miles from her native Wales and prevented by shame from returning.

I reread the cruellest letter of all, the one I had learned by heart, the one in the thin, cheap envelope addressed in small, mean writing, the one whose lines were so coldly pious.

'No, Stella, you have made your bed and you must lie in it. Do not come home again.' Then there were the God bits . . . some God, to insist that a mother shun her daughter when she'd got herself in the family way and without a man to support her. It was horrendous, quite horrendous. And although I had never been there, it didn't take much to imagine that little grey village set round the chapel, where everyone knew everyone else, women peering under their headscarves. They called it the Swinging Sixties, but in that dour little place it was still the Dark Ages.

No wonder Stella was bitter, no wonder she resented me when she'd given up so much that I might live. I never failed to ask during our lonely Christmases with the plastic tree and the telly on—where was the rest of our family? Why didn't we have the joyful times, the get-togethers we were so busy watching?

'Some people have no-one at all,' she would say. 'Be grateful. Don't always think of yourself.'

And I thanked God now, that while she lived Graham and I had never failed to invite her.

There were three photos of my father Stan. One at the register office which showed his face most clearly, and two on the steps of some caravan, wearing dirty jeans and a T-shirt, holding a fish in his hand. Not even a fish to be proud of: a tiddler which anyone else would have thrown back in the water. This must have been taken by Stella herself. Not much of a pictorial history—not a lot of fun. There was a temporary air about him. How long had they known each other before the dreadful deed was done? Was I really this man's child?

No wonder my life was one terrible debt of commitments that I had not sought. How I wished my mother and I had been able to talk about things like this.

*   *   *

A soft knock on my bedroom door.

'Yes?'

'There's someone downstairs to see you,' said Graham.

Martha? Could it really be her? Could such a miracle happen?

'Hilary Wainwright.'

No no no. My heart plummeted like a shot bird. Hilary Wainwright from number four; a smart, cultured woman. God. I hardly knew her from Adam.

'Why is she here?' I whispered.

'*Ssh. She'll hear you.* She says she wants to talk to you.' Graham sounded as puzzled as me.

I shoved Stella's box back under the bed. I needed to wash my face, somehow I must compose myself before I faced this stranger, the counterpane was crumpled, my hair was greasy . . . Too late, the woman was at the door.

172

'Jennie,' she said quickly, before her nerve failed her. 'I won't stay if you'd rather I went, but I just wanted to say that I feel dreadful about what happened and I should have spoken up at the time. You must be feeling so rotten, but some of us do understand, you know . . .' She paused to catch her breath. She smiled shyly. 'Some of us have been there. I just wanted you to know that. And now I've said that, I'll go.'

How could I let her leave, after she'd been so kind? I moved my blouse from the bedroom chair and smoothed the seat for her, a courtier to a queen.

I didn't know what to say.

She played with her hands, as nervous as I was. 'I'm not trying to say our experiences are similar but two years ago I had a breakdown, so I know about feelings of desperation . . .'

I was astonished. This cool person in soft beige Jaeger, with a Moschino belt clasped round her waist, was she really saying she'd lost it? 'Really? Did you? Nobody knew. Martha never said.'

Hilary said, 'She never knew.'

'But Martha and Sam are friends of yours'—I had suffered such pangs of jealousy—'they're always round at your house for supper.' So many times I had watched them arrive and cheered if they left before midnight.

'Nobody knew how ill I was,' said my neighbour of the stiff upper lip. 'Or how tempted I sometimes was to strip stark naked and scream in public. So if there is anything I can do for you, Jennie, you have only to let me know.'

Hilary's kindness, though genuine, was badly misdirected. And now I felt such shame at the

173

times I had scoffed at the Wainwrights, at their oilskin macs and their Timberland boots, at their two smart sons at public school and their compulsory Volvo. Even now she was dressed for sailing. Her shirt was silk and the scarf round her neck had yachts printed on it.

They had never invited us for supper.

But we hadn't asked them either. We never asked anyone.

It was only since the swimming-pool project that the Wainwrights had deigned to visit our garden, in shorts and immaculate deck shoes. Slumming it, I told Graham.

Maybe Martha had seen her come over?

I must keep her here, perhaps start Martha wondering.

'I'm getting more frightened'—this was the truth—'less able to keep control, and sometimes the pressure round my head makes it feel like a tin exploding in a pan.'

Hilary's look said she knew what I meant. 'But is there a reason?'

I nodded. I felt as drained as I looked.

'Well, that's a start,' she told me in her schoolmarmy fashion. She taught at the tech and I wondered which subject. Elocution? Navigation? Her silky smile went with her outfit. 'You can't call your behaviour irrational when there's some logic behind it.'

'To me it feels like madness,' I said. Now that the ice was broken, it was easier to talk. I needed her detachment and I appreciated her cool control. I struggled against a violent urge to throw myself at her feet and confess, to bring it all up like vomit, to clear my system of acute distress. 'And my outbursts upset the children.'

But would she understand if I told her the way, when I was tired and things went wrong, I would stand and scream at myself, at God, at fate, at the red handkerchief that had run and ruined my load of white washing, at anything and everything that conspired to hold me in this trap from which there seemed to be no escape? If Martha gave way to hysterical shrieking, nobody would have turned a hair. Letting go of her feelings was just part of her nature . . . I had seen her smash plates and rip towels in half—and after raising their eyes, people laughed. So did she. It released her tensions. It made her feel better. But I wasn't Martha. My screams of anguish looked like total collapse and I knew how they terrified Poppy and Scarlett.

'Yes. I started to panic in certain places,' Hilary confided in me, as I sat on the edge of my crumpled bed and stared at her sleek, beige hair. 'I couldn't breathe, I was fighting for life. Post office queues were endless, traffic lights stayed red till my eyes were bulging. Panic attacks,' she said, 'are very common.'

Enlightenment slowly dawned. Hilary thought her symptoms were the same as mine. She was going to tell me the heartening story of how she had beaten her demons, but my madness was nothing like hers. I decided, then, that I would be called sane if I'd fixated on God instead of Martha, if I'd taken the veil, been made holy. Become a true bride of Christ. Or if I was obsessed by a man, I would be sad, yes, but understood. History is littered with women who have idolized men; and Victorian women actually died under their aspidistras, sprawled on their velvet *chaises-*

longues, the cause being unfulfilled love. So maybe, unlike Hilary's, mine was not strictly a mental illness. All I had done was make someone unsuitable the pivot of my life.

Devious with my fixation, I spotted an opening, another chance. If I admitted to Hilary's illness, if I called myself mad instead of bad, I might escape the penalty of death and be accepted in the Close once again. If Hilary could sympathize with that, then so would everyone else. I clutched at this new reasoning as a drowning man grabs hold of a floating log.

'I feel exactly the same,' I told her. 'Panicked. Breathless. That's what happened this afternoon. I lost control. I thought I was dying. But look at you now. *How did you do it?*'

'Tranks,' she said. 'Can't beat them. Therapy sessions, self-help groups.'

'And they worked?' I asked in a troubled voice, appalled by the thought.

'It took time, it took patience, but in the end they did the trick.'

Martha would be encouraged to think that I was seeking the help she'd always said I needed. I would deserve all the support I could get. And how would it look if she turned her back and refused to aid my attempts at recovery?

My tears were genuine tears of relief, but Hilary—as I had intended—interpreted them as despair. 'I don't know what to do about Martha,' I sobbed, and Hilary laid a cool hand on mine. 'My best friend—you heard what I said—you all heard how I screamed at her . . .'

'Oh, I'm sure Martha will understand.'

'No,' I said quickly, 'that's just it.' My interruption

176

was feverish but my voice came soft as a whisper. 'She won't understand. How can she? I've used Martha through all this: she's had to endure my moods, my rages, my hysteria . . . She's been such a brick, you'll never know, but this last episode was too much for anyone.'

Hilary's hand was stroking mine now. I had her total attention. People like it when fellow sufferers follow their advice. 'Would you like me to talk to Martha?'

'Oh, I don't like to involve . . .'

'Really, Jennie, I don't mind. Anything that might help. You're going to need your friends more than ever if you're really going to conquer this.'

'*What will you say?*' I averted my eyes.

'Well, I'll tell her how very sorry you are and how you're going to seek help for your illness. I'll say that, because you are ill, you can't be held responsible for your outbursts . . .'

'But Martha won't want me to babysit Scarlett or Lawrence again. She'll think I'm not fit . . .'

'Well, it might be wiser to give that a break, create more time for yourself.'

I shook my head and hugged myself. What must I do to convince my kind neighbour that this was desperately important to me? 'If Martha decided she no longer trusted me to look after her children, well, I think that would finish me.' I went on sobbing quietly. 'That's the one thing I know that would undermine me completely.'

Sensibly, Hilary said, 'All I can do is see what she says and whatever's decided I'll let you know. But don't take Martha's attitude to heart. Martha's a wonderful person and very fond of you, I know, and I'm sure she is not as upset as you think. It's a

177

great shame you feel you can't speak to her yourself.'

'Martha wouldn't like that.'

'Why are you so sure?'

'I just am. We've done so much talking lately and it hasn't got us anywhere.'

Graham came in with two cups of tea.

'Oh no, I won't stay, if you don't mind,' said Hilary. 'You two sit and drink it together, and I'm sure if you mull over what we've said, Jennie, you will see that the answer lies in your own hands.'

I smiled sadly at her. 'You're right, Hilary. I'm going to take your advice. I'm so grateful you came, it's made such a difference. I'm going to make an appointment tomorrow.'

She gave a pleased nod, smiled brightly at Graham and said, 'I'll let myself out. And stop worrying.'

*   *   *

'Better?' Graham came to sit beside me.

I gripped his hand. 'I'm so sorry . . .'

'You've been so unhappy lately,' he said.

So I told him what I intended to do and he was relieved to hear it. 'And Hilary's going to talk to Martha.'

Graham's smile was uncertain. *'Why Martha?'*

'I was so horrid.'

'It's Martha Martha Martha, that's all I seem to hear from you. And I can't help thinking your friendship with Martha is part of the problem.'

'But, Graham, *I have to have a friend.*'

'I know that. Of course I know that. But this friendship is so intense. Either you've upset her or she's upset you, and I can't understand what pleasure you get from such an uneasy relationship.'

'I need Martha,' I told him flatly, alarmed that he'd come so near the truth. I removed my hand from his, feeling unjustly attacked.

Graham sighed glumly. I knew he needed no-one but me and I'd felt the same until I met Martha. How would I have reacted, I wondered, if he had found the alternative companion and was spending all his spare time with him, preferring his company to mine? And I also know that Graham wasn't overkeen to spend every holiday with the Frazers, especially with me and my moods.

'The children are asleep,' he said.

All that concerned him was my happiness.

* * *

All I could think of was Monday.

CHAPTER EIGHTEEN

Martha

All I could think of was Monday.

* * *

'Absolutely no way is that freak having our kids.' That was Sam at his most dominant.

Scarlett went to sleep at last, still worrying about Poppy next door, and leaving images in our heads of social workers and tragic cases, and parents blind to their children's suffering. But although I agreed with Sam completely, I was left wondering how much of his agitation was aimed at getting me to stop work. And this was so unfair. I never could manage an ordered household, but his meal was invariably warm in the Aga when he came home, his shirts were cleaned and pressed, and his special chair was kept clear of cats. Mostly.

He need not have worried. With Jennie out of action, I would have been far happier, anyway, to find a childminder for Lawrence, and Scarlett could go to nursery for two or three full days a week. I would have my freedom at last. Sam would moan on about the money, but I'd be earning enough to pay—so sod him.

The knock on the door broke through Sam's torrent about the weirdos he would lock up if he could . . . Hilary Wainwright stalked in and had the nerve to start preaching to me about my attitude towards Jennie Gordon.

Sam was so gobsmacked he just sat there, dumbfounded, listening to her well-meaning advice, as she advocated our support, criticized the Close as small-minded, and managed to make us sound responsible for Jennie's future mental stability. She didn't have the vaguest clue about the true nature of Jennie's distress, let alone the nightmare times we had already endured.

After she'd finished, after Sam and I had listened patiently for a good ten minutes to this crap, I said, 'I think we probably know Jennie better than you do, Hilary.'

'No,' she argued, 'you're too close. You can't see the wood for the trees.'

Although Hilary's motives were pure, I sensed

Jennie's scheming behind this visit.

'And you can't seriously intend to undermine poor Jennie any further by not trusting her with your children? You must know as well as I do how much your friendship means to her.' She gave me an accusing look. 'And you must also be aware that your help at this vulnerable stage will do Jennie more good than a doctor could. She needs you, Martha. She trusts you.'

I did not want to play an important role in Jennie's so-called therapy.

She was not needy the way Hilary meant.

I wanted no part in her life.

I resented being relied upon. I wasn't a rock to be battered at whim.

'I do wish the poor woman had felt able to come and see you herself,' said Hilary accusingly.

'She knew she'd be shown the door,' said Sam, stung by the injustice of this. 'Quite frankly, Hilary, we've had it up to here with that crazy woman and there really does come a time when you feel you're doing more harm than good.'

Hilary drew herself tightly together and huffed her way out of the door, disgusted by our Nazi-type attitude towards the psychologically stricken. 'I told Jennie I'd let her know what you said,' she threw back over one padded beige shoulder. 'I can't let her down, I will have to phone her.'

'Well, good bloody luck to you, mate,' snorted Sam, after he'd closed the door.

*   *   *

It was almost dawn when Graham called from Casualty.

181

The phone was on Sam's side of the bed.

I was too befuddled by sleep to make sense of what was being said, too busy squinting at the alarm to make out the blasted time.

He turned on the light and sat bolt upright.

'Right,' he said, offhandedly.

'Sam? Who is it?'

'Jennie's been taken to hospital. Overdose . . .'

'Jesus Christ!'

Our silence was aghast, although neither of us believed for one moment that this had been a serious attempt. And then Sam said, 'Now listen, Martha, this is where we stand by our convictions and leave well alone, or get back on that sodding bandwagon, led by the nose by a woman whose cunning appears to know no bounds.'

'We can't just ignore this, Sam!'

'You do what you like, sweetheart.' Sam thumped his pillow angrily, but I was too weary to cope with a row. 'This time, Martha, if you get involved you'll be on your own. She's got you in the palm of her hand, you're being jerked about like a brainless puppet and,' he continued with two fierce lines above his nose, 'what's worse is that pandering to Jennie is encouraging her mad illusions. One day she really will kill herself and then what? Who'll be to blame?'

He was right, and anyway, I couldn't deal with any more of this. I passed a tired hand over my eyes before lighting the first fag of the day. 'But what did Graham actually say?'

'The usual crap. You ought to be told. He didn't have the gall to ask, but he expected you to rush straight over.'

I dragged comforting smoke down my throat. I

spluttered and wheezed like an old bag lady. 'Perhaps they'll keep her in. They might make her see a shrink.'

'Not long ago you were telling Hilary she didn't have that kind of mental problem.'

I ignored him. I puffed out angrily. 'I'll have to have her kids.'

'So what about work?'

'Just for today. I've got no choice, until I can think of something else.'

And I might as well get up, because I damn well knew there'd be no more sleep while I tussled with the whys and wherefores of leaving Jennie to her own devices.

*   *   *

We were the only ones in the Close not to visit Jennie in the psychiatric unit. Hilary had done a sterling job rallying the troops. And when I mentioned to Graham that I couldn't carry on minding the kids indefinitely, I felt like the lowest form of life imaginable.

'Well, no, Martha, of course I didn't expect you . . .' he stuttered, embarrassed.

'It's just my job,' I added, exasperated at having to apologize. 'But I've found a babyminder for Lawrence, and if you were interested she could take Josh, too. And could Poppy go with Scarlett to the nursery?'

Graham scratched his head and stared at me blankly. 'I suppose there's no other option. Until Jennie comes home, at any rate.'

'How long are they keeping her in?'

'She is voluntary, you know. *She can come out*
183

whenever she chooses.' He covered his irritation with a quick apology of a smile. 'They're not sure yet.' He looked so tired, so pale and worried. Just another poor soul in need of comfort and that bloody Jennie ought to be giving it instead of playing her sick mind games. 'She's not too happy at the moment.'

'I'm sorry.'

'She misses you, Martha,' he said tersely.

I nodded. 'Yes, I expect she does.'

He tried to laugh but it didn't work. 'She seems to believe you've been mortally wounded by her aggressive outburst.'

I wasn't indifferent to Graham's misery. 'To be honest, Graham, it might be better for Jennie's peace of mind if I stayed away for a little while. I'd rather not say any more, right now. But give her my love. Tell her I'm thinking of her.'

'A message from you—she'll be so relieved,' said Graham, perking up, and I felt that I'd given him a bunch of white roses.

*   *   *

So that's how the rift began.

That's when the ranks were first drawn up: the Wainwrights and the Fords took up arms in the Gordons' corner; the Gallaghers, and the Harcourts at number six, were for us. How ridiculous it was that we let it go so far.

It was surprisingly hurtful, too. All those looks of blame I was thrown as I struggled to get the kids into the car. Poppy and Scarlett to nursery, Josh and Lawrence to my new minder two days a week, and I gave up all ideas of doing extra work while

184

Jennie was still in hospital.

If I stopped to ask Hilary how Jennie was getting on, she would say, 'At the moment she needs all the help she can get. It's such a shame we missed the first signals, those first cries for help.'

And I felt like lunging out of the car, grabbing Hilary by the arm and shaking her wits to life. *Jennie Gordon is obsessed with me, dammit. This is another of her bloody games to get me where she wants me.* But how could I blame Hilary? She and the others didn't know Jennie, they hadn't seen the depths she could sink to in order to manipulate everyone around her.

And Angie Ford, briefed by Hilary, clearly believed I alone had driven poor Jennie to suicide. Why did she never stop to consider why I would do that to a best friend? It wasn't as though Angie and I were strangers, we'd been quite close before this crisis, so how could she jump to such hurtful conclusions? What other lies had Hilary told her—or Jennie herself, for that matter?

Sam was right. 'Never mind what those daft sods think, we're the only ones who know the truth and we can't come clean because of Graham.'

'Tina knows,' I reminded him, 'and Tina's probably told Sadie Harcourt and that's why they're on our side.'

'We are the only ones who know just how ruthless that woman is,' Sam insisted. 'And Christ Almighty, it does take some believing that a woman would make an attempt on her life just to get revenge on a friend.'

'Am I a friend?' That word felt wrong, but what other expression was there to describe my relationship with Jennie? An object of worship? A

185

great earth mother? I felt more like a graven image.

If I was all-powerful in Jennie's eyes, then why couldn't I use my influence in a more positive way? Why couldn't I work something out, so we could end this dangerous passion?

Sam said it was time to talk to Graham and let him in on the truth. 'Not all of it—we can't wreck their marriage. But how can anyone really help her when they haven't a clue what it's all about? We're keeping her secret for her. I bet none of her doctors discover the truth.'

'We might know more when she gets home. Maybe they'll put her on drugs, which'll put this fiery light out for good. Dear God, there must be something.'

'ECT? A lobotomy?'

'Don't be so unkind, Sam,' I said. But I shivered.

*   *   *

Sod Jennie. My job kept me sane; it got me away from the eerie, suspicious world that the Close had become since the forces were split down the middle.

I felt bad enough leaving Poppy with Mrs Tree and her helpers at the Humpty Dumpty Nursery. Her little face was a picture of grief the first time I said, 'Now you stay here with Scarlett, then I'll come and get you when you've had your afternoon nap and your drink and your biscuit . . .'

There was a certain defiance about her. 'I don't want to be here. *Where's Mummy?*'

Scarlett's eager eyes were fixed on the Wendy house and the dratted pots and pans shining so brightly above the cooker. But aware of Poppy's dismay she held back, waiting, touching her hand, saying the odd encouraging 'Come on, Poppy, you'll be all right with me.'

'*Where's Mummy?*'

'Poppy, you know that Mummy's in hospital and she's not very well, but she'll soon be home . . .'

Time was passing, I was late already. I looked at Mrs Tree and rolled my eyes for help.

'Just go, Martha,' she whispered. 'Poppy'll be fine when she gets to know us. It's just a bit bewildering to start with, isn't it, Poppy dear?'

Poppy pulled a face and tried to hide under my skirt. If she'd been my own I'd have taken the risk and left her crying, in the belief that once I'd gone she'd be fine. I had checked up on the place, of course; it had a brilliant reputation. I'd been lucky to get two places at such short notice and that was only because twins had suddenly moved.

I left the miserable, white-faced child in the quiet of the book corner. 'Look, Poppy,' I said, pointing out the familiar books she had at home. I patted one of the jungle cushions. 'Now, why don't you and Scarlett cuddle down here together and look at the pictures until you feel like joining in with the others?'

Poppy, pale and shrinking fast, all miserable and dimpled, sobbed, '*I want to come home with you.*'

I was careful not to sound impatient. 'Well, Poppy, I'm sorry but you can't. I have to go to work.'

Jesus! Where was her spirit of independence? And immediately I felt guilty for such uncharitable thoughts. She was just a frightened baby and I had no right to feel so cross.

187

'I don't like it here. I want Mummy.'

I had driven the mother suicidal, and now here I was being cruel to the daughter. Bloody hell, the ultimate betrayal.

She had her mother's pleading eyes. 'And I don't feel very well, Martha.'

How long could I hold out? Thank God for the sensible Mrs Tree. Sweetness and light flowed from her. 'You come with me now, Poppy dear, and you too, Scarlett, because I think you're going to like the surprise I've got for you in the kitchen.'

She sounded like a paedophile, but that no longer concerned me. Faint with relief, I was off. She led the children away and I made my cunning exit. I imagined the pain in Jennie's eyes if she'd seen what I had just done . . . the blame, the guilt, the accusations that I was making them grow up 'hard', the predictions for future disaster. Jennie trusted me to look after Poppy as kindly as she would herself—*but if she was so bloody concerned, she shouldn't have done what she did . . .*

All day long I worried. I couldn't concentrate on a thing, imagining Poppy's pitiful sobs—alone, bullied, left out. I surrounded the child with the mantle of her mother's worst defects, all brought on by her mother's behaviour. I told myself what a fool I was: Scarlett would never allow her best friend to be treated that way, and she was a forceful, capable child. She'd soon go and alert Mrs Tree if anything bad was happening.

God bless Scarlett.

*　　　*　　　*

Scarlett, strong and confident, marched to the door

to meet me, animated by new experiences and friends. She flapped a floppy wet painting at me. 'Look, Mummy, you've got stilts on.'

But where was Poppy? I hurried inside to find her still gripping Mrs Tree's hand. 'Oh dear,' I blurted, appalled to find my worst fears justified.

'Don't worry, Martha, Poppy's been fine. This is all for your benefit.' Mrs Tree looked down understandingly and gave Poppy a loving smile. 'Isn't it, Poppy, my love?' And then she whispered an aside. 'They can be terribly knowing, my dear, even at this tender age.'

Hah. Like mother, like daughter. But I smiled at the gentle Mrs Tree as I held out my hand and took Poppy off her. I coaxed her to tell me about her day. 'I don't like it there,' she said in the car, interrupting Scarlett's babblings. *'And I'm not going again.'*

I didn't answer. Let her sleep on it. There are ways and means of manipulating kids to do as you want, and that's what Jennie had been doing to me from the first day I met her. But I wasn't a kid. I was the stronger one, a mature grown-up—anyone could see that. But was that really the case?

In nature, some weaker animals adapt themselves to live off the strong. They learn to do this over the ages, through discord and dilemma, and finally they get carried along: the krill that surrounds the whales, the fishes that clean the mouths of sharks, and the birds that peck the ticks off bison.

I was tired. I was worried. I thought a great deal about Jennie, lonely and unhappy in her hospital bed, but I almost envied her weakened state that was turning her into a tyrant.

189

If I wasn't careful, she would devour me.

CHAPTER NINETEEN

Jennie

If I wasn't careful, she would devour me.

*   *   *

I knew exactly what she was thinking—that I took the overdose just to spite her. But she was wrong, I deny that. How could Martha be so hostilc towards me?

I did it because I wanted to die—my life seemed futile, simple as that.

I didn't rig it, as she supposed. I was found entirely by accident because Josh woke at four in the morning, a habit he had long grown out of, and Graham tried to wake me so I could feed him. So contrary to what *they* think, that's how I was discovered. And the doctor told Graham that in a couple more hours I would have been dead.

After I'd made my decision, I sat up until long after midnight deciding which method to choose. Hilary Wainwright had rung me earlier, saying she had spoken to Martha. She tried to be gentle but it was obvious that she had been snubbed.

Martha refused to become involved.

But she was involved.

190

Up to her neck.

So I lay down on the kitchen floor, sobbing. Desperate for a way out.

What good was Hilary's common-sense concern? It was the caring of a vicar's wife—polite and sincere but horribly limited—baskets of plums and new-laid eggs. Martha was the only person who could actually share my feelings.

My hand slipped on the wet razor blade. I firmed my grip, bending my fist so the blue vein stood out gorged with blood. And then I knew I must slice it in half, like a fat garden worm. My teeth were clenched. I looked away, sickened by my brutality.

'So sad, so sad, she was in her twenties when she died.' That's what people would say when they heard.

Stella, my mother, had done much better: she had reached her fifties. Guns would go off in heaven for Stella.

I couldn't do it like that, not a slash to the skin. I was too much of a coward, although that particular stigma didn't bother me. I wasn't a man, though I wanted one woman as badly as any man ever had. But Martha's feeble friendship was not unconditional. And nor was it, as I'd hoped, everlasting.

I had pushed it to the limit. I knew, then, where that limit was.

There was no question in my mind that I could live with her as my enemy.

She hated me.

She abandoned me.

And, according to Hilary, she wasn't even willing to talk.

And I can't describe the anguish of that.

When thoughts of my children crossed my mind, they were like wildebeest on a dusty plain, on the far side of the river, half hidden in a haze of heat, and nothing to do with me.

I must die.

I'd kept the painkillers after Josh's birth. I had them because of a swelling in my breast—something to do with that word lactation. The pills were massive, monstrous things you had to dilute in water. I had never used them, the pain and the swelling went on their own, but I guessed they were strong enough to be lethal. I took the lot, twenty-four in all, in two foul-tasting, sludgy glasses of water, and then I crept up to bed.

*   *   *

I woke up in hospital.

'*Where's Martha?*'

Graham leaned forward and took my hand. 'Martha's not here, Jennie.'

'*Does she know?*'

He shifted on the bed uneasily so his carrier bag slipped off, and he said, 'Yes, I told her.'

'*What did she say?*'

He answered as kindly as he could, but I saw his eyes filling with water no matter how hard he tried to prevent them. 'Well, I spoke to Sam. Jennie, it sounds as if they have both had enough. They can't take any more. I'm sorry, Jennie, I really am sorry.'

And wordlessly he buried his head in my lap.

So I had not died. I was not in heaven. I would not have to face my mother. Things were exactly as they were, just as unbearable, just as hellish.

I knew all about Graham's pain—that's what

makes me so detestable. Of course I ought to have woken up and asked about the children at once, hugged him, blessed him for staying so staunchly beside me and wept with mortification over how I was hurting the person who loved me most.

He looked so tense and distracted. He took the grapes from the carrier bag and tried to set them out temptingly on the nasty table across the bed. He unfolded two of my favourite magazines—as if I was in there for appendicitis. 'The Wainwrights have been bricks,' he said. 'Hilary's at home now, minding the kids till I get back.'

I listened vacantly to what he was saying, unable to meet his sad eyes. I should be saying more, giving some explanation for my behaviour. I firmly believed that suicide was the most vengeful action anyone could take; I thought that until I did it myself . . . Mine hadn't felt like revenge.

There was no reason on earth for me to inflict my revenge on Graham, the man who had saved me the day we met. He needed an answer to his unspoken question, but he wouldn't understand if I gave it. I knew why I was here. There was nowhere else for me to go.

*   *   *

Every day was like Sunday. The ward was soporific and it was crowded with creeping women. It was named after Dame Maud Bell, a name which made her sound more like a patient to me—and a dangerous one at that—even though she was a doughty far-sighted woman, who must have set up this ancient unit in the days when fruitcakes were baited like bears.

Since then, the old Victorian wing had been replaced by a red-brick asylum, and the one redeeming feature about it was that everyone could be mad as they pleased. Compared to most of my fellow patients, I was as together as the Queen.

Swept from the streets for a brief interlude, here were the shufflers, the dribblers, the self-abusers and the nodding buffoons. And there was I calling out silently, '*Make her love me, God, make her love me.*'

When I told him I was in love, Mr Singh, the consultant, gave a bored, patient shrug.

'And I've been like this for years.'

He tapped his pencil quietly and waited.

'But the person I'm in love with loathes me.'

'And that must be painful for you,' he said.

'She's tired of all the attention-seeking. She's got her own worries, her own life. She's sick of my dramas, she needs other people . . .'

'And what d'you think made her loathe you? Hatred is a strong emotion, every bit as exhausting as love. By assuming she hates you, you are suggesting that you dominate most of her thinking.'

'Oh God, I wish I did.'

Mr Singh was not being sarcastic, merely stating the facts. 'So she doesn't hate you, does she, Jennie? Let's get that straight from the start. Perhaps what makes you so unhappy is that this person you love is indifferent?'

God, that hurt. He was right.

'But from what I understand, apparently you were once close friends.'

My eyeballs ached and my head throbbed. 'I must sound so ridiculous when there're people out there with children dying, loveless people, handicapped, the victims of disasters, and here I am losing the plot because of some freakish passion. We were never equal, that was the trouble—in my eyes she was always special and I worshipped her.' I nodded as if my head was on springs, like a toy dog in a car's back window. I bit my lips, I pulled at my fingers, in the perfect role of deranged patient. 'And I can't understand how this happened, or what I can do to stop it. I've got kids, I've got a husband who loves me . . .' It was just too much. I collapsed in a storm of tears, a spasm of ugly crying, while Mr Singh sat back and observed me from behind his sane brown desk, over the top of his gold-rimmed glasses. *And I'm so tired of it all,'* I cried lamely.

After a calculated pause to allow me to regain some control, the consultant passed me a tissue and asked, 'Tired enough to die?'

'Yes, yes I am. Tell me, does my illness have a name? Is it somewhere in a book which I can read and understand? *Is it chronic? Is it fatal?'* But I didn't have much faith in him because he was not of my culture. And, to be fair, even someone from my own background would find it hard to get to grips with my dilemma, let alone a man from the East with such inscrutable eyes.

*   *   *

I found a quiet place in the hubbub. Beside a radiator next to the coffee machine.

Time heals, I told myself, drinking somebody's stone-cold tea.

She lowered her voice. 'How are you, Jennie?'

Hard to answer when you resent your visitor and

the answer she is wanting is 'fine'.

I wished Hilary would stop coming. We'd run out of subjects to talk about and we had nothing in common.

Hilary Wainwright was 'nice' and there aren't many people like that. She brought an air of decency into this sad and hopeless place. Her eye contact was all about trust. In some ways she was inspirational, she made you want to rise to her level: it was important to please her. This depressed me. I was not nice; I was cunning and deceitful. Hilary's eyes were kindly, she had an air of nurture about her and she didn't seem to mind my lack of interest or conversation.

But what was even worse was that she'd started to bring Angie Ford along, dressed, as ever, in pink denim—jacket, skirt and even bag matching—and her hair streaked with a purplish blue. Was there safety for me in numbers, in the knowledge that the Close was not one hundred per cent against me?

I wanted to talk about Martha.

They sometimes brought me snippets, and they were better than nothing.

'Martha asked after you . . . she says Poppy's settled at school. Little Josh is fine, of course, but then Graham must tell you all this.'

'Did Martha say she was coming to see me?'

Hilary took evasive action; I saw the shift in her honest brown eyes. 'I get the impression that Martha has rather a lot on her plate right now, managing the children and working two days a week, as well as taking care of the house. She doesn't have a cleaner, you know.'

'I suppose she is busy, yes.'

'You'll see her soon, when you get home, and by

then she might not be feeling so raw.'

'Is that what she's feeling—raw?'

'Jennie, dear.' Hilary leaned forward to impart some new wisdom. I did the same in anxious response and my nose brushed against Angie's freesias. I so needed to understand exactly how Martha was feeling, so that I might start the process of planning my next campaign. 'You have to understand that some people find it easier to deny life's unfortunate realities. They would rather stick their heads in the sand than confront situations that threaten them. And do you know, I think Martha is rather like that. Certainly that's the impression I get. So you really must stop upsetting yourself by imagining she is being personal. It is your illness that bothers Martha, not you.'

Jesus Christ.

The humiliation of my position.

At the mercy of naive do-gooders.

But I finally had to face the fact that I was getting no better and Martha was not going to come.

*   *   *

When I arrived home she wasn't there.

The house next door was empty. They were at Martha's mother's place in Dorset.

Was this because they knew I'd be home?

There was no message.

No instruction to feed the cats.

No welcome home card—not from them at any rate, and no-one else's counted. We had kept my illness from Ruth and Howard, Graham's bungalow parents.

No nothing. A slap in the face.

Graham took Josh to his minder, and poor little Poppy, conditioned by now, went off happily to her nursery.

But it's no good wishing time back, as Hilary repeated so tediously, you must live life from day to day.

So I was home alone with pills in my pocket, but not enough and not the kind to do any damage even if I downed the lot. They might as well have been homeopathic, hardly worth taking. But I didn't need pills any more. I knew what I must do.

*   *   *

Taking care not to be seen, I let myself into Martha's house with the key I always used. After I stepped inside there was a stirring around me, as if the house itself was aware of the sudden intrusion. I moved from room to room, disturbing only the weary petals from flowers left to stagnate in their vases. I smiled fondly at the mess. When Graham and I went away everything had to be left spotless, as if we might die and someone would criticize the state of the place when we were no longer there. We'd defrost the fridge, change the sheets, tidy the airing cupboard, disinfect the loos and, last thing, just before leaving, we would hang a brand-new dishcloth over the gleaming taps.

My last memory of my home would be an aroma of undiluted lemon or pine.

But when we returned, time after time, we found the smell homely and familiar, whereas Martha's house smelled of garlic and herbs, unwashed bedding, cats and blocked drains.

What I was doing felt far more right than anything I had ever done.

I was her servant and her slave. I was not worthy. I would make myself worthy. Maybe then she would love me.

My feet padded on the fur-strewn carpets, and clicked on the varnished pine. I paused as I went, touching everything—it all had the feel of Martha about it. I fingered the towels in the bathroom, still wet, and the closeness of Martha made goose pimples rise on my arms and my legs.

Love me!

My own face was haunting as I passed Martha's mirrors like a watching ghost, or a cat creeping through the house all alone. I listened and heard her clocks ticking, her curtains breathing, and the rustling of Martha's wild garden pushed by me into the house.

Nobody saw me.

Love me!

The linen basket was typically full, so I moved the lid and lifted the bundles, and then buried my face inside them as if they were as refreshing as water. And nobody saw me.

Love me!

I sat at Martha's dressing table, an altar within the shrine: eyeshadows, gold and purple, silver, amber and jade. I unscrewed the jars and bottles and sniffed each one in turn until I was hypnotized, stupefied and entranced by Martha's perfume. And nobody saw me.

I started at the top of the house and worked my way down, beginning each day after Graham left for work and not stopping until the children were delivered home by taxi at half past three. Progress was slow, bearing in mind that I had to stop again and again whenever anything grabbed my attention. Compulsively I had to investigate every detail of her life, or be left unsatisfied and wondering. I daren't overlook the slightest clue that might give me more insight into Martha's secrets, lift the veil from my own eyes, and take this fantasy away.

Martha was only human.

I must dig for the flaws that might relieve me.

How could I spend the rest of my life obsessed by an ordinary person?

*   *   *

How could I spend the rest of my life being thought of as pathetic?

CHAPTER TWENTY

Martha

How could she spend the rest of her life being thought of as pathetic?

*   *   *

'Poor Jennie.'

Incredibly, this came from Sam. But if Jennie had smashed our house up in our absence, to me that would have been less sinister.

Instead, the house was one big public convenience, undiluted pine from the kids' bedrooms to the downstairs loo, from bathroom to utility room, and every drawer had been tidied so fastidiously it looked like a Benetton window display. Every item had been washed, ironed and pressed.

I noticed with awe that she'd dusted the light bulbs. The hundred-watt bulbs shone eye-achingly and even the sixties gave a garish glare. There were no familiar fingerprints left round the switches, no dull sheen to the pictures, and even the cat tray sparkled with a kind of grey sterility.

The curtains had been washed and rehung, the wooden floors resealed to a glow. The sofa covers had a brand-new look and a fluffy conditioner smell about them. You name it, it had been through the washing machine, Jiffed or Pledged. But my house was not my house. I felt like I'd been invaded.

Jennie's act of penance: the stifling constraints of duty again, those little tasks that Jennie, with her lack of self-esteem, excelled at. And there on the cooker, all prepared and ready for heating up, sat a delicious-smelling, home-made asparagus soup.

'They didn't help her then,' I said distractedly. 'So it looks like there isn't a cure.'

But Sam was impressed. He had never imagined our house could approach these heights of perfection and neither had I. 'I think she's entitled to a little compassion. The poor sod's trying to make amends and this is the only way she knows how.'

My laugh was a short sharp bark. 'Sam! *What are you saying?* You've been doing nothing but slagging her off for the last few weeks . . .'

'But remember the article Alice found. If that

was right Jennie can't help what she's doing, and it has got a name even if it is too long to remember.'

*   *   *

In Dorset I had jumped at the chance of confiding in Mum, someone detached from this crazy mess, a stranger to the goings-on in the Close.

Alice remembered an article she'd read in the *Observer*: a terrible story about a woman who made a spectacle of herself obsessing over her evening-class art teacher—stalking him, pestering him, lying in wait to see him. He took out an injunction in the end, so the article said, and I thought, how cruel to do that no matter how dreadful she'd been. And it went on to say how her life had disintegrated from happily married with kids to abandoned and poverty-stricken, washing up in a transport café. There was a picture of her, too, Alice said, like a hag, and it was obvious that she'd been to hell and back.

I wanted to find out more, but apart from the fact that this syndrome had only recently been discovered and that there was no easy cure, Alice couldn't remember its name.

'She's not doing this from choice,' said Alice. 'She is ensnared in this ghastly phenomenon. They thought it was some kind of transference.' She seemed concerned and disappointed at my lack of sensitivity, and particularly with my sneering attitude towards Jennie's suicide attempt. 'You, with your intelligence, Martha, you ought to be able to rise above this.'

'You haven't lived with it, Alice,' said Sam. 'You can't begin to imagine how stressed out Martha has

202

been.'

Being back in Dorset for just a fortnight had been more refreshing than going to the Seychelles. I adored going home, sleeping in my own bedroom again, although I'd never quite come to terms with making love in my room overlooked by my childhood pictures and shone on by the innocent light of my Eeyore bedside lamp. The smell of gym shoes and ironed cotton still hung around in there, along with my precious sticker albums. The only downside was my mother's refusal to let me smoke in the house.

How different my childhood had been from Jennie's. And what an important role in development I was certain surroundings could have. Look at all this space and countryside, a parkland of woods, meadows and streams before whose beauty I had stood in awed silence, even as a small child. Here was peace. Here, even the fronds of bracken held sunlight in their hands.

Sam spent his time sailing with Dad.

My parents were close, thrilled to have us but very far from needy—so unlike poor Stella. One day, I supposed, this might be different, when one of them died, or grew senile or ill. But what was the point of worrying—those thoughts were cold and frightening.

This was the nostalgic influence that had drawn Sam and me to the cottage in Hertfordshire, the one we'd originally wanted to buy before we moved to the Close. Since then we'd reconsidered. Country life was not the same . . . no work, communities broken; leaving pretty pickings, such as old chapels and schools for the rich, retired or elderly, who fought like dogs on committees to preserve the stagnant picturesque, something to hang on their walls and stare at, while the dying went on all around them.

'Perhaps we ought to move,' I told Sam.

He thought I'd gone mad. 'Where to?'

'Just anywhere . . . for a change.'

'But what for?'

'Because of Jennie, of course.'

'I'm not being sodding well driven out of my house for anyone,' Sam said.

'Just listen to me for a moment. If what Alice has read is true and there's no easy cure for this fixation, then how long are we going to be stuck with it?'

'That's their problem. Let them move.'

'They'd never go.'

'Well then, maybe we've got to learn to be tolerant.'

'Hah!' I was staggered. *'Listen to who's talking!'*

But I understood his new attitude. From the woods and hedgerows of Dorset our problems at home felt unreal.

*   *   *

That was until we set foot inside our spanking clean house. Then we were back on dangerous ground.

'It's like it's all brand new again,' shouted an excited Scarlett, exploring her neat-as-a-pin toy cupboard and finding things she'd forgotten she had. But I couldn't help feeling unaccountably disturbed to see that even the paintboxes had been cleaned. None of the colours ran any more.

It was just as if nobody lived here.

'What are we going to do, Sam? I think we need a new strategy.'

'What we need is a drink,' he said, but he paused for a moment over my question. He was still amazed by the transformation and kept wandering round the kitchen, opening cupboards and peering into the fridge where even the clogged-up light worked again. 'We could do one of three things,' he announced. 'We could try to start from the beginning and pretend that nothing was wrong.'

'If Jennie would let us.'

'Or . . . we could ignore her completely. Cut her off. Send her to Coventry.'

'Out of the question, she's too near. I couldn't live like that, and what about the kids?'

'Or,' he turned and smiled at me, 'we could give her a job as our char.'

'And that,' I said, smacking him on the head, 'would be pandering to her masochistic desires, compounding her low self-esteem, and I'm not going along with that.'

But I couldn't help my growing unease. Even the way she had made our bed was disturbing. No place for cosy love-making, it was more suited to deathly repose.

*　　　*　　　*

Before we knew it, we were on normal terms. I use the word 'normal' loosely, but we did seem to have found a way to rub along together.

There wasn't much choice—we lived next door and our little girls were closer than sisters.

'And we won't discuss what has happened,' I told her, ticking off what felt like an errant child.

'But I can't pretend I've stopped loving you . . .'

'No, I know that. But I don't want to hear about it and I won't have any more histrionics.' I shook my head disbelievingly, knowing I sounded like a tight-arsed headmistress. 'For the kids' sake, Jennie, you must see that. They're older now, they're aware of atmospheres and they sense if there's antagonism. So let's agree, I'm aware of your feelings and will try not to make matters harder, but, in return, don't burden me with them. If you feel yourself cracking, go home, shut the door, put the music on and scream, dance, shout, punch the cushions, whatever you need to do until the urge subsides.'

Jennie nodded obediently, and I thought Alice would be proud of her daughter's command of the situation.

Now that I'd started, I might as well finish. 'And I'm telling you right away that Scarlett is going to the nursery for five days a week next month, and Mrs Cruikshank will have Lawrence so I can work full time. I won't be around in the week, Jennie, and there's nothing you can do, so don't try . . .'

'No, Martha, I won't.' And she stared abjectly down at her feet.

'Come off it! Don't start on that fawning respect crap. Haven't you heard a word I've been saying? Games! You're so bloody transparent, it's pitiful. If you want us to be friends again, you're going to have to pack that in. I just can't take it, Jennie, I don't know how to react to that shit.'

'I didn't mean to, *I'm sorry I'm sorry.*' She looked up and smiled at me normally. 'I swear this is going to be different.'

'Good, I'm glad that's out of the way.' And then

I tried out my only idea. 'Why don't you go back to school, get some qualifications, get a life, get some courage? That'd stop you wallowing in self-pity.'

She shocked me rigid by staying calm. 'You're right, and I'll do it tomorrow.'

'You will find out about courses?'

'I promise.' She looked pleased and this odd pleasure came from her obedience to me. I was still delicately balanced on that pinnacle of power. So I turned away, defeated.

*   *   *

But Jennie was as good as her word.

And incredibly it appeared to be working. We spent time together—whole families, whole weekends—and it was fine, really fine. We had good times again. We laughed and I was beginning to trust her, just as I had once before. She could be sweet, very lovable and hilariously funny. Graham was relieved just to see Jennie happy and enthusiastic about the timetable they were working out for her at the tech. Back To Work was the course, specially designed for women who had missed out first time round and needed to find new confidence. Jennie showed me the prospectus, which looked perfect in every way.

'You're not alone,' I reminded her. 'See how many other poor sods are desperate to climb out of the trap. You're going to feel so different, your life is going to take off from now.'

'Do you honestly think so?'

I wasn't going to let her turn morbid. 'I know so, Jennie. If you stick with it, you're going to get there.'

'*But only with your help,*' she said shyly.

Damn her. 'You've got it,' I said.

*   *   *

And she did have my help.

Almost undivided.

She still kept her house as antiseptic as a hospital, while mine was like a council tip. Her kids left home with a proper breakfast, while mine left chewing floppy toast. Every morning we delivered the kids, first the babies to Mrs Cruikshank, and then we rattled on to the nursery where Poppy was as keen as Scarlett. Then it was on to the town centre, where the technical college was a five-minute walk from the offices of the *Express.*

Mostly we had lunch together. If I had somebody with me, Jennie stayed well behaved, normal if a little reserved. But then she always found it hard with strangers—you could never call Jennie a social animal.

'If I'm not at the pub by one, then I'm on a job,' I told her, 'so there's no point being wounded and saying I didn't explain. My mobile won't be on, so there's no way to warn you.'

She accepted this, she seemed contented.

I kept hoping she'd bring a friend of her own.

Hilary Wainwright still called on Jennie on a regular, thoughtful basis like a prison visitor; and so did Angie, the builder's wife. But as far as I was aware Jennie wasn't telling fantastic tales or putting untruths about.

The outside world was absorbing her more than her old life in the Close and this had to be healthier. If either Hilary or Angie still questioned my cold reaction to Jennie's lethal cry for help, then I was too busy to notice. The support I was giving her now was far more useful than sympathy and tea—both as dangerous as Twiglets and booze—and that self-indulgent twaddle, stirring up the wriggly pond life it was better to be ignorant of. Naturally, I stayed cautious.

*   *   *

One day at a time, I told myself, let's not run before we can walk.

CHAPTER TWENTY-ONE

Jennie

One day at a time, I told myself, let's not run before we can walk.

*   *   *

This was the person I wanted to be: I went to Martha's hairdresser, Snips, and they chopped off my childlike shoulder-length bob. I had it highlighted in rich rusts, and cropped, and I was transformed into a Dickensian urchin, so thin by now that I looked anorexic. I didn't know what to do with it.

'Just let it stick up,' said Martha, laughing. 'That's how it's meant to be.'

Secretly I was thrilled with the look, just so long as I didn't appear to be mutton dressing as lamb, or slightly clownish. That winter I went into stylish rags as befitted my student status, wearing long, shapeless skirts, clumping boots and skimpy tops which made me look thinner and, I suspected, more interesting. I lined my eyes as Martha directed; I didn't need shadows, they were already there.

Every day I walked my tightrope, knowing that one stupid mistake would launch me into a chasm of despair from which there would be no reprieve.

How I scorned the small concerns of my schoolgirlie colleagues, my fellow students, some of whose computer classes we mature women joined, sticking out of the crowd with our bigness. I hadn't noticed before how long it took teenage girls to grow to full adult size. As the smallest and boniest of my group, I felt I almost fitted.

It was hard to remember that I'd once been normal like the rest of these middle-aged mothers, inhabiting a world of pot plants and potpourri, worried about sterile surfaces and whether the mint sauce would go round, or if Mr Muscle would live up to his promises. But you needed such concentration to enter the world of Windows and Quark, not a head bulging with passions and anxieties of a fantastic kind.

It was so incredibly boring.

I had no capacity for learning, not one spare patch of my brain was free; it was dangerously overloaded. Anyway, Graham could teach me all this on his emerald iMac at home. My daughter had already begun to learn.

Fantasy gripped me. Any quiet moment—time given for reading, note-taking, attending lectures— and my eyes glazed over. I was back with Martha again, planning what to say and how to say it during the next blissful telephone call or the next agonizing journey to town.

In many ways I'd been kept busier and had more to distract me at home.

And what the hell was I doing here learning to be a dogsbody again?

They must have thought me dull-witted. I spent my time alone, not mixing, rushing off to the pub at lunchtime to be sure not to be late for Martha, hanging around after four o'clock to catch her for a lift home.

'Are you having an affair?' asked one middle-aged stop-at-home who had clearly been watching too much TV. 'You've got that look about you.'

The others smiled awkwardly. I froze, telling myself, *it's a joke, it's her sense of humour,* before I bit back my guilty fury. 'How did you know?' I asked archly. 'The only trouble is there's too many offers to know which to choose.'

'You can always dump one on me,' joked the group jester behind pebble glasses. I nailed a monkey grin to my face.

I found their mindless world nauseating.

There were times when I longed to strip, dance on a desk, shriek depravities, just to bring these deathly classes to life.

I reminded myself I was here for Martha and there was satisfaction in that. I was here for Martha and so must endure, not miss one seminar, attend every lecture, hand in my homework on time, and make her believe I was improving. I couldn't get over how lucky I'd been landing on my feet again, after exhausting everyone's patience. For the time being, I controlled my feelings and all was going to plan.

There was something about me my group distrusted, and I learned to deal with some sudden attacks. 'And you leave your baby with some minder—at his age. The poor little mite won't know who you are.'

I used Martha's arguments to shoot down my old opinions. 'Better a contented mother than a vegetable.'

'Well,' said my self-righteous friend. 'I managed to wait until mine were in school before I enrolled.'

I wouldn't be undermined by her censorial comments. I turned the other cheek like Jesus, the victim, and sat at the back until lunchtime.

One hour to go until I saw Martha.

I was proud of how well Poppy had settled at the Humpty Dumpty Nursery. 'She's a very popular little girl and certainly one of my brightest,' Mrs Tree told me. 'Of course, she and Scarlett won't be separated so it's rather like dealing with twins, confusing to know what's coming from who. Rather too much huddling and whispering for my liking.' If Scarlett hadn't been so dark and Poppy so contrastingly fair, it would have been hard to tell them apart because their build was the same, their clothes were the same and so were their hairstyles. They rang each other up every morning to discuss what to wear; it was so sweet to hear them. I went along with the dungarees and the bicycle shorts, but I stopped short at the teeny skirts and glitter sandals so beloved of Scarlett. Clarks Start-Rite for Poppy: I did insist on those and refused to listen to her furious cries. Care of growing feet is important and Scarlett did lean towards the tarty—navy nail polish and vulgar tattoos, at her age, ridiculous.

But one of the blessings of my hospital stay was the new independence my daughter was showing.

It looked as if my shy little girl wouldn't suffer as I had done. She'd manage to avoid my frantic desire to please. Next term she'd be in the infants' school along with Scarlett.

And Josh was a more settled, happier baby. I put his earlier problems down to colic and teething difficulties which, luckily, he had now grown out of. Mrs Cruikshank was a gift, Martha was right, and even Graham accepted the fact that children can be happy when loved and cared for by more than two people.

Howard and Ruth, Graham's mum and dad, were put off from visiting quite so often because there was no-one at home to wait on them. Their stays were limited to weekends which, between us, we could just endure. And with me away and busy all week, their mean criticisms over the lack of home-made cakes and puddings, and my new dependence on fast food, fell on deaf ears.

'Have you made your blackberry and apples yet, Jennie?'

'No, Ruth, and it doesn't look like I'm going to get round to it this year.'

'Oh, what a pity,' she'd say. 'My freezer is already full, what with the plums and Howard's string beans.'

I was immune. She could no longer touch me.

Martha and I laughed about this. 'You're a different person already, you're free of all that old crap.'

Martha would never understand why so many women weaker than her used this trivia as stabilizers to stop them wobbling. Because who is brave enough to confront that vast, unfulfilled void in their heads? And if I let go of my obsession with Martha, neither plums nor blackberries—nor cleaning the windows—would fill the empty universe that would be left inside me. *Where would I put my passion?*

*   *   *

That day, confident, strong and beautiful, she presided over chaos: slicing tomatoes, searching for glue, answering the phone, bawling instructions about clean socks. I knew I could never tell her that only last night I had seen Sam almost eating a woman alive in the jeep, down a side street, outside the China Garden.

When I got home with my takeaway I wasn't hungry, I couldn't touch it. Why had I gone myself? Why hadn't I let Graham collect it?

Pity and sorrow did not suit Martha's image—those descriptions were mine, not hers. I couldn't abide the idea of a Martha made weak. And, quite apart from keeping quiet from a selfish point of view, I knew I was on shaky ground; I had no illusions—Sam's betrayal of Martha was no worse than mine of Graham. And going on past experience, Sam's flings were normally brief.

But I did confide in Mr Singh on my next monthly visit to the clinic.

'And does this discovery make you feel powerful? You are obviously more in control of your life than your idol, Martha, is.'

I said, 'I don't see it like that. If Sam left her she would recover—she runs the house single-handed, shops, cleans and pays the bills. Sam doesn't lift a

214

finger. She moans about him but he gets away with it.' I was curious to note that I found it threatening to diminish Martha in the doctor's eyes. 'She'd find someone else, she's fun, she's lovely. With Sam she asks to be taken for granted, she fusses over him, cooks his favourite meals, drives when he's pissed, and you should see the trouble she goes to to find him exactly the right present. It takes her hours and he's never grateful.'

'Jennie, are you jealous of Sam?'

'It's the kids, even the cats,' I blurted out without thinking, and in Mr Singh's pause I had the time to realize how silly this sounded.

'Could this be because they belong to Martha in a way that Sam does not?'

How could I know? I was annoyed. All I had demonstrated were my unhealthy feelings: suspicious and abnormal. I hated this intimacy with a virtual stranger. Talking about Martha was fine; I loved to talk about Martha and I did half hope he could cure me, but I wasn't even certain that I did envy the cats and the kids, and now he would labour the point, wasting time on me.

'Let me rephrase my original question. Are you saying you're not jealous of Sam, but you are jealous of the cats and the children?'

I felt my eye begin to twitch; there was no way I could control it. The man would be bound to interpret this as some deep, subconscious response. *Leave me alone, let's talk about Martha.*

But I thought of the times I had kicked the cats when Martha wasn't looking. Surely this was mere annoyance because they would jump on my shoulders or sharpen their claws on my knee? Cats frightened me and they sensed that. Hers were

215

assertive, menacing cats, and the only time Martha ever smacked Poppy—well, more of a tap, but even so—was when she was tormenting Honey. I couldn't share Martha's blind devotion to these stealthy, flea-ridden creatures, and it irked me. No big deal. That's all.

I told Mr Singh, 'I love Martha's children like my own, more sometimes, and that's awful. They're so like Martha, you see, perfect little carbon copies.'

This could be because her kids loved me back, unlike the cats who verged on the hostile. And, of course, Martha's children and mine were one way of keeping us together.

And I wondered how I would feel if they ever gave us cause to part.

Mr Singh glanced at his watch to signal five minutes left. Presumably he gave this warning so his patients could pull themselves together and not start diving too deeply before the end of the session. He used this time as a summing-up period during which he withdrew some of his sympathy. It slipped like a shadow under his door. 'So you've decided to say nothing to Martha about Sam's little infidelity? Although she's your friend? Although she might rather be told about her husband's latest fling?'

'Yes, I've decided. Whoever told her something like that, she'd resent them for telling her. And knowing Sam it'll soon blow over.'

*   *   *

'Mummy!' Poppy was jumping through the puddles, the water lapping over her boots. She clung on to my hand and in her other she held a

216

small, useless umbrella.

'Yes?' She ought to stop messing around, the blasted shop closed at five thirty.

She gabbled on. 'D'you like Scarlett better than me?'

'What on earth gave you that silly idea?'

She kept on jumping, jarring my arm. My sleeve was pulled over my wrist. The rain sheeted down in full force now and the buses, brilliantly lit, sloshed past us as we struggled and huddled, and Poppy's umbrella kept nudging my face. 'Mummy?'

'What is it?' Sometimes her chatterings provoked me to tears. I needed to think—I'd forgotten my list but I knew what I wanted was important.

'D'you like the way I have my hair?'

'Of course I do. It suits you.'

'When Josh grows up, will he look like Lawrence?'

'I dunno, Poppy.'

'Mummy?' My patience was exhausted. I didn't bother to answer. Rain was dripping down my neck and my right hand, in Poppy's, was going numb. I would call in and see Martha when I got back, but only if Sam's jeep wasn't there. If we didn't hurry, we might not make it.

'Scarlett says that when we go to big school next term, we can sit at the same table together.'

'Well, that's nice, you'll like that.'

*   *   *

At last we were out of the shop and hurrying homewards. My strides were too long for Poppy, so she skipped along by my side.

217

Damn and blast! Damn. *The jeep.*

I couldn't pop in to Martha's now. Sam was on his way home. I blamed Poppy for dawdling, for keeping me at the counter while she took so long to choose her sweets, and now there was the jeep—it pulled out of the line of traffic and stopped at the bus stop.

We kept walking, but I watched as a woman in a mac got out. It took them a while to release hands, it took time to finish what she was saying— something urgent. They smiled, then laughed; she slammed the door and hurried towards the shelter.

So Sam's indiscretion was still going strong and I felt a sickly blob of terror as a new threat presented itself—*a disturbance in the status quo.* What if the Frazers' marriage broke up? What if they got divorced and had to sell the house? What if Martha, ambitious and capable, moved to another part of the country?

And what would become of poor Poppy, having to cope without Scarlett? Parting would break their hearts.

Sam's behaviour could prove lethal, and he wasn't too bothered about being discreet. I had seen him twice now, so it was quite likely that somebody else, some meddler like Tina Gallagher, would be the next one to catch him at it and hurry to Martha with the news.

These possibilities were terrifying. I couldn't allow this affair to drag on until Martha somehow found out. Time and again, she had promised she wouldn't have him back if he cheated once more. 'And it's different now,' she told me the last time we discussed it. 'I'm stronger, I'm working, the kids are older. Once, I couldn't have done without him,

218

stuck at home with a baby. But not now. Oh no. There's no way I would take any more of that.'

Had she meant it?

I fretted, but what could I do?

Damn Sam and his lecherous urges.

It might be that Sam was in love this time and would demand a divorce. In that case, confrontation would only bring matters to a head. But whatever the circumstances, Sam wouldn't take kindly to me interfering in his life.

I would have to be subtle. I would not criticize. I would issue a friendly warning.

*　　*　　*

It's only when women are normal that plums and blackberries have a place in their lives.

CHAPTER TWENTY-TWO

Martha

It's only when women are normal that plums and blackberries have a place in their lives.

*　　*　　*

If plums and blackberries had a place in my life, I might be one of those enviable people whose lives cruise along on an even keel, no storms to confound them, no waves to unseat them and no half-hidden icebergs lying in wait. People like my mum and dad, theirs was a blueprint for marriage,

219

and as a child I used to dream that one day I'd be as contented as them.

I should have married a less dangerous man whose love for me was greater than mine for him.

Like Graham, for example. But like most women so blessed, Jennie failed to appreciate her luck.

Was this another of Sam's flings, one that just lasted rather longer, or was this the time it would turn serious? As years flew by—Poppy and Scarlett off to school and Josh and Lawrence to playgroup —pride and terror stopped me from asking. I had no-one to share my misery with since I'd stopped confiding in Jennie. Although she'd improved over these last few years and taken several jobs as a temp, I was still nervous around her, of her troublemaking abilities, which weren't deliberate— I understood that—just part of her uncanny fixation. She didn't deny this was true; poor thing, she couldn't even trust herself any more.

Angie Ford was an expert at turning a drama into a crisis. And anyway, since she had sided against me over Jennie's lame suicide bid, we weren't as close as we once had been. As for Tina next door, she would look for the funny side and I knew I couldn't cope with her jokes—I didn't want to compare our marriage to her own troubled one with Carl, and nor did I want a toy boy to screw, or to put up with her coarse laughter.

I loved Sam. I adored him.

There were any number of giveaways, and I was wise to all of them because of past experiences. I refused to be the last to know. Sadly, like some suspicious old shrew, I seemed to be programmed to pick up clues, prying in back pockets, sniffing round crotches. Sam was unnaturally considerate, over-enthusiastic in bed, and he'd ring to warn me if he was going to be late instead of just letting his supper burn.

I responded in my old pitiful manner: cooking up his favourite dishes, baking his beloved home-made bread, waxing my legs and plucking my eyebrows; and even checking the oil, water and tyre pressures.

I blessed Jennie's Back To Work endeavours, they were doing the trick—she stayed on the rails and there was no more excessive behaviour. That straw would have broken this camel's back.

She grumbled, of course; that was her nature. 'Me, the slave of some paunchy man stuck behind a desk all day, that's all I'll ever be. Out of the house, yes, OK, but still servicing the male of the species.'

'That's not right. This is just a start; you must reach for higher things. Stick your name down now. Get a degree.'

'Oh yeah? *With what qualifications?*'

'They don't count. You're a mature student. They'll take you on the strength of an interview, if you make an effort to be slightly more positive.'

'Would you come with me?'

'Of course I would.'

*   *   *

At the school sports day I missed him terribly. I went with Graham and Jennie because Sam rang at the last minute to say he couldn't make it. Scarlett would be heartbroken and I cursed the bastard's selfishness. No matter how desperately he was bonking, you'd think his daughter's feelings might still mean something. The wanker.

221

'Cheer up, mate,' said Jennie, too self-absorbed as usual to notice the cloak of sadness around me. 'Most of the women are here on their own. At least you've got a husband at home, unlike some of them, poor things.'

I've never been keen on competition, especially when it comes to kids. They don't enjoy beating each other. Winning is learnt behaviour and I'd seen enough of their games to know that they'd rather encourage each other and lose than gloat over a win. Winning can be a lonely business.

Scarlett and Poppy came a marvellous first in the three-legged-race, and I was weak with laughter as they hobbled home. I looked round to share my amusement with Jennie, but she was standing up, clapping frantically, and all she could give was a tight, tense smile.

Scarlett, six now, was a natural, and when she bragged, 'Look how high I can jump, Mummy,' or, 'See how much faster I can go,' I probably played it down too much with my 'Well, you're lucky to have such fast little legs.' Rather too dismissive. Maybe I should have made more of her talents, but she was big-headed enough already.

So there I was, chatting to the mums, sitting on a bank of daisies, missing Sam on such a beautiful day. Although I barely noticed when Scarlett and Poppy lined up at the start of their running race, I managed to give them a quick, cheery wave before I went back to the gossip.

But what was this weird change in Jennie?

She was ramrod straight, sitting up like a meerkat, and her knuckles were such a ghastly white it looked as if they were diseased.

People were talking—she took no notice.

222

You could almost imagine she was praying.

I followed her stare. What could be happening? *Some accident? Some argument?* No, as far as I could tell, the only thing going on was the running race.

I nudged her. 'Jennie, are you OK?'

Perhaps she was silently choking.

She didn't even hear me.

They were off. Jennie rose to her feet, taut and tense, a creature possessed, and her fists went straight to her mouth where she chewed at her knuckles. 'Come on, come on,' she hissed with menace and her mouth formed a perfect snarl. *'Oh Poppy, come on!'*

It was a relief to notice that her performance was not unique. A number of mothers, and most of the fathers, were on their feet, howling at their kids as if this was the Olympic Games, not a class of six-year-olds having fun.

When the race was over Jennie sagged, collapsing like a sack beside me, in a genuine state of despair.

I asked her, 'How did our lot do?' In the frenzy, I hadn't been able to see.

'Scarlett won,' Jennie told me, with a rictus smile stuck to her face. 'I don't think Poppy was placed, she came in the middle with the rest of the masses.'

It was hard to know what to say. Should I apologize for Scarlett's success? Would that make Jennie feel better?

'Well, they did win the three-legged—' I offered what comfort I could—'so they'll win a box of Liquorice Allsorts.'

It was not a good moment for Scarlett to come rushing over, red-faced and breathless. *'Did you see me, Mummy, I was way out in front and then . . .'*

I lowered my voice. 'Well done, well done! And how about you, Poppy?' I thought my question innocent enough.

But, oh no, poor little Poppy was crying. 'Poppy, what's wrong, did you hurt yourself?'

She wouldn't answer—one of her sulks.

'She's cross because she didn't come first,' said Scarlett unhelpfully. And I nearly said, *For goodness sake, what the hell does it matter how fast you can run,* but luckily I stopped myself just in time. Scarlett was listening, I'd be letting her down.

'Maybe next time,' I said brightly.

'Poppy's no athlete,' said Jennie seriously. 'She's more of an academic, I'm afraid.'

'Of course she is,' I quickly agreed. 'Maybe she'll win a prize at speech day.' My God, my God, how could coming first assume such bloody enormous proportions?

During all this heavy stuff, we were trying to control Lawrence and Josh who tumbled together like a couple of puppies as soon as they set eyes on each other. What makes people say boys are easier? That wasn't my experience. These boys never settled to anything, no quiet crayoning, no cutting out shapes—it was kicking balls, it was fighting, climbing . . .

Although this was natural and I laughed to watch them, there was something worrying about this little friendship. I'd already mentioned it to Sam: 'Lawrence always comes off worse.'

'He's smaller, he's bound to,' said Sam, indifferently.

'Josh does get carried away . . .'

'He's a baby,' said Sam, 'testing his strength.

224

Don't worry so much. You'll turn poor Lawrence into a sissy.'

That was the last thing I was doing. And even if I'd wanted to, it wouldn't be possible. That boy was a monkey, a rubber ball of energy: if he fell he hardly noticed. He was smaller than Josh who had yet to lose his puppy fat. But it wasn't only these tussles that concerned me, it was the way Josh wrenched Lawrence's lorry away, or tripped him up almost deliberately, or nicked his Smarties, or knocked down his bricks.

How laughable, I told myself, to be so paranoid over three-year-olds.

*   *   *

It was Jennie who persuaded them to enter the little brothers' race.

And this time I watched, concerned over wiry little Lawrence in such an excited scrum. He might get confused over which way to run, he was such a soppy laid-back kid.

The little terror set the pace, paddling away with his nutbrown legs, tongue between teeth but still giggling, while behind him thumped the chubby Josh, so determined for such a baby. By some fluke, God alone knows how, Lawrence was going to win, and I worried about the effect on Jennie. But at the very last moment we were saved from what could have triggered a tantrum, because Lawrence glanced behind him and then collapsed in a frenzy of laughter. All the mini athletes shot past him, and the dope was still laughing when I picked him up.

Josh hadn't won, but he came fourth and got a

225

tube of Smarties, which went a long way towards pleasing Jennie. Her mood lifted. She was sweetness and light.

But even after these niggling incidents, even when Lawrence showed such a preference for playing with other toddlers and not Josh, I still didn't worry about my kids' friendships with the little Gordons. Hell, they were more like family than friends, Scarlett and Lawrence grew up with them. Naturally they would want to be close.

* * *

I had hoped that eventually Jennie would find a permanent position and decide to work full time. Her various employers seemed pleased with her. She'd be quiet and conscientious, I knew. Either that, or do a degree which I thought would challenge her, use up her spare energy and absorb some of that raging passion. When she said she was thinking of giving up work altogether, I went into an immediate panic. Understandable in the circumstances.

She said, 'It's OK for you, Martha, your job's fun.'

'Only because I make it fun.' I was horrified. 'But you can't want to go back to square one, stuck in the house on your own, with the sprogs out all day. What will you do? You'll end up in bed with the Emva Cream.'

'Contrary to accepted opinion, some women do enjoy home life, Martha. People like us just aren't given credence. We don't all yearn to wear pinstriped suits and sit in swivel chairs.'

'Fair enough,' I had to agree, and I sometimes

wished I was more like that—the stress of a full-time job and two kids wasn't funny. 'I just feel you're wasting your talents.'

'*What talents?* Don't keep patronizing me.'

The last couple of years had been so much calmer with Jennie's mind and energy focused, and I dreaded a relapse with her brain free to churn. We would see less of each other than ever because the pub lunches would have to stop. And how would that affect her?

'I'll still be able to meet you at lunchtime,' she confounded me by adding.

'So you're not keen on the degree idea either?'

'It was your idea, not mine. I've decided to wait until Josh starts school proper.'

'Oh? I thought . . .'

'Keep your hair on, Martha, I'm not about to start screaming and stalking. Anyway, they've made that an official offence and I'm not about to get put away.'

'That never crossed my mind,' I lied.

'Liar,' she said.

She was making a mistake, I was certain. Look at me, for example. Even with the nagging heartache of Sam's indiscretions going on in the background, work made it possible to half forget. There were people to be interviewed, stories to write and deadlines to be met. It would be so easy to dwell on my fears and, yes, even wallow in that black mire, but work put a stop to that fatal option.

*　　　*　　　*

If this was an affair, it was no quick bonk.

At the worst times, Jennie used to waffle on

about how I could never understand the enormity of the passion that drove her. That was shit. Sam and I started off like that—on my side, anyway. I adored him to the point of worship; he was godlike in my eyes. I'd have given my life if he'd asked me. I was the typical lovesick cow, I was the woman in a Mills and Boon romance, I was the subject of all those tragic love songs. I was as close to insanity then as I was ever likely to get. And after we were engaged and I found him with some office floozy, if it hadn't been for my mum and my friends I think I'd have topped myself.

When I told her this, when I tried to explain that I had once been obsessed like her, Jennie was contemptuous of what she called my servile behaviour. I didn't see it that way—I saw it as loving, caring. I enjoyed cleaning his shoes; I didn't bother about my own. Sam was master of the house; at the end of the day, what he said went. OK we had our disagreements, but I liked to let him win.

Now even Tina told me, 'If you were less of a doormat he might respect you more.' But Carl's roving eye was worse than Sam's, so I don't know how she formed this opinion, or how she had the nerve to advise me. Jennie called me 'the doting wife' and said I was worth a hundred of him.

Over the years, my intense, mad passion had turned into something more mellow. But even so, underneath, that first enchantment was still there and the thought of living without him filled me with desolation.

Sex was part of his magic.

The bastard was led by his prick.

In bed, he took women to ecstasy and I'm sure

228

that's why they clung on so desperately when the sod finally dumped them.

He swamped every fibre of their being.

But who was the bitch this time? If I knew who she was, I would tear out her eyes.

Probably some whore at work. I kept my eyes peeled at the firm's Christmas party, but there were so many lusty young women and Sam gave nothing away. He was more attentive and loving than ever.

It was hopeless. Was it some bitch he'd picked up in a pub?

So yes, I did understand about Jennie's yearnings, but just as mine turned into a gentler fire, so I believed her ardour would cool to something more manageable over the years. And let's face it, there's so much to do, one has to keep going.

*   *   *

'Pottery,' said Jennie.

'Is that Singh's idea? You sound like a nutter.'

'Pottery was the only subject I excelled at at school. And I'm going to learn to do it properly.'

'Swear not to give your offerings as Christmas presents.'

'You can scoff,' she said. 'One day you'll be glad to give a year's wages for one piece of work by Jennie Gordon.'

'I hope you're right,' I said, and meant it. But I couldn't see how watching a wheel go round or slapping about with wet clay could soak up such hopeless passion.

If that worked, then I would enrol.

229

*   *   *

Time went faster. It sometimes seemed a waste of time to put the Christmas decorations away.

CHAPTER TWENTY-THREE

Jennie

Time went faster. It sometimes seemed a waste of time to put the Christmas decorations away.

*   *   *

In Mulberry Close we bucked the trend. The place turned into a time warp, with the same six families settled so long and nobody moving away. True, the school was good, most people had well-paid jobs and high mortgages, but the main reason for our permanence was the escalating notoriety of the nearby estate. While equivalent houses, not that far away, saw their prices soar, ours tumbled dramatically. We'd been warned this might happen when we bought the house. To move would be a backward step. The council promised to take action: evict some of those neighbours from hell, appoint wardens, improve public services, tackle crime and drugs. So we marked time until they obliged, thanking God all the while that our school catchment area was different.

The Wainwrights had a FOR SALE sign up for weeks, but they took it down when no-one showed any interest. I also gathered that some money

Anthony Wainwright was expecting had failed to arrive. The saintly Hilary was Anthony's third wife, and not only were there two other families for him to support, but their own lifestyle was expensive and their two young sons went to private schools. Oddly, the swanky Wainwrights seemed to have more money worries than the rest of us.

'The Child Support Agency have milked the man dry,' said Angie Ford, who knew these things. 'They're even talking about selling their boat.'

'Quite right too,' said Tina Gallagher, giving lanky Carl a sideways look. 'Men must be made responsible.'

I was so lucky. No money worries. No straying husband.

Pottery? Why not.

I wasn't going to be made a fool of by being turned down for a university place. Martha seemed convinced they would take me, but I knew damn well they wouldn't. I would fail every test they gave me, and when she found out I was thick she'd despise me.

I couldn't go wrong doing pottery.

I might talk intelligently about current affairs, but this was a deliberately acquired skill. I gleaned it all from the newspapers and the telly in order to impress. Unlike Martha and her cronies, I didn't care about the world around me. I had no interest in governments, despots, refugees, plagues or pestilence. I wasn't proud of my petty-mindedness, it was just that there was no space for anything else in my head except Martha and my devious schemings. Inside, I burned up every day with a yearning I couldn't control, and I'd long since given up on the idea of a cure. For now, I just had to live with it.

I invented little tasks for myself so I could forget Martha, lose sight of her for a few moments—let her slip away, find some relief. But whatever I tried didn't work.

She gave me life; she was the source of my animation.

My mentor and saviour, Hilary, was wounded by my renewed friendship with Martha, who had abandoned me in my time of trouble. I grabbed every chance to be near her; and as summers came and went, we spent more holidays together, the children lived in each other's houses, and we sat for hours in our gardens drinking wine, swimming and laughing.

The swimming pool was a triumph. The project proved a terrific success. If some of the neighbours treated me carefully, I just didn't notice—not then. The weekly rota meant that everyone shared the maintenance work; there were strict rules about running and diving and bringing your own towels and drinks; and because everyone loved the water and wanted to be in it, there wasn't much awkward social stuff which I would have found hard to cope with. It was difficult to get jealous over games with a beach ball, or water polo with table-tennis bats. After half past eight at night it was ours, and those late summer evenings, when Martha stayed and we talked about nothing, were quite unforgettable.

But Hilary Wainwright was feeling left out. My crime was my ingratitude. All the kindnesses shown to me, all those confidences, grapes and hospital visits should have been rewarded with more than occasional smiles and trays of Jammie Dodgers. In spite of her style and charm, in spite of her part-time teaching job, Hilary, I realized, was lonely.

I firmly believed that everyone I knew was determined to get close to Martha. I went round thinking they envied me and my special relationship with the Frazers. So if anyone showed an interest in me I suspected their motives at once—they wanted a channel to get through to Martha.

'These days that woman is never at home,' Tina Gallagher moaned. Her coffee-time calls were becoming a nuisance, but I put up with her visits as long as she indulged me and got onto the subject of Martha. I wondered why Tina made such an effort over her appearance, in her hard, glossy, shell-suited way, with make-up immaculate and accessories perfect. After all, she worked from home on a computer and wasn't planning to see anyone. And then I realized that, after me, she felt Martha's absence most. She said, 'I wonder that Sam puts up with it.'

'Puts up with it?' I didn't agree. 'It makes not the slightest difference to him if she's there or not, so long as his needs are pandered to.'

'But I get the impression that Sam's not too happy.'

'Oh?' I must be discreet. 'I wouldn't know. But he's moody, he's always been moody.'

'You're very fond of her, aren't you, Jennie?' Her voice was too casual and I guessed she knew something about my abnormal obsession. Had Martha told her or had she guessed? Or had my behaviour been so transparent that it was the talk of the Close? 'The Frazers don't seem the sort to hang around here indefinitely, particularly Sam. He's so ambitious, the itchy type who needs to

233

move on. I'm surprised they've been here so long, to be honest.'

The reasons were clear to me—why not to her? The kids enjoyed school; Josh and Lawrence, five years old, were full time at the infants' now. Martha loved her work, so did Sam, and then there was the estate problem and the house price dilemma. 'It's disruptive to move unless you have to.'

'Would that worry Sam?'

'It might worry Martha.'

'D'you think they'll last?'

Her question came as a surprise, although I'd wondered the same myself.

'Who can tell these days?'

'I dunno about us,' Tina confessed, 'what with Carl's smutty habits. I don't know how long I'm going to be able to stick it. That rabid sod should have his balls severed.'

'But you're OK at the moment?'

She made a face. 'I never know, Jennie, quite honestly.' And those maudlin thoughts seemed to carry her off.

I got up to make more coffee. I stared out of the window across to Martha's empty house. I looked at my watch: five hours to go until she came home, and how could I fill them? I asked Tina, 'Would you want to be told if Carl was having it off with someone?'

'Why? You haven't . . . ?'

I spun round to reassure her. 'No, no.' A pause would have been too cruel. I'd been a fool, I ought to have realized that was how she'd take such an odd question. 'I wouldn't have asked you if I had. Of course not. But seriously, how would you feel if

234

a friend kept that information from you?'

'Livid,' she said firmly.

'You'd rather know?'

Her lip curled. 'Only a woman who hasn't lived through it would think otherwise,' she said with contempt. She agitated her teaspoon, ramming it into the sugar lump. 'I might not like it but I'd not blame the messenger, if that's what you're suggesting. If I heard that a friend of mine knew what was happening but kept her mouth shut, I'd never be able to trust her again.'

'What if she'd been mistaken? What if it had been harmless?'

'It's never harmless,' Tina snapped.

'Maybe if you'd had children . . . ?'

'That's rather an unkind remark.'

'No, no, I didn't mean it to sound like that.'

'Carl can't,' she said bleakly. 'That's why he scatters his seed indiscriminately, trying to prove everyone wrong.' She shrugged and stirred a fresh cup of coffee. 'I'd miss the Frazers if they left.'

'Oh, so would I,' I said.

*　　　*　　　*

I fell out with the Harcourts at lodge number six over operatic arias.

Arty-farty, Graham called them. They ran an antique shop in the arcade in town and specialized in old books. I thought they acted superior. I'd never been inside their house. Martha had—she called it refined. With their two serious teenage daughters they came swimming, dried themselves and left; I always felt Sadie Harcourt was nervous of me, but Martha said I was being neurotic.

235

Some people can tolerate noise. I can't. And because I was at home all day I was the one who suffered most. Tina said the row never bothered her. The closer you lived to the source, I thought, the worse the awful distortion. And the Harcourts' house was the last one in the circle, opposite ours which was the first.

The Harcourts, friends of the Gallaghers, used the swimming pool least of all and were self-contained, almost distant—although not with Martha, of course. I tried to be reasonable. I bore it for weeks, closing my windows and doors to warbling, incomprehensible Italian—not pleasant in that warm weather. There were times when I put the sunbeds away and moved in from beside the pool, but it went on and on and on . . .

'The last thing I want is to make a fuss,' I told Graham. 'I don't want to fall out with anyone, but . . .'

'Say something, Jennie, if it's really that bad. You don't have to be rude. If she knows she's disturbing you, she'll probably feel worse than you. She seems a friendly sort, even if she is a bit quiet.'

'She probably just doesn't realize,' I said. 'And in the evenings the family come home, so it's her only chance to listen properly.' I knew that problem. I loved to listen to loud, mad music and lose myself . . . I was making excuses for her, anything rather than go and complain. I'm a coward.

And Martha wouldn't be there to support me.

What would Martha do?

Well, after shouting and swearing, she'd stump over there with her fag dangling from her lip and her newly dyed hair under towels, and shout, '*Shut up, for Christ's sake, you're driving me mental.*'

And she'd end up sharing a glass of something.

Martha had the knack of complaining to anyone—British Telecom, post office staff, traffic wardens. She did it and got away with it. She could tame the most officious official and get everyone wanting to please her. *But me . . . ?*

That afternoon I was trying to read, difficult for me at the best of times because it was so hard to concentrate, and unless the author was terrifically strong the mantras in my own head took over. Sadie's music was the throb of a headache, the pressure before the thunder came, the sucking gust of an oncoming train. I could counter-attack by playing my own music, by squeezing out every decibel, but it was peace and quiet I was after, and why should I have to make noise to drown out hers?

The main thing was to keep calm.

Holding my breath, I went over.

I rang her doorbell. No response, and no wonder.

I walked round the side of the house and saw her through her sitting-room window engaged in some ungodly ritual, kneeling in a faded nightdress, both arms raised to heaven. And swaying.

I had stumbled upon some shameful secret.

I knocked on the glass, puce-faced.

Sadie either heard me or caught my reflection in the window because she leapt like a rocket into the air and rushed to turn off the sound.

Now, the silence was deafening.

She came to the window and opened it.

'I'm really sorry . . .' I started.

'What the hell are you doing in my garden?' she asked coldly. Her face was white, dull like her

nightie.

'I tried the door but you couldn't hear . . .'

'But why are you here, of all people, hanging around private property?'

'I'm sorry, it's just that the noise . . .'

'Spying on me.'

'No, I'm not.'

'Oh?'

She sounded more like Poppy than a sensible married woman. I must act grown up, act natural like Martha.

'I don't mean to say you shouldn't play it, but if you wouldn't mind turning it down?' I couldn't have been more polite.

'Jennie. If you don't leave immediately I'm going to ring the police, right now.' She was frightened. Her shoulders were shaking. She kept checking the door as if she might make a run for it and her eyes were wide and starey.

She was scared of me! *She was terrified.* What did she think I was going to do? Did she think I made a habit of sneaking round gardens and knocking on windows? *What had she heard?* What had Tina told her? What sort of things had these two talked about when I was in the hospital?

I burned with embarrassment as I backed away, shaking my head at my distraught neighbour and trying to smile reassuringly. I heard her shouting something about 'head cases creeping about', and my eyes stung with shame when I let myself back into my house. It was horrible, really horrible. If only I'd put up with the noise.

I told Graham when he came home.

'Embarrassed to be caught performing . . . wouldn't you be?' he asked.

'I suppose so.' Had it been like that?

'And you must have given her quite a fright. That always makes people furious.'

'I don't know what to do now. Maybe I ought to go over . . . ?'

'Leave it alone,' said Graham. 'It's really not that important. And if she keeps her music down, so what if you've upset her?'

But I didn't want enemies.

It preyed on my mind.

I had to do something to make it right, I couldn't leave it alone. What had Sadie been so afraid of?

*   *   *

When the kids were in bed I went to see Hilary. 'Please tell Sadie that I didn't mean to disturb her. It was just that her music was so loud.'

She didn't invite me in for coffee. She just asked me, 'Why didn't you ring?'

This was silly. 'I don't have the Harcourts' number, going over was quicker.'

'Sadie can be a funny girl, you never know quite where you are with her. But she's genuine, she's good fun, I like her.'

'But why was she so nervous to see me?'

Hilary paused and then said, 'Don't take it personally. You gave her a fright, that's all.'

'Will you tell her from me that I'm sorry?'

Hilary turned frosty. 'Listen, Jennie, it's no big deal. Don't make such an issue of it.'

'Hilary,' I pleaded, *'that woman thinks I am dangerous.'*

'Rubbish,' Hilary said, eager to withdraw, and I could smell roasting chicken behind her. 'You're too wrapped up in yourself, too busy imagining things. It really is time that you tried to pull yourself together.'

Hilary used to be my friend. 'So you won't speak to Sadie for me?'

'I won't get involved—you'll only cause trouble. Jennie, please, just leave well alone.'

A troublemaker as well as a nutcase? Oh yes, I see. So that's what they were saying. A whispering campaign. All against me. If I'd wanted to keep Hilary's friendship, I shouldn't have gone back to Martha. Hilary was over her breakdown and she thought it was time I recovered from mine.

*   *   *

I was coming out of Safeway's, loading the car on the following Friday, when they stay open till nine.

A path runs alongside the car park. It is fenced off, strewn with Safeway carriers, paper bags and cartons. When it gets past Safeway's the path becomes more appealing, with seats and picnic tables set up by the prettiest bits of the river.

I had loaded the car and was wondering if I'd remembered the Edam. I turned on the headlights and the beam lit them up—arm in arm, cheek to cheek, hip to hip, enlarged like lovers on a cinema screen.

If I'd blinked I would have missed them, because one second later they were out of the spotlight and I'd never have known who they were. Only lovers would use the path at this darkening time of night, under such a leaden, lifeless sky.

Why me?

Why did I have to see them?

I felt as if I'd witnessed an accident. The ground shook, I couldn't move.

Tina and Sam—well, why not?

Why hadn't I recognized her when I'd seen her in the rain at the bus stop, getting out of Sam's jeep, all that time ago? Her hood had hidden her then. And I'd been too flustered and wet to care. And Tina must have been using me to track Martha's movements. I was better than any timetable. No wonder she called for coffee so often.

*   *   *

I was haunted by the question. Should I leave well alone or make matters worse?

CHAPTER TWENTY-FOUR

Martha

I was haunted by the question. Should I leave well alone or make matters worse?

*   *   *

My ongoing worries about the kids—Poppy's reliance on Scarlett and Josh's bullying of Lawrence—would have to wait; I'd sort it out eventually. I had a damn sight more than that on my mind.

This sordid little intrigue of Sam's was dragging on too long for comfort—if I could believe what

241

he'd sworn to me after the others, which supposedly lasted for no more than months. This was years. It was exhausting. And why would he lie after the event, after he'd been forgiven again? Maybe I should have confronted him with it—but I had no proof, nothing but instinct, nothing substantial enough to slap on the table. He was tired, worked too hard, and felt like a stranger, but how could I tear him apart over that? If I was right, he was dipping his wick and being mega-crafty about it this time. It began to look as if we might end up like those sad couples who lead separate lives, but stay together for the sake of the kids.

I hoped to God I was wrong. What if I asked him and he said yes? What would my next question be?

*   *   *

We'd lived here for too long. It was time for a change. There'd been trouble in the Close again and I couldn't help thinking that if our life was more normal, we would have done more about moving on. It was nothing we couldn't cope with, of course, but because of the characters involved, the results were unpleasant and unpredictable.

The main problem was Jennie, needless to say. The other protagonists were Angie Ford and my now frighteningly grown-up eight-year-old daughter, Scarlett.

When I was at work Jennie took charge: she had my house keys, she averted domestic dramas, she let in the plumber and the electrician; she took in parcels, she switched the lights on when it got dark early on winter afternoons. And she'd pop over and turn on the heating if it suddenly grew extra cold.

She'd done this for years now, without complaint, ever since that appalling crisis when she'd ended up in a mental ward.

If the kids were ill, it was Jennie who turned out to fetch them from school, took them to the doctor, tucked them in, kept them warm and medicated until I got home from work at six.

Scarlett's fall was her own silly fault. It was time that child calmed down. She broke all the rules. She shouldn't have gone anywhere near the boiler house, let alone on the roof of the caretaker's hut, and when she fell off and slid down the coke pile, breaking her leg in the process, it should have taught her a well-deserved lesson.

The school had Jennie's name and number for emergency contact, so how come Angie Ford was sent for?

Nothing, it seemed, could right that wrong in Jennie's thwarted eyes. And what was even worse was the fact that after Scarlett's arrival home in Ken Ford's battered builder's van, Jennie was not even informed. Scarlett used her own key to get in.

No amount of explaining would calm her—she had been personally affronted, 'that woman' had acted deliberately to spite her. And I had to admit I was surprised that the school had gone against my wishes. Why fill in forms if they're going to be ignored? But to Jennie it was more than that; it was part of a campaign being waged against her.

Poor Angie, on the other hand, was forced to spend a wasted day hanging around the casualty unit, queuing for hours amongst the ill and dying arrayed on stretchers knee-deep in the corridors, with a moaning Scarlett at her most dramatic. The school had been lucky to catch Angie at home—

mostly she worked down at Ken's yard—so on top of everything else, she missed a day's work. I couldn't apologize enough.

But how had it happened?

'God knows,' said Angie, 'but you could have knocked me down when that crazy Gordon woman came over here with her sleeves rolled up and accused me of muscling in on her act . . .'

Poor Angie hadn't had much option, she'd merely done what was asked of her. She'd picked up Scarlett and dragged the child from hospital department to department, from X-ray to bandaging, and from shop to canteen so that my daughter could stuff down Mars bars and Coke.

'I've never been yelled at like that in my life,' said Angie, 'and it came completely out of the blue. I'll tell you something for nothing, that nutter ought to be back in hospital where she belongs.'

'She's not so bad, but she does get these bees in her bonnet and she won't stop to think before she explodes . . .'

'That's a bloody understatement! You didn't hear what she said. She can keep her frigging pool and her obnoxiously designed garden, she can keep them and boil her head.'

*　　　*　　　*

I had to find out what had gone so wrong. Why did the school contact Angie? 'Did they say anything to you, Scarlett? Didn't you tell them to call Jennie?'

Scarlett shook her head guiltily.

Oh no—was the child stupid? 'You told them to call Angie? Is that what happened? Why? *Why would you do that?*'

244

'Because I hate going to Jennie's,' Scarlett quietly admitted. 'And because I didn't want her fussing round me all day, flapping and being bossy. And she'd have taken Poppy from school to come with us and I didn't want Poppy fighting over the comics and always needing the loo. Angie was much, much better. She gets things done, like you do. She's sensible.'

This put the cat among the pigeons.

'It's not my fault, Mum, and you can't blame me. How was I to know Jennie would crack? Why does she get like this anyway? She's always shouting or crying. You'd think she'd be pleased to get out of the drag of being bored and sweaty all day in that hospital.'

'I know, Scarlett, and I do understand. It's difficult for you and it's not your fault.'

So the gaffe was Scarlett's doing.

But what reasons could I give Jennie?

'Scarlett felt she'd be putting on you too much,' I said, confronted by Jennie's mournful face.

She stared, open-mouthed. *'Putting on me?* What does she mean? She knows she would never be putting on me.'

'Oh Jennie,' I said, trying to pass it off, 'you know what kids can be like. They get these ideas in their heads.'

She stood square on and accused me as if I'd been caught at some heinous crime. 'It was you, wasn't it, Martha? You must have altered the form. You changed it because you don't trust me . . . You've been listening to what people round here are saying.'

'Jennie, that's stupid.'

'Well, someone told the school to call Angie.

Her name didn't drop out of nowhere.'

'Just listen to us both.' I laughed—a brittle, nervous sound. 'What the hell are we going on about? It's so bloody trivial. Scarlett's OK, so what happened is really no big deal.'

'It might not be important to you,' said Jennie at her most woeful, 'but it is to me and you ought to know that.'

*   *   *

She had such a capacity for making enemies. After the loud music incident Sadie loathed her. Jennie had frightened her out of her skin that day and Sadie knew she'd overreacted, but as she told me later, 'You don't know what that woman is capable of. And I've heard some pretty odd rumours.' Even Hilary Wainwright, who had befriended Jennie and defended her, was stiff and offhand with her now, seeing her as a troublemaker and a loser.

Dear God, I was glad to be out all day and away from this petty feuding. Men don't seem to get caught up in these kinds of tangles: this spiteful, emotional stuff that is usually best forgotten.

But Jennie would not let things go. She kept on about Sadie's opera, how loud and disturbing it had been, how thoughtless and selfish Sadie was . . . but she couldn't hear herself ranting on, which to me was more aggravating than any loud music could be.

And the business of Angie picking up Scarlett—on and on she went. 'They knew I was responsible, they knew I had your key, they knew I had your work number . . .'

'Jennie, please leave it,' I begged. 'It all

happened so fast they didn't have time to think straight and when Scarlett came out with Angie's number . . .'

But the damage was done. Jennie, mortally wounded and at her most volatile, had stormed over to Angie's house and accused her of undermining her role and slandering her in public. And instead of merely shouting 'sod off', Angie, who was used to dealing with builders, counter-attacked with a string of obscenities and told Jennie to get back to the bin.

'I've never liked her,' Angie said darkly. 'There's something about her I just can't stand . . . "something of the night", as that Widdecombe woman so rightly said.'

Hopelessly, I tried to defend her. 'She's insecure, very low self-esteem . . .'

'Balls, you should have seen her esteem when she came over here. Inflated, I'd call it. Near to bursting. Martha, you just can't talk to people like that.'

'She does tend to dramatize . . .'

'Well, she's no right to. Going round insulting people. You might let her get away with it, but not me. No way. And I thought there was some talk at one time of her messing around with Sam?'

'That was a misunderstanding.'

'And then she slagged you off in public.'

'I said she could be difficult.'

'And then she tries to top herself.'

'She was desperately unhappy.'

'Well,' said Angie, unconvinced, 'what I said still stands. She should go and get the appropriate treatment and stop flinging her weight about. Nobody round here can stand her.'

247

And that, sadly, was true. Apart from Tina Gallagher, who Jennie had palled up with, at last. But the fact that she had managed to upset everyone else in the Close, when she so wanted to be liked and was so put out if she wasn't, was tragic. She who had actually built a swimming pool in her garden to attract not just me but 'friends'. Lately, the pool was hardly used; partly because of the wetter summers and partly because no-one wanted to sit in Jennie's pristine, orderly garden, never knowing what her mood would be.

'Stub out a fag in an ashtray and you're made to feel like a rapist,' Sadie said to me once. 'Let alone if you forget and drop it on the grass. And they're so fixated about cleanliness—that damn footwash . . . the shower if you've got a tad of oil on . . . You wonder if you ought to be swimming at all if you're on, and I'm always terrified some poor kid is going to piss and be caught. Pissing in that pool would be a drawing and quartering offence.'

Such a shame for Jennie, and all the more reason why she should get herself out and about. She went to her pottery once a week but that was hardly stretching herself, and she insisted on meeting me for lunch whenever I was free.

What she did with the rest of her time was beyond me, and when I asked she passed it off with 'I'll get round to it when I'm ready. Give me time, don't nag.' I guessed she was frightened to take on anything too ambitious in case she failed, or was rejected. Anyway, I told myself as I wrestled with my guilt, how could I be expected to look after her when my own life was in such a sodding mess? How could I take on anything else? What was the point in looking for trouble?

*   *   *

I just couldn't stand the not knowing. Every time I sat alone, I wondered if I should come straight out and ask him, breaking a silence that was becoming intolerable. Sometimes I actually got as far as opening my mouth and forming the words, but then I clammed up and was left staring daftly. If Sam denied it I wouldn't believe him, but if he admitted it—what then?

After all the promises I'd made to myself. Convincing myself I was stronger now. That I didn't need him any more.

And I certainly could do without living with such humiliating insecurity. It was like being tortured, day after day.

I was reaching the end of my tether.

*   *   *

How long could I go around pretending that nothing was happening?

CHAPTER TWENTY-FIVE

Jennie

How long could I go around pretending that nothing was happening?

*   *   *   .

Another Christmas came and went. Scarlett was given the role of Mary in the school nativity play, while Poppy was relegated to shepherd and spent the whole time behind the manger. She had no lines. She brought no gifts. She appeared to be in charge of the lambs. At the Frazers' traditional Christmas Eve party Graham was the life and soul, while I was virtually ostracized by three of the women of the Close.

Graham said to take no notice. 'If they don't know any better, ignore them.'

I made out I couldn't care less, but inside I felt mangled up. This was so unjustified—how come I was always picked on? I made an effort to be warm towards them—Hilary, Sadie and Angie Ford—but they returned such a frosty politeness that I thought: let them go to hell.

Martha and I were good friends again, so why should I care about three losers who were green because of our closeness? We had managed the almost impossible—years without major trauma. And most of those years I had spent on a high, assuming this bliss would go on for ever. But everyone noticed the change in Martha; everyone said how peaky Martha was looking compared with her usual bouncy self. Of course, I suspected this was Sam's doing. I waited for her to confide in me, but was disappointed when she didn't. I knew why, I understood her reasons: it would take time for her to trust me again after all the hassle I'd caused her. This hurt, but how could I blame her? I wasn't sure if I trusted myself.

I had seen Sam and Tina with my own eyes, I had the proof and I hadn't gone seeking it. So why had nobody else got wise? Tina's comings and goings had always been unpredictable because her work for the tourist board involved dashing about all over the county, but these days her Citroën was rarely in her drive.

Did the philandering Carl suspect what was happening?

Was he keeping quiet for his own protection?

Tina's calls to my house were regular, for a chat and coffee before she set off. She came to keep tabs on Martha, knowing that every move Martha made was known by me because of her children. It was me who collected them both from school and kept them at my house until Martha returned, and if either of them was too ill for school, she would hand them over the fence, still warm in their pyjamas.

Oh yes, Tina was cunning. And cunning was something I knew all about.

The time came when I had to speak out, but I was so anxious about making things worse. Would threatening Sam with exposure be enough to end this worrying affair? Indignant on Martha's behalf, and resentful, I'd watched them both at the last Christmas party. They'd been bold enough to smooch together. There were even whispered conversations . . . a ploy to convince any doubters that this fooling around meant nothing. Just casual fun. What a nerve.

That night Martha was abnormally quiet. Tired, she said, working too hard. And although she often went over the top with her make-up and outfits at parties, this time she'd outdone herself—she glittered like the Christmas tree. Brittle and bright, she flashed on and off as colourfully as the fairy lights, and I worried that she might snap at any

251

moment and rush from the house in tears . . . But that was my behaviour, not hers.

I heard Sam laugh. I saw him grinning impishly like a schoolboy. I wanted to reach out and slap his face, as he had once slapped mine. How could he torment Martha like this?

Every time Tina came round for coffee and every time I failed to confront her, I felt an acute sense of failure, of weakness, and I became determined to face the truth—next time. I would hang back nervously, waiting for the next opportunity, but there were no right moments for such revelations. I'd kept quiet for too long, hoping, stupidly, that this dark cloud would blow over, or that any of the unlikely miracles I had been praying so desperately for would occur.

Next time Tina called, I'd be ready.

*   *   *

'You say you can't trust Carl and I wondered, have you ever been unfaithful, Tina?'

The merest flicker of shock gave her quick denial away. There was no change of expression when she said, 'No, and I wouldn't. *The pain it causes . . .*'

I resisted the urge to leave it at that—for Martha's sake I had to go on. My palms were sweating and my mouth was dry, but above all I wanted to hide in bed. 'Tina, I'm sorry, but I know for a fact you are seeing Sam Frazer. And it's been going on for some time.'

Her eyes flicked to my face and away before she said, 'That's not true.'

I moved from cooker to cupboard to bin and

252

then round to the table, trying to carry out everyday tasks—preparing the supper, stirring the casserole. Half for us, half for the Frazers, and there might be enough left to freeze.

She sat at the head of the table as usual, smug and in a wide-shouldered outfit I'd always disliked. The fact that it was scarlet I considered appropriate, and the trainers today were a shimmering pink. I couldn't face her, I had to keep moving.

'But I've seen you together,' I said, squirming, peering into my bayleaf jar. 'Twice, actually.'

Suddenly we were enemies. 'You don't miss a bloody thing, do you, Jennie? Peering through those sodding nets.' And I was surprised to hear such a firm voice from out of the mouth of the condemned.

'You admit it, then?'

'*Admit?* What does that mean? How do you see yourself, Jennie? Some arbiter of other people's morals?'

'I see myself as Martha's friend,' I said nobly.

She shot me a sly look. '*Friend?* Oh, that's an interesting one, not quite the word I would have chosen.'

This was awful. No, worse than awful. I'd been dreading this encounter and now I was on the receiving end. I'd never imagined that. I was made fragile when I needed my strength.

'I don't mean to judge you, I wouldn't judge anyone, but it does seem rather cruel.'

'Cruel?' she said through a sickly smile. 'So how about you, Jennie? Are you rather cruel, or off your head?'

I couldn't find the words. In the end I stuttered,

'*We're not talking about me . . .*'

'Oh? That's convenient, isn't it? So you are conducting this investigation from an impartial position, is that it? You are not, and you never have been, sexually involved with anyone else's spouse?'

It appalled me to think that this woman might know about my feelings for Martha. She must know, *she did know* . . . 'Sam must have told you.'

'No, Jennie, Martha told me. I walked into her house the moment after you'd damn nearly raped her and she opened her heart to her friend, as you do. At least I make sure that my passions are reciprocated.' The viciousness of her last remark stabbed me and stained me like a rusty dagger.

I asked softly, '*So who else knows?*'

'Who doesn't would be easier to answer. I doubt that Martha was particularly discreet, repulsed as she was by the whole sordid business.'

My world might be collapsing around me but I wasn't about to accept defeat. 'That happened years ago. What you're doing is happening now . . .'

'So what do you propose to do, Jennie? Go next door and tell precious Martha? She wouldn't thank you for that, you bitch.'

My head spun, I felt drunk. 'I might do that, yes.'

When she folded her arms, her shoulder pads bulged. I hadn't noticed before what a cold, spiky person she was, or the depth of that hard veneer. 'And then what d'you imagine would happen? What the hell would you gain from doing that?'

'Sam would be forced to choose.'

'He might choose me.'

I managed to give her a scornful smile. 'Never. Not in a million years. This isn't Sam's first time, you know, he's renowned for his weakness for silly

254

women who throw themselves at his feet. He's gone back to Martha every time. He's just that sort of man. You should know, you've got Carl.'

'So should you, from what Angie says. You didn't turn Sam down when he carried you, drunk, into the bedroom, not that many moons ago.'

I went weak with shame. 'That wasn't true.'

Tina laughed, not pleasantly. 'That's the trouble with you, isn't it, Jennie? Nobody knows if it's lies, attention-seeking or just straightforward madness. So I wonder if Martha would really believe you if you told her about me and Sam, especially when we'd both deny it. I wonder who she would rather believe. She might think you were up to your old tricks again. Trying to get rid of Sam, maybe, so you could take his place in her bed.'

'You're foul.'

'You said it.'

'It's nothing like that . . .'

Tina sat back while I took the chair opposite, hunched with the cheese-grater still in my hand. And I felt grated, every piece of me as spindly and wrinkly as the spirals that hung from the metal holes. I must have looked ashen, while Tina, I noticed, had a bright orange tinge to her face and a line faded round her neck where the make-up stopped.

A fake tan. Pathetic.

'Come on, Jennie, be honest,' she said, 'what did you expect me to say? Did you think I would promise to give Sam up out of fear that you'd go and tell Martha? Are you honestly that naive? I can't believe it—nobody is. Sam knows all about you and Martha. Since that abject letter you sent, she's told him everything, you know that. So what

255

the hell did you hope to achieve by threatening me this morning?'

'I'm going to achieve what's best for Martha,' I managed to croak through her sneers. 'I'm still going to tell her, and I'm sure that if Sam finds out, he'll drop you like a stone.'

'But you're not sure about that,' said Tina.

'I'm pretty certain.'

'Going on past experience?'

'Yes, that's right.'

'Well, please bear in mind that Sam and I have been screwing on the side for more than four years. I wonder if any other women have lasted that long in Sam's life?'

My mouth was parched. *'That long?'*

'So you have to agree this is something different?'

'I suppose so, yes.'

'And that my influence over Sam is more than just a passing passion?'

I plucked at the shavings of loose cheese and gave a toneless 'Yes.'

'Let me put it like this,' crowed Tina. 'Let's be fair. If Martha was to find out from you about Sam and me, Graham would also have to be told about that rather unpleasant business that took place in Martha's bed. That would be one distressing result. No, wait, there'd be others: Sam would leave Martha; Martha could not keep up that house no matter how many hours she worked; and Martha,' Tina finished sweetly, 'would move away from the Close.'

'But why this deceit? You don't want Sam,' I exclaimed, 'else why don't you come clean, split and divorce? Why don't you and Sam set up house

256

together?'

'Because this arrangement suits us both. It's as simple as that,' said Tina.

'And what happens if Martha finds out for herself?'

'We'll deal with that when the time comes,' she said with patient malice. 'But I warn you, Jennie, if by some chance Martha did find out, I'd insist on dates, times and places before I'd believe it wasn't you that went creeping to her with your wretched tales. So all I can say is, it's in your own interest to keep your mouth shut and make sure Martha remains in blissful ignorance.'

'You are disgusting.'

She was remote, self-possessed. Why could I never argue like that?

'And there are words for you, too, Jennie,' she said, 'but personally I'd rather not use them.'

*   *   *

Life without Martha would leave me deaf, blind and crippled.

And so I was grateful for her lack of trust. If she'd chosen to share her anxieties with me, I couldn't have kept the secret, not even for self-protection. But now I was a party to the deceit, disloyal to the person I loved best.

Maybe I was being kinder? Perhaps she would rather not know. And I tried to console myself with these thoughts while I watched her suffering in traitorous silence. All I could hope for was that the affair would fizzle out by itself.

But naturally Tina told Sam about our hostile conversation and his attitude towards me grew more aggressive. When Sam was around I was made unwelcome, and I wondered if Martha noticed the change from his normal indifference.

'Sometimes, Jennie,' Sam said to me, arriving home one evening, 'I have to wonder if you've got a home to go to.'

I jumped up. 'I'm just off.'

'Sit down! Take no notice of Sam,' said Martha, laughing. 'You know him well enough by now to ignore his appalling rudeness.' And she gave her husband a strict, cross look.

But he carried on. 'Doesn't old Graham feel abandoned sometimes?'

The silence was uncomfortable until Martha broke it cheerfully. 'Graham's not home yet. Get yourself a drink and stop interfering. Jennie and I won't say no either. The kids are busy playing outside, so there's no need to disturb them yet.'

'I have to go anyway,' I said. 'Things to do . . .'

'Never a dull moment, is there, Jennie?' Sam said, his mouth straight and tight. 'The rich tapestry of life and all that.'

Not knowing how to respond to this, I pretended not to hear. I collected the children and fled.

He was not only laughing.

He was threatening me.

God, what did Martha see in that man? Why did she need him in the way she did? Was it just sex? Surely she would have no trouble finding someone else for that. But then she would move in with that someone else . . . *no, no* . . . that was intolerable, *she must stay here with Sam.*

I sat on the edge of my bed, clenching and unclenching my hands. My whole world had turned unfriendly. All I had left was Martha, but then all I needed was Martha . . .

*   *   *

'But you have your children,' said Mr Singh, as if I needed reminding. 'And your husband. These are realities while your make-believe Martha world is delusion, an intoxicating vision you won't let go of.'

He was right. At the end of the day, the one who would be there for me was Graham. But not if I'd been misbehaving, not if I was still misbehaving.

'Why not give it a try?' said Singh, offering a rare piece of advice instead of leaning back with his eyes closed.

I was astounded. 'What? *Risk telling Graham what I've told you?*'

'You don't think he's big enough to take it?'

I blew my nose violently. 'I know he's not. Graham is normal, Mr Singh.' I was annoyed at being forced to explain. Wasn't it obvious? The doctor should know that by now. 'An ordinary man who likes black and white houses, reads biographies, loves cricket, plays golf, votes Tory, watches *Ground Force,* and considers any eccentric behaviour to be not just unnecessary but ridiculous. If he chose a dog it would be a spaniel. He's embarrassed to watch Tina Turner.'

'Ah, well,' sighed Mr Singh, 'you know him better than I do and it's up to you, of course. But you're in a virtual blackmail situation. Life would be so much simpler for you if you . . .'

I groaned aloud. 'There's no question of me confiding in Graham, so talking about it is a waste of time.' I was impatient, eager to be gone. Mr Singh and the hours I had spent with him—

259

expensive hours, paid for by me—had achieved nothing at all. I wanted comfort like a naughty child, but Mr Singh wouldn't give it.

*   *   *

I must be very careful now or I knew I was going to be hurt.

CHAPTER TWENTY-SIX

Martha

I must be very careful now or I knew I was going to be hurt.

*   *   *

The killer question was—how long? And it haunted me day and night. How long could Sam and I play mind games? The kind of games favoured by Jennie back in those dreadful times, during those years of trauma. I started to lean on her heavily now, but I wished so much I could trust her in the doting way she trusted me.

*   *   *

Alas, Jennie was due for one of her ghastly confessions.

I was so tuned to it, I could smell it coming.

'But don't say anything you'll be sorry about afterwards,' I reminded her for the tenth time. 'I

260

know you have this compulsion, this confession thing which you have to obey, but please try to be selective.'

Her mood-change was instant. 'You're not interested. You find me boring.'

Jennie told so many conflicting stories, depending on who she was trying to impress, that I'd stopped taking much notice when she launched into one of her make-believe modes. And her fantasy tales ranged over all subjects—from her childhood to her wedding day, from her 'big house with grounds' to her meeting with Graham. This time, she warned me, she'd be telling the truth and it was how Graham and she had first found each other.

'Jennie, I don't find you boring, however you tell it, whether you and Graham met in the loos of the biscuit factory, or over the counter at the bank, and then there's the picnic version. I don't care where you met him; I'm just relieved that you did. You mustn't feel you have to justify everything you say, even lies, to me.'

'I just worry I would be betraying Graham.'

'Well then, that's easy, let's change the subject.'

The weather was icy and I was driving. The car was fugged up with throat-parching heat. Every so often Jennie leaned forward and wiped the screen with her glove. We were on our way back from the Marks superstore, making the most of a precious hour free of kids. We had reached the blissful stage of being able to leave them to play in the Close, just so long as they had a house to go to and Angie promised to keep a lookout. It was a Saturday morning: they could watch TV or play on the green with the other kids, in safety. Most likely, as it was

261

cold, they'd all be huddled up in our house, eating crisps and watching cartoons.

Poppy and Scarlett were nine years old; the boys were only six, not really old enough to be left alone, but the Close was a very safe place. There were lots of responsible adults around and all well known to the kids. Although the prestigious Close was surrounded by a sink estate, we'd never had any trouble from there. We wouldn't be gone longer than an hour. Graham was playing golf. And God only knew what Sam was up to; I'd stopped asking.

Jennie went on, sounding ominous. 'I've never told anyone this before.'

I groaned. 'So are you sure you want me to know?' I wasn't remotely interested in what had happened in Jennie's past—or in anyone's past for that matter. Today was all that counted.

'I have to tell you. *I need you to know.*'

'But maybe I'd rather not hear it.'

I was concentrating hard on the road. They'd given black-ice warnings and I never understood what black ice looked like. The whole road could be sheer black ice, for all I knew. I wished she would shut up or get it over with quickly. I couldn't wait to get home in the warm and make a huge mug of hot chocolate, with a flake. Or two. Or three.

'Graham and I met in a car.'

'That's a new one,' I said, from a distance.

I gave her a glance, just a quick one. The driver behind was becoming frantic, infuriated by my crawling pace, and I feared road rage might be imminent. Should I accelerate and throw caution to the wind? The bastard behind clearly thought so. Maybe he knew the road better than me. Jennie said that there had been times, hair-raising times she could never forget, when she'd been coerced into driving at breakneck speed to pacify the pig in the car behind. Risking her life to please some turd.

It happens. I'd done it.

But Graham, when pushed, would drive slower, while Sam gestured obscenely out of the window. And I wondered how much was given away by a person's reaction to driving pressures.

'*He was kerb crawling,*' Jennie said.

I started with amazement. Then I laughed. 'A habit of his you forgot to mention.'

It took time to register that this was no joke. My woollen gloves itched my fingers. I took the tip of one in my mouth and struggled with a hairy tongue to tug the damn thing off. I prickled all over. Jennie's imagination was wild. What the hell was she going to say next?

'Light me a fag, will you, Jennie? Front pocket of my bag.'

'I know where you keep your fags,' she said crossly, annoyed by the interruption.

Did she know what kerb crawling meant? Perhaps not. Maybe she'd misunderstood the term? She had been known to be silly like that. 'What do you mean, kerb crawling?'

The hand that passed my cigarette shook. 'Come off it, Martha.'

'You mean, kerb crawling to pick up a pro?'

'Yes,' she said firmly, 'that's what I mean.'

Graham? That was laughable. That quiet, gentle, studious man—a manager with Essex Water —whose sandals and brown socks heralded the first chirpings of summer? Whose knitted scarf signified

263

winter?

'Jennie, shut up. This is outrageous.'

'He picked me up,' she said. 'That's how we met.'

'And I'm Cherie Blair.' I refused to indulge her.

She hissed her annoyance. It looked as if it might snow at any moment; the black wires of the power lines cut into a greying sky. I opened the window a fraction. The air was so cold it seared the throat, but I needed to puff out my smoke.

'He picked me up and I was glad I'd found another punter.'

'OK, Jennie, OK . . . if that's what you want me to believe for some strange reasons of your own . . .'

'I was lonely. So was he. We'd both decided we'd not find anyone, nobody could love us. We were both looking for comfort.'

'OK, Jennie, so that's how you met?' I didn't need to look at her. I knew she would have her eyes closed in the way she did when she got intense. She'd be missing the squiggles on my kitchen table which she liked to trace when she got emotional.

Damn damn damn. What sort of reaction did she expect? The only natural one was humour, but I knew she wouldn't appreciate that from the depths of her special slough of despond. If I took this too lightly I would wound poor Jennie, but what I couldn't understand was the way some people guarded their secrets, nursed them, wrapped them and hid them away—I could never do that. Sam might call me a prima donna, and yes, when I had pain I let everyone know, so it didn't assume such an enormous significance or turn into a closeted skeleton.

264

So why not tell the world about Sam?

That was different. Perhaps I'd been wrong? If I'd shared it, maybe I wouldn't be feeling so hellishly ill with it all.

'I got in his old blue Metro and we drove to the car park beside the bakery. I usually took the punters there.'

I kept my eyes glued to the road. Was Jennie telling me she was a whore? And did she really think I'd believe her? *'Usually?* So this was not a one-off?'

'I was in business on Formby Road for six weeks.'

She sounded sincere, but she was expert at lying and fantasizing—I knew that to my cost. I'd play along just to humour her. 'Good God, the risk, *you could have been killed.'*

'At the time I wouldn't have cared.'

Could this be true? Could all that crap about being a virgin when she married Graham be a lie? All that high-handed moral stuff . . . I was so stunned by what she was saying that I couldn't have been more shocked if she'd said she'd once been a serial killer. It was too fantastic for words. This wasn't like Jennie, this was far too extreme.

'You see these,' Jennie went on calmly, as we passed a row of Thirties houses with red brick porches and bay windows. The lights from within made patterns on the otherwise colourless scene. 'See how they look, so warm and inviting . . . all the happiness in the world behind those safe, closed doors.'

'But how wrong you'd be if you believed that,' I told her firmly.

'Especially when it's cold out here. But that's

265

what other people's lives looked like to me then. When I saw couples holding hands, some with babies in prams . . . and in the shops when I watched busy women filling their trolleys and rushing off to somewhere special, while I shopped for just Stella and me—liver, cabbage, tinned rice pudding—and I knew my trolley was missing something, something I wanted so much for myself.'

'I know what you mean. We've all felt like that . . .'

'No, Martha! You haven't! Not like me!'

There was no point in interrupting, even to help her along. Jennie was determined to hold centre stage and from there she stumbled and blundered on, although her words were so strained, her heart was so pained for her own sake that I wished she would stop, whatever the truth.

'I was twenty-one,' she said, 'and had never had a boyfriend. When I'd finished work, I'd get something for tea and go straight home to cook it. Then when Stella was watching her soaps I'd say I was going out for a walk, just to get out of that flat for a while and spend some time on my own. She didn't like it. But walking the streets alone in the evenings—and I even sat down in pubs—made me feel more lonely and cut off from the world. The only people who talked to me were dirty old men or yobs who would shout unkind remarks.'

I could hardly bear to hear this. That she'd been lonely I could easily believe. 'What about the cinema, with someone from work?'

'I didn't get on with the girls at the bank. It was cliquey. They all had social lives, I knew that, it was all they talked about. They were friendly but we had nothing in common.'

'Like that Back To Work course at the tech?'

'I don't seem to get on well with women.'

'Well, that's no tragedy . . .'

'Don't patronize me!'

'Damn you, I'm not. I'm agreeing.'

'So I picked up my first punter by accident. I didn't know he was looking for sex. He pulled over, really chatty and nice, not bad looking, though his face was a bit pitted. He bought me a drink and for half an hour I could pretend I had a lover, too. Did I want to go for a ride in his car? God, I was so naive! Incredible, when I look back, but I went for fear of upsetting him—what if he wanted to see me again?'

'The bastard.'

'No, he was kind, he was patient. It was only when he drove me back and gave me a twenty-pound note that I realized what it had been about; I realized that I had a new name. And he wasn't going to ask me out, not ever.'

'But you, a virgin, and so prissy, you must have been horrified to do that with him after only half an hour. You're so disgusted by bodily functions . . .'

'It was vile. I'd never seen a man's prick before, only children's on beaches. I couldn't believe the size of the thing, and the colour, all veins and wrinkles. I was so glad I didn't have one. I closed my eyes and I thought: if this is what I must do to keep from feeling so lonely, then I'll do it, I don't care.'

This was just too fantastic, but something about how she told it rang true. And yet I couldn't be certain this wasn't one of her games, a bid for sympathy or a cry for attention. 'Poor you. No

267

wonder you're so anti-sex—having used your body for barter. Poor you, poor Graham.'

She didn't even hear me. Jennie's wounds went deep, much deeper than I'd realized. She was still reliving the whole ghastly mess while I crept round icy roundabouts, turned on the wipers to clear the sleet and wondered if my lights should be on. The people we passed were rubbing their hands and turning their coat collars up. If only we could get home. If only we could have this bizarre conversation in front of a fire with a bottle of wine. I couldn't give the responses she needed with my mind on so many other things.

'We were like computer parts,' Jennie said, 'both products of sterile environments. He'd led much the same sort of life, huddled round *Coronation Street* with Howard and Ruth, joining in with their social life . . . garden centres . . . church fêtes . . . coffee mornings. A full-grown man, and that was his life. Howard couldn't drive, you see, so Graham bought the Metro. He even drove his father to work rather than let him go by bus.'

'No wonder he's so shy,' I said.

'We both were. That was the trouble. We didn't know how to make friends, we'd never acquired the knack.'

I gave her a quick look of affection. 'Oh Jennie, you're both so much better now!'

She shrugged her shoulders. She gave a sigh. 'That's because we're together. Finding each other was a miracle, we needed each other so badly. But one thing we agreed on and that was we'd never have sex till we married. I hated it and he was ashamed that his first experiences had been paid for. I didn't want him to see me as some slag who did it for money.'

'Well, no. Definitely not.' Sod it, sod it. Why did nothing go smoothly for Jennie like it did for most other people? She was always being cheated or disappointed or misunderstood.

'So keeping sex for Friday nights seemed like a sensible thing to do.'

'It never got any easier?'

'It's something we don't talk about. We don't want to bring that old stuff back.' She paused for a while, eyes still tightly closed. The sleet was coming down more thickly—thank God, we were almost home. I could have murdered a brandy. Jennie had finally managed to convince me and I knew no-one more cynical than me. 'If Graham knew I'd told you, he would kill me.'

'You don't have to worry about that.'

'But you went and told Tina Gallagher about what happened between us that day.'

This sudden statement was a slap in the face. It wasn't expected. I was guilty as hell and there was a moment's embarrassed silence. 'How do you know that?'

'I don't know for certain. I guessed it.'

What did it matter how Jennie knew, it was my betrayal that I had to put right. 'Tina caught me at a terrible time,' I told her, at my most coaxing. 'And I'm sorry I told her, I regret it now. I don't normally go around shooting my mouth off over tricky situations, but that was an extreme. You can trust me as far as Graham goes and I'm glad you're able to talk about it with me. But I think you should have told Mr Singh.'

She was angry, as if I'd thrown back a precious gift, or suggested she give it to somebody else.

'Why would I tell Singh? What good would that do?'

'It could be that these awful experiences triggered off your fixation on me.'

'So if I'd confided in Singh I'd be able to leave this obsession behind?'

'It's possible, I suppose. Your childhood and all those repercussions, well, they're not things you can look back and laugh at, are they?'

At last we drove up to the house. I slumped over the steering wheel, gasping with relief. My neck muscles had seized up like crane chains.

'*You hate me now, don't you?*' cried Jennie.

Oh no, not that old chestnut. She had returned to her manipulative ways. I sat back in the driving seat, physically and mentally crippled. 'I'm not even going to answer that.'

'You're disgusted. Tell me. For Christ's sake, be honest.'

'*Jennie!*' I shouted. 'If you give me so little credence, it's hard to know what you see in me. I'm not an insensitive cretin, dammit.'

'*I'm sorry, so sorry,*' she said quickly. 'I'm just so afraid you'll find me disgusting.'

I fixed my eye on her fiercely. 'If we don't get inside this sodding house, get the bags in and get these boots off in one minute from now, I will never speak to you ever again,' I yelled. 'So let's go. Let's do it. And, Jennie, I really couldn't give a toss about what anyone's been or is likely to be. I see you as you are now, my friend, and I need you. So leave it there, will you, just stop.'

*   *   *

It was so cold that winter the fire couldn't warm me.

CHAPTER TWENTY-SEVEN

Jennie

It was so cold that winter the fire couldn't warm me.

*   *   *

'It never used to be like this,' said Graham.

We sat in the hotel dining room overlooking a cheerless grey sea, the colour of the morning porridge that Poppy refused to eat.

'Jennie, it can't have been like this then, or I'd never have . . .'

'It must have been something like this,' I snapped crossly, trying to attract the attention of a sour-faced waitress. 'They can't have rebuilt the whole place since the Seventies.'

'It looks the same, it smells the same, but in those days it wasn't crammed full of crusties.'

The dining room bristled with walking sticks, electric wheelchairs and tweed, lace-up shoes, and moustaches both male and female. An Agatha Christie haunt of brown Windsor soup, polish and sprouts.

I tried to be forgiving; Graham meant well, he usually did. Perhaps Sea World would be open today. 'It must be the time of year, normal people don't come to Llandudno in March.'

But this March felt more like January. Arctic winds cut the tops off the waves and hurled them up through the streets of the town and on to the Welsh hillsides which were hidden in sheets of rain. Prepared for some blustery walking, I'd packed the fleeces, boots and anoraks, but nothing kept this weather at bay. It was Graham who had suggested this holiday alone, our first without the Frazers. He had happy memories of this place. 'Even with Howard and Ruth you could keep well ahead and pretend to be separate, make out you weren't with them.'

*   *   *

The Frazers were in the Austrian Tirol for ten days. They'd gone with Emma and Mark as usual, but this time the Harcourts went with them as well. Sadie of the arias, and Crispin, her antique-shop husband, along with their two serious teenage daughters. Sam and Crispin played squash together and they were both expert skiers. This was the first time that Graham and I had not been invited.

It'd all been explained to me kindly.

'Now I want to talk to you about this, Jennie, because I know how you're going to feel, and I do understand, whatever you say. But we can't always have holidays together just because it's become a ritual . . .'

'I know that,' I sobbed, feeling raw and despairing.

'You and Graham don't ski, but Sam learned when he was little and I used to go every winter from college. Fulpmes has some nursery slopes, but we're after the more difficult runs. Mark and

272

Emma have been there before and they say it's perfect for what we want. We reckon we're all pretty much the same standard and it's time Scarlett and Lawrence had a go.'

How could Martha do this to me? It was so plain they didn't want us. Her mind was made up, probably by Sam, and there was nothing I could do to change it. They had booked the trip before she told me. 'I always wanted my children to ski,' I told her bleakly.

More excuses came tumbling out one after the other. 'Scarlett and Lawrence will stay with the ski school; the Harcourt girls will be in charge. Now you just listen to me, Jennie: Poppy and Josh would hate that, being left all day with strangers, and you know that as well as I do.'

'So you're saying that mine couldn't cope.'

'Damn you, no, that's not what I mean. You're so determined to make this an issue. Your kids aren't like mine, that's all. Not worse, not better, but different. *And that's nice* . . . that's nothing to moan about. But I'm pretty sure they wouldn't enjoy skiing.'

'You might have let us decide about that.'

'And you and Graham would loathe it too, it's a very sociable night life.'

'How can you say that when we've never been?'

But Martha was determined. Nothing I said could move her. 'I can say that because I've been so often and because I know you both so bloody well. You would not enjoy the skiing and you would hate the way most things are done in groups. Not just groups, Jennie, but *lively groups, loud, drunken groups.* Imagine the *après-ski* and the sitting around one huge table. Communal eating, too. Come on,

273

admit it, that's your worst nightmare.'

And she even had the nerve to laugh.

'We could book separately and come anyway.'

'Certainly you could. But it would be a complete waste of money and I would not be prepared to give up my holiday to pander to you.'

'This was Sam's idea,' I said, 'wasn't it?'

'Now you're being paranoid. Why would Sam take that attitude?'

I knew the answer to that. 'Because he can't stand me, that's why.'

'Oh, nonsense,' said Martha crossly.

At least Sam had had the decency not to invite the Gallaghers. And I wondered how Tina felt, forced to endure ten days without him. I couldn't give up. I nagged on, I had to. 'I can stand the idea of Emma and Mark, but why did you ask the Harcourts? You know what Sadic thinks about me, surely you know how that makes me feel?'

'That wasn't my doing,' said Martha. 'Crispin was having a drink with Sam when they caught sight of the brochures. The Harcourts go skiing every year and it seemed a good idea to team up. And I have to admit that Jasmine and Clara will make the holiday easier for me. Built-in babysitters, and Scarlett adores them.'

'*But Sadie?*' I couldn't get over that.

'She's OK,' said Martha coolly.

'She's bitter, she's precious and she's a snob,' I retorted.

'That's Crispin's problem, not ours.'

'And she hates me,' I added. 'She lies.'

'Now you're being childish.'

'*But I'll miss you so much.*'

This cut no ice. 'What's stopping you and

274

Graham going away? Maybe that's what you need—time together. I've been thinking a lot about what you told me.'

'I wish I hadn't said anything now.'

But Martha ignored my sulks and suggested, 'You've never been away on your own as a family, so why not give it a whirl? Who knows, it could help.'

So we decided we'd go to Wales the day before the Frazers left.

*   *   *

I wished I hadn't confided in Martha. I had betrayed Graham in a way that was totally unacceptable, when I knew that even under torture he would never have done that to me.

At night I tossed and turned, anguishing over my stupidity, hoping to God she'd keep her promise and keep our secret to herself. *But what if Martha told Sam?* She'd blabbed before, she'd confided in Tina over what had happened between her and me in bed. I could never be totally certain she wouldn't give away Graham's and my closest secret.

What sick urge had made me tell her?

It was like I wanted to give myself to Martha.

If only I could take back what I'd said.

Graham would be destroyed if anyone found out what I had been saying about him. I owed him a damn sight more than this mean little betrayal. And I also owed him a holiday together, without the Frazers, in a place of his choosing.

Guilt made me agree to Llandudno because of his happy memories of it.

*   *   *

I was not the only one who suffered because of the Frazers' unkindness. When we told Poppy about Llandudno, she wore her closed-up, mulish expression. 'I don't want to go, it sounds horrid. If I can't go with Scarlett, I'm not going anywhere,' she said. And I saw how hurt Graham was by that.

Josh was the same. 'We won't have fun, we never do.'

Furiously, I shut them up. 'Don't talk like that. If you only knew how spoilt you sound. Of course we have fun as a family . . .'

'When?' asked Poppy defiantly. *'Go on—tell me when.'*

'I'm not getting into this, Poppy. If we can't enjoy ourselves on our own, it's a pretty poor situation to be in, don't you think?'

'It's true,' she said sulkily, 'and you know it.'

*   *   *

What Poppy said was proving to be right. We weren't having fun, it was purgatory. Ten years married and we'd never been away on our own before. It seemed extraordinary then and I hadn't realized what it would mean. We had no formula to follow. We had nobody to provide the ideas, or the laughs. When we were away we followed the others, and the children were happy to go off and play, leaving us adults to do our own thing. This time they hung around our feet all day, moaning and asking impossible questions like 'When's it going to stop raining?' and 'What do people usually do here?' and 'Why is everyone so smelly and

276

old?'

Perhaps we'd chosen the wrong hotel.

I hoped that Scarlett and Lawrence, in Austria, were giving Sam and Martha the same kind of hassle but I doubted it—it seemed unlikely. It wasn't a fair comparison because they'd be busy on the nursery slopes, not bored like my kids. But, reluctantly, I had to admit that if Martha's children found themselves here in this drab and lifeless place, they would manage to entertain themselves: they'd have made friends somehow, they'd be racing down the pier on skateboards, because that's just how they were.

The hotel meals were endless, catering for the toothless who had nothing better to do than eat and were happy to spend two hours at it. I cursed the fact that we'd paid full board.

Night after night we ended up, silent and staring, in the windowless TV room and the sense of failure was overwhelming. I knew, by the way he looked at me, that Graham felt it, too.

We were often in bed by nine.

We tried going to see a film.

We walked along the gale-torn front.

In our desperation we even booked for an old-time music hall. 'Stop moaning, Poppy, it's a new experience.' The blue-rinsed performers were all senior citizens, the singing was in northern club style, the costumes tatty, the MC crude, and the one act we might have enjoyed, the ventriloquist, was corny and raving drunk.

What a flop.

'I wonder what Lawrence is doing now,' said Josh. And I conjured up a picture of an ecstatically happy child dressed in red with a blue bobble hat,

277

flying over sunny snow on skis.

We spent a fortune on games and toys so that Poppy and Josh could play in their rooms while Graham and I, next door, lay for hours on our beds and read. I must be honest, I tried to read, but jealousy ate me up over Martha.

Walking was out of the question.

We made the children send postcards, but they refused to lie and say that they were having a wonderful time.

We spent hours driving around in the car, stopping at cafés for unwanted drinks, looking in bookshops and dragging the children around museums and country houses—the few that were open to the public. Nothing got into gear until Easter.

The children quarrelled constantly.

'I wish I could be adopted,' said Poppy, deep in misery, after we'd hauled ourselves around some bleak town centre in the rain for half an hour, searching for the toilets.

'That's unfair,' I said. 'You don't mean that.'

'Oh, I do,' said Poppy. 'When I get home, I'm going to ask Sam and Martha if they'll have me.'

No-one else was having a good time either, by the look on people's faces. What would Martha do if she found herself stuck here in the rain? All I conjured up was her looking around and saying, 'That's it, this is a dump—straight home!' But I couldn't go home early, face everyone and admit that we'd had a terrible time.

When I suggested moving on and finding somewhere more exciting—Alton Towers, for example—Graham said, 'We can't do that, we've paid to stay here. And anyway, that might suit the

278

children but how about us?'

'Well, London then,' I ventured.

'We can go to London any time we want.'

'But we don't go, do we? That's the point.'

Perhaps we'd be bored by ten days in London, get tired of it and be branded as a family tired of life.

'When can we go home?' Josh finally asked me, having been turned out of the TV room at ten o'clock in the morning so the cleaners could come in.

*   *   *

'It was fine,' we said, when people enquired. 'It was fine, but just too early. Another month would have made all the difference. You can't trust the weather in March.'

I didn't want to hear about the Frazers' skiing holiday although the children insisted on telling me and I had to look through the photographs and pretend to be thrilled. They said it all—just as I'd imagined—laughing people, pine trees, mountain cafés, *Glühwein* and horse-drawn sledges.

Our holiday seemed to have upset Poppy in more ways than one. When we got home she was scratchy, overtired, not keen on school—unusual for a child who had never wanted to miss a day and couldn't wait to leave every morning. The earache that she had suffered from when she was much younger came back in full force.

The doctor examined her but said he could find no reason for this. 'Could she be worrying about anything in particular?' he asked, before prescribing the drops.

279

What could Poppy, at her age, possibly be worrying about? She'd tell me if there was anything wrong. More likely it was proving difficult to leave her warm bed on these freezing cold mornings.

Easter came and went. This summer Scarlett and Poppy would be in their last term at junior school.

I still took charge of Martha's children after school, as before, but she was rather thoughtless to allow Scarlett to bring friends home and expect me to give them all tea. Harriet Birch, an unattractive child, given to whispering and nudging a lot, had terrible manners and was 'knowing'. That's how Stella would have put it, and it seemed just right for Harriet Birch. She was the sort to empty toy cupboards but not dream of putting anything back. She could commandeer a PlayStation for hours on end and even eat while pressing the buttons. What on earth did Scarlett see in her?

I was informed that Harriet was going through a difficult time, following her parents' traumatic divorce. That was what must have made her so sly. I tried to be more charitable towards her.

Poppy didn't take to her.

'Why don't you say she can't come?' Poppy asked me.

'It's not up to me,' I told her. 'Martha's working, and I suppose it's only an hour until she gets home and then they can go over to her house. If you don't want to join them, you can stay here.'

But she did want to join them; in fact, she made a point of staying at Martha's until Harriet left and I wondered if I should have kept her here after all. Harriet was Scarlett's guest and Poppy the uninvited intruder. But Scarlett didn't complain, so

I decided to let it go.

'Why don't you bring a friend home for a change?' I asked my daughter.

But Poppy just gave me a fierce look and I was sorry I had interfered.

'You worry too much,' said Graham, when I shared my misgivings with him. 'Scarlett and Poppy are still best friends and probably always will be. But Scarlett is such an extrovert she's bound to need other people, too. You only have to look at her mother.'

How lucky I was to have Graham—stable, steady, sensible Graham—while Martha, I knew, suffered so over Sam.

No, that affair had not fizzled out as I'd hoped.

Damn him, damn him. As far as I could tell by the comings and goings of Tina's car, Sam's affair with that woman was as intense as ever.

*   *   *

Perhaps we weren't quite so sad after all.

CHAPTER TWENTY-EIGHT

Martha

Perhaps we weren't quite so sad after all.

*   *   *

Sam was changing so subtly nobody else would notice. One evening he spent the whole night in, working on a robot for Lawrence. It was a construction-kit present from Mum last Christmas that we hadn't got around to fixing. And as they sprawled on the carpet together, their likeness—dark and wiry, tight curls, and with the same sexy grin—struck me with such quiet pride.

To stop me cracking up completely I'd taken up painting again: every lunatic whirl and loop, not to mention the thickness of the oils, managed to dilute the worst of my terrors, briefly, at any rate. While I was thrashing about on canvas Jennie was slapping her clay around. She'd stuck with her pottery sessions, a marvel for someone as inconstant as her, and what was even more remarkable was her natural flare for shape and texture. She'd even dabbled in casting small bronzes which she gave away to admirers at local exhibitions. She was commissioned to make a statue of a dolphin on a plinth for the new Sainsburys at Stamford Way, and after this confidence boost she started selling her stuff, first on a stall at the county show and then at serious craft shops. Her work was appealing, it sold like hot cakes; someone compared her to Barbara Hepworth. And when she signed a contract with Henry's Place, an arty-farty London gallery, she was more staggered than any of us.

*   *   *

'Who'd have thought she had it in her?' Sam said nastily, his tolerance of Jennie always fragile. He had no patience, he was even uneasy in her presence. She'd been right about Austria—Sam wouldn't have them. I'd pleaded their case, but in

282

vain. One more holiday with the Gordons and Sam swore he'd have a breakdown.

'I'm not bloody well giving in this time, Martha. Just cast your mind back . . . they're a drag and you can't have forgotten the moaning and groaning. Every single holiday for the last nine years has been ruined by that family one way or another, and I've had it up to here. No way. Forget it.'

But I hadn't lied when I'd told Jennie they'd hate it: skiing was just not their style—they'd wither and die in the cold, for a start. And, as it was a group activity holiday, too much of the Gordons' silly fussing would have affected us all. When I tried to argue the case for Poppy and Josh, Sam flipped.

I was so pathetically eager to please him that I didn't push the issue. I secretly hoped that the holiday might bring the two of us closer together, and without Jennie tagging along, without all the worry her kids would cause, this plan of mine would be more likely to work. I had to think of myself, for God's sake; my sanity was at stake here.

I think the holiday did help. Sam was back to his old self as we screamed with helpless laughter, tackled some satisfying runs and finished each day exhausted and aching, singing songs raucously and making love gently.

Reacquainting himself with his kids again was a slow process for Sam—he'd been withdrawn and distracted for so long—and if I'd believed in God I'd have flung myself on the ground to thank him. This time Sam's liaison had been so protracted that I honestly believed I'd lost him. The best thing for all of us now was to try and forget absolutely. I didn't want confessions, soul-searchings,

283

outpourings. I just didn't want to know.

*   *   *

When I told Sam Jennie's story about being on the game, he snorted, 'But you didn't believe that crap?'

'Not at first, of course not. We know what she's like, she'll say anything. But this was different. She gave so many details, and I couldn't see what she'd achieve by letting me in on all that.'

'Sympathy? Attention? She might have modified her behaviour for her own devious purposes, but she'd chop a leg off for one ounce of sympathy.'

'You've changed your tune,' I reminded him. 'There was a time, first when Stella died, and then later, after Jennie came out of that hospital, when you were all for forgiving and forgetting.'

'Time moves on,' said Sam. 'Jennie Gordon is seriously unbalanced and you should never take that one at face value.'

'But she wouldn't have included Graham in her lies, she's never sunk that low before. Imagine if it ever came out, if Graham heard what she'd said about him—a sad kerb-crawling sicko—that would be the end of them, surely.'

'You're a fool, Martha. When will you learn? She'd sell her own kids to keep you sweet.'

'She's a different person. She's so much better. Sometimes she's great to have around.'

'You're entitled to your opinion,' said Sam.

And I had noticed an uneasy atmosphere whenever Jennie was in our house. Sometimes it was embarrassingly hostile. 'She's got more on her mind than me these days, with all her successes, all this new acclaim.'

'That's a blind,' he said convincingly, 'and you're naive not to see that. Why do you give her the benefit of the doubt? That woman's got some hold on you, Martha. I mean, Graham screwing his arse off with whores, think about it, I ask you.'

'When I think of Jennie I always feel guilty.'

'You can't carry guilt with you for ever.'

How convenient for Sam to think that.

'You're the only one around here who's got any time for that cow,' he went on, determined to convince me. 'The Fords, the Gallaghers, the Wainwrights and the Harcourts, they all see her for what she is—but not you. She's dangerous, Martha, remember that.'

*   *   *

Dangerous? Rather a loaded word for poor, infatuated little Jennie, but Sam was right about everyone else. Hilary Wainwright called her disloyal, Angie Ford just couldn't abide her, to Tina she was a drama queen, and Sadie swore she was out for trouble. All this aggression directed at one small inadequate person, with a thin pixie face and cropped streaky hair. If only Jennie could get over her crush, the Gordons would do better to move. Even with the estate nearby, house prices were rising.

I still defended her whenever I could.

But even Scarlett was turning on Poppy. This dislike appeared to be catching like some virulent type of flu, and Lawrence had long ago asserted his preference for any child rather than Josh, who had still not outgrown his puppy fat. Josh was a fat child and he suffered as most fat kids do. In Josh's case it wasn't just genes: never without his bag of crisps, he ate like a horse, and when the chip van did its rounds he was mostly at the front of the queue.

Scarlett moaned, 'Poppy's forever round here, Mummy, and sometimes me and Harriet just want to be together, without her. It's not fair. She even keeps her things in my room. And why do we never go anywhere without her . . . the zoo, the flicks, Pizza Hut . . . Why do Poppy and Josh have to come?'

'Don't talk like that, Scarlett, you sound so horrible. Just because you've found a new friend doesn't mean you dump the other. And I hope you're not being unkind to poor Poppy.'

'I'm not, but she makes me sit beside her at school. She cribs my work. If she didn't use mine, she couldn't do hers.'

This didn't sound like Scarlett. But as usual I was too busy to concentrate on Scarlett's complicated social life, trying to do a hundred and one things before getting them off to school, scraping together the damn packed lunches, finding a clean shirt for Sam, and searching for my wretched shoes. Scarlett would have to sort things out. It would be a useful learning experience.

Maybe next time I saw her I'd discuss it with Jennie.

*   *   *

We did discuss it.

We got nowhere.

Jennie blamed my kids for everything. I was unsure how to react to this. *Could she be right? Were*

286

they being unkind? But before I could take any action, lo and behold she was up at the school, blabbing on to Mrs Forest that Scarlett and Harriet were bullying Poppy.

This was a first, and a serious one. We'd never really fallen out over the kids before and I didn't want it to happen now, but something made me so furious . . . I could put up with most things—I had proved that—but when she dragged my kids into the picture . . .

Jennie had acted slyly. She had interfered unnecessarily and I felt that this was an important matter the children should sort out for themselves.

What was more annoying, her behaviour solved nothing.

*   *   *

Jennie had no reason to come round at six. Scarlett and Lawrence came home on the bus now, they let themselves in, made a drink, grabbed a biscuit and started on their homework until I got back from work. They insisted that they would rather do this than wait for me at Jennie's.

The reason Jennie kept coming over was so that her children could play with mine. And, maddeningly, she would leave them at my house while she went back to start on the supper.

I was going to have it out with her. I had decided to get the kids round the table and have a grown-up, honest discussion about how everybody was feeling. I would put up with no nonsense from Poppy, the air must be cleared before this got out of hand. Everybody must have their say and be listened to and understood.

I had only just poured the wine and lit a relaxing fag when Sam burst in and shot Jennie a look. How could he be so appallingly rude? She couldn't have missed that face . . . I felt awful. *What the hell had got into him?*

'I'm just going, Sam,' she said meekly.

'Good,' said Sam. 'I can't wait.'

Was he joking? He must be! But hang on a minute—I had wanted to talk. It was essential we sort matters out. When Sam noisily poured a drink and pointedly ignored Jennie, I was forced to say, 'He's had a bad day and he doesn't mind showing it.'

'I have not had a bad day, actually, Martha, and I really don't need you to speak for me.'

'I'm making excuses for your rudeness, Sam,' I told him firmly. I'd have a real go at him afterwards. He didn't stay and finish his drink but slammed it down and went up for a shower, after first asking how long supper would be.

'When I get round to it,' I snapped.

'Well, I'm bloody hungry,' was his awful answer.

I felt for Jennie. I shrugged. 'What the hell has got into him?' She stayed silent but looked pale and troubled.

Suddenly she seemed to explode. '*Why do you take it?*' she asked.

This was not like her. 'You know Sam . . .'

'I don't know what you see in the bastard and I never have,' said Jennie. She followed the woodworm trails with her finger, usually a sign of worse to come.

'He can be wonderful,' I told her, 'at times.'

'But he uses you, Martha, he laughs at you.'

'He has done in the past, that's true, but just now

288

things are working out . . .'

'No, they're not,' Jennie said quietly.

'They're not?'

'No, and that's the reason he's being so atrocious, because I know all about what's going on.'

My heart drummed against my chest. It was like I had bitten something sour and wanted to spit it out before swallowing. But I had to ask, *'Know all about what?'*

'I know what the pig has been up to. And he's turning you against me, Martha. I know that and so do you. He's not being particularly subtle.'

Did Jennie know something?

My God—*was this true*? Or was this Jennie's way of tarnishing Sam so that I would take her side? But surely, no matter how passionately Jennie felt about me, no matter how desperately she wanted my friendship, she would stop short of wrecking our marriage? I wanted to stop her. *I couldn't.* Didn't she know that whatever she told me, true or false, wouldn't matter? *I would hate her.* Had she no understanding of my love for Sam?

'He's been cheating on you for years,' she said, following the squiggles with that stupid finger. 'I've known about it for half that time, but I decided not to tell you because I hoped it would blow over.'

'What's been going on, Jennie?' But I knew! *I knew!* Why did she feel she had to tell me?

She changed tack, raised lowered eyes and gave me nervous, fluttering glances. 'Did you suspect? You never said. You never trusted me that much, did you?'

This was my pain she was making her own. How could she be so mistaken to think that even now, in this dire situation, I'd be feeling sorry for her because I, Martha, hadn't trusted her? Her self-absorption was so ugly it defied belief. And the only reason she was doing this now was to take her revenge on Sam and ingratiate herself with me.

'Perhaps I did know all along, but didn't want to believe it.' I clung to my last shred of self-control. 'That's quite a human reaction, I'm told.'

'But, Martha, while you keep denying it he'll just go on and on . . .'

'*Who was it, Jennie?*' She was dying to tell me.

'Tina Gallagher,' she said.

That made sense. That added up. Tina, all curves and lips, was Sam's type, for sure. But I couldn't move my eyes off Jennie. I was getting tenser and tenser, near breaking point.

'Why are you looking at me like that? The last thing I wanted to do was hurt you.'

In this roaring chasm I felt so alone. I stood up, swept the glasses off the table. They smashed to smithereens on the floor. I screamed like a savage at the top of my voice, '*GET OUT OF MY FUCKING HOUSE . . .*'

'Wait, Martha . . .'

I could hardly bear to speak to her. 'I said, get out of here . . . oh Christ, I've been so wrong, you evil, warped bitch from hell. Everybody was right about you but me—I'm so stupid I just couldn't see . . .'

She was deathly white, half stunned, bent in half as if from a blow. She backed towards my door like a dark and ugly spider. '*Martha, Martha, please . . .*' she cried.

If she didn't go now I would kill her, I would bludgeon her face until she stopped speaking. I would pull out her hair, gouge out her eyes, shut that sobbing, slobbering mouth. I clawed at the air in front of my face. '*YOU WILL NOT PULL ME DOWN. DO YOU HEAR WHAT I'M SAYING? YOU FUCKING CRETINOUS LIAR.*' And I kept on shrieking as she backed to the door, 'You'll stop at nothing, you'd see your kids dead just to vindicate your own sick desires . . .'

'Christ! Martha!' Sam hurried in, saw the mess on the floor and Jennie cowering at the door. 'What the bloody hell's going on here?' He was naked save for a towel round his waist.

'Jennie's just leaving,' I managed to hiss. 'Aren't you, *sweetheart*? And you're never, ever coming back. I never want to see your face again.' Just the feel of her poisonous name in my mouth made me want to vomit.

'But—'

'Shut up, Sam!' I shook with rage. 'Let me handle this on my own. This vicious little bastard won't be—'

'She's gone, Martha. Calm down, calm down. She's gone. *Look, Jennie's gone.*'

Shaking like a jelly, I let myself fold into his arms. I allowed myself to be comforted. I stuttered out exactly what had happened. 'She said . . . she said . . . she tried to make me believe that you and Tina . . . you and Tina . . .'

'Bitch,' snarled Sam. 'Bitch.'

'You were right,' I told him as he dried my eyes. 'You were dead right. I did, I felt guilty, I felt sorry for her and responsible in some weird way . . .'

'You were never to blame for Jennie's sickness,' Sam said, as I shuddered in his arms. 'It took time to realize what a freak she was and you were too

291

involved to see. As for that evil story about her and Graham . . .'

I sniffed and blew my nose on a tissue Sam found on the table. 'Poor Graham,' I started to say, 'and those poor, poor kids . . .'

'Those kids you feel so sorry for are giving our kids hell. They've been sucking them dry for years and you've been blind to all of it.'

'I know, I know that now.' My voice had turned childlike. 'And I didn't tell you before, but Jennie has been complaining to Mrs Forest and saying that Scarlett has been unkind. And Mrs Forest has been on the phone to me about it.'

'Shush, Martha, shush, it's over now.'

With a rush of relief I hurried to tell him. 'I had to go and bring Scarlett home and talk to her about it. But it wasn't Scarlett and Harriet at all—it was Poppy, trying to get them into trouble. No wonder they were so worried and so wary of her friendship.'

Sam looked furious. 'It's a good thing I didn't know.'

'Scarlett kept trying to tell me, but I was always too busy and then Jennie went behind my back . . .'

'Well, she would, wouldn't she? True to form as ever. But now you know the truth, you can take a very different attitude.' He was stroking my face, calming me down.

'But how could she, Sam? *How could she lie about you and Tina?*'

'There are no limits to Jennie's schemings where you are concerned, I'm afraid,' said Sam. 'Poor cow.' He kissed me softly, lit a cigarette and said, 'It's over now, Martha. Come on, come on, it's all over and I love you.'

And I knew without doubt that he meant it.
I only wanted to sleep in his arms.

*   *   *

I knew I couldn't take any more. I was an emotional wreck.

CHAPTER TWENTY-NINE

Jennie

I knew I couldn't take any more. I was an emotional wreck.

*   *   *

My work was my salvation.

I needed no calm interior for that—the more tumultuous the turmoil, the better the results; the more anguish, the quicker I worked; ideas flashing like forked lightning as I formed and hewed and nurtured some sort of order out of chaos into my moonscapes of a tortured soul.

The classes were behind me since Josie said she had no more to teach me, and yes, that did thrill me then. 'You're on your own, Jennie. You'll make it,' and she held out a hand encased in red clay. 'I envy your talent, I really do.'

But nothing could lift my spirits now.

I watched dully when Graham cleared the garage in preparation for my new firing oven, a birthday present from him. He set it up, built shelves and racks and then tiled the floor.

'Don't you need planning permission for that?' shouted Sadie as she stalked past.

Graham took no notice.

There was so much ill feeling now, and all directed at me.

And then, of course, the planners came round, alerted by a petition signed by every resident which said my studio would cause local nuisance—just one of the petty attacks we endured. The chief planner, Mr Jackson, saw no problem as we weren't changing the external aspects or putting in a window. 'But change of use?' he wondered aloud. 'That could be a tricky one.'

No window. No looking out.

I worked all the hours God gave under that stark fluorescent light. I moulded, I twisted my shapes of wire, I sliced, I fashioned; I fircd with the inside of my head all broken and my brain whirring round with the wheel. Of course, I had to explain to Graham about this frantic behaviour, so I told him truthfully about Tina and Sam, and Martha's angry denial.

'So Martha believed them, not me. She honestly imagined I made it up.'

'But why tell her, Jennie? Christ, you kept it from me, *why not her?*'

Why? How could I tell him? How could I explain? 'Because she was being made such a fool of.'

'Better that than torture,' said Graham, with a knowing that surprised me. He drummed the table with his long fingers, concerned that I was being turned into this *persona non grata.* 'But this animosity can't last, it's far too time-consuming.

294

Persecution uses up energy. The only answer is to ignore them and get on with our lives as normal.'

There was no 'as normal' about it.

It was never going to be that easy.

'Don't let them see you're upset,' I told Poppy and Josh with a breaking heart. 'Just don't give them the satisfaction.' It was anguish to watch them being ostracized through no fault of their own, cold-shouldered by kids on skateboards and bicycles; Poppy not collected for school and coming home alone. And when, of an evening, the green turned into a playground, if Poppy or Josh crept out to join in there'd be sniggers and nudges and rushes inside the nearest unfriendly house.

Look what I'd done to my children.

Dear God, how could I answer their innocent questions? How could their mates turn on them like this? Someone had eavesdropped, as children do, as the angry gossip flew round the Close, and they must have caught on to the undertones. We were vilified as a family of troublemakers and common decency no longer applied. Intelligent and manipulative, Scarlett was a natural leader.

It was quite a shock to realize just how much I was disliked in the Close. It hadn't occurred to me before how much Martha's protection had meant; these women held on to their various grudges, bitter old vultures pecking at morsels, poised to pounce and drain and tear, and I was astonished to see normal adults conspiring in this vicious way.

I tried to approach them as individuals, but as public enemy number one I didn't achieve very much. Hilary Wainwright turned and stalked off as if I didn't exist, Angie Ford acted the same, and I didn't have the guts to tackle Sadie because she was the least well inclined of them all.

I went across to Martha's house with a speech carefully rehearsed. The door stayed closed in my face.

I tried to ring her.

She put down the phone.

I sent her reasonable notes, pleading for sense for the sake of my children who Martha had always been fond of. I couldn't get my head round the fact she was happy to see them so cruelly treated.

The men remained polite but distant. Although they took no part in the feuding they weren't blind; they must have accepted it. When Graham tried to sort things out, man to man, across the road with Anthony Wainwright, he was told he didn't know the half of it, that I was being taught a much-needed lesson and that I was a vindictive woman.

He was told his kids would get over it. 'It might be easier for everyone,' advised Anthony, 'if you moved your family somewhere else.'

*   *   *

Finally, after six weeks of this, we both decided we had no choice. We couldn't go on living like this: the children would have to be moved before any lasting damage was done.

Swimming pool, brand-new studio, a safe and stylish place to live—all down the drain through one foolish mistake. We'd had such high hopes when we came here and now we were both broken-hearted. The FOR SALE sign went up and we started looking for houses nearby within commuting distance of town. New schools for the children seemed like the sensible option—this

September Poppy would have gone to the comp; she'd been assessed and placed in the C stream, two below Scarlett, with rough types not interested in learning. A private school was the obvious answer, and I felt the same about poor little Josh who already missed Lawrence so much that he cried for him every night and refused to give his Buzz Lightyear back.

The kids in the Close, hyped up by the feud, got wise to the kind of trouble they could cause. Led by Scarlett and Lawrence, the little gang consisted of Harriet and other school friends, the Wainwrights' two boys and Angie Ford's nephews. They were pissed off because they'd been banned from the pool—not by us, but by their parents. So when we had our first couple of viewers, these little tormentors played football on the green, making sure to kick the ball in our garden, targeting the car and the front windows, finally wedging it in our gutter.

'This open-plan arrangement,' mused a Mr Gregson, eyeing his wife, 'I'm not entirely sure I'm in favour.'

His neat little wife was more direct. 'How do you tolerate this behaviour? They're so uncontrolled, so cheeky! They must come from that awful estate. The agent said it was improving, but obviously he was wrong.'

So we cut the viewing to daytime only, avoiding the summer evenings when the kids tended to hang about. But then some yob came up with a new ploy—and scarlet paint was tipped into the swimming pool.

'Right,' said Graham, 'time for the law.'

They were useless. What could they do? they

said. 'You're lucky if this is your first time,' said one. 'At least you're insured. Some poor bastards put up with worse than this every day.'

Graham insisted, 'But this is a personal vendetta and we're suffering daily from petty vandalism.' He sounded so tired, so pissed off with it all.

They had summed us up as paranoid, probably deserving all we got, because why else would the neighbours turn against us? 'Before we can act we have to have proof and that's not easy to obtain. Our hands are tied. Without the proof, we can't get these buggers to court.' I didn't offer the two coppers tea.

They were undermanned, under pressure, the force was certainly not what it was; these two would get out when they got the chance.

Where could we turn?

We felt so alone.

We were prisoners in our own home. When they came home, Poppy and Josh crept up to their rooms and shut themselves in.

'It'll soon be the end of term,' I said, 'and then maybe we could go away.'

'School's not so bad as it is here,' Josh said. 'At school they leave me alone.' And I imagined him in the playground, abandoned.

'Poppy? How about you?'

My daughter was crying silent tears. Resentful and angry, she sobbed, 'Don't ask me, it's hell, don't make me go . . .'

'It's only for another two weeks . . .'

'One day is too long,' she cried, and oh how I felt for her distress. 'Mrs Forest lets me stay in the office. Sometimes I help Mrs Gould, typing envelopes and that, and sticking stamps on.'

Unable to go on, she buried her head. God, I was angry. *What sort of education was that?* What was the point in putting her through it, but to take her away would be total surrender. I just hoped she wouldn't start skiving and end up vulnerable in the mall again.

'This is all my fault,' I told Graham. 'You just don't know . . .'

'I don't need to know, Jennie. Nothing you did could justify this.' Again he was my strong protector, defending me and soothing me, the way we were before I loved Martha. 'This is an evil vindictiveness, the kind you expect from some mindless underclass. These arseholes ought to know better.' He was pale and utterly furious. I rested a hand on his knee and we dropped back into uneasy silence.

But what if he did know? *What if they told him?* They had so much ammunition to use if they chose to annihilate me completely—all those betrayals, our private sex life, that story about our shameful first meeting, my fumbles in bed with Martha. For God's sake, my worship of Martha, my suicide bid.

And then the secrets nobody knew: I'd deliberately hurt my child to get Martha's sympathy, I'd faked a miscarriage and frightened the children in my care with my bouts of frenzied screaming; I had even welcomed my own mother's death.

At weekends, in an effort to protect the children, we took them for days out—anywhere. Anything was better than sitting around at home and feeling all that hostility closing in on us; anything rather than gaze out the windows to where our enemies gathered. We attempted a kind of enforced joviality, but, of course, that never worked—even at the best of times we weren't really like that.

We tried to anticipate future attacks and guess what form they might take. Who was at the heart of this devilish revenge? We failed to find any answers. We only knew that when we went out, we had to keep our heads held high.

The silent phone calls came from the children. I could hear them laughing behind their hands. We never knew how much vandalism was caused by our neighbours, and how much by the estate kids whose troublemaking on the way home from the pub had escalated since last year, to every home-owner's horror.

My washing line was laden with clothes when somebody sliced it in half.

Our flowerbeds were trampled into mud. The heads were cut off our roses.

They slashed the tyres of Graham's car. Some of my pottery tools were stolen.

A dirty old mac was left on the doormat. Graham was nonplussed but I knew what it meant and I detected Sam's hand somewhere in this. This was the ultimate stab in the back. Martha must have told Sam my story of how we two had first met, and Sam would not hesitate to turn this into public knowledge. But this didn't cause any more dismay; I already lived in a fog of horror.

My pleasure came in the few split seconds I was relieved from pain . . . those moments before waking up every morning.

I deserved this vilification. Over the years I'd brought it on with my appalling behaviour, but my family were innocent. Maybe I should go away for a while, perhaps until the house was sold. My brain played around with this new idea. The thought of flight was appealing—any action seemed attractive, any action promised some hope of relief.

Graffiti was scrawled on our garage door; Graham painted it over. It came straight back.

And all the time I marvelled—how could Martha have a hand in this?

Did she honestly know what was happening?

But she wouldn't see me: she refused, even when I called on her at work.

'Martha is busy,' was the message that finally reached the front desk. What was she—cool, amused, hostile, controlled?

*   *   *

I even turned to God, to the stern God of my mother. 'Forgive me for all that selfishness, oh God, please tell me what to do.'

There was no point in crying out loud.

Nobody wanted to hear me.

On weekdays I was alone in the house with nothing to do but think, or work. I rocked, I moaned, overwhelmed by the thought of my children being turned into victims, like me. I thrust my fingers into my mouth and bit them to cause some alternative torment.

Then I would force myself into action. I worked from the moment the family departed until the time they came home. And often, at night, after they were asleep, I wrapped up warmly, turned on the studio lights, lit the heater, and worked myself senseless till dawn, experimenting with new forms, new glazes, while I moved around the howling corridors of nightmare.

The house alarm didn't cover the garage and I was in mortal fear of some child creeping in and destroying my work. Slowly, it became very precious to me. I went overboard with padlocks and bolts.

'I don't care what they smash up just so long as we stay safe,' said Graham.

'But they wouldn't seriously hurt us, would they?' I was astonished that he might think otherwise. It was me they were after, it was me they detested. What might they do—shave off my hair, tar and feather me, break my kneecaps? This was absurd.

'I just don't know anything any more,' Graham confessed without expression. 'How can I know, how could anyone know? This is all beyond understanding.' He kept a poker beside the bed.

'I've had it before,' I reminded him, 'most of it. And it felt just as bad when I was bullied at school and nobody bothered. At least this time there's two of us. Imagine if we were alone and didn't have each other.'

*   *   *

We were so used to abusive calls that Graham always answered the phone in the evenings. That screaming sound was so threatening then, and that jerk of anticipation the phone seems to give before it actually starts to ring. Everyone jumped when the phone rang; we all stopped what we were doing and stared around with frightened eyes.

Total relief. We breathed again. This was a dealer called Hamish Lisle, a bit of a joke between us, and Graham gave me a wink.

'Thing is, old dear, I've got someone here who would just adore to meet you. Wondered when would be a good time?'

Hamish, with his gaudy silk waistcoats, ran a London art studio with his great friend Tomikins.

I instantly panicked—evenings were out and so, just lately, was every weekend. And if anything ugly did happen, I'd hate to have to explain our position to an almost total stranger. 'It's tricky just now, I'm not too well . . .'

'I wouldn't bore you with this, my darling, but it's all rather exciting at this end. Demetrius Hogg? Name ring a bell? Big in the trade in the USA, wants to meet with a view to buying for an important client from Baltimore. Catch my drift? Not one to turn down . . .'

'Who did you say?'

'Demetrius Hogg.'

I'd heard of him. Who hadn't?

'I presume you've got something to show him?'

'There's quite a bit of stuff hanging around. I've been working hard just recently . . .'

'Splendid. Say no more. Why don't we make it Wednesday. I'll run the guy down and we'll have some lunch after he's taken a gander. What d'you say?'

'Wednesday sounds fine.' What else could I say, faced with an opportunity like that?

'Lovely, darling, must go. Chin chin.'

I put the phone down slowly. It was a voice from another world and sometimes it was hard to imagine that there still was such a place. The Close was all-encompassing when you rarely left it, like me. Even the children: I'd allowed the Close and its people to become all-important in their lives.

We were trapped here, flies in a web.

I was never more sure that we must escape.

If only I could live without Martha.

I abhorred myself, loathed and disgusted myself, for even thinking that way.

*   *   *

I had to get shot of that woman.

CHAPTER THIRTY

Martha

I had to get shot of that woman.

*   *   *

But was this the way? Was this cold-shouldering fair or acceptable? Sam told me to leave it alone; my judgement had been warped for so long when it came to that scheming woman, it was time I shut up and toed the line. Group pressure would force the Gordons out and that was the unanimous aim.

'But the kids? They can't be included in this.' I can honestly say I had no idea at this stage of the level of cruelty towards the Gordons. I would not have tolerated it for a moment.

'Children survive, they're hardy animals,' Angie Ford assured me—she who knew nothing about them, because she didn't have any. 'Face it, Martha, if the Gordon kids stay around here they'll suffer much more in the end. Nobody genuinely likes them, they've been mollycoddled for far too long.'

'*But I like them.* I'm very fond of them.'

'They wouldn't thank you in the long run for keeping up this pretence. Let them make their own friends for a change, let them be themselves instead of just shadows of others.'

So I was being thoughtless by worrying too much. But I couldn't stop aching for poor little Poppy, although I'd never forget the way she'd performed at school, dropping Scarlett in it like that for something she'd never done. It was just the fact that my kids were being used that I couldn't stomach. Anyway, Jennie's kids were OK, no pressure would be put on them, my neighbours weren't that sort of people.

We'd tried discussing this rationally at first. Anthony Wainwright had talked to Graham and suggested it would be best if they moved, but Graham, apparently, wasn't convinced. Everyone in the Close had their reasons for wanting the Gordons out, on top of the general agreement that Jennie was a scandalmonger, unbalanced, volatile, and a snake in the grass. She'd fallen out with everyone, causing all kinds of unpleasant repercussions. She'd lied about bedding Sam years back, and now she was after splitting the Gallaghers, not just me and Sam. And I understood it was generally known that Jennie was infatuated with me. Tina, no doubt, with her big mouth at its busiest.

*   *   *

To her shame Scarlett coped well without Poppy,

but then she'd been trying to distance herself for so long that her freedom came as a blessed release. Lawrence, of course, never turned a hair. 'Just so long as there's no unkindness,' I stressed. 'Staying at arm's length from the Gordons does not mean teasing. It does not mean tormenting them.' But surely Scarlett knew better than that; she was not an insensitive child.

'Some people *are* being horrid,' said Lawrence.

'You don't know what you're talking about,' Scarlett quickly shut him up.

'I hope that's not true. Scarlett? *Is it?*'

'Lawrence is just goading you. Nobody's bothering much at all.'

'Because I couldn't stand that kind of wicked behaviour.'

'*But you do it*,' accused my daughter. 'You're not speaking to Jennie.'

'That's different. You know why I won't speak to Jennie, and that's because she sometimes twists things that people say and causes all sorts of misunderstandings.' I'd explained this to Scarlett already. I'd told her the adults were dealing with this, that the youngsters must keep out of it. 'But I'd never be deliberately cruel and I know you wouldn't be either.'

Sam was too outspoken. I worried about his attitude. Listening children take things at face value, and he didn't bother to curb his anger. 'They've been telling malicious tales . . . from the moment we met that sodding family they've hung on to us like leeches—bloodsucking, draining energy . . . and those bloody kids are no better.'

'Graham's OK,' Lawrence put in mildly.

'Graham's as bad as the rest of them. It's time

306

that wanker put his foot down and realized just what a cow he married. They're losers, the lot of them, they deserve all they get.'

Scarlett's eyes gleamed in bright fascination. Neither of them had heard Sam or me raving in this hostile way before. This was an eye-opener for them both, and for me, too, to be honest.

It was weird how this unhappy campaign began to take over our lives. Soon our main topic of conversation was the goings-on with the Gordons and we'd gossip over fences like gnarled fishwives; we'd sneer down the phone, reviving old rumours, mulling them over and pulling the Gordons to pieces. It was appalling how it became so absorbing.

It verged on the thrilling. There were enemies in our midst.

Collective hatred was so easily fuelled. I worried the children would be infected.

Sometimes at work I'd look forward to six, so I could get home to hear the latest. It was more intriguing than *EastEnders.* And when the FOR SALE sign went up next door, it left us feeling thwarted rather than triumphant.

We had achieved our aim so simply.

What about Jennie's violent love . . . did this mean it had left her? Could a miracle have occurred overnight? She must be resigned to living without me.

'That place won't sell in a million years,' said Hilary Wainwright unkindly. 'Not now they've put up interest rates as well as stamp duty on these types of houses.'

There was a perverse sense of relief; we were reluctant to be deprived of our prey.

307

Sadie summed up the communal feeling. 'For all their airs and graces, what are they? One old slapper and a dirty old sod.'

No, no, this was crass, I couldn't accept this level of spite. 'That happened a very long time ago and it was told to me in absolute confidence.'

'Martha—she lied!' sneered Sam. 'Just another bid for attention. What a squalid imagination that woman's got—did she ever speak the truth, one wonders? She's even gone as far as to throw red paint in her own swimmimg pool to exact some mean revenge, that new copper told me. Jesus Christ, Martha—get wise. She's going around slandering us as we speak. They've got to go to stop any real damage.'

By the way everyone looked at me I could see they thought I was spoiling their fun—one good word for Jcnnie put a dampener on the proceedings. In my neighbours' eyes, I was the victim of a vicious and mean-minded attack.

A delicious community fear was born, which left us all imagining that Jennie, in her madness, possessed special powers to hear and see through walls, to cast spells. Everyone loved to speculate on what her next evil deed would be, which one of us would be ill-wished, when would the next wicked spell be cast? Improbable, I realize that, but that was what happened.

'How pretentious she is, turning that garage into a workshop,' sneered Tina. 'And what she does in there is rubbish. I mean, has anyone seen it? It's so spooky. God knows what sickos are buying it, if what we hear is true. No, the real truth is that Jennie's using that garage to spy on us. There'll be complaints about the youngsters soon. We'll hear what scandalous acts they've been up to. She's so transparent, the woman's pathetic.'

'She can't see out, there's no window,' I mentioned.

'That woman has ways of seeing through stone.'

What started as a mild idea to suggest to the Gordons that they weren't welcome fed off itself over the weeks and turned into a witch hunt, the kind of hatred that leads to tragedy, when emotions are encouraged to run too high. I was afraid it would end with someone blabbing to Graham about Jennie's fatal attraction and then we'd see, and presumably enjoy, the explosive flak from all that. And as her passion for me was the underlying cause of this chaos, and as everyone but Graham now seemed to know, it was obvious that that particular secret was out.

'She's a dyke and that's all there is to it,' said Sam.

Always a threat to the male of the species. An ingenious way of involving the men.

If only she hadn't confided in me.

'Nobody likes Poppy at school,' said Scarlett, pretending to sound concerned for my sake. 'She's thick. She came last in the maths test. Thirty-two out of thirty-two.'

'Well, that's not your fault, Scarlett,' I said. This was the very reaction she had wanted and my daughter purred like a cat. It did sound quite sensible the way I put it. 'Poppy's teachers need to know exactly what standard she's at, for her sake. Nobody wants her to go up to the comp in September and find herself out of her depth. That's how some children slip through the system and end up illiterate and innumerate.'

'She's been bragging about going private.'

I smiled sadly. 'Maybe that's her way of defending herself. It might be the best solution for her. It might mean she'll get special help.'

'Is Poppy special needs, Mummy?'

'Of course not, don't be silly.'

But when Lawrence came home from school with a bloody great bruise on the back of his head, it was almost a matter for rejoicing because it was Josh who had thrown the stone and that justified our position. This incident was added to the list of transgressions that we could gang up together to chew over.

'Josh has an aggressive streak. He never could play properly,' said Sam with a fair amount of triumph. These were my own words of years ago, now turned into weapons. My betrayal of Jennie was absolute. 'Always determined to be the best and the strongest,' said Sam. 'Temper tantrums if he didn't come first.' Sam would never have noticed these flaws if I hadn't pointed them out.

'What were you doing to make him do that?' I had to ask my wounded son.

'We were all throwing stones,' he said innocently, blind to his encouraging audience.

'Did Josh get hit?' I asked him, knowing he would tell the truth.

'No, Josh was behind the boiler-room door.'

'Well, that's a blessed relief,' sniffed Tina, 'else we would have had the police round by now.'

Yes, it was so easy it was frightening—so simple to turn and destroy a person we had known for so long, especially when it came to protecting our own in the noble cause of righteousness.

I had liked to imagine I would stand alone against the abomination of victimization, or the singling out for suffering of any one person by any group, guilty or not. But Jennie's barefaced gall, how she sat and told lies about Sam and Tina at my own familiar kitchen table where I had welcomed her so often, changed me. It brought out all those destructive feelings and turned me into a stranger. I had never known so much rage was lying dormant inside me.

She had deliberately attempted to wreck my marriage.

Not only that, but her sly approach to Mrs Forest, trying to blacken Scarlett's name behind my back, as if she had forgotten how much I cared for her children, hurt me and repulsed me.

I saw that as unforgivable.

And after all we'd endured together, all those scenes and trauma sessions, the explanations, the forgivenesses, the passions and the truths and the lies, the laughter and the tears . . . *Who would have thought it would come to this?*

It wasn't my fault, it was Jennie's. If only she'd taken my advice and gone on to get a degree that might have led to a job she enjoyed . . . If she'd done that she could have saved herself—she was just too feeble, or too bloody stubborn.

But even bearing all this in mind, the group offensive would not have happened but for the personalities involved.

Sam, for a start, could never relate to such a withdrawn person as Jennie. Sadie was trouble—bored and unhappy—with no other interests save

311

the shop and her opera; and Tina thrived on the pickings of gossip. At home all day on her PC or driving long distances, she had too much time to dwell on trivia.

Hilary Wainwright, with her part-time career, was far more interested in playing the good fairy, and like so many people with wings on their backs, the misfortunes of others gave her propulsion. Maybe I was being unkind, but her vehement dislike of Jennie had started when her goodness was thrown back in her face.

Angie's dislike was more reasonable. Jennie was unforgivably rude after the incident of Scarlett's leg and it was Jennie who'd kept that pot boiling in her worst high-handed manner.

And me?

Well, I was riddled with guilt.

So eager to pander to Sam.

To show him whose side I was on and to demonstrate in the strongest way my belief in him, and my fury at Jennie.

'She thought I was turning you against her,' said Sam. 'That's why she made up that hideous lie.'

I still found this hard to understand. *'But she must have known that I wouldn't believe her.'*

'Why?' Sam asked mildly. 'You've believed her before. She's told more extraordinary porkies than that.'

'That's true.'

'So you've finally got to admit it,' he insisted. 'You were duped by that freak, you were her puppet for ten years, and the irony was, you believed *she* was the needy one.'

After all that, it was me who was weak, not Jennie, and I was taken by my new image—an unworldly, brainless, credulous fool. It was nice to be called 'child' again, it relieved me of so much responsibility. I enjoyed the new coddling, the tutting and shrugging; I was no longer a knowing old bag. No-one could say of me, 'No flies on that one.'

Sam said, 'Tina's not my type. Give me some credit—an Essex girl, common as muck. And she's so busy chasing after Carl, when would she have the time for any extra nooky?'

I longed to ask: *Who was it then, Sam?* I knew for sure there'd been somebody. I wasn't such a cretin as that, whatever he might like to think. But I guessed that all I needed to do was wait until he made his confession. He always did. A creature of habit. Baring his soul was part of the thrill.

*   *   *

It was me who brought home the scoop of the week.

I brandished a copy of the paper like a flag. 'You're not going to believe this.' And I read aloud to a startled Sam: '"LOCAL POTTER'S WHEEL OF FORTUNE! An obscure local potter, working from her garage at home, hit the big time this week when she accepted an important commission from US dealer and art connoisseur, Demetrius Hogg. This means a whole change of fortune for housewife and mother, Jennie Gordon of Mulberry Close . . ."'

I read on quickly, tumbling over the words in my pleasure at seeing the amazement spread over Sam's face. '"'Of course I couldn't believe it at first,' said Mrs Gordon, thirty-four, mother of two. But teacher and author Mrs Josie Magee, who taught Mrs Gordon for two years, said, 'I knew that if Jennie kept going, one day she would make it big. She's a one and only. The magic touch. For her this is just the start.'

' "Mr Hogg, with connections to the world's most prestigious auction houses and whose clients include wealthy collectors, studios and stores, told the *Express*, 'I am delighted to have discovered such excellence. Jennie's beautifully formed and textured sculptures make an important contribution to the ancient craft of creating with clay and must be exploited fully. Only then can they be properly admired by those who appreciate such unique talent.'

' "It is understood that Mr Hogg has purchased several of Mrs Gordon's pieces and these include works entitled 'Sky through the Eyes of God', 'The Wings of the Wind' and 'Hound Howlings'. When asked where her inspiration came from, Mrs Gordon said, 'It comes from anguish.'

' "There will be an exhibition of Jennie Gordon's work at the Hamish Lisle Gallery at the end of this month." '

'Read that again,' said Sam, so I did.

'It's no good. I can't take it in.'

Neither could I. Wait till the neighbours heard. At last Jennie had somewhere to put her passion.

*   *   *

So why did I feel so sad?

CHAPTER THIRTY-ONE

Jennie

So why did I feel so sad?

*   *   *

Look at me now, I was successful, with appointments in my diary other than dentist and smear.

I felt so sad because it had required an almost intolerable level of misery for me to discover my art, to stumble on this magic talent never awakened before. I had to reach rock bottom to find it. The passion that drove me to work every morning was due to a total collapse of the spirit and I could only vaguely recognize the acclaim my work received. Graham was prouder of me than I was and made sure I saw the articles and write-ups that catapulted me to fame. It was my anguished sculptures that made it, not my humble everyday pots.

I prayed for the equanimity that would let me get back to my pots again.

As the fastidious Stella would have said: 'How could you expose yourself so? What do these ugly forms mean?' And her lips would pleat over her teeth just like a Cornish pasty.

But the main benefit of my phoenix-like rise from the ashes of lowly housewife and mother was the diversion it caused for me and my family. And, my God, we desperately needed something. I also have to admit to a sense of revenge lurking somewhere in the hotchpotch of emotion—I had survived in spite of the odds. We had risen above a malicious campaign aimed at our destruction and so long as I could keep plying my trade we would do a hell of a lot more than survive.

It looked as if we might make a fortune.

Far too good to be true.

Martha was contemptuous of humbler winners of the National Lottery when they stood beaming daftly in front of the cameras, swearing that their lives wouldn't change. 'Why do these morons buy tickets?' she'd ask. 'Why don't they give the money to me—at least I'd know how to spend it.' And Martha did love to dream like that: imagining how it might have been if she'd gone to drama school as she'd hoped, or if she'd kept up her tennis, or if she'd married that queer MP who had once proposed at a drunken party, but who she'd turned down because he was too old.

She certainly liked to pour scorn on me. 'You don't have a clue when it comes to taste. I mean, of course that dress doesn't suit you, it's tacky, it's dated, it does nothing for you.' And over the years she had influenced my buyings, from upholstery fabrics to Graham's new suits.

When she went to buy clothes for her children, I would go with her and buy the same makes.

'And do stop calling it "sweet", Jennie, please. Whatever's the matter with pudding?'

Could it be—and I shrank from this thought— that Martha's influence came out in my sculptures, that they were nothing to do with me at all? And as I had now lost contact, would my talents peter out? Had I soaked up enough to last me? It was so difficult for me to believe that my creations,

316

admired by so many, came from the dull and heavy heart of frumpy Jennie Gordon. There was no doubt that Martha was my inspiration.

Had she heard about my little success?

'She knows all about it,' Graham reassured me. 'They all know. They'd have to be hermits not to know. Your face is splashed over every local paper, and then there was that *Guardian* interview last week.'

'What do they think? How do they feel?' It gave me pleasure to try to imagine, especially Sadie Harcourt with her arts degree and her hand-made earrings.

'Don't spare them a thought,' said Graham contemptuously. 'Knowing them, they'll be green. Pretentious prats.'

'Jealous? Of me?' The idea was preposterous.

'You've got to get them out of your head.'

Was Graham jealous? What would I have felt like, I wondered, if he had been the one suddenly to be called an amazing talent by the *Sunday Times* magazine? Would I change my attitude towards him? See him as a brand-new person, a stranger, stronger, who had grown a new part like an extra leg which was nothing to do with me—*not mine?* I might have found this stranger threatening and have worried that he might find somebody else more worthy. But I secretly wished it had been Graham; he deserved to triumph so much more than I did.

Now whether it was my fifteen minutes of glory that weakened the will of my neighbours, or whether they were just getting bored or running out of ideas—whichever it was I don't know—there was nevertheless a marked reduction in vicious

317

behaviour; more of a cold and stony silence. Stares and whispers. Their prey had been shown a hole in the hedge large enough to take all of them. And in this calmer climate we were at last able to sell our house. We sweated as the deal went through; in those days you heard such alarming stories.

I had hoped that Martha might bend enough to congratulate me, just a note or a phone call for old times' sake. But no.

Nothing.

*   *   *

Filled with a new and startling energy, we set off for the gallery where I was to be introduced to the world. Great preparations were under way. White carpets, walls and windows. Hogg, Hamish Lisle and Tomikins rushed around seeking perfection. I felt foolishly out of my depth in this precious environment, yet I couldn't deny the flushes of pride when I saw my pieces out of the garage and displayed to their best advantage, made bolder and richer by clever lighting. They were big, big and getting bigger as my passion and anger grew, especially the heads of the two black rooks, which even I found disturbing.

'My God, it's so dark. Is it sinister?' I asked Hogg, as I followed him round and watched him directing the handlers where to place another haunting piece. 'People will see these and think I'm a freak.'

'No, they won't, they'll love them, like I do,' he said. And I saw how much the right angle mattered and how a fraction of an inch could make all the difference. My mentor was a fat little Texan, bald as the American eagle, with round gold spectacles hooked over his chubby ears.

They were asking unbelievable prices, when you think that most of these were knocked up crazily in a week or even a matter of days. This must be some fluke, I thought. I lived with a fierce premonition that something would go disastrously wrong: they would discover that I was a fraud and the critics would expose me to an angry public.

'Why don't you ever make something nice?' asked Poppy, as awed as I was.

'Nice?' boomed Hogg, overhearing. 'No art should be nice.'

'Well, pretty then,' Poppy insisted, reverently touching the arm of one of my favourites and maybe the darkest—'Battles with Shadows'—and I noticed her dreadfully bitten nails. 'How can you describe a thing like this?'

'Frightening,' said Hogg emphatically, 'wonderfully eccentric and menacing.'

I would have liked to ask Martha what I should wear.

I didn't look much like an artist.

These London people gushed words like fountains—heavenly, marvellous, gorgeous, magnificent. For them it seemed a constant struggle to find a new way of lavishing praise. It was hard to take them seriously. If I believed one word they said, I'd soon be bloated by self-esteem and lose all sight of reality. But although I knew this, I couldn't help it—I relished their sugarsweet praise, wallowing in the warmth of it, savouring every second of it. These were people from glamorous worlds so far removed from mine. This might never happen to me again.

We went off to enjoy a sumptuous lunch, wine, more praise, simmering excitement, and I was heady with all of it, keyed up and dreading going back to the Close and losing this feeling of being wildly alive. Even Poppy looked happier now— she'd been given a catalogue to take to school and she underlined my name on the front. 'They'll all want to be friends with me now.'

*   *   *

Not only this, but if Hogg's estimates on the likely sales resulting from this one exhibition were anywhere near correct, we'd be able to afford the very best private schools in the area, the ones I'd dreamed of sending the children to.

I had done to Poppy the very thing I'd sworn never to do. She had been through hell because of me. It was only right I should help to put her back together.

Poppy might not be first in class, but even Mrs Forest admitted that my daughter was far from stupid. 'You will see,' she'd told me when we'd discussed Poppy's future, 'that although this might seem like a nightmare for her now—being moved away from her friends and classmates—in the long run Poppy will benefit. She'll learn to use her own brain again and discover a truer identity.'

This was hard for her to accept. She was truly, utterly miserable as the final term drew to an end, and her hatred of Scarlett knew no bounds. 'I wouldn't help her if she was dying, and when we get rich I'm having a pony and then she'll be sorry, you watch.'

'That's not the attitude . . .'

320

'It is, and I'm taking it,' she said, wriggling away unhappily and going to sit on her own in front of the silent TV. 'Why are they being so unkind? Why don't they speak to you any more? Why does that cow Hilary Wainwright turn away when she sees you coming?'

What could I say that would sound convincing? How could Poppy, aged ten, understand when I hardly understood this myself? But I made an effort because I was forced to. 'Sometimes people don't like hearing the truth.'

'What truth? Did you say something horrid to Martha?'

'Yes, Poppy. Yes, I did.'

'What was it?'

'That's between Martha and me.'

Suddenly she raged at me, her mood-swings as rapid and rabid as mine. 'No, it's not just to do with you. *It was you who made all this happen. We were happy here until you went and spoilt it. You have ruined my life for ever and I really really hate you . . .*'

'That's not fair, you were having problems at school long before I fell out with Martha.' I tried to cuddle Poppy close, and before she pushed away I could feel the tremors in her breathing. There was so much of myself in this unhappy child, the same insecurities and self-doubts that I had passed down like a ghastly legacy. I had failed in my determination to make her childhood a happy one. My heart broke for her; I knew what she was suffering and ten years old was too young. I wished that I felt less for her. How could I ever forgive Martha for causing my children to be so hurt?

'You always wanted me and Josh to be exactly like Scarlett and Lawrence and we never could be,'

Poppy sobbed. 'And you wanted to be like Martha because she was strong and she made you feel good. She made you feel important. Well, Scarlett made me feel that way too and now I don't know what to wear in the mornings and I hate you more than anyone else in the world.'

Remorse struck like an electric shock. Horror and shame. Had my behaviour been so transparent that even my children had watched and mocked me? I confessed, 'Well, maybe it is my fault.'

She was so anguished that she begged, 'Please go round and make it up with her. *Make friends with Martha, make Scarlett like me . . .*'

Dear God, if only I could. 'It's not as easy as that, I'm afraid.' And I thought of the time I had dosed this child with Benylin, rubbed her head with sandpaper and pretended she had fallen out of her high chair, just to grab Martha's attention.

Any justification of this would be sick.

Poppy went on. 'And Scarlett says I'm common. She calls you a witch, all the kids do. And now we are running away and going to live somewhere else because nobody likes us, even Daddy . . .' Looking more vulnerable than ever before, Poppy collapsed into spasms of crying.

And then, dear God, not content with wounding my child, I had tried to take my own life with no thought for Graham, Poppy or Josh. How could I call myself a mother?

Pity for Poppy made me cross. 'Those stories you made up about Scarlett and Harriet, they weren't very nice, were they? It wasn't all my fault, you see . . .' I tried to reason gently. I tried to apportion the blame.

But Poppy saw right through me. 'Don't try and

blame me, it was you, *it was you.* You made a stupid fuss over Sadie's music, Hilary tried to be friends with you but you just told her to sod off, and then you wonder why everyone hates us. You told silly tales to Martha—yes—*yes, we all know about that.* You told her you'd been to bed with Sam when that was a lie—it never happened! *Did it? Well, did it?* It was you who turned Scarlett against me and everyone else against poor Dad and Josh.'

I turned away. To the window. My only view was of Martha's house, a dead spot in my memories. I rode a colossal wave of despair that curved and foamed but refused to break.

'Don't you ever let me hear you speaking to Mummy like that again.' Graham turned up just in time to save me, as he usually did.

*   *   *

Snow powdered the mulberry tree.

We were the only ones in the Close not to be asked to the Frazers' party.

We stayed and played Scrabble round the fire, trying not to listen as cars arrived and left. We closed the curtains against the merriment of headlights.

Poor Josh, he was more introspective than Poppy, and boys don't tend to form such intense and dependent friendships. Josh could protect himself if it came to a scrap, but he was overweight—down to me—and so I had caused all of his problems. Had I overfed him to compensate for something . . . not being able to love him enough, trying to make it up to him because my child could not be like Lawrence no matter how

323

hard he tried?

If we managed to buy the new house, if our finances stretched to that, I would work all hours in the studio-barn to make sure he, too, got the best education, the best second chance I could give him. And I'd do my utmost to help him lose the two stone he could do without.

I owed them all so much.

Especially Graham, who never reproached me, who remained indignant on my behalf, and at a loss to understand exactly why everyone had suddenly turned on us with such fanatical fervour.

'One of these days, Martha's going to find out that what you told her was perfectly true. Are you sure it was true—Sam and Tina—*are you certain?*'

'I saw them together, I saw them quite clearly, and Tina admitted the truth to me. But it is possible Martha will never find out.'

Graham said, 'For your sake, I hope that she does.'

'For my sake?' I couldn't help it, my voice faltered.

'I know how much her friendship means . . .'

'Not half as much as yours.'

'You'd never lose that,' said Graham, 'unless you decided to leave me. And there'll be plenty of opportunities now, once your new career takes off—you'll have the whole world at your feet.'

But why would I want the world? The world was something I'd rather run from. 'I need you more than the whole world,' I told him. And that was true. I wasn't lying. It was just that Martha . . .

*   *   *

I turned and drew him gently towards me.

CHAPTER THIRTY-TWO

Martha

I turned and drew him gently towards me.

*   *   *

This was the first time I had seen Sam cry, properly, genuinely. He needed all the comfort I could give him. He needed me—he needed me now.

After so much work on building it up, UK Marketing Ltd was on the rocks: eleven people thrown out of work and the bank was refusing to give Sam a break. Advertising was notorious for its risks. Sam had never once breathed a word about the difficulties he had been facing for the last six months—he'd believed he could pull off the impossible, but late payers and two big customers going bust had combined to strangle the firm to death.

Within one week of me finding out, UK Marketing Ltd, Sam's pride and joy, Sam's reason for living, went into the hands of the receivers.

Maybe more warning would have softened the blow? Perhaps we could have pulled in our horns that much earlier, taken out some suitable insurance or even moved to a smaller house, I don't know. But here we were with a mortgage that took more than half of Sam's annual income—my wages on a weekly rag hardly counted for much—and up till now we had lived very well. A privileged existence, you could have called it.

It had taken the Gordons a while to sell theirs, so how quickly would our house go? Sam said, 'Their buyers haven't signed the contract yet. We could try and lure them over here for a few grand less.'

He couldn't be serious. 'Stop it, Sam, we might be in a sodding mess but we're not going to stoop to that sort of level.'

He wasn't joking. I couldn't believe it when he edged over to our neighbours' would-be purchasers as they got out of their car the following day, with their surveyor in tow.

Jennie must have seen them chatting mysteriously out on the road and I cringed in shame. But I felt even worse when Sam crawled back, tail between his legs, to tell me the guy was after a pool. 'I told them that one leaked,' Sam said, 'but I doubt if they believed me. I could tell they were pretty pissed off when they heard my alternative proposition.'

'*Are you surprised?* Christ, how could you? I can't believe you stooped so low. What if they had taken the bait and the Gordons had lost their sale?'

'Sod the Gordons,' said Sam defiantly.

*   *   *

In so many ways we seemed to be losing our grip. What was happening to us lately?

The Close had become a stagnant pond; hatred caused that rotten smell, that green slime of shame that seemed to cling to every single thing we did.

For the first time our Christmas Eve party was not a success. Quite frankly, it was a bore. We'd overdone tradition and it felt like a meaningless ritual where once it had been such fun. I was painfully aware of the lights across in the Gordons' house, and of the feelings of those two kids, of their bewildered faces, and how essentially wicked we were to exclude them in this hurtful way, especially at Christmas.

I'd been surprised when the invitation arrived for Jennie's London exhibition. I stuck it on the mantelpiece where all invitations went, but Sam chucked it on the fire. I shivered as I watched him do it. So mean. So vicious. 'That was rather unnecessary. We could have refused. There was no need for that.'

Corrosive as rust, this communal vengeance had seeped into all of us with a violence hardly merited. Still our conversations focused on what the Gordons were doing: if they'd chosen a new house yet, if they'd decided on which private schools to send the children to, and which, in their right mind, would take daft Poppy? We voiced our concerns about their potential new neighbours and hoped they would be strong enough to withstand Jennie's scheming—as if we honestly gave a toss. For God's sake, when they'd gone they'd be gone, but who would the rest of us talk about then?

I despised the way our active dislike had infected our children and wondered over Scarlett's seemingly natural vindictiveness, although I did take Sam's point that she, of all people, had suffered from Poppy for far too long. Personally, I would be relieved when the Gordons' contract was signed and sealed, when the removal van was packed and gone.

There would be such an odd emptiness . . . such a vast space to be filled.

For so many months they had entertained us.

Tina Gallagher had no such qualms. 'Don't go soft on us now, you're forgetting how bad it was.'

'But, Tina, when you stand back and look at everything that has happened, when you think of what we've done . . .'

'Think of what that woman has done to us,' Tina retorted, 'and you of all people should find that a cinch.'

I still tried to reason, 'But there is a limit. Good grief, don't you think the time has come when we could bend a little and wish them good luck? They have been our neighbours for over ten years . . .'

'*And have them change their minds?* Not likely,' sneered Tina, and I sensed that they were all watching me in case I betrayed them and gave Jennie a smile or asked the kids over to play. Oh yes, Jennie's lie about Tina and Sam had been absolutely outrageous, but no harm had come of it, and it wasn't her fault—she was sick, her illness had a name I'd forgotten, and instead of retribution my neighbour needed counselling.

For our behaviour there were no excuses.

And interestingly, that good Samaritan, Hilary Wainwright, with her meals on wheels and her Christian duties, was the meanest of all.

Look at the Blitz and the sense of togetherness, united against a common foe; then look at us—this little vendetta was so unhealthy, it sapped us and made fools of us all. I ached for the Gordons when they got in their car with their heads held high, eyes straight ahead, and I ached again when I noticed the kids only looked round when they'd left the Close.

Jesus, what had we done?

I couldn't share in the pouring of scorn on Jennie's work by those who had never seen it— particularly Sadie Harcourt, a self-proclaimed artist herself, just because of her art degree and her tacky animal earrings which she sold at the market on a Friday morning.

'She must have something. She can't have conned everyone.'

'She conned everyone here for years,' snapped Sadie, 'especially you.'

'You're wrong, Sadie'—I had to get this straight—'Jennie didn't con me, she made her feelings clear from the start. I would rather not have known, but she told me anyway.'

'But, Martha, the lengths to which she was willing to go in order to impress you! The way she ignored the rest of us, shouted her mouth off, caused so much trouble . . .'

'Quite honestly, Sadie,' I said, 'your music can be annoying.'

'Well, Martha, you could have mentioned it.'

'What? *Like Jennie?* And have you slag me off ever after?'

'That's not fair,' said Sadie.

Oh God, it was all so petty. And such old hat by now. Time is supposed to move on, but not here in Mulberry Close.

If we had to move out because of Sam's business, then I wouldn't give a damn.

*   *   *

329

My main concern wasn't the money although that was catastrophic enough, it was the effect of failure on Sam's macho image—he was provider, team leader, gifted designer and entrepreneur. And if work had given me an antidote to insanity and lack of self-esteem, then Sam's need was imperative. What would he do? How would he face rejection time after time, competing with four hundred others for work in an industry that prefers the under-thirties, and cope with being humiliated before panels of judges who, according to his lights, would know fuck all about it?

The prognosis did not look good.

He'd been so scathing about unemployment: the underclasses should get off their arses, he'd say. I hadn't bothered to contradict him because his attitude was so ingrained. His ghastly right-wing views were pathetic, but, more importantly, would he clean the bath while I went off to work, would he cook a meal, fetch the shopping, sort out the garden? *No, he wouldn't.*

Sam would be all hell to live with.

*   *   *

I knew I would agree to go the minute the chief reporter gave me the office invite. 'Jennie Gordon's your neighbour, isn't she? So take more of a human angle: hubby, kids, reactions to Mum's success, that stuff . . . have they inherited her natural talent?'

I felt I was spying on my country. If Sam or any of my neighbours discovered I was going to Jennie's exhibition, I would be stood against a wall and shot. No trial, nothing. I would certainly not insist on a byline for this little job.

I hadn't a clue what to expect. The last time I had spoken to Jennie I had barred her from my house for ever, but I guessed that the sickening tie that had bound her to me over all these years would not have broken overnight. She would not ban me from the gallery as I had banned her from my life and I hoped a meeting might give us both a chance to end this ludicrous farce.

It was a shock—I hardly recognized her. She'd been out and bought something suitable from Ghost and she looked spectral in that gauzy grey with a string of silvery beads. Her hair was as it used to be, straight and loose to her shoulders. There was a quality of grace about her; she looked confident, almost demure, enjoying herself in this high society with a glass of champagne in her hand, chatting away as if nothing fazed her, as if she'd never known a life of scrubbing, cleaning and skulking about, peering at the world through cautious nets.

The publicity people. I accepted a drink from some purple-haired chick.

I recognized a fellow hack and we agreed how incredible it was that someone like Jennie could come from nowhere and take the art world by storm.

'What's she like, this nymph?' he asked me, when I explained that I knew her. 'That's what everyone wants to know. She's so enigmatic, without a past it seems, or none that she wants to lay claim to.'

'What's she like?' I considered. 'That's hard to define. Quite ordinary, I would have said once. No-one could have imagined she had this kind of talent lying dormant inside her.'

I smiled at Graham. He glowered back and made no attempt to come over and speak. Fair enough. Why should he?

Poppy and Josh both noticed me, whispered something, and then Poppy went off. I guessed rightly that she'd gone to find Jennie.

*   *   *

Her smile was tense when she said, 'Hello, Martha.'

'All this.' I gestured towards the impressive display—weird, wonderful, dominant and disturbing. It was easy to see how special her work was. 'All this down to you. It's amazing.'

'You find it surprising?' She was quiet, pale.

I was honest. 'Where you are concerned, there are no surprises.' These formal exchanges were uncomfortable. 'How are you, Jennie?'

Her answer came without expression. 'You've got one hell of a nerve to ask.'

'I'm sorry you think that.'

Then her eyes turned cold. 'No, you're not sorry at all. So why come here and pretend that you are?'

The words almost stuck. 'I hoped that we might . . .'

'That we might what, Martha? Be friends again?'

'I suppose . . .'

'You and I were never friends.'

'You make me sound like the guilty party.'

'Guilty? *Guilty of what?*'

Confusion made me vulnerable. I was uneasy. People were looking. She was obviously still twisted up, still obstinate. I shouldn't have come. I certainly should not have offered the hand of friendship so readily. 'Guilty of lying . . .'

'Go away, Martha. I'm tired of all this. Go back to the Close where you belong. Go back to Sam and the rest of them.'

*   *   *

Sam rattled the *Observer* hard before throwing it down beside him. He had only bought it for the jobs and found himself unexpectedly face to face with his despised next-door neighbour. Someone was doing well even if he wasn't. He said, 'I wonder if anyone would pay to know the sordid truth about Jennie Gordon?'

'What truth? *What do you mean?*' I gave him a hard look and moved away. He was after making some money, OK, but to involve his wife in a tabloid scandal was surely a step too far.

'Jennie and Graham—how they met—I can see the headlines already.'

'*You denied that was true,*' I told him, incredulous. 'You called that one of her fantasies, you said I was mad to believe it.'

'I said that at the time, you're right, but all this has got me wondering.'

'Don't bother, Sam, it's sick. I promised Jennie total discretion and I wish I'd never told you.'

'But you did tell me and everyone knows. Somebody's bound to jump on this bandwagon and why shouldn't that person be me? Why shouldn't I make something out of it? After all, that slag did lay my wife.'

I stiffened. So that was it. He had never got over that affront to his manhood. 'How can you think of such a betrayal, let alone talk about it? Hell, we might be on our uppers right now, but we don't have to act like scum. And anyway, if Jennie told the truth about her first meeting with Graham, what about you and Tina? *Maybe there was more to that than you led me to believe.'*

The words were out before I could stop them. Something about Jennie's demeanour, the genuine hurt I saw in her eyes in the gallery where she reigned supreme and where there was no place for infantile games, had made me face some difficult questions. And now Sam had this grotesque idea in order to make a few quid . . . I hoped to hell he was joking, and I hoped to hell Jennie was lying.

*   *   *

I wished that life was only a dream so I'd have a chance to wake up.

CHAPTER THIRTY-THREE

Jennie

I wished that life was only a dream so I'd have a chance to wake up.

*   *   *

We moved house.

I still can't discuss it.

There is an illness—what it's called doesn't matter—when obsession is caused by a need to

334

focus on one supreme being who can define the world for infantilized adults, in the way that a parent does for a toddler.

Infantilized? Was that really me?

And was Martha my supreme being?

And now, just when life was turning around, giving us all new horizons, new hopes, I found myself staring at the studio wall, defeated and empty of all inspiration. This could only happen to me.

Dead from the inside out.

The princess who never spun straw into gold. The hidden magician had done it all for her.

'This happens,' Graham told me. 'Too many high expectations, not just from Hogg but from you, too. It will pass. Relax, it's just a block. Wait and see. If you do nothing else for a year it won't matter. The school fees are paid, the new house is ours.'

How could he be so accepting of disaster? 'But that's not the point. *I've lost it.* Was all that energy just a fleeting gust which I've used up in one go?'

'Stop it before you convince yourself. Sit down and read some of your write-ups. The experts know what they're talking about, and no, it's not just a flash in the pan—you're going through a natural phase, that's all. And moving house is meant to be the third most traumatic event—'

'That's nonsense.'

Nothing Graham said could help me.

*   *   *

He was still disgusted by Martha's effrontery in turning up at my exhibition: 'Flamboyant, overlarge, like some prima donna from Covent Garden.' He called her a nosy, jealous old tart, 'trying to soft-soap you now you're famous'. But I knew Martha wasn't like that. Poppy and Josh were all for throwing her out on the pavement, or telling the press about the campaign to evict us from Mulberry Close. 'They'd be interested in that, wouldn't they, Mum? The way we were treated? Go on, Mum, tell them.'

But Graham warned Poppy, 'If we want to make a fresh start, what's the point in hauling that old baggage with us or washing our dirty linen in public? You have to learn to rise above it. After next term it won't matter anyway.'

*   *   *

We'd been a bit intimidated when we'd taken Poppy along for her interview at Birkdale House, what with its wood panelling and black and white tiles. I was scared she'd fail the entrance exam. While she sat in a daunting room full of strangers, head bent over the papers, we were shown round with the other parents, some in designer jeans and sweatshirts. Graham and I had dressed carefully in suits.

I prayed—my habit in times of stress, when me and God were in constant contact—and offered to do anything if he would just give Poppy this second chance. Oh, let her not be defeated by thinking the odds were stacked against her—as I would have been. Oh, please let my daughter, just this once, overcome her negative thoughts. If I could triumph, if only briefly, then so could Poppy, and apart from a massive boost to her ego, passing this exam would mean smaller classes, better results and a vast range of out-of-school activities. Birkdale House put the comp to shame.

Apart from that, she'd look great in the uniform.

Apart from that, I wanted to prove the Frazers and Mrs Forest were wrong.

She came out of the hall, pale and dejected. 'Well, that's it, I've had it, I couldn't answer one question. And anyway I hate it here and the rules are stupid.' Poppy stomped off ahead of us as if it was our fault, as if we had forced her to endure the ordeal for some demonic motive of our own.

*   *   *

We had heard on the grapevine that Sam had gone bust and I couldn't prevent a mean stab of joy. If what we'd heard was right, then the Frazers would have to leave the Close, and this knowledge was such a relief it was hard to express it adequately. I'd have no need to look back and yearn once we'd gone. I wouldn't be missing those marvellous times because they wouldn't be happening. The Frazers were going. There'd be nothing there for me.

And they wouldn't be buying a smart house like ours.

Ours was a Georgian house in the country, with a fairy-tale garden and a small field behind. Wisteria draped in clusters around the porch. The old barn next door was a ready-made studio: the previous owner had been a painter.

With my extra income we'd been able to buy a house that would normally have been way out of reach. How Martha would have loved it. It was probably more her style than mine and her furniture would have suited it better than our small, modern bits and pieces which we hadn't changed since we got married. My obsession had blinded me to such trivia as interior design.

For the first time in my life I had stood up to Martha and the memory of that still made me tremble. I'd been on a high, flushed with success and strengthened by the sight of my work which had looked so impressive, magnificent even. To see her there in the gallery was startling; I'd been so sure she would ignore my invitation. If I had known I'd have spent weeks rehearsing exactly what I should say and it would have tainted the whole marvellous experience.

Damn her, damn her.

Why did she have to turn up like that? It had been so hard to live without her.

I refused to let those old wounds reopen.

The only way forward was to concentrate on more work—but I couldn't work, my mind was a blank, all passion spent. Bewildered and vacant, I sat in my studio and blackness stared at me off the walls. Obliteration. *Where had I gone?* The dark feelings that nourished me had been unhealthy and horrible, they had deadened all normal emotions, they had demanded constant attention—but I needed them back to survive.

I was far more pathetic than Poppy. How could I pray for my daughter's small triumph when I couldn't rise to the challenge myself?

*   *   *

'You've passed! You're in! *Poppy, you did it!*'

I remembered to say a quick thank you to God

as I rushed up the stairs with the precious letter, half blinded by tears.

Her sleepy face was a joy to behold.

'Don't kid me.'

'I'm not, I'm not. Would I joke about something like this?' I took her in my arms, kissed and hugged her, and I could hear her heart pounding away nineteen to the dozen while my own head was buzzing with thoughts sweet and good.

'I don't believe it.' She read the letter. She reread it again and again. *'But how could I have passed?'*

'Quite easily, it would seem. They say your results were excellent, so there we have it, on paper—if you have to do it alone, you can.'

'Can I have that pony now?' But I knew she didn't really care; for the time being, this success was enough.

I dabbed at my eyes. 'We'll see. We'll see.'

*   *   *

I wouldn't have seen the article if Demetrius Hogg hadn't taken the *Mirror* because he had heard a rumour that something dastardly was afoot.

He didn't call me, he waited until we arrived for the dinner his wife, Gloria, had organized at their enormous Cadogan Square flat.

'Look at this—sensational!' he boomed. He spread out the centre pages.

I reeled back with shock. It was libel. It was vicious.

And worst of all it was my lie.

I wanted to hide my face and weep. I glanced at the newspaper with utter revulsion; it could have been covered in maggots.

'*What's this?*' asked Graham from over my shoulder.

'Don't look,' I begged him, trying to cover the lie with my hands. 'It's vile.'

'Don't be an ass, let him see,' commanded an excited Hogg. 'The more folks see this, the better. You can't be small-minded now, you're a star.'

'The children!' I cried, appalled by his attitude. How could a man of such taste have such a warped view of the world? 'How are they going to cope with this—*their own mother was once a whore?*'

'It can't be,' said Graham, snatching the paper. 'For God's sake, let me see what they've done.'

'Graham,' I cried—this was worse than a nightmare—'*what about your job*? You might lose your job over this.'

'That's crap,' said Hogg. How could he stay so calm?

Graham looked up, aghast. '*But how can this be possible?*' he demanded, ashen-faced. 'How can they print such blatant lies? Surely they'd know we'd sue? I mean, this says that Jennie was on the game. It says I was kerb crawling down Formby Road. This is mind-boggling. Listen—look—*this says that's how we met.*' His eyes were sunk in his head. They were hunted eyes, haunted. 'We'll get the law on this right away—'

'Cool it, my friend,' drawled Hogg, resting a calming hand on Graham's shoulder. 'If you really want a fight we'll have one and we'll win, I'd bet on that. But I've had two phone calls already from TV stations keen to do interviews, and it's worth remembering they allege these happenings took place before you two got hitched—too long ago to

340

count for anything. All this publicity means is that Jennie's appeal is no longer confined to the narrow world of art but extends to the man in the street . . .'

I snapped back, 'I don't need this kind of infamy. Christ, I'm amazed you think I do! Your attitude beggars belief. I can't have wicked slurs like this printed and not deny them outright.'

What other angle could I take? If Graham found out that I had used this lie to seem more colourful in Martha's eyes at a time when I felt her friendship was cooling . . .

But Hogg, cucumber cool, refused to be convinced and his worldly wife with the glittering black eyes agreed with him whole-heartedly. 'These days it helps a celebrity to have a chequered past. Look at the rush to claim child abuse. Look at the glamour of a criminal background—nothing too offensive, of course. It's what Joe Public demands of his heroes.'

'Christ, that might well be, but there is a difference between child abuse and tottering about in stilettos with a skirt halfway up your arse, selling your body to Tom, Dick and Harry.'

'But you didn't do that—*that's what you're saying.* So the mystery remains unsolved. Who can tell if it's true or not? You must admit, Jennie, it's a far more romantic image than the blank persona of wife and mother.'

'You might call prostitution romantic,' I turned on Gloria and told her. 'I see it as sad and pathetic.'

'Not the way they've got it here. You come across as a real survivor, a vanquisher of the odds of life.'

341

Damn them both. *This was unreal.*

'But who would have said these awful things?' Graham was still in shock, stupefied. 'Who'd be sick enough to go to the press with this sort of crap? And why would they print it without checking?'

Hogg was almost rubbing his hands. He clearly saw this as a golden day. 'That feud you mentioned, the feud in the Close. Who's to say one of those guys didn't go to the papers with this load of garbage in order to make a few miserable bucks?'

'That's possible,' Graham said with a groan, his normally neatly combed hair standing up in tangled disarray on his head. 'So you're standing there, honestly telling me that anyone with a grudge can say what they like and get it printed without any comebacks? Come on, get real! There's got to be some research, there's got to be some smattering of truth. In this case, it's just a tissue of lies.'

'Don't deny. Don't agree. Just give a few knowing smiles,' advised Hogg. 'Darling, you're an artist and meant to have a tortured past. These little people have done you a favour. Be wise. Be grown up. Use it to your own advantage.'

'I suppose it was a long time ago,' I started mildly.

Graham exploded. *'Jennie!* What the hell are you saying? You can't mean that.'

'Graham, what else can we do? If we took it to court there'd be more publicity. It could drag on for months, there'd be more nasty lies, the children might be drawn into it . . .'

'But, dammit, we can't just let these people . . .'

'Relax, darling,' cooed Gloria, attempting to win Graham over with her perfect smile. She laid her jewelled hand on his arm. 'Your wife is about to become a big name. Relax and enjoy.'

To Graham this reaction was anathema. He spluttered, *'Enjoy it?* The very idea . . .'

'Graham,' said Gloria gently, batting her long black eyelashes at him. 'I do understand how you feel. After all, Jennie is your wife and it can't make you feel good to know your wife was anyone's for the price of a McDonald's.'

'No, no. You've got me wrong,' he tried to explain, while I listened, burning with shame. 'I wouldn't care what Jennie was, that's not the point. It's the fact that these scumbags can get away with these lies, that's what bugs me. And what if this kind of libel was used against you, you and Demetrius, how would you feel?'

'If Jennie's OK with it, what the heck?'

An aproned woman appeared in the doorway. 'Dinner's ready,' said Gloria. So Hogg slipped an encouraging arm through mine.

I tried to find some calm place, but everything was chaos inside me. *How could Martha have done this to me?* As a punishment after the exhibition? Or was Sam the perpetrator of this great betrayal? Had she passed on this confidence in the way she had passed on so many others? I was cold inside, my tongue tasting the corrosive flavour of a real and deadly hatred. Had Martha always betrayed me, even when I'd thought her safe? For all I knew, the whole Close believed I'd been a whore and Graham a punter, and the only person to blame was myself.

The food they served was magnificent. Like something you see in the supplements.

The wine flowed and I shivered.

A distinguished man in spite of his shape, Hogg's deep drawl was authoritative and I watched how his heavy gold watch glowed on his hairy wrist. In the prismatic light shed by the chandeliers, this bald-headed connoisseur shone—he hypnotized us with his stories of places he'd been and people he'd met. Behind his glasses, his eyes were sea-green. And then he turned his attention on me. 'You rarely see such illusive longings expressed so clearly in a work of art. Some of your sculptures are quite exquisite, they mesmerize with their primitive truths. They moved many people at the exhibition and I feel privileged to have found you.'

And so he went on . . . and on . . . and on . . .

Tipsy already, I drank more of the heady red wine and wondered drunkenly about changing idols. Could I transfer to someone else? Images came togethcr and dissolved as they do on the edge of sleep and gradually I felt some life returning. The numbness that blocked me was penetrated as I sat there watching and listening to the man, my thoughts disturbed and yet letting in some new delight. If I could surrender to love again, to that awful aching, yearning fantasy . . . If I could break free from this stony prison and come out into the menacing light . . .

But Hogg?

Did the subject really matter?

The disorder inside me felt like an earthquake.

Could I actually choose my supreme being?

Was it really as simple as that?

I tried my utmost to plunge again—for the sake of my art, for the sake of my soul . . . I did admire this incredible man who had talked with kings and walked with knaves. My knuckles were white against the cloth as I tried to transfer my passion, so that I could get back to my studio where so much work was waiting to be done.

Martha was gone. She would not come back.

Perhaps I could work for this man's approval. Perhaps he could love me if he knew how I felt . . .

*   *   *

This was how I found my strength. I had done it before. I could do it again.

CHAPTER THIRTY-FOUR

Martha

This was how I found my strength. I had done it before. I could do it again.

*   *   *

If only Sam would let me.

When he told me about his outrageous plan I knew he'd gone raving mad. 'What? *Did I hear you right?* Ask the Gordons for money, after what you did? After going to the press behind my back and annihilating that family in public—quite apart from the fact that we and the rest of them smoked the Gordons out of the Close? I don't recognize you any more, Sam. You're turning into something unnatural, they talk about people like you in the Bible.'

He poured another Scotch, his third, quite

unfazed by my disgust. 'A loan, that's all I'm asking. Just enough to tide us over . . .'

'Till when? When will we be able to pay back a loan? And why the hell would the Gordons consider giving us one in the first place? Us of all people?'

'Because she's completely obsessed by you, because she's sworn to be your slave until the day she dies.' He sounded so bitter. 'And all that crap.'

I hadn't told Sam that I'd been to Jennie's exhibition. I hadn't told anyone how she snubbed me. When it came to the Gordons he was irrational. Sam, more than any of us, appeared to miss their presence next door, as a hunter might curse the escape of his prey, and this aspect of Sam made me shiver. They'd gone. It was time to move forward. Morosely he watched the new people move in, a couple called Watson with three young boys.

When I got home from work I asked him, 'Have you spoken to our new neighbours yet?' I hardly had time to take off my coat before starting on the backlog of work: the day's washing-up, peeling the spuds, sorting out the coloureds for the machine.

'This time we will not get involved. This time we will leave well alone.'

I was only asking.

'Any luck?' It was a regular question.

He stared at me under folding brows. 'What the hell d'you think? Of course I've had no sodding luck and there's no need to rub it in with such glee the minute you get home.'

'Sam, I'm so sorry.'

He snorted. 'Your ignorant brand of optimism I can live without right now.'

'We can't both wander around depressed. This'll pass . . .'

'Shut up, Martha, *for God's sake, shut up.* You'd have done better to cultivate the lovely Jennie Gordon when you had the chance. She would have made damn sure you were looked after in the manner to which you are accustomed. And how you must be regretting that now.'

I didn't answer. I carried on clearing up the kitchen. I'd never known Sam sound jealous before—in our relationship that was my prerogative—and for him to be jealous of another woman, when he knew the circumstances perfectly well, was mean as well as callous.

'Perhaps I should have flogged that to the papers.'

If he only knew what he sounded like. This wasn't the Sam I had fallen in love with and stayed true to for all these years. I tried to feel pity instead of anger. 'Well, you failed to destroy Jennie with your first crude efforts. Since your little contribution, interest in her has reached dizzy heights. She's had the wit to ride over that whole seedy episode, so any lesbian connection would no doubt only add more mystique to her image. Do what you like, Sam. I don't give a toss.'

'Dyke,' said Sam with a tipsy slur. 'That vamp tried to wreck my marriage.'

And so he would rant and rave, unable to leave old wounds alone; he was irritated by that itchy scab which got worse as he worried and scratched at it. 'Yes,' I said, 'she did try, but she didn't succeed, did she? We're together in spite of Jennie. So why the hell don't you leave it alone?'

Last night we watched our former neighbour on

347

a late-night chat show with Melvyn Bragg. I imagine all our neighbours watched and I wondered if their reactions were mine, bowed by the weight of a terrible guilt? Did they worry like I did that Jennie might launch into a story that would ruin us all? Bring the wrath of God down on us? Sam watched, slumped forward, drinking in every word. And whenever Jennie spoke, he muttered, 'Stupid cow,' while all I could do was marvel at her new-found self-confidence. Seeing her there, holding her own among all those experienced media people, it was hard to remember the Jennie I knew.

She looked so good, so astonishingly composed.

She handled all this far better than I could.

'Bitch—she even sounds like you,' said Sam.

In this vengeful mood he had insisted that we drive past her house to see what it was like. Naturally I was reluctant, especially with the kids in the car. What was his morbid fascination? But maybe if Sam saw where the Gordons lived, he might finally manage to let them go.

'Christ,' said Sam when we drew up. 'She's rolling.'

I just prayed that no-one would see us. This was the worst kind of envious snooping—how ghastly if Jennie were to come out. 'It's probably not all her money,' I said, mainly to calm him down. 'Graham's got a management job, hasn't he?'

Too late—I'd said it. A direct comparison between Graham's success and my husband's abject failure. Sam sulked all the way home and Scarlett went on about the field at the back. 'And it's got stables,' she informed us. 'Someone from her school told Daisy Masters. I bet she'll be given a pony. Poppy always gets what she wants.'

'But that would be nice for her, wouldn't it?'

'She's too wimpy to be able to ride.'

'Why couldn't we go in and see them?' Lawrence asked, confused. 'I bet Josh's got some wicked computer games.'

'Shut up, Lawrence, we don't like them. Haven't you worked that out by now, cretin?' said Scarlett.

'So why did we bother to come here?' asked Lawrence, who seemed to miss the Gordons in his own quiet way as much as Sam did.

*   *   *

I wasn't allowed to forget the Gordons.

It was just as difficult at work, now that we had a local personality made good. The handouts and press releases flowed in: Jennie in America, Jennie in Germany, Jennie at the Getty museum, or in the Hepworth garden in Cornwall. At all times she was accompanied by that weird, bald American guy called Hogg. Perhaps he was coaching her with her public speaking and image, maybe he was choosing her wardrobe, because how else would she have the nous to cope with all this?

And I wondered how poor Graham was managing, left out in the cold at home.

The insurance was paying our mortgage, but only for six months. Sam was on benefit. We sold the jeep and my second-hand banger. Mark and Emma invited us to Betws-y-Coed again, but Sam said he'd feel bad comparing his situation with their privileged lifestyle, fast cars and lobsters. I know they were hurt when we turned them down.

A holiday abroad was out of the question.

We'd drawn apart from the neighbours soon

after the Gordons left. It worked out as I suspected it would; suddenly our main connection was severed and everyone felt embarrassed when the last removal van left the Close. We had all behaved appallingly badly and we were sheepish around one another. It felt like the end of an era.

*   *   *

Our FOR SALE sign looked as rooted as the standard roses in the front garden and the riotous hydrangea. Because Sam was showing our viewers round I was not surprised there were no takers—he was surly and resentful and showed it. The fact that we had been forced to move he blamed on Jennie Gordon.

He'd blown the whole episode right out of proportion to disguise his own sense of failure. Nothing was his fault, but some of it was mine.

So when he suggested asking them for a loan, it seemed he believed that they owed him.

'If you can't do it, then I bloody will,' he told me bluntly. 'Maybe that cow wants reminding of a few sordid incidents she might have forgotten.'

I lit a fag. My hands were shaking. 'Blackmail, is it?' I had to ask.

'No, not quite blackmail.'

'As near as dammit. Money for silence. Sam, what you're saying, it's loathsome.'

He sounded so bloodcurdlingly hostile, and in this mood there was no humouring him. 'Graham deserves to know what went on. We ought to have come clean at the time.'

'Oh? To what end? Graham is a dear, sweet, boring man, but he adores Jennie. And nothing but

350

terrible pain could come from him finding out.'

'He needn't find out if Jennie pays up.'

I got up, making out I was searching for an ashtray, but really giving myself the time to sum up just what Sam was getting at. 'Are you suggesting that I go to her house and threaten her, like some low-life mobster?'

'Why not? I doubt you would need to threaten her. She'd give up her life if you asked her. You only have to smile nicely.'

'You're sick.'

'I could have sued her, you know, she slandered me and Tina. We could have got her back then, cleaned her out.'

I said, 'I doubt that.'

'Martha, you're wrong.'

'You would have needed to prove financial loss . . .'

'Fuck you.' When Sam stood up heavily, he wobbled. His voice was thick with drink, or was it anger? He was wagging a stupid finger at me, but I felt he would rather have used his fist. 'Whose bloody side are you on? Don't you start lecturing me, just because no-one will pay me a sodding wage while you—'

'Don't!' I said. *'Oh don't.'* I went towards him, held him in my arms, and I felt the shudder where the sobs should have been. 'Don't make out I'm against you just because of a lousy job. Things can only get better. We'll find somewhere else to live, you'll see, and before you know it, it's Sod's Law, you'll be on your way up that old ladder again.'

'No, Martha. Not this time.' His voice was drowsy, so tired of it all. 'That's not the way, not these days. Education, hard work, shit.' His breath

351

was boozily warm on my ear as he whispered furiously, 'It's not like that now. If you don't want to go fucking under, you've got to grab any chance by the bollocks and squeeze till you get what you damn well want.'

'No, Sam.' I helped him drop back into the chair, his weight on me felt so heavy.

'Money,' he moaned hopelessly. *'Fucking, bleeding money.* You've got to have it . . . you've got to get it . . . whatever it takes you've got to . . .'

*   *   *

Sam didn't know that I had appealed to my father for help, seeing how desperate we were. I hated doing it. Debt was something my parents had never experienced and would not understand. According to them, it was simply a question of living within your means. Accounts at a few reputable stores were the only debts my mother ran up and they were paid off every month.

'A few thousand, darling, that's all I've got free.'

I tried desperately to make Dad understand.

'Our money is tied up in long-term securities, Martha, sweetie,' he said.

'Couldn't you, for my sake, get some out?'

I might as well have asked him to kill.

'No question, Martha, we'd lose too much. It's long-term planning that's all-important.' And that staid remark suggested to me that we should have been more circumspect and not gone around spending more than we earned.

'What about a small mortgage?' I begged him. 'Couldn't you and Mum take one out?' They'd gone on safari last year, and this year they'd already booked for Alaska. Their house was stuffed with priceless antiques. They might not approve wholeheartedly of Sam—flippant, too arrogant, they'd warned years ago—but they needn't take it out on me. 'Just to tide us over this difficult patch?'

My father was far from heartless—he'd been over-indulgent in his time—but now it was 'No, dear, you'll just have to cope as best you can and sell that expensive house and those cars, eat sensible food instead of that rubbish you buy, and maybe it will do the children good to appreciate that money doesn't grow on trees.'

Ah yes, we were feckless, they'd always known it: we chucked socks away instead of mending them; we didn't stick slithers of soap together; we failed to use up every dried-up scrap in the fridge; we bought a new washing machine this year while Mum had had hers since she was married . . .

Ah yes, we were reckless: we bought gifts like computers and new mountain bikes; we went round Safeway's and M&S and picked up lemon and garlic chickens, prickly pears, and avocados with sauce; we even bought pre-wrapped carrots and salads, and all for such a shocking price!

'Why all these foreign sauces?' Dad would ask. 'Whatever's the matter with gravy?'

Dark days. Hard times.

Sam would die before he asked his own father. They'd always been so competitive—that was their relationship since he'd been a small boy and he'd thrived on it. But now, since this catastrophe hit us, he'd not even told him that the firm had gone down.

*   *   *

So I said I would try for the loan—just to placate him. 'But not in any threatening way. I'll ask Jennie to come and have lunch and I'll try and bring it up casually. But don't hold out much hope, Sam, will you? Things can't be the same between us, not now, not after all that's happened.'

Sam's smile was far from pleasant. But he didn't follow up my promise with scathing remarks or sarcastic sneers. I had finally agreed to his mad request and he had to be satisfied with that. Maybe I could approach Jennie in a way that didn't sound like begging—make it sound as if lunch and a reconciliation were all I was interested in. But following on our last meeting there wasn't much chance she would believe me. Would she suspect some ulterior motive?

I had to try, for Sam's sake.

But if Jennie refused to see me, then that would be the end of the story.

*   *   *

The thought of it actually made me feel sick.

CHAPTER THIRTY-FIVE

Jennie

The thought of it actually made me feel sick.

*   *   *

Meeting with Martha. Should I? After everything ...?

This wasn't love else I wouldn't have gone. Love requires respect, and how could I respect a woman who collaborated with her husband to bring me and my family down by betraying such a confidence? The fact that it was a lie was irrelevant. I guessed that Sam was the one who gave the *Mirror* their centre-page spread. And Martha was still with him—still, no doubt, his uncritical and all-worshipping chattel.

It wasn't love and it wasn't transferable. I had struggled hard to replace my idol, my long-term supreme being, with Hogg, but to no avail. Hogg had the hallmarks of a far more suitable champion—male for a start, sophisticated, amusing, worldly and, what's more, a success, while Martha still grubbed around for peanuts on the *Express.* Nevertheless, after her surprise phone call, all struggles for freedom ceased. She was interested in me again, she wanted to meet me, I didn't care what for, and I found to my horror that my block disappeared merely on the strength of one stilted communication.

Our meeting at the gallery didn't count, that had been impersonal, she was there because she was press; she had not replied to my private invitation. And that took place before I realized the terrible truth that I now accepted—without her and the anguish she brought me, I was empty, I simply couldn't work. Martha's phone call was different ... she gave me no clues as to the reason for meeting and this provided hours of fascinating speculation.

Could it be that she missed me?

Could it be that she had finally found out about Sam and Tina, and was desperate to apologize and make up for that revenge campaign which had surely been instigated by her? No-one else in the Close would have had enough influence to turn the others so completely against me.

My life was full now: I travelled, I dined, I socialized. This made me an *interesting person*, so maybe Martha wanted part of the action. What laughs we would have if we travelled together— we'd go shopping, she could choose my outfits; I could drop Gloria with her strict advice and too glossy image, and revel in Martha's company again.

*   *   *

'I was afraid you wouldn't see me after . . .'

'The *Mirror* exposé, or the Close campaign?'

Martha bowed her head, closing her eyes against my accusations. She hadn't changed. *Had I feared she might?* She was blowzy, fat and beautiful, and her silk strapless dress was her own design— nobody else would have mixed those colours. We were sitting in the window seat at the town's best restaurant, Willies. That was Martha's idea. She knew I travelled around; this local venue was convenient for me—I could walk there from my house.

Where was her car?

She arrived by taxi.

The change of status was apparent at once. For all those years, I had been the needy one and Martha the bountiful giver, and I was shocked by the subtle reversal. I stared at her as she studied the menu, as the firelight played over her face, and

356

I thought how I'd wanted to end my life, how I'd yearned to change places, and how I'd even hurt my child in a sick bid for this woman's attention . . . But instead of remorse, there was nothing but a perverse sense of joy to discover that my passion still lived—there could be nothing worse than the death of it; there could be nothing worse than the disillusion of seeing the adored one as mundane, almost distasteful once obsession had died. And I knew this, as everyone knows it.

I adored her.

'I don't know what I can say to you about what went on in the Close,' said Martha. 'I wasn't happy with it then, and now I can hardly believe it happened.'

I didn't like this inferior approach. I didn't want to see her made weak.

'What's the point in talking about it? It happened. We've gone. That was another life.'

She shook her head, closed her eyes again, and I hated this new subjection. As if unable to meet my eyes, Martha twisted the stem of her glass and watched that instead. 'It just snowballed out of all control,' she went on, in spite of my stated lack of interest. 'It sickens me, I can't explain it and there are no excuses for it.'

I went along the route she had chosen. Maybe she needed to know where I stood. My anger was still there, fuming inside, but all I said was, 'The children were miserable. Very hurt.'

She fumbled with her unwieldy bag, delved around for her fags, offered me one and then said, 'Sorry. I was forgetting . . . do you mind if I do?'

What? What was this? Now it was my turn to look away. This was abject surrender on her part.

Her fake subservience was intolerable.

I said, 'I heard about Sam, about the bankruptcy. It must be horrendous—you must be shattered.' In the old days she would have collapsed dramatically, raved on about creditors' meetings, bailiffs, settlements, receivers and liquidation. Her experiences over the last few weeks must have been horrific, not least the fear of losing her home . . . but all she said was, 'We're in a mess, Jennie, it's been quite a shock.' And then, for the first time, she met my eyes.

I thought I'd convinced myself not to bring this up, but her reserve riled me so much that I tried to break through it by asking, 'And Sam, how's he bearing it, and has he told you the truth yet?'

'Isn't there enough shit between us without you digging around in that? Can't you and I forget the past?'

'Hah!' I still admired the nerve of the woman and her resistance to facing reality. There was no future for either of us if she still believed I could shatter her marriage with a lie so outrageous as that. But could I blame her, bearing in mind the story I'd told about Sam and me in bed that Christmas? What demon inside me invented these lies and was he still there scheming, biding his time . . .?

I didn't expect her question. *'Was that true, Jennie—Sam and Tina?'*

If I said I had lied she would forgive me and I'd see that fond look in her eyes. But if I insisted I'd told the truth, she might get up and walk away. I tried to avoid the decision. 'Does it matter any more?'

'It does to me.' It was then I first noticed how

drained and weary she looked under that clever make-up.

'Yes, at that time it was true. He was seeing Tina, I saw them together. Twice. Quite apart from the fact that Tina admitted it herself. But now I haven't a clue if it's finished or still going on. Maybe the fact that I told you stopped them in their tracks. They would have been pushing it after that, if they'd gone blithely on. You ought to know, would Sam be so stupid?' Had she taken this message on board, or was she still in denial? Would she answer me, or turn round and stalk off? I held my breath and waited.

'No,' said Martha, 'I don't think he would.'

'You still adore him, don't you? It doesn't matter to you what he does.'

It took her a while to answer. It wasn't like Martha to be so hesitant. 'It's not the same any more, Jennie. It hasn't been for a while now. Most of the viciousness heaped on you came from Sam and I believed he was genuinely furious because you'd set him up so unjustly. But now I'm wondering if it was guilt . . . and sheer rage . . . which drove him.'

'It doesn't take much to work out that answer.'

Martha toyed with a marinated prawn—again, nothing like her greedy self. 'But that's not the worst part of what's going on, the mess I told you about isn't that.' She held her fork to her mouth and stared at me. I had to wonder what was coming. 'It's *money*,' Martha confessed in a whisper. 'Or the lack of it. All this is killing Sam, and it looks as if when everything's over we're going to end up homeless.'

'*Money?*' Stupid as ever, I still couldn't get my

359

head round why she was talking to me about this.

Money? Is it really one of the most important things in life, important in the simplest sense? I don't think so. I think it is only important as a lie, the biggest lie that civilization has ever told mankind. I think it's the giant token for all the rubbish in the world and a false one at that, like a one-armed bandit paying out tokens that you can't cash anywhere else but in the pub where you're playing it. A promise of power that produces paralysis; a promise of happiness that leads you into the uneasy world of the opium-eaters, the false friends, the false lovers—that false and exquisite environment; a magic talisman in a world of unreality.

The chink of gold. The rustle of notes. And money had handed Martha to me.

'Nobody is prepared to help us,' Martha went on pathetically. 'We've tried everybody we know, every loan company—but Sam's a bankrupt and they won't touch him.' There were brilliant tears behind Martha's eyes. 'It would mean so much to us if somebody trusted Sam now—of course he would repay any loan with interest, given the time to get back on his feet. He's an enterprising person, you know that, Jennie. He's full of energy and ideas, he works himself into the ground. It wasn't his fault that the company failed . . .'

'Where's all this leading, Martha?'

'This is so degrading,' she said. 'I told Sam I wouldn't do it, but to see him so destroyed, so despairing and getting worse, is more than I can stand . . .'

'You want my money? *Is that why you're here?*' Why did she think I would sympathize with Sam

360

after the years I had spent with begging bowl in hand, not hoping for money but for Martha's attention, drip by drip. And who had cut off the source of my sanity? Sam Frazer, with no compunction. He'd been to blame for every bad thing that had happened to me and my children. But Martha was ahead of me.

'I understand that you'll find it hard to forgive Sam for what he's done. But don't forget, Jennie, for years Sam and I put up with one hell of a lot from you. Not your fault.' She held up her hands as if to provide a buffer for any angry denial. 'Not your fault, *I know that*; we both understood that you couldn't help what was going on inside your head. We were as patient as we could be, not just me but Sam too, particularly when Stella died. We did what we could to help you, Jennie. We tolerated all kinds of shit from one year to the next . . .'

I said, 'You were very kind.'

'I couldn't love you back, Jennie, which is what you really wanted. I had other commitments—the kids, Sam, my work—and I hadn't the energy or the will to give you everything you demanded. You can't call me unreasonable, I forgave you so many times.'

'No-one can love me like I want them to,' I said with a sudden, deep sadness. 'I make sure I choose people who can't. Who else would give all their love to their next-door neighbour—a woman, at that?'

Martha smiled wryly. 'I did give you something unique and important. I gave you the anguish you needed for your work.'

She had obviously read the article when I'd gone

on about pain being a spur. She had known and understood at once what I was referring to.

'You gave me that,' I had to agree. 'But I might have been happier without my work, just being normal, at home with my children.'

'Being normal and at home with your kids was the reason you had all that spare passion.' She sounded annoyed that I still hadn't sussed it. 'More on your mind and you might have stayed sane. You mustn't blame me for your inhibitions, or for their painful release.'

'Anyone but you and I would have been fine. Any other neighbour and I might have lived a contented life. I would have enjoyed being a good wife and mother and been satisfied with my lot. But you came along and the madness took over. You were everything I wanted to be, I envied you, I admired you, I needed you . . .'

'Not any more,' said Martha firmly. 'You're assured, poised, assertive, confident.'

'But, Martha, you gave me all that.'

'No. No.' She slumped in her chair and it looked as if I had depleted her with my relentless assertions. It looked as if I had sucked her dry like bats suck from the legs of donkeys, like spiderlings feed on the entrails of their mother.

'We did have some laughs, though. We had some fun, didn't we? There was that, too?' I could tell by her eyes that she hadn't laughed much lately. 'How's the job?' I had gone too far, I had to bring some light to this meeting.

'Boring,' she said. 'Pitiful pay. Our debts are incredible, they go up daily.' Flames flickered over brass and glass and the shire horse tablemats. Martha sounded like me, not her. Negative vibes, totally hopeless. I had fed off her for so long, now she needed a food source, too. For the first time Martha needed me.

'You are asking me for money.'

'I don't know, Jennie. I was going to, that's why I came today. But I see now that it's impossible. It was Sam's idea, by the way, not mine. He's drinking a helluva lot at the moment.' Her face tightened up with the kind of quiet anger I had seen directed at me in the past, particularly the time I spread the rumour that her drinking habits were out of control. She went on tiredly, 'Sam convinced me that you owed us something after that wicked lie about him and Tina.'

I pitied her then, really pitied her, and I hated this new experience. This was Martha sitting dejectedly in front of me, Martha demeaning herself—Martha who for so long had been the one solid feature in my tortured mind.

'Jennie, you should turn to religion,' she finally announced as if reading my mind. Were my feelings so transparent? And then she refilled her glass once again. 'Let's face it, it's a God you're after, not some feeble human relationship. Jesus wouldn't hurt you. Jesus wouldn't walk away.'

'Jesus was weak. They crucified Jesus.'

'But God's not. God's a bastard. He fixed that crucifixion himself.'

'But now you're trying to foist him on me?'

Neither of us smiled. 'Worship somebody from afar, that way you won't be fucked up by their foibles. Some celebrity, some footballer or popstar, and yes, I would foist them on you if it meant the traumas between us would end.'

Her own life wasn't such a success when you

thought about Sam's treachery and now this lamentable poverty threat. Her own love life wasn't so enviable, so what made hers more valid than mine? Just because it was less outlandish.

'But you are dealing with the stuff of pain. You design your requirements with that aim in mind.' The way she said pain made it sound like a dart with the tip soaked in a deadly poison. 'And if you need to release the creative, the pain level has to rise even higher. Yours isn't a pleasant passion, Jennie, and it has a repellent effect on others.'

One minute she was after my money, the next she was on the attack. I had to admit, 'I don't choose to be like this.'

'At some subliminal level you do,' Martha answered hotly. 'You go for it in the same way junkies go for their fix. Your drug is unrequited love, and it's sick. It's a killer, it's as bad as heroin.'

'What do you want?' I asked her. '*How much?*' We might as well reduce this to the basics. I might as well admit that her reasons for wanting to see me again were no more personal than going to the hole in the wall for some cash.

'It might sound a lot . . .' she started, fiddling with her glass once more.

'*How much?*' With every question, I reduced her. With every question, our roles were reversed.

'Two hundred and fifty thousand pounds. To be paid into a Guernsey account, under a name to be decided. Don't worry, I won't let Sam touch it. To be kept completely separate, to be managed by me for personal expenses . . . a home, for a start, food for the kids, some kind of old car . . . to be paid back over twenty-five years at an interest rate to be agreed on . . .'

364

Jesus Christ. But my latest work, which excited Hogg, was going to the US and with a price label not far off that amount. I knew that Graham wouldn't care—what I did with my money was my affair. And he would understand if any decision of mine concerned Martha. We had our house, no mortgage needed. Our investments would keep us comfortably off, and our pension and insurance plans were sufficient for anyone's needs. Even if my block came back, even if I stopped working today, Graham and I were secure . . . he wanted to keep his job anyway . . . and wasn't this all thanks to Martha?

Didn't I owe her this much?

*   *   *

Who has the last word? This is my story after all. Shouldn't I have the last word?

CHAPTER THIRTY-SIX

Martha

Who has the last word? This is my story after all. Shouldn't I have the last word?

*   *   *

So here I was in Piglets Patch, the house Sam and I had originally wanted before the deal fell through and we decided to move to Mulberry Close. And here I was playing personal assistant to the famous sculptress, Jennie Gordon. I didn't get paid much, but the rent, council tax, water rates and the use of a new Vauxhall Corsa were thrown in to compensate for that.

This was the turning point in my life when I stopped stepping out of the vicious circle. The pull of the vortex had beaten me. 'Here we go round the mulberry bush' . . . and all that stuff.

When I got home after lunching with Jennie, I found Sam had packed his bags in my absence, sodded off and left me with his iMac and a box of CDs. A note said he could no longer tolerate living under the same roof as a dyke, and other malicious insinuations.

I think he knew the truth would come out.

This was so sudden, so jarring, just as unexpected as the firm going bust; and I must have been going around with my head in the sand because, once again, he gave me no clues. And according to Carl Gallagher, who seemed quite excited by the whole idea, Sam and Tina had a flat in Glasgow. They'd arranged this escape for months. Glasgow—of all places?

'But Tina's an Essex . . .'

'Yes, she is,' said Carl, 'no call for niceties now. But she's got her own income, she works from home, and it's never mattered to Tina where she lived. Flats in Glasgow are probably cheap.'

Carl was wearing that pleased silly look—cat got the cream—and it was obvious why. All Tina's fears had been justified; he'd been screwing some other woman for years, and she wasn't slow in moving in, either.

But me, poor me. What was I going to do now? Talk about getting out while the going was good, dumping your garbage on the mat with your front door keys and a pile of bills.

'Where's Daddy?'

'Daddy's gone to live in Scotland, Scarlett.'

'For ever?'

'Darling, I just don't know yet.'

'He's left you, hasn't he?'

'Yes, he has.'

'But he hasn't left us,' she told me triumphantly. 'We had a talk about divorce at school. Daddies who leave still love their children and want to keep in touch, it's just the mummies they can't stand.'

'Well, that's good, so long as you understand that, Scarlett. And please make sure that Lawrence does too.'

But when I tried to tackle Lawrence, he was too engrossed in Tomb Raider Four and groaned, 'Hang on, I'll be there in a minute.'

'It's about Daddy, Lawrence,' I said in a meaningful tone, the same one I'd used for the facts of life and why head lice only choose clean hair.

'Oh God,' he said, 'I know all about that. I'm nearly there, Mum, I've reached level five.'

So against all the expert advice, I left him.

*   *   *

The owners of Piglets Patch had gone to build a dam in Peru, leaving the cottage with an agency for a three-year contract. Jennie dug out this marvellous information after I rang her to confirm the loan and admitted that I was leaving the Close and looking for somewhere to rent. 'It's no good,' I told her. 'They want me out. They want me out now. And anyway, I can't afford it. I'm handing in my keys and going.'

'Hang on,' she said, 'don't do anything, let me check with Hogg. He has a list of places for clients who come to the UK on courses or sabbaticals. Let me check this out and I'll ring you back.'

She did more than that, she was amazing: she organized everything, paid the deposit, removals, the lot; and said I could stay here rent-free provided I did some work for her. 'Higher rewards than a small-time hack.' Blackmail, no other word for it. But who was I to argue?

In other circumstances I'd have laughed at her, scorning this manipulative streak—now more forceful than ever—as she used me in her weird games like some disposable lighter.

And as if she expected some argument, she was quick to defuse it with a positive approach. 'Think of the fun, like the best of the old times. I need a PA, you need a home and space to find your feet again. This is a professional arrangement, signed and sealed, legal. Straight. And, Martha, you need me now Sam has gone.'

She didn't have to put it that crudely. The offer was tempting from the word go; I hardly needed convincing. And she was proving a forgiving friend after all the damage Sam had done to her, supported by my weakness. I was still disgusted with myself at what I had allowed to happen. Jennie had never meant to be mean, never meant to hurt me.

*   *   *

The bailiffs came round the following day. I

suspected Sam knew they were coming and pissed off just in time. They called when I was at work but Hilary Wainwright told them what time I was expected back, and the devils came an hour earlier to make sure they caught me. Scarlett and Lawrence were terrified.

I wouldn't have minded this rough intrusion if I had been intending to fight tooth and nail, but I'd already come to terms with the fact that nothing was mine any more. They were rude and they were threatening, and I was an innocent party. How can these bullies be legally entitled to ply their terrible trade in any civilized society? The bastards tried to make off with Lawrence's bloody computer. They took the kettle. They eyed the cats—all toothless, worthless, thank God. I screamed at them and I cursed Sam for abandoning us to this dreadful fate. I detested him for all he had done.

And so the idea of Piglets Patch, starting afresh in the way I had originally dreamed—elderflower wine and bluebells for the kids—was doubly attractive to me after that. A real refuge from hell. And although I knew she was using me—Jennie made no bones about it—I wasn't going in with my eyes closed.

Funny, I'd have called myself strong before this. I thanked God that Jennie didn't have money when she was at her most passionate.

*   *   *

So here I was, installed in comfort with a new computer and fax machine. There might be no mulberry tree in sight, but Jennie was still going around as if she found that old treadmill irresistible. The cottage, full of the children's friends or empty, according to their social diaries, was a constant delight; an enchanting place with its fringe of thatch, flagged floors, peeping windows and bread-oven fireplace.

'But what do you do all day, Martha?' asked Peter Taylor, my old editor, calling me on the phone to see if I was up for a feature.

'Oh, I drive over to Jennie's if she needs me. I make reservations, write letters, keep books, consult her diary, e-mail her clients all over the world, and when she travels I'll be free to go with her. Graham's job, of course, is to look after the kids whenever he's at home.'

It was not a stretching schedule and left me with time on my hands for reading, freeing bits of the unruly stream and getting back to my painting again. The financial pressures were off me. I didn't long for work like I used to; I was fonder of my own company now. And, if I wasn't summoned to her house, invariably Jennie would come round for coffee. Here, contact with people was not so important as it had seemed in the Close. There was more of nature going on, a buzzing of colourful life, a living and a dying which made boredom impossible, and the cats were in seventh heaven.

'As long as you're happy,' said Peter, surprised, 'but there's always a job for you here, in case you change your mind.' I think he saw me as Jennie's stooge or a flunkey who had lost all ambition, identifying with the vegetables I had planted in the garden. But if I was empty of enterprise I was content with my new-found peace.

I missed Sam, however. I wept at night for the empty place in the bed. I carried out long conversations, trying to make matters right. I forgave him. If he'd found someone else, then it must be my fault. I saw Tina as the enemy, not him. The only communication we had was through infrequent letters demanding money. I had not taken up Jennie's loan, although it was there should I need it. But not for him.

Sometimes, unable to sleep—when everything was quiet save for the cries of the owls in the wood, when the wind in the trees sounded mocking, when defeated by exhaustion—I wondered if I'd given up my soul. I wondered if that was possible. Was Jennie, so single-minded, so obsessed and so determined to keep me, draining me of the life I had left?

Was I now exclusively hers?

Or was it me who was feeding off her by giving in, too weary to fight? Who was the parasite, her or me? Had I subconsciously fed on her unhealthy worship for years, and was I now too weak to resist?

*   *   *

But as time went on there were changes.

I began having nightmares and strange dreams. The dream feeling kept following me even when I was awake, and it brought a strong sense of unreality.

The crocuses appeared again under the old apple tree by the gate. Thrushes flew to and fro, collecting twigs for their nests. New life for them, but for me? For her? Sometimes, alone at home so much, I was convinced I was losing my mind. The meaningless chatterings in my head sounded like the wind as it gusted down the chimneys. The innocent light of shadows on grass tired me like my own thoughts; the rain cascading on the windows turned into mocking laughter. Solitude became too much and I longed for Jennie to come.

Jennie came and cried on my lap, and her tears were tears of hopeless longing.

'I love you,' she insisted, 'how I love you.'

So selfish, so remorseless was she, and yet now, all resistance gone, I held her and comforted her. Like a grotesque parody of a motherly embrace. But the mother was only a vacant lump.

CHAPTER THIRTY-SEVEN

The difference was—we seemed to be equal. That superior/inferior relationship between us had dwindled away to stagnation. It was wrong. How could anything work like this?

She came to my house and I watched her.

'What are you doing?' she asked, that last day.

She looked lovely in that bright summer dress, with the straw hat down her back on a string. Quite poised and peaceful.

It was just an ordinary school day. In a week's time we were flying to New York for a meeting with Demetrius Hogg, and I was already half packed and looking forward to a change of routine. We might have some fun there, like the old days. We'd both been shopping for the trip. I rubbed my temples hard as I looked up against the sun. A headache coming on? The sky seemed a peculiar colour. 'Just reading the paper,' I told her. 'Join me.'

'Don't get up. I'll make the coffee.'

I watched her.

There was a sudden cold gust of wind that did not suit the warm morning. That snort of laughter—did it come from me?

As she left I watched her shadow as she ducked to avoid the apple tree. She expanded, contracted, broadened and thinned like a character from *Alice in Wonderland.* She gyrated inside me in nightmare. She looked out of a livid mist and took on a distorted, deformed appearance. One minute all was beautiful, and the next, as my breathing increased, I sensed an evil presence that felt as if it was throttling me. And I had a breathless sense of being on the brink of some discovery. I had handed my soul to the powers of darkness. It was then that I began to fight to control the swelling panic in my chest. I struggled to find normality, but this terror filled the whole of my consciousness. Was I having a heart attack? Was this a stroke—at my age? Would I wake to find myself paralysed, dependent on others for ever? Dear God. I tried to clear my throat just to hear that comforting sound. These were bad feelings, I could smell them, like flesh decaying behind hedges.

The laugh that exploded out of me while I waited for her to return was more like the gasps of a convulsive fit. After so many years, hilarity and grief finally met in one circle and that was the sound they made. And volcanic anger caused the trembling. So much ferocity in so feeble a container.

I watched her.

She came back. She sat down on the wicker chair

and put the tray carefully on the small table. She brought the phone out with her. She'd important calls to make.

But now the pain was coming again, the blade of it twisted inside me and ripped up towards my guts. I fought to control the bile. She looked over and asked, 'Are you cold?'

Stupid question—nothing more than a gesture of possession. If I was cold, she must be too. We were as conjoined as Siamese twins, not at the stomach, the chest or the back, no, we were conjoined at our souls. We should have been aborted—that would have been the kindest way out. Foetuses for the incinerator. No human beings could survive like us, playing a frantic game of blind man's buff, bumping into the edges of life, tumbling into mountains of obstacles with no real identity of our own. We drained the lifeblood from each other. All I needed was one scalpel; sharp metal, shiny. One slice, one deep and bloody gouge to complete the separation.

I watched her.

'Need a blanket?'

I think that this silly question caused the detonation. The force sucked everything out of me and the light left my eyes and my brain together. Now everything was swallowed up by a vast and unbearable vacuum of rage.

'I'll get one.'

'There's a rug in the hall.'

'I know.'

I went.

The mahogany knife block stood proud in the kitchen. And down the side of the butcher's block was a miniature axe for chopping off fat. She used it for splitting coconuts, too, and she used the blunt end for cracking nuts. It was a most useful tool. I'd been round here for enough meals to know where everything was in this house. I knew that she kept it sharp; all her knives were regularly checked.

I picked it up and stared for a while—like you stare into those 3-D pictures and find a pattern hiding there. The metallic shine broke up in my head and turned itself into a million stars. When I touched the blade my finger bled, but it was a tiny wound, no more than a paper cut.

I was a child again, in the kitchen with my mother, polishing the silver with black stains on my fingers. I was weary, so very tired. To be an object of desire, to be the ultimate beloved must be just as exhausting as being the obsessive. We had both of us suffered so much for so long.

With a plan firmly fixed in my mind I collected the tartan rug from the blanket box in the hall. Hidden beneath it, in my hand, I gripped the handle of the axe. It was a pretty weapon, sometimes used to chop kindling, quite light—not hard to gain the right impetus, as if it had been honed and balanced especially for a woman's hand. A man might well have scorned it as a murder weapon.

We were joined at the head so it was the head I must aim for, as careful as any surgeon choosing the line of an incision.

She never looked up when I brought it down, aiming for the parting which separated the right side from the left side of her brain. I brought the axe down with all my strength and it stuck in her skull. She fell forward, then jerked back and stared inanely into my eyes. And then she lurched towards me, fighting, struggling for her right to devour me.

There was a scuffle. Fearing a second blow would be necessary, I desperately tried to free the axe, but each time I pulled, I heaved with such strength that her whole body weight shifted and eventually she fell off the chair. If she had a sense of danger, it was only for a second. There was blood. Her head was sliced open to reveal chunks of brain with hair attached to the pieces. What had I expected to see, cupid hearts in a river of scarlet? I stayed with her in that garden so long that evening came, the buzzings increased, and her face turned from deep red into a black fur of flies.

The separation had been successful. I sank to the ground unable to move. When she finally closed her eyes I knew that the love had always been real for her. Dying left a trace of warmth like my tears on shredded paper, like the last of the snowdrops on the grass. *It was over, dear God, at last it was over.*

*   *   *

The Crown Court. The final judgement. And then we were left, one of us dead, the other alive to serve the life sentence for us both.

Murder with intent. In court it sounded cold-blooded, inevitable.

Who was the victim, who was the killer? I still can't answer that question with honesty.

Prison seems to suit me. I have been confined for so many years—*she kept me a prisoner*—the routine meets my needs.

The children are well and growing up fast, in the care of the reliable Graham to whom forgiveness comes naturally because he's a decent man, and wise. Sam visits them when he can and sends over-indulgent gifts when he can't. They don't have much contact with me, I'm afraid. I never miss a birthday or Christmas, but the prison visits were not a success and we decided to let them peter out unless the children changed their minds. By the time I'm released they'll be married with children of their own, no doubt. I keep a photograph on my cell wall behind my bed: all four of them are smiling, lying there in the long grass when we went on holiday to Betws-y-Coed, and I think about what innocent fun it all could have been.

AUTHOR'S NOTE

This story is based on edited extracts from the diary of the victim with permission from her next of kin, and from the transcripts of statements by the accused, both to the investigating officers and to the police psychiatrist before the trial.

The author thanks all those who, by way of opinion or professional expertise, contributed to this work.